GW00788621

Orange Moon

Also by Srianjali Gunasena

Luk in Sri Lanka
A children's travel guide to Sri Lanka

Orange Moon

Srianjali Gunasena

First published in 2019 by Srianjali Gunasena

Text © Srianjali Gunasena
sripgun@gmail.com

ISBN 978 – 955 – 44588 – 1 – 9

Cover Illustration © MelTing
www.melissagunasena.com

Cover Design © Nuria Lamsdorff
www.nurialamsdorff.com

First printed in Sri Lanka by
M.D.Gunasena & Company Printers Pvt Ltd

1st Edition

All rights reserved. No part of this publication may be
reproduced, stored in a retrieval system, or transmitted, in any
form or by any means, electronic, mechanical, photocopying,
recording or otherwise, without the prior written permission of
the author.

To all those affected by events
out of their control

The Civil War in Sri Lanka raged from 1983 to 2009. The total number of dead and missing people is still unknown. This novel is set in 2006, in the aftermath of the 2004 Asian Tsunami which killed over 35,000 in Sri Lanka. Although the Civil War and the Tsunami were actual events, and provide the background to the story, this novel is a work of fiction. All characters, locations and events are fictitious. Any resemblance to actual events, or locales or persons, living or dead, is entirely coincidental. In this story, the Moon Rise Hotel is located in a village on the Central East Coast of Sri Lanka. Muslims, Sinhalese and Tamils, with a variety of religious beliefs, live peacefully in this village side by side.

Contents

1 Cinnamon Biscuits

Rushani stood contemplating the hole in the road. A trench, four feet deep, two feet wide and five feet long, providing drainage for the relentless rains that battered down with the coming of each monsoon. Already there were several serious injuries associated with this hole and she was pondering whether there was a sinister force at work, or was it just poorly managed roads?

A purple and pink sky spun above her, and a breeze whipped the dust around her ankles. She hoped the bus would not be full. There was always more chance of wandering hands on a crowded bus. On her feet since dawn, she had not processed the day's events and felt bothered by it.

The road was empty except for an old man cycling towards her, the chain squeaked with each rotation. Rushani stepped aside to let him pass, nodding in recognition. He was wheezing, but she knew the man was as strong as a buffalo and cycled over twenty kilometres a day.

Rushani's eyes followed the man until he became a dot on the horizon. A terrifying squeal of brakes from behind broke through her reverie and her feet propelled her into a run. With remarkable instinct gained from a tumultuous life she leapt into the hole with a single bound, crouching down low as the thunderous, hulking body of a lorry skidded towards her, blocking out the sun as it crashed down over her head.

Rushani didn't breathe as she collected herself and listened to the silence. The walls around her felt damp against her skin and she detected a rotten odour, probably the carcass of a wretched animal that had fallen to its fate.

She forced herself to breathe out. A crack of light was shining onto the back wall and she moved closer, peering up. An eye staring down at her made her scream.

"There's someone down here," a voice said in Sinhala. "Hurry! Let's get this lorry moved."

There were more voices now, some Tamil, some Sinhalese and then English.

Vehicles were arriving, and five voices became ten, then twenty. The muffled sounds from above became louder, and she tried to understand what was happening. The pocket of adrenalin borne from her flight burst inside her skull, making her momentarily deaf and light-headed. She could hear someone screaming and the fear of their injuries made her retch. Claustrophobia crept over her skin as her sanctuary betrayed her, crushing her into a tiny dungeon, and she tried desperately to regulate her shallow breath.

There was a loud screech as the lorry shunted forward, forcing her to cover her head with her arms as gravel rained down on her. The noise stopped abruptly, and she opened her eyes. The evening sun sent gentle warmth through her shivering body, and a silhouette of onlookers stared down at her. Arms reached in to help pull her out and suddenly she was back standing on the road looking down at the hole.

Everybody started talking at once. There were some people she knew from her village and others she didn't recognise.

"Oh, the driver of the lorry, he's in a very bad way. You should see, blood everywhere."

"No-one else is hurt, but we all thought we'd find a dead body under the lorry, and here you are, not even a scratch on you!"

Rushani let the rest of the comments hail onto the tarmac as she walked towards the injured driver. His screaming subsided into moaning. There was glass strewn around his body, it looked as though he had gone through the windscreen. Next to him was a four-wheel-drive pick-up, attached with rope to the front of the lorry, presumably to which she owed her freedom.

A foreigner was kneeling down over the driver, tying his leg to a wooden plank. The driver had something in his mouth and was biting down hard.

"Look, she, hole woman!" another man said in broken English, pointing to Rushani.

The foreigner looked up, his kind face cracked into a smile. "Well, I'm very pleased to meet you hole woman."

Rushani nodded but was unable to smile back.

"Sir, I will take this man to the hospital," another man spoke to the foreigner in English. "There are no ambulances here. Do you want to come, or find somewhere to stay until I can pick you up?"

"I've had enough travelling for the day, I'll find somewhere to stay here. Call me from the hospital."

They carried the man onto the back seat and the foreigner pulled out a rucksack from the trailer and hoisted it onto his shoulder. The pick-up drove off at an alarming speed and the crowd dispersed into their waiting vehicles now the show was over. The road was suddenly empty again but for the abandoned lorry lying on its side.

The foreign man turned to Rushani who was still staring at him.

"Are you ok?" he asked. "Injured?"

"No, no, ok" she managed to reply.

"I think you might need to sit down, have a cup of sweet tea for the shock."

"No, no, waiting bus, go home."

"Really, I think it might be better if you sat down."

"No, no, daughter waiting."

"Oh right, are you sure you'll be ok?"

"Yes, ok."

"Do you know anywhere I can stay?" he said, glancing behind her down the deserted street of boarded-up shops and abandoned teahouses.

"Go there, nice hotel, Moon Rise Hotel"

She indicated a rocky path leading towards the beach and her place of work. The man looked travel weary, his messy blond hair bleached almost white by the sun was stuck with sweat to the nape of his neck. Dust from the road covered his boots and rucksack and he had blood on his hands and down the front of his shirt. She watched the tendons in his forearms tighten as he heaved the rucksack a little further up his back.

"Thanks," he said, creasing his face into that smile again, that softened his frown, "take care."

She watched him walk away, down the path and out of sight.

The squealing breaks made her heart stop for the second time as the bus pulled up in front of her. Rushani gazed past the scratched and dented paintwork and through the grimy windows to the packed interior. She had forgotten it was market day. She pushed her way on past rice sacks and baskets bulging with vegetables. A chicken could be heard protesting its imminent fate.

There was one seat left, and she sat down heavily, holding on to the rail with white knuckles, closing her eyes to block out the hot sweaty body next to her. She'd caught sight of the blood-red saliva leaking from his mouth as he chewed on betel nut and prayed that she wouldn't have to endure any nonsense from him. A waft of particularly offensive body odour forced her to lean over the man and open the small window above them. He grunted and shifted in his seat, pressing his leg tighter against hers.

She turned her back to him and stretched her legs out into the aisle. They were trembling, so she pulled them back under her seat. The rest of the passengers were crowding the windows trying to glimpse the overturned lorry, chattering excitedly about the blood splatters on the ground and guessing the death toll. She saw a tuk-tuk[1] arrive and three policemen get out. She was glad no one had thought to call the police sooner, or she thought it unlikely they would have let her leave. Several of the passengers tried to engage her in conversation. Had

---

[1] Tuk-tuk – three-wheel vehicle

she seen the accident? How many people were hurt? Had anyone died? She told them she had run for the bus and not seen anything. Eventually they gave up their interrogation and she let her mind return to the events that morning.

The army had turned up brandishing rifles with a smirk of authority that chilled her. They were sweeping the area, looking for terrorists, due to the arrival of a junior minister, one Mr Jayasuriya. The soldiers looked seventeen, maybe eighteen years old. She wondered whether they had killed anyone. What would they be like if they did? She doubted they would still strut like that.

Opening her eyes to the lush green of the paddy fields racing past her window made her relax. She thought back to her childhood and of the hours she would spend with her father in the fields. While other village girls were at home learning how to make roti, she would plough the land and harvest the crops. Life seemed easy then. She had grown up as the only child of a Sinhalese farmer, a kind and patient man who loved her in a way that bundled her up and held her tight, even in the aftershock of his early demise. Her mother had desperately wanted more than one child and after several traumatic miscarriages, that had her haemorrhaging and almost left for dead, had inflicted shame upon herself, when it seemed the gods had decided that just one was all she deserved. Her pain turned into jealousy when she realised that in her emotional absence, the bond between her husband and daughter had become impenetrable, and she withdrew more and more until her bitterness shrouded her like a cloak. After her husband's death, and against Rushani's wishes, she married her only daughter off to the son of a neighbouring farmer who took over the working of the land and their finances. Rushani had made repeated attempts to persuade her mother of her ability to work the land herself, but her mother had simply raised her hand to her daughter and slapped her hard across the face.

"You're a fool," her mother had said, "and so was your father. Now it is left to me to pick up the pieces of this family."

Rushani moved her hand up to her face to trace the memory. She caught hold of the wisps of hair that had escaped their detainment, now fluttering across her cheekbones, and twisted them back into the bun she had worn every day of her adult life. She had a young face, but the odd strand of grey hair implied her thirty-eight years. Her eyes were wide and long-lashed, giving the appearance of innocence, but on closer inspection, her irises took you to a place where innocence had long been abandoned. She had a beauty spot on her cheek, vanishing into the crease of her dimple when she smiled. She looked down at the front of her sari and adjusted the hem; it was her favourite, emerald green with a delicate design of petals in turquoise and purple thread. Her employer, and owner of the hotel, a Muslim by the name of Mr Ali, had brought it back from Colombo, along with shirts and trousers for the male staff, to commemorate the reopening of the hotel after the tsunami.

The sari highlighted her curvaceous body. She had a tiny waist with full round hips, balanced out by generous breasts. She was not unlike the frescos painted on the cave walls in Sigiriya. Not that she had visited there, but she had seen a travel book once in the hotel, illustrated with colourful photos. Her brow creased, and she tutted when she noticed a rip in the hem and the scuff marks and frayed threads on the front from where she had climbed out of the hole.

The bus turned a corner and Rushani bit her lip. Her precious daughter Meena was waiting for her at the bus stop, her beautiful eyes creasing as she spotted her mother. Rushani's mother stood behind Meena, smoothing down her granddaughter's flyaway curls. Rushani grabbed her bag and pushed her way off the bus, grateful for the reprieve from the stench of her potential assailant, the shock of the accident, and a day full of guns.

She caught Meena up in her arms and kissed her again and again. She was still so light even at the age of nine that Rushani could swing her around. Meena giggled in delight.

"You are my everything," she whispered.

The rocky path led to a simple wooden gate. Chris pushed it open with his foot and walked in. He admired the rows of flowers and sweet-smelling herbs. He felt comforted by the care that had been taken in the garden and was looking forward to a meal made with the same attention to detail.

The restaurant had stunning views of the ocean. He dropped his rucksack on the floor and headed towards the sink in the corner. He scrubbed his hands with soap then picked up a rock and rubbed it on the remaining stubborn blood spots until they were gone. Finally, he dropped his weary body into a hammock.

The sound of the waves lulled him into semi-consciousness, but he blinked himself awake when he felt a shadow standing over him.

"I didn't want to wake you," she said as he squinted his eyes open. "You looked very peaceful, what can I get for you?"

An attractive woman was leaning over him. She had coffee-coloured skin and straight black hair in a shoulder-length bob. She was petite with an impish grin on her face.

Chris grinned back "a coffee would be great."

"You've got good timing we're just roasting some beans now. We also have some cinnamon and cashew biscuits straight out of the oven. Shall I bring one of those too?"

"Sounds perfect."

The woman's face turned to a frown as she noticed his shirt. "Is that blood on your shirt? Are you injured?"

"Oh no, it's not mine."

Her face took on a new look of alarm.

"Oh no, don't worry, I haven't murdered anyone. There was an accident on the road, a lorry overturned, the driver got injured."

"Oh god, I thought I heard something, but strange noises are not that uncommon around here. What's happened to him?"

"My driver's taken him to hospital. He'll call me with any news. There was a woman as well, who got trapped by the truck, but she appeared to be ok, just in shock."

"What did she look like?"

"Mid to late thirties, hair in a bun, purple and green sari."

"Oh god, that's Rushani! Where is she now?"

"I suggested she should take it easy, but she wanted to go home."

"Oh, poor Rushani, that must have been awful. Let me get your coffee."

Chris watched the woman head back to the kitchen. Her accent sounded English, possibly from London. He settled back into the hammock and breathed deeply as the smell of roasting coffee beans filtered past his nose. It was good to just lie there, doing nothing. He wasn't on his way anywhere, didn't have a deadline to meet. He had simply just stopped, and it felt good. He knew he was on borrowed time and intended to make the most of his enforced holiday. His work was hectic. There was so much to do and not enough time, money or resources. He was really tired.

Chris heaved himself out of the hammock and walked down the path and onto the beach. To the right was a wide cove, several kilometres long, edged by high sand dunes that travelled back to meet a dense forest. To the left of him was an outcrop of giant boulders weathered smooth by the wind and the water.

Chris took off his bloody shirt, shoes and trousers and ran into the turquoise water in his underpants. He let himself float face down for as long as he could hold his breath and then flipped himself over and stared up at the dusky sky, feeling utterly peaceful. His grumbling stomach forced him out of the moment and up the beach to the restaurant, grabbing his clothes on the way. Lying down on a reclining chair, he let the water slowly evaporate from his body.

He was not a happy man. He hadn't felt good for a long time. Even the gratification from his job could not bring him out of his melancholy. He knew

10

what was eating him up though. It was clear as could be and staring him straight in the face when he looked in a mirror. He was gut-wrenchingly lonely. Not the common kind of loneliness that he was used to and could rectify by a brief fling with a transient colleague. This was to the core of his being, so much that it hurt. It was a loneliness that swamped him last thing at night and first thing in the morning and it was this loneliness that pierced his entire body until his fingers and toes cramped up with the pain.

In the kitchen there was pandemonium. A rat had been spotted, and Aruna, the Sinhalese cook, was on his knees with a cricket bat in his hands.

Suresh, who had been in charge of the roasting was now stabbing violently behind the freezer with a broom handle and the beans were in danger of being burnt to a crisp.

Marni grabbed the pan and took it over to the blender, tipping in the contents. With an ominous whirring, the motor spat and hissed its way through the beans, choking itself on every grain. Surprisingly, the beans mutated into a fine powder and the blade slowed to a stop.

She made a pot of coffee and carried it out to the restaurant. She guessed the man was here for work, not pleasure. She could see it in his eyes. He looked fatigued, with the worry of the world on his shoulders. He had a European accent that she thought was Scandinavian. She placed the tray down on the table and watched as he poured himself a cup.

Bringing it to his lips, he breathed in the aroma and then sipped it gingerly, wincing as the brown nectar burnt the back of his throat on the way down.

"Wow! That really hit the spot. It's been a long time since I've had good coffee:"

"Try a cinnamon biscuit," she said, pushing the plate of gooey biscuits towards him.

She watched the crumbs fall against his chest as he bit into it. She paused for a moment while he savoured the mouthful. She knew how good they were. They had that little bit of magic that reminded people of loved ones left behind, Christmas past, and home-cooked food. Well, that's how they made her feel anyway.

"Where have you been?" she asked.

"Working up North, I haven't had a break for almost six months."

"Well, you've come to the right place, rest and relaxation are what we do best! You should hang around here for a while, take a few weeks holiday, or at least until your driver can pick you up."

"Do you have any cabanas free?"

"You're in luck! The threat of being blown up keeps most tourists well away from here! Let me show you one."

Marni led Chris to a stilted cabana. From its rickety veranda, the ocean spread out as if it was there just for him. Inside was a gigantic four-poster wooden bed with a white mosquito net draped around it. He wanted to crawl in right then and there and sleep for a week.

"I'll take it," he said.

"Great, I'll leave the key in the lock. Dinner will be at 7 pm."

"What's on the menu?"

"Barbecued red snapper, pumpkin curry, roasted aubergine salad and milk rice."

Chris smiled, and his tummy growled again. "I'm in!"

Marni left Chris and returned to the restaurant. She swept it and emptied the ashtrays. She wondered where Jake was, as Zoe would need feeding soon. Her breasts were enlarged and beginning to leak through her cotton dress. They'd gone almost three hours ago to pick up the post from town. She was annoyed at being left to get the dinner ready. She felt Jake did that a lot these days, skipping out at the busiest times and swanning back in when the last plate had been dried.

She wandered out to the beach and sat down. The sun had already set, and the stars were twinkling down on her from the cloudless night sky. She picked up a handful of sand and watched it trickle through her fingers. The day had been stressful. The army had been in again demanding a list of all their staff. Their waiter Suresh, a Tamil who had grown up in a village an hour north from there, had been taken for questioning for most of the morning. She wished they'd leave him alone.

Marni was grateful to the anonymity of her mother's English surname. Otherwise, there would be too many questions. She enjoyed having the cloak of foreign woman labelling her. Even she didn't know the answers of her Tamil ancestry. Who was her father? Where does he live? What does he do? Is he alive? These questions she had been asking herself all her life. There had been some discoveries since she had arrived in Sri Lanka, but it was a frustratingly slow process. Her mother hadn't tried to stop her. She knew, for Marni, this search was inevitable.

Her mother, Lara, had come to Sri Lanka in the summer of 1978. She was young and carefree and looking for adventure. She had met Marni's father, an intelligent man with a twinkle in his eye. He had recently arrived in Colombo to attend university and they spent a glorious month together, basking in the sunshine and in the light of their mutual respect. They talked of politics and of a new country that was forming. Pravish was excited at the future that was emerging for him. He was proud of his country and was looking forward to a career in politics. He had plans to take his career to parliament.

He spent the days studying while Lara went on day trips to visit temples or shop in the markets. The nights were spent skin on skin. In his cramped, single bed in Fort, they discovered themselves through each other's touch. Lara would marvel at his smooth dark skin stretched over taut muscles. The kisses that made her shiver and the wild, energetic expressions of love that made it so hard to unwrap her legs from his when it was all over.

Lara knew that this would not last. They were on two different paths and neither wanted to give up on their own journey. Her ticket was booked home, and she knew that she would be on that plane.

Lara and Pravish were unable to foresee the hand that fate would deliver. Several months after arriving back in England, Lara discovered that she was pregnant. She cried for a week, torn in the indecision of her future and the life that she was carrying inside her. She wrote to Pravish asking him for help in reaching a decision, but week after week, as she waited for the post to arrive, she realized that the decision would be hers alone.

Marni left the beach to shower and dress for the evening. She chose a green batik halter-neck dress the tailor had made for her, that fitted her slim body perfectly. She wound a scarf around her sleek bob and tied it at the base of her neck. As she left the room, she saw the lights of a tuk-tuk pull into the car park. Jake and Zoe were just arriving back from town. She took Zoe from Jake's arms and went back to their room to feed her.

"Have I done something wrong?" Jake asked, following her in.

"It's really late and there was a load of things to get done which I could have used your help for," she replied crossly, pulling the straps of the dress off her shoulders to expose her leaking breasts.

"I was doing things, I was looking after Zoe and getting an oil drum BBQ made."

"There are other things to think about rather than random DIY projects!"

"It isn't for me, it's for your precious guests," Jake replied as he slammed out the room.

Marni looked down at Zoe as she suckled and wondered whether she imagined the look of disapproval that crossed her daughter's deep-set eyes.

"I know Zoe, he does do things, but why do I feel like I'm trying to do everything alone?"

She listened to her daughter's contented noises as her belly filled up. Her eyelids flickered until eventually shutting tight as she relaxed into the rhythmical breathing of deep sleep.

Marni laid Zoe in her cot, her small pink fist clenched tightly. She closed the door quietly and followed the stepping-stones to the restaurant to start the evening shift.

The night was humid with a scent of jasmine in the air. There were several guests already in the restaurant. They were mainly staff working for non-government organizations (NGOs). There were very few tourists around anymore. There hadn't been since the tsunami. Business was poor, but the hotel was muddling through thanks to the huge influx of foreign aid workers needing somewhere to stay.

They were already the headquarters for International Response (INR), a network of skilled professionals covering projects from engineering to conflict resolution. There was a full-time manager, Niraj. He was Tamil and had gained a senior position in the company through hard work and dedication.

There was a French woman, Claudette. She had arrived from Colombo several weeks earlier. She was an elegant woman who looked young than her 48 years. Marni, who normally found a way to communicate with everyone, found her personality difficult. She had a sharp tongue and gave her opinions freely and loudly. She was responsible for a substantial tsunami aid budget, which she frequently bragged about. She had come to build housing but was stuck in a heap of red tape, so had ordered in fishing boats by the lorry-load, to get rid of the budget before the end of the financial year, so as not to have to return it to the donors. She was currently negotiating with the school in town to build an extra classroom.

Prior to Claudette arriving, Marni had not come across a single guest who didn't eventually let their negativity melt away the longer they stayed. She wasn't sure if it was the therapeutic water or the stark reality of life here. Maybe there simply wasn't time to behave like an arse.

There was an elderly Australian couple who bought land just before the tsunami and were now building a modest holiday home for their retirement. They were staying at the Moon Rise Hotel until the building work was completed, but three months had turned into four then five and the house was still not finished. Marni had set them up with some voluntary work in a local school and they seemed content for the time being.

Claudette's cigarettes hung in the air of the restaurant. She had accosted Chris and was leading a discussion in the shocking prices being charged by the building traders.

"I mean, don't they know we are here to help them and their people? It's outrageous the prices they are charging us!"

Chris was trying to back away from the smoke she was blowing in his face whilst attempting to explain the hand-to-mouth situation that many people were in and the lack of funds that had been directed to this area.

Marni went into the kitchen to help bring out the food. Aruna had barbecued the red snapper and the smell of garlic and lime fused with the evening air. The food was laid out and the guest's low murmuring voices lulled as they savoured the delicious spread.

"Good evening Marni," Ali's smiling face greeted her as he walked up the path.

"How is everything?"

Ali was her business partner and confidant. He had grown up in the local town, a dedicated Muslim who won his battles through kindness and compassion. She knew that without his patience in teaching her the ways of the country she was adopting, she would have returned to London long ago.

"Everything seems well this evening Ali, but the army were here again this morning."

"There has been some rallying and protesting in town today. The people are not happy with the army presence. There is a curfew tonight and people are being stopped on the street and harassed for just going about their business. The local restaurants are working overtime to feed the extra army, and of course, they are not being paid what they should be. All because of a state visit, that will last half an hour, by a junior minister. I'm not even sure why he is coming."

They sat thoughtfully, sipping sweet, spicy chai, infused with cinnamon, cardamom and local honey.

Ali broke the silence. "We need to dig a beer cellar. We can access it by a trapdoor we keep hidden with leaves. The police are becoming more aggressive with hotels and just yesterday hauled off Lakmal, from the Reef Hotel to court, and fined him Rs 100,000 because he had refused to entertain the excise police the night before. Whether or not we get a licence, it will be the same story."

"Yes, I'll get Suresh working on it tomorrow," Marni replied. "Tell me Ali, do you think it's possible for peace in this country?"

"I believe there is already peace in the villages, in the homes, in the fields. Look at our hotel, we are all living peacefully with one another, Tamils, Sinhalese, Muslims and foreigners. We are the United Nations! This war is about money driven by greedy politicians. If we, the people, don't stop them, then why should they care? They will just carry on doing what they do."

Marni watched Jake take his plate to the kitchen and slouch off to bed. He had been moody all night, probably because he felt he was owed an apology. But Marni didn't have the energy. She had too many other things on her mind. The responsibility of the business, the needs of the guests, the staff's squabbles and Zoe. He would have to wait in line.

"That food was delicious!" Chris said, breaking her thoughts. "My belly is very happy."

"I'm glad you enjoyed it. Can I get you anything else?"

"No thanks, I'm going to find my bed, it's been a long, crazy day today, following a whole succession of long, crazy days! I will need to get some washing done tomorrow though. Where can I take it?"

"We can do it here. I'm hoping Rushani will be here early if she's ok, so give it to her when you wake up. You'll find her working in the garden."

"Perfect. Thank you for the food and your great hospitality. Good-night."

"Why would Rushani not be ok?" asked Ali after Chris had left.

"They were involved in the accident with the lorry today. Apparently Rushani was trapped down one of the drain holes underneath the lorry."

"Ah yes, I heard about it in town. They were saying a woman had been very lucky, that it was a miracle she had survived. I saw them moving the lorry just now. Did the driver make it?"

"Chris' driver is still with him at the hospital. He's badly injured and needs surgery. We'll know more in the morning."

Ali cleared away the dishes while Marni closed down the restaurant for the night. It was an open design with a roof made of palm fronds and a sandy-coloured cement floor. She carried the computer into the main building and through to the office. This she thought of as her space. Everything else was shared with her guests, even her morning cup of coffee. But the office was a refuge, where she could take five minutes to collect her thoughts. She said goodnight to Suresh, who was making up his bed in the restaurant where he slept for security and snuffed out the kerosene lamps that were lighting the path to the beach.

She wandered out onto the sand to breathe in the sea air. There were no clouds and the stars were bright. The moon was high in the sky, it would soon be full. She lifted her face and closed her eyes. She could feel the moon's energy absorb through the thin skin around her eyes and across her forehead. She understood its power, how it toyed with fortunes and feelings.

Marni shivered involuntarily from a familiar chill. It was now eighteen months since the Tsunami. The day the wave had swept her and Jake away, taken their home and business and a large percentage of the population of the seaside village. In this remote corner of the world, Marni felt alive. The powerful energy she felt radiating from the earth fuelled her, but she now knew how quickly it could all vanish. She wasn't sure how a place could fill up her heart so strongly but ignite such fear in her. She felt there was more to come. There was an anxiety in her that made her doubt her commitment to stay. Jake had long since expressed his desire to return home, especially now they had Zoe. He didn't like the heightened powers of the army or the threatening presence of the Tamil Freedom Fighters.

But Marni couldn't leave, not yet, but for this reason, she and Jake were slipping apart. He couldn't understand her stubbornness to stay and she couldn't explain it. She walked back to their hut and watched Jake as he slept. This was the closest she'd felt to him all day, but she knew tomorrow would stir up the same emotions that festered between them; fear, anger and resentment. She wasn't sure how they would make it through this.

2 Roti and Dhal

Vish was unknotting fishing nets. He found it relaxed him enough to focus his thoughts on the task ahead. They would definitely need four extra people to travel through the night to Colombo for back-up, but he had not yet decided who those four should be.

That was the hardest part. These proud Tamil soldiers were dedicated, trained and ready. They had sworn themselves to the cause and were honoured to be on the front line. But the front line these days always meant certain death. Who was he to make that decision? The line had become blurred and he no longer knew which side he was on. What was happening to him? Was he losing the courage of his convictions?

But there was a job to be done, and he was responsible for it. He folded up the untangled nets and left the tent to relieve himself in the woods. This was the part of his life that he loved, living free like this, always moving, a simple life as nature intended. He loved the sound of the forest, the evening chorus of crickets shouting from the thick vegetation that surrounded him. As the sun began to set, birdsong rang from the trees as they called their loved ones to return to their nests.

There was a lull over the camp that evening. Everyone content in their own thoughts. A large pot of dhal[2] was bubbling away on the campfire and essence of roasted cumin seeds hung in the air.

Kumar approached Vish and asked to have a private word.

"What is troubling you, Kumar?"

"Head office is calling for a recruitment drive. We need to visit some villages."

Vish could feel his headache coming on. It was becoming a familiar feeling. The pain moved up around his eyes and closed down on his skull like a vice.

"I'd be happy to head the project if you have too much on," added Kumar.

Vish hated the village raids. In the beginning, he could understand the need to recruit in secret. Young men and women were taken from the villages to the camps and trained as soldiers. They couldn't risk letting the positions of their camps be known to the families of the new recruits. Thus, the new soldiers were never heard from again.

By the time they became soldiers, they too believed in the ideology and would not break the code of silence.

But it was different now. The deaths were becoming more frequent, so the new recruits were just replacing dead ones, only to be led off to duty in a production line of wasted lives.

Vish had not thought too much in the past about the families that were left behind. The soldiers

---

[2] Dhal – a dish made from lentils and spices

were respected, fed, clothed and highly skilled. What would have been their fate if they had stayed in the villages? Schools had few or no books. They couldn't even learn in their mother tongue. Resources made their way to Sinhalese schools with leftover crumbs thrown to the Tamil areas.

It's true they were scared when they arrived. Who wouldn't be when faced with the unfamiliar? It was the job of the supervisors to show them the true value of their lives.

But now these details troubled him. How does a mother or father survive the loss of their son or daughter? Aren't these the people they were trying to protect? Wasn't it the rights of the mothers and fathers, the sons and daughters that they were looking out for? Where was the justification? Vish no longer knew.

Kumar would be able to organize the raid without him. He was a fine soldier but Vish worried that his humanity had been depleted. After witnessing the murder of his parents by government soldiers when he was only nine years old, Kumar had wrapped his heart in stone. He had survived their village being burnt to the ground by hiding in a woodpile, with only a viper for company.

This made him a tough supervisor. The new recruits feared him and he had no patience for weakness. He had the qualities to carry out these orders.

"Yes Kumar, you go ahead with organizing the recruitment drive and I will finish the preparations for Saturday."

"Thank you, Vish Uncle, for your trust in me. I won't let you down."

Vish couldn't sleep that night. He dreamt wolves were chasing him. They were hungry and salivating. He could feel their breath on his heels. It was dark, and he didn't know where he was going. Suddenly the ground vanished from beneath him and he was falling, tumbling to the water below. He plunged in and a feeling of calm washed over him; he didn't want to find the surface; he wanted to sink deeper. The water comforted him; it was taking away the pain; he didn't want to resist…

Vish woke up violently and gulped the air in strangled breaths. He had been so close to letting go. He felt robbed and desperate. He got up off his sleeping mat and opened the door of the tent. There was a cool breeze that slowed his breathing to a regular pace. The light from the moon brought a sillouhette into focus on the far side of the camp, sitting on a fallen tree. He went to investigate.

It was Banita. She was taking the night lookout shift.

"Did something wake you, Sir?" She was cradling the rifle that lay across her lap. He wondered if she yearned for that cold metal to be the warm flesh of a baby, to experience the kind of love that a mother has for her child.

"Only memories of past lives haunting me."

"She smiled quizzically and then dropped her eyes to her feet. Will you be sending the next group to Colombo Sir? I would like to volunteer."

Vish's body tensed. He wanted to cry out: NO, I WILL NOT ALLOW IT! But this was not what he was here for. This fearless woman prepared to risk her life. It would be disrespectful to try to prevent her.

"If that is your wish, I will support your decision."

The young woman smiled gratefully up at him and idly stroked the muzzle on her rifle.

"Thank you, Sir, you won't regret it."

———————— ● ————————

Leela pulled the sheet over her little brother. She loved watching him sleep. He would pout his lips and suckle as if still drinking from their mother's breast. Leela thought he must be dreaming of being a new-born when the world still held open all its opportunities.

Her two sisters lay side-by-side, mirroring each other's position as they slept. There were two-and-a-half years between them, but they were more like twins. The younger one was of a strong disposition and grew quickly despite the limited food on their plates. She had soon caught up with her delicate older sister.

The moon was bright and shone through the window onto a cobweb in the corner of the otherwise gloomy room. She could see the spider weaving her magic as the silk thread moved in and out of the moonlight. Through the wall, she could hear her mother and grandmother snoring. The walls of her house were mud, baked in the sun to provide a protective shelter. The roof was corrugated asbestos-sheets. Leela had preferred when it was covered in weaved palm fronds. It was cooler, and the sound of the rain had not kept her awake at night. She shifted slightly on her mat, making sure that she didn't disturb her brother. His small fist was curled tightly around her nightdress. She was his heroine, protector and carer. Their mother worked long hours and their grandmother was now almost blind. She had cataracts in both her eyes, and they could not afford both the cost of travelling to a hospital and the operation to remove them. Leela spent all her free time with her brother when she wasn't at school. In grade ten, but looking older than her fourteen years, learning came easily to her. Fascinated by the sciences, her teachers often discussed the possibility of a scholarship programme to send her to school in Colombo. So far it had come to nothing. The funding wasn't there, or the criteria did not fit. Red tape had wrapped it up.

Leela was a quiet girl with deep, questioning eyes and a set of big, white teeth that protruded from her thin face when she smiled. She was of average height with a slim build. She thought she could pass for pretty. Her mother told her she was. Comments from boys were always directed at her two best friends, who curled their mouths in a way that made the boys more eager, emitting confidence that Leela could only admire. She watched their mannerisms, the way they flicked back their pigtails or held their hands over their mouths when they giggled. Leela could see it was a mating ritual that she herself stood firmly on the outside of. Thus far, she had no urge to participate.

Maybe, one day, she thought, starting to feel the weariness of inevitable sleep wafting over her. She rolled onto her side and placed her palm over her brother's fist. She closed her eyes and was instantly asleep.

The hand over her mouth was the first thing she was aware of. At first, she thought she was dreaming but as her eyes flicked open and adjusted to the light, and her consciousness kicked in, she realised this was no dream. She saw the silhouettes of three men, two at her feet and one above her head. The man bent down and whispered to her in Tamil.

"Don't make a sound, if you don't want your family to get hurt." The man's mouth was so close to her ear, that she felt the wet of his lips graze her lobe. His breath was rancid, and she almost gagged on his hand that was still covering her mouth.

Her instincts overcame her as it dawned on her what was happening. She tried to kick violently with both legs, but the two men were holding on tight. She tried to shout but the other man still had his hand over her mouth.

Her brother woke up screaming. This was too much for her to bear. She started twisting her body, trying to release herself from their grip. They held tight around her ankles, so she bit the hand that covered her mouth. The man cried out in pain but grabbed her shoulders and suddenly she was airborne. They were running with her now through the front door. She could hear her mother's cries, and then Leela saw her, hanging on the man's arm, begging him to release her daughter. The man pushed her with one hand and she fell to the ground, but she was up again almost immediately, holding on to his ankles, screaming and yelling. He kicked at her, but she held on tight. They were almost at the van now. The doors were opened, and she was thrown in the back. They slammed shut behind her. Her mother's fists were pounding on the white metal and Leela tried desperately to unlock the doors, but she already knew it was futile. She became silent and pressed her palms against the glass trying to touch her mother's hands in vain.

Leela knew her neighbours would be out of their houses by now, holding their children tight to themselves, wondering when their turn would come.

The back of the van was separated from the front seats so Leela could not see anything, apart from the occasional light flick past the patterned glass panes on the back doors. She huddled in the corner of the van, her knees bent, and her arms wrapped around her legs. She wasn't even sure in which direction they were driving. She rubbed her ankles where the men had held her. She was angry and frightened, but it was the thought of her little brother that upset her most. His screams were still ringing in her head and she pushed her ears hard with the palms of her hands to try to block out the noise.

The van came to a sudden stop. She could hear voices talking in Sinhala. An army roadblock; she was saved. She shouted and hammered on the walls of the van.

"Help me, help me," she screamed in both Tamil and Sinhala. "Let me out! They've taken me."

She stopped screaming to listen to what was happening. The voices became raised. She could hear the Tamil men in the front seats arguing in broken Sinhala, and the Sinhalese voices arguing back.

"Yes, I'm here," she began shouting again. "Help me, please." She was crying now, large racking sobs. She was wailing and shouting and kicking at the doors. The engine started and the van screeched off.

"No, wait, help me. Let me out."

Leela stopped abruptly and wiped away her tears, trying to understand what had happened. Why hadn't the army saved her?

They were travelling faster now. Minutes turned into hours until eventually they slowed down and turned off the road. She could hear sticks and leaves crunching under the tyres and the van wobbled from side to side on the uneven ground causing her to bump and crash into the sides. Eventually, the van stopped, and the engine turned off. Leela crouched in the darkness, not knowing whether the locked doors were a better alternative to open ones. She could hear someone moving around the side, a key was coaxed into the lock and the doors flung open.

"Come out," said a gruff voice, in Tamil.

Leela pushed herself out the van and winced as she trod on a sharp rock with her bare feet. There was jungle surrounding them 360 degrees. She strained to hear any traffic noise but there was nothing. The man pushed her forward.

"Follow him," he said, indicating the man in front. She walked forward with her head down. It was hard to keep up with the men in their sturdy boots, but she didn't want to show weakness to these repulsive men. They followed a trodden down path for some time until it opened out into a clearing. There were several large tents around a fire and a few smaller ones dotted in between. The camp was quiet except for one woman holding a rifle. She looked directly into Leela's eyes as if to convey something. Maybe this is how she arrived here, Leela thought. Now she was guarding the place that had once been her prison. Leela shivered, there no way she would let that happen to her.

They showed her a tent where she could sleep. There was a woman watching over her. The first night was always the hardest, the woman told her. Sometimes the new recruits tried to run, but the forest was unforgiving. "You'll never find your way out," she added.

Leela looked down at her sore and shoeless feet. She knew her best option was to surrender to a night's sleep.

She had always felt this day would come. She didn't know why but she wasn't surprised. She didn't want to be a soldier. She didn't want to kill anyone, and she definitely didn't want to die. But she was curious. They had heard a lot about these camps in the village. She knew of children who had vanished. She had seen the terror in the parents left behind. She didn't want that for her mother. She knew her mother would never recover from this.

She was scared, but fear was an emotion that had run along beside her, throughout her short life, so much so she now found it made her feel alive. She was scared when the first wave of the tsunami washed through her village, lifting her high above the roofs and into the branches of a mango tree. She was scared when they carried her father's body to dry land, he who had not been so lucky. She was scared when they could hear the shelling to the north; they were sure it was coming closer, but they didn't know where to run. She was scared when the men came with their guns demanding money and food in return for protection. She was scared when the army came in tanks, searching houses and threatening them. And she was scared now. She didn't know what they would ask of her and she didn't think she would want to give it.

Leela fell into a deep and fevered sleep. She dreamt of her mother waving to her, beckoning her to come closer. As she tried to reach her, the earth tremored and the land split in two. Her mother was moving further and further away. The gap was getting bigger and bigger. Her mother's smile was turning to horror. She screamed at Leela, "jump, jump before it's too late!" But even in her sleep, Leela knew it was already too late.

Vish heard them arriving back last night. He had not heard screaming or crying, which was easier for everyone. He was anxious to find out the mental state of their newest recruit, to know when and how to start the training programme. Some needed more time to adjust to their new life than others. The more resilient ones resisted for as long as they had the energy, but with the help of mentors who were little older themselves, most of their recruits came to accept the new direction of their lives within a few weeks.

He saw Leela with her back to him, rocking slightly and staring at the towering canopy. She was sipping black tea and munching on a roti. At least she's eating, he thought. A full stomach lines the way for a smoother ride. He had noticed those who could eat on their first morning fared better, due to their strong constitution. They were, above all else, survivors.

Vish approached the girl. He walked in front of her, blocking out the morning sun on her face and putting himself in shadow.

"My name is Vish. I am the supervisor in this camp. You are now a serving member of the Tamil Freedom Fighters. I will be responsible for you while you are here."

Leela looked up at the looming figure above her. He didn't seem that threatening, but what would she know. He must have killed people, maybe even hundreds of people.

"Why am I here?" She asked.

"You will know the answer to that question soon enough," he replied.

"First, you need uniform. Follow me."

Vish led Leela to a large canvas tent. Inside there were stores of food, weapons and clothing. He handed her over to a female soldier.

"When you're finished, come and meet me and we will have a talk."

Leela was dressed in green trousers, green shirt and boots. She felt more comfortable now she was out of her nightdress, and she knew there was a greater chance of escape with some decent boots on.

She walked out of the dark tent into the brilliant sunlight. The camp was buzzing with activity. There was a group sitting in the shade of a tree cleaning and loading weapons, food was being prepared and a more serious group of men and women were pouring over maps around a makeshift table made from a large tree stump. Leela could see the supervisor Vish. She hung about wondering what she should do. One of the men who had carried her last night noticed her and covered the maps.

"Move away from here! Your eyes and ears are not welcome. Or do you want me to remove them for you?"

She scuttled away towards the kitchen area to the sound of taunts and laughter. Her heart was beating fast and her throat was dry.

She had no idea what these people had planned for her. Fighting for justice they said, but this was not justice: taking her away from her family, scaring her half to death. How could they be righteous in their beliefs? They were thugs, bullies, kidnappers and murderers.

She walked to the far edge of the camp. At the perimeter there were guards on duty, their rifles propped up against their legs, watching her with idle curiosity. She wondered what they would do if she ran? Would they shoot her?

There was a large rock, and she climbed it to get as far away from these people as she could. Behind the rock, in a sheltered dip, a shrine had been built with a lot of care. There were flowers arranged around the centre and candles in glass jars had been lit. In the centre of the shrine there were many photos. She looked closely and saw that they were all youths. Wide-eyed hopeful faces staring at her. She thought she recognized one of them. A boy from her village, yes it was him! She looked closer to see the writing underneath. 'In Memory'.

She gasped, a cry escaped her throat as she realized this was a shrine to dead child soldiers.

Suddenly men were on her.

"You shouldn't be up here," one of them said. "It seems you can't be trusted to be by yourself."

They took her back to her tent and one of them remained outside guarding her.

She was shaking but glad to be by herself. The shock of seeing those faces, the boy that

she once knew, was too much. She couldn't stay here.
She had to find a way to leave.

The flap on her tent opened and Vish walked in.

"I have been told you saw something you were not ready to see," he said.

"I wouldn't ever be ready to see that," she replied.

"One day you will understand more."

"Do you understand?" she asked.

She thought she saw his eyes flicker with sadness, but his face remained passive.

"Some of our group will move out tonight. You need to keep your head down and not cause any more trouble. There is enough going on without you adding to it."

Vish walked out feeling uneasy. There was a lot of attitude for such a slight girl. In time they would be forced to break her, but right now there were more worrying matters at hand.

The four had been chosen. They would travel with all the equipment. There were already three in place in Colombo who had done the groundwork, and now they had all the information they needed. The job would be executed at nine in the morning. Most of the businesses would be open by then so numbers should reach as high as they could hope for.

They would travel part of the way through the forest to avoid roadblocks, then be picked up by vehicle, where they had a good stretch of unmanned roads.

Vish shook their hands solemnly and blessed them. As they walked off into the night, he wished silently for their safe return. He watched the slim figure of Banita vanish into the undergrowth like a ghost.

3 Fish Curry and Pol Sambol

Like a tidal wave flooding a desert, Colombo swamped Gaya's senses. Stepping off the plane, the familiar, warm, humid air shot up her nostrils and opened the pores of her face. She had been in America, studying at University. Having completed her degree in Conflict Resolution and securing a job with a non-government organisation called INR (International Response), she was back in her beloved homeland of Sri Lanka. She was impatient to get to the frontline and finally make use of all the years of books and theory.

She knew Ammi[3] and Thathi[4] were not happy about it. They worried about her safety. They wanted her close to them in Colombo, where they could keep an eye on her. She had always been fiercely independent, happy to start and finish a discussion, however heated, and not likely to settle down anytime soon with a nice Sinhalese boy who would look after her. This they worried about daily. They didn't want

---

[3] Ammi – mother (Sinhala)

[4] Thathi – father (Sinhala)

her to become too old for starting a family or repel a prospective suitor by becoming too successful in a career. They were proud of her achievements so far, but the combination of her beauty and qualifications were all she needed to find a suitable husband. In their plan for her life, she didn't need to work once she married.

She didn't want her parents to worry, but she intended to live her life her way. She was planning to stay a few weeks in Colombo and then head to the East to join the team in the field.

She found her bags and pushed her way through Immigration into the throngs outside. Suranga was there waiting. He had worked for her family for over twenty years and was now near to retirement, but Gaya didn't think he would ever actually retire. Where would he go? He waved at her and took her bags.

"Oh Miss Gaya, we have missed you. Your parents will be so happy to see you. It hasn't been the same here since you left." He was gushing in Sinhala to her and she thought she saw tears in his eyes, but maybe they were just watering due to his age and failing health.

"I'm thrilled to be home Suranga. America was a very interesting place, especially when you get out of the cities, but there is no place like Sri Lanka! I can't wait to eat some of Nima Auntie's food. What are we having for dinner?"

"Naturally she is making your favourite; string hoppers, fish curry and pol sambol."

Gaya's mouth salivated at the mention of it. She thought Sri Lankan food the best in the world, but it wasn't the same outside of Sri Lanka. She had joined the Sri Lankan Society at University and they regularly cooked for each other, but it never quite hit the spot.

She watched the lights of the city filter past the car window. It never seemed to change much, just more cars and more pollution. She was distracted by a wretched dog trying to cross the street. There was not much hope for the poor or the ill here. No social security like in America. The vulnerable members of society shunned rather than cared for. At least she would be able to try to do something for the peace process, to carve a better future for Sri Lanka.

They pulled up to the gate. It opened electronically now, that was new. Suranga explained they needed to put more security around the house since the ceasefire had ended. There were daily threats and army presence was on the rise in central Colombo.

Gaya jumped out of the car and into the open arms of her mother.

"Oh Putha,[5] I've missed you," her mother cried. She pressed her face close to Gaya's cheek and took a deep breath of her daughter, through her nose down into her belly. "Come inside you must be hungry."

"Hello Thathi," she said, getting a big bear hug from her father.

The smell of home hit her as she walked into the house, fish curry lingering with freshly polished floors.

Nima Aunty was in the kitchen. She was not really her aunty but their housekeeper. She had come to them from the hill country ten years ago when her children had grown up, and her mother had passed on,

---

[5] Putha – baby / darling

leaving her with no-one else to care for at home. Her husband had left to work as a driver in Saudi but never returned. She spent many years asking questions and demanding answers, but none were given, and she eventually stopped wondering about him for the sake of her own sanity.

"Nima Aunty!" Gaya gave her a big hug from behind as she stood stirring her curry pot. "I have missed you and your beautiful food so much!"

"Well, don't waste time, bring a plate and serve yourself," said Nima.

Gaya piled five red rice string hoppers[6] onto her plate. Next, she ladled on fish curry, chunks of fresh tuna simmered in a spicy red sauce. Last, but definitely her favourite, was the pol sambol. Chilli and grated coconut bound with lime juice. Her saliva glands were already working overtime, and she hadn't yet brought it to her mouth. She pulled off a bite-sized piece of string hopper and mixed it with the pol sambol and fish curry. She flicked the ball of food into her mouth, using her thumb as a catapult. Gaya gorged herself. She was famished from travelling, and the taste and smell of the spices were nourishing her emotionally and physically.

As she licked the last delicious drop of curry from her fingers, she thought about phoning Saman. She had been thinking about him a lot on the flight home. He was her childhood sweetheart, a love that turned sour in the last few months before her departure to America. It had started at Devika's birthday party. They had finished their exams and were drunk, not only on a ludicrous amount of alcohol but also on the joy of the unknown that lay

---

[6] String Hoppers – rice noodles weaved in a circle

ahead. They were young, good-looking, rich and smart. They were the next generation of doctors, politicians and managing directors. They knew it all.

Mojitos were mixed and lines of cocaine racked up. The buzz was electric. The sexual tension was reaching a peak as they strutted, preened and exhibited themselves around Devika's house.

Saman had started early. He had arrived high on ecstasy and was pouring his attention on a new girl. In those last few weeks, Gaya felt Saman pull away from her. Maybe he couldn't handle her leaving, maybe he was falling out of love with her, she wasn't sure. But she didn't want it to end like this. He was being spiteful, and she didn't feel she trusted him anymore. Drugs were becoming a big part of their lives. They no longer went out without them.

She walked over to him. Saman was massaging a girl's back. She was expected to be cool about stuff like this, everybody was. Under the influence of drugs, there were no rules, everyone knew that. She didn't want to appear childish.

"Hey," said Gaya, sitting down next to them. They didn't look up, lost in their own fantasies of the touch of a stranger. Gaya shivered. She felt so alone.

She left the party soon after asking him to come with her. He refused. People told her they had seen him leave the party with the girl. He told her he went home to sleep, but he didn't seem to care if she believed him or not.

Things between them never returned to the way they were and a few months later Gaya left for America. They kept in touch for a while by email, eventually becoming more sporadic and then stopping altogether.

Now she was back, she wanted to see him. She still cared for him and wanted to regain their friendship. She had missed him.

She called their mutual friend Ranjit.

"Oh Gaya, babe, so good to hear your voice, come over. We're all heading out tonight but come to my place first for a drink and a catch-up."

She went up to her bedroom to change. Her parents were already in bed and she tiptoed past their room. It was easier if they didn't know she was going. Fewer questions and promises she wouldn't keep.

She took off the clothes she'd been wearing on the plane and stepped into the shower. She turned on the cold water to remove the sticky layer of thick Colombo heat. She could feel her travel weariness wash off her and vanish down the plughole.

She chose a short, sexy black cocktail dress with emerald green around the hem, that she'd bought in New York. She wanted to show off her new confident self. It was a long time since she'd seen her friends and she was no longer the awkward teenager that she had been when she left.

She took a last look in the mirror, pleased with the person who looked back. She grabbed her purse and headed out the house to flag down a tuk-tuk.

Ranjit opened the door wearing loose cotton trousers and no shirt. He had grown into a man since she'd last seen him. He threw his arms around her and she caught the scent of whisky and cigarettes.

"Gaya, it's so good to see you. No one's here yet, but they're on their way, no rush to head into town."

He poured a drink and passed it to her, Absolut Citron and Sprite. It clinked, fizzing and spitting bubbles on her nose as she put the glass to her lips. It was strong, and she enjoyed the alcohol flooding her veins. He offered her a cigarette, and she took it. She had stopped smoking in America. You'd be hung, drawn and quartered if you tried to light up in somebody's home. But here it was just too familiar.

Ranjit lit it for her and slid on to the cushions beside her.

"So, tell me, how was America?"

"It was great, really great. I missed home though."

"And what are your plans now you're back?"

"I've got a job with INR. I'm heading out East in a few weeks to start the contract."

"You're crazy to go out there, you'll probably have your head cut off by terrorists within a week. Why would you want to do that?"

"Well, I'm not planning on having my head cut off. What's the point of me studying Conflict Resolution for three years and then working in Afghanistan or somewhere else when my own country is in dire straits?"

"I don't know why you'd want to help the terrorists."

"Don't be ridiculous, it's not the terrorists I'm going to help. I want to help ordinary people: Tamils, Sinhalese, Muslims, Burghers, Veddahs. It doesn't matter what race they are. They are all Sri Lanka's people. Ordinary Tamil people are being bullied, kidnapped and murdered by both the Sinhalese government and the Tamil terrorists. Don't you think they need some help?"

"Well, I just think you should stick to helping your own people."

"I do consider them my people. Don't you get it?" Gaya breathed deeply. She knew she would get a lot of this opinion from people, including her parents. She would have to argue her corner over and over and still, they will hang on to their own ignorant narrow-minded thoughts.

"How about a line?" Ranjit grinned cheekily at her.

"Now you're talking," she said, relieved to divert the awkwardness.

Gaya's stomach turned over in anticipation as Ranjit cut two lines of cocaine on a CD case and handed it to her. She rolled up a note and inhaled the white powder. She lit a cigarette and savoured the mini explosions emanating from her brain.

"Wow, this stuff has some kick."

"I saved the best for your return Gaya." She thought there was a hint of something more in his voice. Perhaps he was flirting with her. She wasn't sure, and she didn't care. All was well at this moment in time.

"So enough about what I'm doing. What's been happening here? How's Saman?" she asked.

"He's changed Gaya, you'll get a shock when you see him. He's got too heavy on the drugs and let himself go. I've spoken to him about it, we all have, but he won't listen. He's not working, he's just living at his parents and partying day and night. Rack up another line babe."

She did so. She wanted to get wasted tonight. Blow it all out the water. Rid herself of her claustrophobic reins of dutiful daughter and conscientious student.

"Coming right up, babe."

People started to stream into the house. There were good friends of hers and new people she didn't recognize. There was a lot of squealing and hugging and then clucking at how much she had changed and how gorgeous she was looking. She could feel a few cats' claws come out and she remembered how competitive and jealous her friends could be sometimes.

"Saman will regret throwing you out with the dirty laundry," was one comment.

"Talk about ugly ducklings," was another.

Gaya let it all go over her head. She didn't want to regret coming home. She had made some solid friendships in America and she now understood what to expect from a true friend. As she turned around to head for the bathroom, she saw Saman walk in.

Ranjit was right. His skin had paled. He had lost a lot of weight and his eyes were shallow. A girl was hanging off his arm. High maintenance, Gaya thought.

She collected herself and walked over to them. Saman looked at her, first without recognition and then with surprise.

"Oh my god it's you Gaya, you've changed so much. It's good to see you." The girl scowled and tugged on his arm. "Oh, and this is my girlfriend Rajani." The girl managed a grimace in place of a smile and extended a limp hand towards her.

Gaya shook it gingerly, in case it snapped off, and managed a grimace back at her.

"I'm just on my way to the bathroom, we'll catch up after."

"Yeah, sure thing Gaya," Saman said, sloping off towards the drink and the drugs, dragging his alley cat behind him.

The party raged on until they moved to a hotel nightclub and Gaya danced for the rest of the night, letting herself go. No cares, no worries, just her in that moment. She left the dance floor to get water and go to the toilet. Saman followed her and caught up with her in the rest-room corridor.

"Hey Gaya, we haven't had a chance to catch up yet." He moved closer to her and breathed into her neck. He had been watching her all night, getting more and more horny, wondering when she had got so sexy. "Let's get back to where we left off," he said, trying to kiss her.

"Oh yuck Saman, get off me," she cried, pushing him away. She was disgusted by him now, repulsed. He had become one of those leering uncles whom she had to hide from at family functions when she was younger. She couldn't believe he had become like that, her Saman, whom she had known all her life.

"Come on Gaya, I know you still want it."

"Fuck off Saman," she said, departing to the bathroom and locking the door behind her.

She splashed her face with cold water and looked in the mirror. She felt like she was in a different world to all these people, her friends. They were shallow, self-absorbed and spoilt. Didn't they care about what was happening in their country? She wanted to go home, be by herself. She saw Ranjit on the way out.

"You're not leaving, are you?"

"Yeah, thanks for the great night but I need to sleep. I've still not had any sleep since I got off the plane."

"I'll come with you," he said.

"No Ranjit, you stay here and enjoy yourself. I'm happy to go by myself."

He grabbed her arm. "I've got more stuff I saved at home. Let's go back to mine and have a private party, just the two of us."

"No Ranjit, I want to go home."

"What the fuck is wrong with you. Have you become a prick tease since you've been in America? You've been coming on to me all night and now you want to go home?"

"What is wrong with all of you?" Gaya cried, tears welling up in her eyes. "What have you all become? Where are the friends I left behind? This isn't what life's about. You've all been given so much and you're just wasting it. I don't want this anymore."

Gaya jumped into a waiting tuk-tuk. She watched Ranjit as it drove away. He looked angry but also confused. What an idiot, she thought. They were all idiots. The rising sun was peeping at her from behind the tower blocks. She wanted to get to the safety of her bedroom and her own thoughts.

She couldn't sleep when she got home. She busied herself with unpacking and sorting through the stuff she'd left behind. The sun was shining brightly now, and she could hear her parents moving around downstairs. The smell of freshly made roti filtered up.

She descended the stairs for breakfast.

"You look tired," said Ammi. "Didn't you sleep well?"

"Not really," said Gaya, "I think I've got jetlag."

She decided to venture into town and get some of her paperwork sorted out for her new job. She didn't really feel like being under the scrutiny of her parents' watchful eye. She knew her pupils were still dilated, and she had lockjaw from chewing all night, so she slipped on her sunglasses and opened the door to brave the world.

The central business district was teeming with people. It was 08.45 and most offices had already been open from 08.00. She walked into the central plaza and took the lift to the tenth floor to the INR office. She walked into the open-plan area and gave her name to the receptionist.

"I've come to meet Jenny Carroway, my name is Gaya Somarasekera."

Jenny stood up from her desk and beckoned Gaya over. She walked towards her, past the large, paned-glass windows that looked down on the square below. Time seemed to slow down and Gaya felt like she was watching herself on a big TV screen. She held out her hand to Jenny but a second before their fingers touched a huge blast came from below; the windows blew in and Gaya was flung across the room. She hit the wall at the back of the office and fell to the floor. There was screaming from all around her. She touched her head and felt a thick, sticky liquid. Broken glass surrounded her. She held her hand up to her face, realising it was blood. The bright blue sky through the huge hole in the wall ten floors up was the last thing Gaya saw before it all went black.

4 Sweet Tea

---•—

"Miss Marni, Miss Marni!" Suresh crashed into the restaurant, panic on his face.

"My sister gone, Leela, gone!"

"Slow down Suresh, what do you mean, she's gone?" Marni put her hands on his arms to steady him.

"They take her, the men, they come night-time. My mother, nothing can do!"

His eyes were wide and startled.

"Suresh, what men? Taken her where?"

"The men, Adhikara's men. They come in white van and take her."

Marni shivered involuntarily. Adhikara was the leader of the Tamil Freedom Fighters. His name, whispered by Suresh, meant only one thing. She had heard second-hand stories of the white vans. News filtered through from the villages. Children taken from their homes, trained up as soldiers and sent out on deadly missions. There were many missing. There were no answers for the families left behind and most of the children were never heard from again.

"Suresh, we need to report this and get help."

"Report to who? If police telling, they coming, arresting my mother like terrorist and then no-one take care my brother and sisters."

"We can report it to INR. They are investigating some of these disappearances and may have some information that can help us."

"I'm scared Miss Marni, I don't want more bad things for my family."

"It's ok, they won't tell anyone else. They might know what we can do."

Suresh reluctantly followed Marni to the hut converted into a workspace for the field office of INR, hovering behind her while she knocked on the door.

Niraj called for them to come in. He was a kind, sensitive man with wide, almond-shaped eyes that looked up at them intently.

"How can I help you? Please come in, sit down."

Marni told Suresh to tell Niraj the whole story, in Tamil, from the beginning and not miss out any details. Marni had picked up some Tamil from the time she'd spent in Sri Lanka, but she was in no way fluent and she watched the two men, trying to pick up words here and there. Niraj did not take his focus off Suresh. He listened closely, writing things down as they went. When they finished, Niraj made a phone call, talking quickly and quietly. He put down the receiver and turned back to Suresh.

"We may know of the camp where they have taken her. We made contact with them before, regarding another case, and we can see if they're willing to talk. First, we need to find out if she's there. Then we will try to negotiate with them for her release."

"But why would they listen to us?" asked Suresh.

"They get a lot of their financial support from the international community. If they think there could be some bad publicity, from an international aid organization like ours, they may rethink their strategy. We have developed a certain amount of trust and we can present it rationally and unemotionally."

Suresh took a deep, slow breath.

"Don't give up hope," said Niraj

The shrill ring of the phone made them all jump, Niraj picked it up. "Yes, yes, this is Niraj, say that again. What? What's happened? I can't hear you properly. Say it a... Oh my god!" Niraj could hear now, his face draining of colour. "How many? Yes, yes ok, I'll talk with you later."

He put the phone down. The sound of the Call to Prayer filled the silence. The figures of Marni and Suresh frozen in front of him, not even their breath released.

"There's been a bomb in Colombo," he said, slowly and evenly. "There are over twenty dead. The INR head office was hit in the blast, but we have no more information yet. That was Fawaz on the phone. He left for Colombo yesterday, but he was out doing errands before going to the office, otherwise, he would have been there too."

The three of them sat in silence, each with their own thoughts. Niraj thought of his colleagues, whom he respected so highly, he hoped all of them had survived. Marni thought of the twenty people who had died so needlessly. Who were they? Who had they left behind? Suresh was longing to see his sister. What would happen to her if they couldn't find her? Would she one day be sent on one of these death missions to kill innocent people and sacrifice her own life for someone else's game?

The camp was in chaos. Vish could not get any radio signal through to the operatives in Colombo. They should have heard something by now.

"Turn on the radio," he said to Kumar. "We'll see if it's reached the news desks yet."

And there it was, breaking news...

"A bomb has exploded in the central business district of Colombo. There are over twenty fatalities, but rescue workers still cannot get into the tower blocks of Central Plaza. Adhikara has claimed responsibility in retaliation for the government air bombing of the Northern territory which accidentally hit a school and caused the deaths of seventeen children. It is believed the bomb was left in a car, parked outside Central Plaza..."

Kumar was slapping Vish on the back in congratulations. "Well done Sir, we have some victory." Vish turned off the commentator and looked at Kumar. How could he be so joyful, when so many people were dead?

"Well, we know the mission was completed, but we don't know the fates of our soldiers."

Just then the radio began to crackle. Vish grabbed it and spoke loudly and clearly. "Receiving, go ahead."

"Five of us got out, two didn't make it. Banita and Raja. They were behind us and got stopped at the checkpoint. There wasn't much time, they panicked and tried to run but they were both shot in the back seconds before the explosion. There was nothing we could do."

"We will wait for your safe return," Vish replied and turned off the radio transmitter.

Vish went to his tent and closed down the flap. He didn't want to talk to anybody. He had a nasty feeling creeping into his stomach that he recognised as guilt and shame. The death of Banita and Raja were on his hands. So too were the deaths of the innocent bystanders. He wasn't fighting for a just cause. He was a murderer, pure and simple. There was no turning back for him. He knew he couldn't do this anymore, but how could he ever make amends for the past?

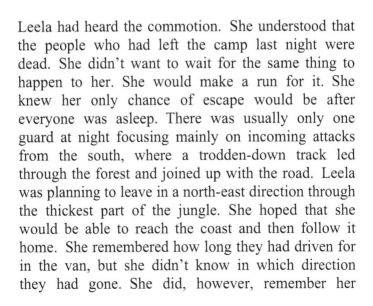

Leela had heard the commotion. She understood that the people who had left the camp last night were dead. She didn't want to wait for the same thing to happen to her. She would make a run for it. She knew her only chance of escape would be after everyone was asleep. There was usually only one guard at night focusing mainly on incoming attacks from the south, where a trodden-down track led through the forest and joined up with the road. Leela was planning to leave in a north-east direction through the thickest part of the jungle. She hoped that she would be able to reach the coast and then follow it home. She remembered how long they had driven for in the van, but she didn't know in which direction they had gone. She did, however, remember her astronomy lessons from school. She knew the north star, and she thought if she kept it to her left, then there was some chance of reaching the sea.

She thought of the jungle at night, full of snakes, leopards and elephants. It was possible she would come across any of these animals. She could get lost or fall and hurt herself and not be able to walk. In reality, there was a chance anything could happen. But at least there was a chance she could make it, unlike if she stayed in the camp. There was only one outcome here. Kill, or be killed, or probably both.

She thought about what she might need, a knife, food and water. She also thought about what would happen if she survived the jungle. In the clothes she was wearing, she would be arrested or worse. She had to get some civilian clothes. She knew there were some in the store. She had seen them when they had kitted her up in uniform. She had also seen a good knife. The cook used one, and he always kept it close.

She would need to be fully prepared, so she decided for the night after next. That evening at supper, she hid a roti in her trouser pocket and took a few bananas back to the tent with her.

She went to bed early that night, hiding the food in her boot, hoping it wouldn't attract any wandering animals looking for a feed. There were several women sleeping in the same tent and she moved her mat closer to the entrance, mumbling something about needing the toilet in the night. She dreamt of a female leopard, walking at her side, showing her the way through the jungle. She felt the warm, waxy fur of the beast beneath her fingers.

Leela woke early feeling calmer than she'd been in days. Today she could take back her life, change her fate. She thought about what would happen after she'd escaped. She realised that she wouldn't be able to stay at home. They would come looking for her. She would need to go somewhere else, but where? Then she thought of her older brother, Suresh. Maybe she would be able to find him. She knew there were foreigners where he worked. Maybe they would help her.

Moving with renewed purpose, she put on her boots, hiding the food under her mat. She pulled back the tent flap and embraced the morning sun. There weren't many people about. A group had left the camp to pick up the remaining soldiers returning from Colombo, and another group had gone into the jungle to hunt for food. She saw the Supplies Officer drinking tea with Kumar. She had her chance and slipped into the supplies tent. She headed straight for the box containing civilian clothes and pulled some out. She found a peacock-blue shalwar kameez.[7] Hanging up next to the box there were some drawstring green canvas sacks. She pulled one down and stuffed in the clothes. She could hear voices coming closer so ran to the other side of the tent, pulled up one side and threw the bag out the back of the tent into the bushes behind. The Supplies Officer came in and pulled up sharp at the sight of Leela.

"Leela, surely you're not somewhere you shouldn't be again! Do you want me to tell Kumar? What are you doing in here?"

---

[7] Shalwar Kameez – a tunic with matching trousers

"I'm sorry Miss. I was looking for boots. These are too small and are rubbing. I came in looking for you, but you weren't here."

"You shouldn't have come in when I'm not here. Go on, get out before I tell someone. And you won't be getting another pair of boots. You need to learn a little hardship. You're too soft. You need to toughen up!"

She watched Leela's departing back. She was firm with her but gentle. She felt sorry for the girl. She remembered how she had been when she first came to the camp and knew this period of adjustment from civilian to soldier was the hardest part.

Leela breathed in deep and long. She was lucky she had got away with it. She wandered over to the kitchen and took a cup of hot, sweet tea. It coursed through her body, soothing her rapidly beating heart.

The day passed uneventfully. The whole camp seemed in limbo. Vish knew he should induct the new girl, but he didn't want to. He had nothing to say to her about their purpose or what they expected of her. Did they really expect death from their loyal soldiers? Wasn't there some other way to fight this war? He was going full circle. This is where he'd come from, wasn't it? Fighting for his people with words. Becoming a political force, taking on the giants that ruled his kingdom. Putting forward argument and counter-argument, discussions, strategies, legislation, but eventually all to no avail. This is what it had come down to. Killing and being killed.

The girl could wait another day. She seemed to be calmer today, her agitation from the previous days easing off. That was one good thing, he thought. She was accepting her fate. Maybe he would feel better tomorrow. Be able to remember why he was here and the future he was fighting for.

He watched Leela sitting with the cook. He was showing her how to use the machete to divide up the deer meat brought back from the hunt. Maybe he didn't need to worry about her, maybe she would fit in well here.

Leela felt the heaviness of the knife. She wasn't used to handling such a big knife, but she knew she would feel safer to have it with her. She had watched the cook last night take the knife with him to his mat and hang it on the branch above where he slept. It was close to the supplies tent and near to where she was planning to slip out the back of the camp. She had managed to get more food. She had been helping as much as she could in the kitchen and taking her chance when she could. She took the shovel they used for toileting, made her excuses and headed around the back of the supplies tent. She found the canvas hold-all and pushed the food down deep, covering it with the clothes. She sealed it up tight and buried it further down into the bush to ensure it wouldn't be discovered. She found an old, plastic soda bottle, which she filled with water and shoved into the bag.

She returned to camp and approached the cook again.

"Do we ever get to eat fish here? We can't be that far from the sea," she ventured.

"Far enough," was the cook's reply, and he gave her a look to warn her not to ask anymore.

That night Leela lay on her mat, watching the insects on the roof of the tent. She thought about her mother and grandmother. It would be so good to see them again, feel their arms around her. She was proud of herself so far to not fall apart, but she was desperate for someone to put their arm around her and tell her she was going to be ok.

She lay motionless for several hours, hearing the rest of the camp packing up and going to bed. The soldiers had returned from Colombo and had continued a de-brief late into the night with the supervisors. She had heard no noise for a while and thought everyone must be asleep by now. She sat up and looked around her. She watched the rhythmic breathing of the other women and felt sure they were in deep sleep. She picked up her boots and tiptoed out into the night. From there she was she could see the silhouette of the night guard. She crept around the back of her tent to be as far from him as possible, stepping slowly to minimise the sound her feet made on the sticks and leaves. There was a wind, and she was grateful for the noise it was making, rustling the leaves on the trees, covering the sound of her footsteps. She slipped her feet into her boots and squatted down to tie her shoelaces. After making sure no-one was checking on her, she headed to the back of the supplies tent and pulled out her bag. She walked on a little further to the spot she intended to leave from and left the bag there. Next, she headed for the knife. She could see it glinting in the moonlight, where it hung limply from the branch. The cook was asleep on his side, snoring slightly. She reached over him and tried to take the knife from the tree. It was stuck, making a scraping noise as she yanked it and pulled it free. The cook stirred and rolled over onto his back, mumbling in his sleep. The guard stood up and looked over, shining his torch on the sleeping cook. Leela slunk back into the shadows and held her breath. She closed her eyes and counted to ten. When she opened them, she saw the guard had turned back to face the forest. Call yourself trained terrorists, she thought to herself, a smile playing on her lips. Outsmarted by a schoolgirl!

Leela slipped out from behind the trees and hurried to her bag. She grabbed it and entered the forest. Her heart was in her throat. She wasn't sure which was worse, the camp she was leaving behind, or the dark, sinister jungle she was about to discover. She rolled back her shoulders, took a deep breath and moved forward.

———————●●———————

Vish woke up to the shouting.

"My knife has gone!" The cook was storming around the camp, lifting up mats and cooking pots, turning over stones and firewood logs.

"So has Leela!" one of the women called running out of the tent.

"Maybe she has just gone to the toilet," said Vish. "Check in the forest." The women spread out, calling her name.

Vish stood in the middle of the camp facing north. He looked left to Leela's sleeping tent, then he looked right to where the cook slept, and the missing knife. He turned and faced south to where the guard's station was. He already knew she was gone. The night guard, roused from his slumber, approached Vish with shame written on his face.

"I'm sorry Sir, I heard a noise and looked, but I saw nothing. I thought it was just Lilath uncle talking in his sleep. It's my fault."

Vish walked over to the perimeter of the camp. Slowly he followed it around until he found scuff marks in the dirt and some broken foliage.

"She went this way. I need a pack made up of food and water, I'm going after her."

Kumar heard this and hurried over. "Vish Uncle just leave her. She won't make it out of this jungle alive and, even if she does, we can just pick her up again from home. You don't need to do this."

But Vish was feeling something he hadn't experienced for a long time. Excitement? He wasn't sure, but he knew he had to go after the girl. Something was calling him from deep inside the jungle. He saw a door open, and he wanted to run through it as fast as he could.

"Believe me, Kumar, I do need to do this. I really do."

5 Crab Curry

———————— ● ——

Rushani swept the leaves from the sand in a rhythmical motion. She enjoyed working outside and early morning was her favourite time of day. She liked the moments before the guests woke up. It gave her time just for herself. She was neither mother nor daughter, nor employee. She was just Rushani. She hummed quietly to herself: An old lullaby that her father sang to her when she was small and she had sung to her own daughter, Meena.

She walked to the beach to pick up the rubbish left by last night's revellers. Food packets, half-eaten, picked apart by crows, an empty arrack bottle and plastic cups. Must be locals, she thought. That was one good thing about the foreigners. They tended not to litter. They didn't like leaving a mess behind them.

She stopped to admire the east coast sun rising over the water, looming huge and orange. Bringing with it silent promises of new hope, a new day. She was unaware that she was also being watched. She stretched her hands up to the sky, feeling the sun's rays on her face. With a smile, she picked up the rubbish and walked back through the gates of the hotel.

Chris had woken early. He lay in bed listening to the sound of the brush on the sand. Rushani must have arrived, he thought. She normally came about this time. She caught the first bus out of the Sinhalese village in the morning and the last bus back at night. Chris knew this because he had observed it. He noticed a lot of things. He enjoyed watching people and this forced vacation had provided a great opportunity in the most ideal setting.

He spent a lot of time watching the proprietors, Marni and Jake. They were always warm and welcoming to their guests, especially Marni, but he couldn't help feeling that the warmness was not there between the two of them. They seemed to have the perfect life: a beautiful hotel in a spectacular place, a gorgeous daughter and the comfort of having one another. But that was what was missing. They didn't seem comforted by each other. They were two separate entities passing like ships in the night, only stopping to exchange information regarding the hotel, their guests or their daughter. He hardly ever saw them in the restaurant at the same time, and he had not seen any kind of intimacy. Maybe they saved it all for the privacy of their room. It must be a strange kind of life to share all your personal time with your staff and guests. He hoped this was the case. He liked both of them. They deserved to be happy.

He had also been observing the other guests. He had ascertained that they were all there for work. Marni had told him they rarely had tourists these days. She said they would have had to close if it wasn't for business coming in from the aid workers. Some were here to rebuild after the tsunami, and some were here for the war. Chris worked for a de-mining company mainly in the far North. His job was to locate and remove landmines from contaminated areas. He had seen the effects of landmines on their victims and the responsibility of this project played heavily on Chris. He was originally from Norway but had lived all over the world during the last ten years. He went wherever the work was. His friends and family worried about him living this way, but so far it had suited him. Until recently, that is. He had started to feel lonely, never quite finding home, and he also worried about being too old to start a family. Of course, he met women and had relationships, but they were always transitory. Either he or they would get posted to a new location and that would be the end.

He was constantly fending off the French woman Claudette. She had set her sights on him and he felt that she was a woman who normally got what she wanted. He, however, did not want her. He had met women like her before in this field. She was a hard-nosed businesswoman who felt like the world owed her something because she worked for an aid organisation. She thought the locals should be grateful for having her input, but she had no idea how to talk to people. She commanded rather than asked and saw herself above the people she was there to help. In the past, he may have slept with a woman like Claudette. Out of loneliness, sexual frustration or boredom. But he didn't want to anymore. It wasn't worth it. He was looking for something deeper, more satisfying. Someone he could feel through his soul, not just his sexual organs.

He got out of bed and went outside to watch the sunrise. He saw the silhouette of Rushani on the beach. Her hands stretched out to the sun. This was a real woman, he thought: elegant, soulful and capable. He knew nothing about her background, but he felt she understood life in a way that only came from understanding death. She moved with strength and pride, always shoulders back and chin up, but up close, the few times Chris had exchanged words with her, he had seen something so vulnerable and worn in the dark recesses of her eyes. He assumed she was married, as she had told him on the first day that she had a daughter. He silently wished for her a good life, one without a struggle.

The sharp tone of Claudette disrupted any further thoughts of Rushani. "Bonjour Christian, what is keeping you so enthralled, out there in the ocean?"

She sat down next to him with a pot of fresh coffee and a packet of Gauloises. "Do you want to share this with me? Shall I get you a cup? Bring a cup would you."

Chris cringed inwardly as Claudette clicked her fingers at Rushani. Rushani turned to look at her with her usual composure.

"Yes, madam."

"Her name is Rushani," Chris said to Claudette as Rushani walked into the kitchen.

"Oh, I can't remember all these names. Here, you want to smoke?"

Chris took a cigarette. He rarely smoked, but he felt he might need one to get through this cup of coffee.

"It's so beautiful here. You must learn to relax a little more Christian. Here let me help you."

She began to massage Chris' shoulders with her long, manicured fingers.

"Ooh, you are so knotted, you naughty boy! You must stop taking the world on your shoulders. Let's meet this afternoon after I finish work. I can give you a proper massage. Show you how to relax Claudette style!"

Rushani returned from the kitchen with the cup. Her eyes rested on Claudette's fingers around Chris' neck.

"Thank you," said Chris. Rushani's eyes flicked up to meet his.

"You're welcome," she said and turned to head back to the kitchen.

"Thanks for the offer Claudette," said Chris turning slightly so that her hands dropped from his shoulders, "but I already feel very relaxed. Also, I'm going on a trip this afternoon and won't be back till late."

"Oh, that's a shame." Claudette looked very put out. "Will I see you for dinner?"

"I'm not sure yet what time I'll get back, but I guess I'll probably be back around dinnertime. Might see you then."

Chris got up from the table and hurried over to the reception counter. Claudette watched him go, pouting and looking dejected.

"Hi Jake," said Chris. "Can you book me in for a trip this afternoon. I'm happy to go anywhere and do anything."

"Sure," said Jake. "How about some elephant and crocodile spotting and maybe a temple or two thrown in?"

"Sounds marvellous," Chris said. "Can't think of a better way to spend the afternoon!"

Chris was happy to be on the open road. Either side of him there were bright green paddy fields. The sun was high in the sky and the wind was blowing the hair back from his face. Muzil was driving the tuk-tuk. He worked for the hotel, hiring out himself and his tuk-tuk to guests.

"We will see a very old Buddhist monastery, Mr Chris. High on a hill with a very nice view."

"That would be great Muzil, any chance of a swim as well?"

"Yes, Mr Chris, very nice beach there. I stay in the tuk-tuk."

"Don't you want to swim?"

"No, Mr Chris. The only time I swim was tsunami time and I don't want to again!"

"Well Muzil, if that's the only time you've been swimming then I'm not surprised you didn't like it. You should come in the water with me today. I can teach you how to swim."

"We will see Mr Chris, we will see."

The walk up to the monastery was hot with little shade. Chris wiped his face on his shirtsleeve.

"How much further is it Muzil?"

"Nearly there, around this corner."

The next corner opened up to a spectacular view of the beach and ocean stretching out in front.

"Wow that looks inviting," said Chris. "I wish I could dive straight in from here."

"Come, Mr Chris, this is the way."

They scrambled up the sheer stone, past a rock pool with exquisite lily pads. There was a statue of Buddha, twelve feet high and a cave in the hillside containing another smaller statue. There were also out-buildings, presumably where the monks lived.

They headed back down on the shady part of the rock and walked through the soft sand to the beach. Chris noticed elephant footprints and dung.

"Should I be looking out for elephants?" He asked Muzil.

"It's ok now but sunset they come."

Chris stripped off his shirt and shoes and ran down the beach, diving into the cool water. There was a good amount of swell and he swam out to body surf a wave back to shore. The wave dumped him onto the beach where Muzil was sitting. He sat up laughing, his face and hair covered in sand.

"Come on Muzil, come into the water. I'll make sure nothing happens to you."

Muzil reluctantly agreed and took off his shirt and sarong, leaving on just a pair of shorts. He took a few tentative steps into the water, holding onto Chris' arm. As they got deeper, Muzil's breathing got shallower. They were now in the dump zone, where the waves were breaking.

"Ok, we need to go either over the wave or under it, depending on how big it is. Here, hold my hand."

They jumped over a wave but as it passed under them, the body of water increased and Muzil was suddenly out of his depth. He cried out just before his head went under. Chris was still holding his hand and pulled him back up to the surface, coughing and spluttering.

"I want to go back. I don't like it," he said in between gasps of air.

"It's ok Muzil, try not to panic, you're safe. But we need to time it right to get back into shore otherwise we will get dumped."

"No, I can't…," he said, pulling away from Chris. His feet found a footing and he tried to make a break towards the shore. Chris looked behind him and saw a larger wave forming.

"No, wait, Muzil, you'll get caught by that wave, we need to stay out deeper." But it was too late. Muzil was already wading into the path of the oncoming wave. Chris hurled himself through the water and threw his arms around Muzil just as the wave came down on top of them. They spun underwater, hitting the gravelly bottom where Chris took the brunt of the impact. His body scraped along the beach under the weight of Muzil, whom he was still holding tight. Just as suddenly, the water was gone.

Muzil was coughing up water in-between sobs. There was a bad graze along Chris' left side.

"The tsunami," Muzil was saying. "We were spinning and spinning like a washing machine. But the water was black. We couldn't see which way was up. I was looking for the sky but all I could see was black. I didn't know how to get to the surface. I didn't know which way to go. I lost my son that day."

Muzil was crying now and Chris helped him up. "I am so sorry Muzil. Sorry to make you come into the water. Sorry to bring up such painful memories."

"Look!" Muzil exclaimed, sucking air through his teeth. "You are bleeding."

Chris looked down. He was bleeding from his ribs to his waist and again down his thigh, but he was ashamed and embarrassed at the distress he had caused Muzil, so felt very little pain.

"We must get your cuts cleaned. We will go to the Sinhalese village. It's not far."

They changed out of their wet shorts into dry sarongs and climbed back into the tuk-tuk. When they reached the village, they stopped at a small shop and Muzil asked if they had any bandages, but they were all out.

"We will go to the village well and at least wash all the sand out."

They walked the short distance to the well. Muzil hauled up a bucket of the cool, clear water and poured it over Chris' cuts. He was just hauling up the second bucket when a voice called out to them.

"You want help?"

<hr />

Rushani was on her way home. She had had a good day. Although that woman, Claudette, annoyed her. It was the way she spoke to people, always barking out orders. And the way she slithered around that nice man Chris. She reminded Rushani of a rattlesnake, noisy and poisonous. Her daughter and her mother were at the bus stop like always, Meena's expectant face searching through the bus windows. Rushani jumped off and smothered her daughter with kisses.

"Wow, I think you've grown since this morning!"

"Come Ammi, I want to show you something, quick!"

Meena dragged her mother from the bus stop and down a stony path, off the main street.

"What is it, Meena? Where are you taking me?"

"Look Ammi, foreigner!"

Rushani looked up and saw a very attractive, half-naked man, standing at the well with his back to them. She recognized Muzil and then gave a gasp when she realised it was Chris, her cheeks flushing as she dragged her eyes from his torso.

Meena was holding her mother's hand and giggling beside her. Rushani's mother was watching the spectacle with a frown on her face.

"You want help?" She called over.

The men looked up from what they were doing and Muzil started speaking rapidly in Sinhala. Rushani walked closer and saw the long graze down Chris' side.

"Please come, my home. I have medicine."

"Thank you, that would be very kind," said Chris.

Rushani could sense he felt embarrassed. Her mother was scrutinizing him with her sharp eyes and being half-naked he was more than a little vulnerable. She showed him into her house and told Meena to run and get him a chair from the neighbours. Muzil went to help her carry it and Rushani went outside to heat some water on the Calor gas stove in their makeshift outside kitchen. Her home was simple, but she loved it because it was her sanctuary. There was one main living area with a small cupboard containing a photo of her late husband

and a small bedroom off to the left where the three of them slept.

"Is that your husband?" Chris asked. "What does he do for work?"

"Yes husband, dead now, murdered."

"I'm very sorry," said Chris. "Do you know who killed him?"

"Yes, I know, Sinhalese terrorists. No money give, so kill."

"Was anyone brought to justice?"

"No justice. We live like this."

"I'm sorry Rushani. It is a terrible thing for you and your daughter to go through."

"Life goes," she said. "Now show me, I put turmeric."

Rushani smoothed on the thick, yellow paste, being as gentle as she could. Chris winced a couple of times but tried to hide it, feeling an urge to gain the respect of this strong but gentle woman.

Rushani's mother called to Rushani from the kitchen. She answered back and then turned to Chris and spoke in English.

"You hungry? My mother find crab from lagoon today, we eat crab."

Chris could smell the spices in the air and agreed gratefully. It had been a long time since lunch. Rushani's mother brought out two plates with crab curry and string hoppers. She gave one to Chris and the other to Muzil. Rushani, her mother and her daughter sat down on the mat and silently watched them. Chris was used to this kind of hospitality as he had been a guest at colleagues' homes in the North. He knew they would not eat until he had finished, so he tucked in. It was delicious. The combination of spices mixed with tomatoes, onions and huge pieces of crab still in their shells. Chris broke the crab apart, sucking out the flesh and spicy sauce. It was by far the freshest crab he had ever eaten. Soft and juicy, it melted in his mouth, the sweetness of the sauce mixed with the hotness of the chilli made his mouth salivate. His body tingled and his brain exploded with the intensity of the heat. By the time he finished, his hands, lap and chin were a mess.

"You not like?" Rushani teased but looked satisfied by the clean plate.

"We go back now Mr Chris," said Muzil. "It's dangerous on the road after dark, too many elephants."

They washed up and paid their respects to Rushani's mother, for the invitation, who avoided eye contact but gave them a nod. Chris gave Meena a tickle as they headed out the door.

"Thank you Rushani, for the first aid, and your hospitality. I guess I'll see you tomorrow."

"Yes Sir," said Rushani and watched the tuk-tuk for a long time as it headed down the main road back to the hotel.

Rushani's mother watched her daughter, hoping she might be wrong about the look she had just witnessed, crossing Rushani's face.

The hotel restaurant was buzzing when they arrived back. The guests had just finished their dinner and Claudette beckoned Chris over.

"Where have you been? We were all getting worried about you. We thought you'd fallen down a black hole or something. And what have you done to yourself? Sit down, we must get you a drink."

"Oh, I just landed a wave wrong in the sea today. I think I'll head off to bed, I'm pretty exhausted, thanks anyway."

"Well, tomorrow we must definitely have dinner together. I want to know all about your projects and pick your brains about funding proposals."

"Ok, well, see you tomorrow." Chris hurried off to his cabana. He showered and lay his sore body on the cool sheets. All pain seemed to vanish as his thoughts drifted away. He fell asleep dreaming of Rushani and how it made him feel when she smiled at him.

6 Watalappan

Gaya stretched, paying particular attention to the tight muscles down her left shin. She was still recovering from the effects of the bomb blast, which had fortunately only left her with a sprained ankle and some cuts and bruising. There was one bad cut along her right temple, which needed five stitches but was healing well.

She had lost consciousness immediately after the explosion due to the bang on her head, but the overstretched hospital had given her the all-clear when she came too, sending her home the same day. The rest of the staff in the INR office had been equally lucky due to the distance of their office from the source of the blast.

The people below them had not fared this well. They knew there were twenty-seven dead, now that all the bodies were recovered, and another fifteen seriously injured.

They were all civilians except for three Sinhalese army officers and two Tamil terrorists who were reported to have detonated the bomb.

Gaya felt sick at the loss of life. She wanted more than ever to relocate to the East and start work with INR. One positive effect of the disaster was that Gaya's parents were more supportive of her plans, realising the risk of living in Colombo was in fact much higher than in other parts of the country.

Saman had visited the day before. He was straight and much more like his old self. He apologised for his behaviour the night they went out and congratulated her on 'climbing out of the gutter' and finding meaning to her life. He wished her success in her new job and said he hoped they could meet when she returned to Colombo. She wanted him to be happy. She hoped he'd find the courage to stand up on his own and create a life for himself. He had such an opportunity. She couldn't bear that he was wasting it when there were so many with so little.

She swung her legs out of bed and padded downstairs to the kitchen where Nima was preparing lunch.

"Good morning, Gaya Putha. I'm about to make Watalappan,[8] get yourself some breakfast and then come and help me."

"Ooh you're the best, Nima Aunty,"

Gaya made herself some toast and went to watch Nima preparing the ingredients. She was melting jaggery[9] on the stove. Gaya hadn't been able to get jaggery in America and she had missed it. She watched the blocks of hard brown sugar melt into a thick, sticky liquid. Next, she added coconut milk, water, sugar and salt, blending them into a smooth mixture.

---

[8] Watalappan – custard pudding (coconut, nuts & spices)

[9] Jaggery – sugar made from palm sap

"Get the eggs from the fridge and break them into this bowl," she said to Gaya. "Now add the cardamom, nutmeg and vanilla and beat them together." She took the bowl from Gaya and poured the rich creamy liquid into an oven dish.

"Now cover the dish and put it in the oven to steam. It should take about forty minutes. Let's make tea while we're waiting."

Gaya placed the dish in the oven and then pulled up a stool opposite Nima. This had always been one of her favourite places at home. Watching Nima bustle about the kitchen, breathing in the delicious smells and being chief taster.

"So Putha, are you ready to go?"

"Yes, I'm leaving in the morning. They are sending a vehicle for me. It will take most of the day, but I should get there by dinnertime."

"Your parents will worry about you."

"Yes, I know, but they will worry about me wherever I am, whatever I'm doing."

"You must look after yourself, a young, single girl. You will be a target and I'm not talking about terrorists."

"Yes, I know, and I will take care of myself. I'm not that innocent, although my parents would like to think I am!"

"No, none of us are that innocent, that's how we know to warn the next generation," she said, giving Gaya a wink. "Just remember that you will never be truly happy if you spend all your energies looking after everyone else. You need to look after your own happiness."

Gaya slipped off her stool and walked around the bench to give Nima a hug. "I will remember that, thanks for the advice."

Gaya watched Nima get the dinner ready. She was preparing murunga or drumsticks, as they were otherwise known, Gaya's favourite vegetable. Green sticks of hard skin around a soft middle, which you could pull off the stick with your teeth. She was boiling them up in a white coconut sauce to accompany a spicy chicken curry and rice.

"I can smell the Watalappan," Gaya said, standing up and taking the steaming dish out of the oven.

"You should wait until it has cooled down," said Nima. "You've always been an impatient child!"

"Sorry Nima Aunty, I can't wait!"

Gaya grabbed a spoon and took a huge helping. She closed her eyes in rapture as the smooth, creamy dessert slid down her throat.

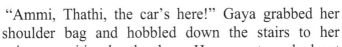

"Ammi, Thathi, the car's here!" Gaya grabbed her shoulder bag and hobbled down the stairs to her suitcase waiting by the door. Her parents rushed out of the living room, attempting to still their hands that wanted so much to grab her and stop her from going.

"It feels like we've only just got you back, and then we nearly lost you for good and now we're losing you again," her mother said crying into her hair.

"You're not losing me Ammi I'll be back in a few months."

Gaya's dad hugged her tight. "I'm proud of you Gaya, just take care and protect yourself at all times."

"I will Thathi."

Gaya was grateful for the absence of a lecture about her naivety in wanting to do this kind of work and she hurried out before he could launch into a sermon. She jumped into the waiting Land Cruiser and opened the window, blowing kisses to her family.

"I'll ring as soon as I arrive," she yelled out, as the wheels rolled forward. She glanced across at Jenny Carroway and hoped her face had an expression of 'I've got this,' rather than the trepidation that was making her heart thump hard and fast inside her chest.

The traffic was horrendous as they made their way out of Colombo, but their driver was an expert navigator and managed a decent speed, dodging and weaving, and several hours later they were on the open road. They began the steep ascent into the hill country. The air temperature dropped considerably, and the views were spectacular.

"On a clear day you can almost see the ocean from here," said Jenny. She was the Project Manager and her direct boss. She was American, so they chatted for most of the journey about the years Gaya had spent in the States. Jenny explained INR's organisational structure to her and told her about the staff she would work with.

"You may become frustrated as there is a hell of a lot of red tape. Our hands are tied in many areas, so we end up becoming information gatherers and social support. We would like to do more, but if we try, then our visas are revoked, and we get kicked out the country. We're in a difficult position. You may hear stories that shock you, that you will want to shout from the rooftops, but we must be very discreet as people's lives are continually at risk. Protecting the people is our number one priority and unfortunately, that means burying a lot of crimes. We hope that one day there will be an opportunity to bring some justice."

Gaya watched Jenny, silent now in her own thoughts, staring at the blue sky through the open window of the Land Cruiser. Their shared experience during the bomb blast had brought them close quickly, and Gaya was glad she had Jenny to support her in her new role. Gaya thought how passionate Jenny must be about her job and how many times she must have been powerless to do anything to help the people she was working with. Gaya had heard stories about the disappearances and murders, which continued daily, with no accountability.

They left the lush green of the hills behind; the terrain becoming sparse and dry as they began the decline towards the East Coast. They stopped at a roadside restaurant for some lunch. With tummies full of okra curry, dhal and rice, they set off on the last leg of the journey.

The sky was turning a beautiful blend of pinks, oranges and reds and Gaya could taste the salt in the air. They must be nearly there. They had driven through an elephant sanctuary on the way, having to stop for one lone bull elephant that was peacefully munching leaves from the trees and blocking the road. Gaya loved the wildness of this part of the country. She felt free and her heart lifted. It was nothing like the polluted confines of Colombo.

They finally arrived at the hotel and parked in a gravelled car park. Gaya got out the vehicle and stood for a moment, taking in her surroundings. A lush, manicured garden, beautiful wooden cabanas, and the great Indian ocean rolling out majestically beyond.

She was enchanted. She felt that she had finally found her paradise. A man, who introduced himself as Suresh, showed her to her room. Jenny told her to have a shower then meet in the restaurant for dinner where she could introduce her to everyone.

The room was delightful. Wooden walls with a weaved palm frond roof, a large four-poster bed draped in a mosquito net and a door leading to an outside bathroom, complete with a frangipani tree and mosaic tiling. There was a frangipani flower on her pillow and pink and red bougainvillea floating in a bowl of water on the table.

Gaya stood under the cool gush of water that sprung from the tree shower in her bathroom. She felt instantly refreshed from the long journey and looked to see which clothes she should put on for dinner. She had gone shopping in Colombo and bought herself several sets of shalwar kameez for work. She needed something modest, that also suited the heat and dust.

She chose a black suit with red embroidery and a red chiffon scarf. She fixed her hair up high on her head, and headed to the restaurant, the soft sand squeezing between her toes.

There were already quite a few people in the restaurant. Gaya felt suddenly shy and hung back a little.

Jenny spotted her and called her over. "And here is the lovely Gaya who has been through so much already for our organisation. I don't think we wrote 'almost being killed in a bomb blast' as a necessary requirement in the job description, did we!"

There was laughter around the table as people released their pent-up emotions, firstly from the news of the bomb blast, and then from the waiting, to hear the fates of their colleagues.

A man approached Gaya and held out his hand. "Welcome Gaya, my name is Niraj. I'm the field coordinator so we'll be working closely over the next few months. There is also Fawaz, but he is still in Colombo and I think you may have met him already."

"Yes, I did, pleased to meet you Niraj," replied Gaya.

"And here we have Nuwan and Champath who are local staff."

Gaya shook everybody's hand and sat down at the table.

"What can we get you to drink?" asked Niraj.

"Oh, I'll take a lime juice please," said Gaya.

"Don't be ridiculous!" cried out Jenny. "She's just being polite, get the girl a bloody vodka in there. This is a celebration. There's no need to stand on ceremony around here. We work hard, and we play hard. Sometimes it's the only way to process the things we see."

Gaya smiled and nodded to Niraj's expectant look. "Yes, go on, pop a vodka in there." She smiled at Jenny, grateful that she would be able to relax into a stiff drink.

Jenny winked at her. "Us girls have got to stick up for each other!"

Several hours later, Gaya was feeling very at home. Her colleagues were kind and welcoming and she felt positive they would support her wherever her work would lead. She also met some other guests who had joined their table. There was a woman called Claudette who had given her three air kisses, and then said loudly, "Darling we must take you clothes shopping, I see you would benefit from some expert advice!" Gaya just giggled and said "ok". She didn't take offence. She thought Claudette entertaining, even though Gaya herself thought she'd scrubbed up well.

A man, by the name of Rakesh, had caught her eye. She only spoke a few words to him as he seemed to need the private attention of Niraj for much of the night, but she enjoyed the thrill of his presence, whenever she could steal a glance at him.

"I wouldn't go there," Jenny had whispered in her ear. Gaya flushed at being caught out. "Not unless you want to join half the female NGO workers currently in Sri Lanka nursing a broken heart."

She also met Chris, who seemed friendly, Marni and Jake, and their gorgeous daughter Zoe, and a lovely Australian couple called Eva and Jo, who immediately took it upon themselves to become her surrogate parents.

The evening was turning into a party, out came guitars and cooking pots turned into drums.

The vodka, beer and arrack were making their rounds and there was an undeniable festive air to the proceedings. Gaya felt like a moment alone to collect her thoughts and wandered out to the beach. The calming rhythm of the waves crashing on the beach in front of her and the noise from the restaurant behind her felt like they were part of her. She breathed deeply and with a rush of euphoria, threw off her clothes, down to her underwear, and sprinted into the water. She dived and swam, playing with the waves that danced around her. This was living, she thought. She floated for a while, drunk and happy, out of reach of the peaking waves. She stared at the stars and wished on all of them.

As she swam back to the beach, she spotted a figure near her clothes. When she got nearer, she could see it was a man, at the same time catching sight of the gleaming barrel of a rifle. She froze, not knowing whether to grab her clothes or head back to the sea. He spoke to her then in Sinhala.

"Are you Sinhalese?" he asked.

"Yes," she replied.

"What are you doing swimming in the dark, don't you know it's dangerous?"

Gaya walked forward, deciding it was better to get dressed and head back to the hotel. She recognized the uniform of the Sri Lankan army.

"I'm a strong swimmer but thank you for your concern."

"I think maybe you like a little danger. You have been partying with these foreigners?" he asked nodding his head towards the lights of the hotel.

"I'm not partying, I'm working there."

She tried to walk past him towards the gates of the hotel. He grabbed her arm. "I don't think that's right. I think you are a party girl, drinking and flirting with foreign men. Maybe you need a reminder who you belong to."

Gaya felt her blood run cold. "I'm going back to the hotel," she said, but he still had hold of her arm. She pulled away from him, but he dug his fingers in tighter.

"Gaya, Gaya, are you out here?" Jenny was calling her.

"I'm here, Jenny," she shouted. The soldier relaxed his grip and Gaya ran up the sandbank to the hotel.

"Are you ok, what's happened? Who was that on the beach?"

"I'm ok," Gaya said, her heart pounding. "I was just foolish to go swimming by myself. I won't be doing that again." Jenny watched the soldier retreat and turned to Gaya hugging her tight. "Well, I'm glad you're ok. You'll probably be on a steep learning curve for the first few weeks. You just have to stay on the right side of trouble!"

Gaya asked Jenny to say good night to everyone for her and headed off to bed. The incident on the beach hadn't scared her. It had just made her angry and sad. There was such ignorance to wade through. She didn't know when they would find peace; for men, women, rich, poor, Tamil, Sinhalese or Muslim. There were so many barriers to integration. But the journey had to start with the first step.

Remarkably, she slept like a baby and woke anxious to begin her first day in the office. She breakfasted on fruit salad and coffee and then went to find Niraj. He was already hard at work at his desk and she knocked and walked in.

"Hi Gaya, I hope you slept well."

"I did, thanks Niraj."

"Jenny told me what happened to you on the beach last night. Unfortunately, it's not a rare occurrence, so women have to be extra vigilant when there aren't many people around."

"I knew that, that's why I feel ashamed and stupid about the whole thing. I think I just got carried away by being here and everything."

"Please don't beat yourself up about it. Society is at fault, not you. Come, sit down and let's get stuck in. I have a project for you."

Niraj explained the story of Suresh's sister, Leela, going missing. He told her they had some leads, which they were following, and they were waiting to hear back from their contacts. In the meantime, he wanted Gaya to contact the embassies and try to organise a refugee visa to get her safely out of the country to somewhere she would be safe.

Gaya got straight on to the embassies. They were sympathetic, but none could provide any practical support. "Do you know how many people are trying to get visas every day?" came their reply. "And you're asking for a visa for someone who is missing. The paperwork is impossible. Find her first and then we can talk."

The phone rang and Niraj answered it. He scribbled something down on a piece of paper, thanked the caller and hung up. "We've got the number for a satellite phone at the camp where they think she is. They're expecting our call."

He dialled the number and sat drumming his pencil against an empty teacup. The phone was answered and Niraj spoke in Tamil. Gaya couldn't understand what he was saying, but he spoke calmly and firmly. His back was towards her, so she was unable to read his expression. Finally, he put the phone down and turned to face her.

"Well, are they going to release her?" she asked.

"They said they can't release her because she's not there. She's escaped into the jungle and they have no idea where she is. The contact says he doubts any of us will ever see her again." Niraj put his head in his hands, wondering how the hell he was going to tell Suresh.

7 Devilled Manioc

Suresh was by the front fence digging a hole to plant a Kombuk tree seedling.

Gaya called out to him as she approached,

"Hey Suresh, have you got a minute? Niraj wanted to have a quick chat with you."

"Yes, Miss Gaya, I come." Suresh washed his hands with the garden hose and wiped them on his sarong.

Gaya turned to walk back along the stepping-stones to the office, Suresh following.

"Go in, take a seat," said Gaya, closing the door behind them.

Suresh looked at Niraj's worried face and knew this was not good news. He sat down quickly, his knees shaking.

"I'm sorry to have to tell you…" Niraj began.

"No!" cried Suresh, gripping the table so hard, his knuckles turned white.

"Wait, Suresh, she's not dead, she's missing."

Suresh released his grip and took some deep breaths. He let the relief wash over him before he spoke.

"What do you mean, 'missing'?"

"It looks like she's run off, into the jungle. We don't know much more."

"How do we know that they are telling us the truth?"

"We don't," said Niraj, "but we've got a good idea as there is no reason for them to lie at this stage. We would have made a good deal for her release. They would have made sure she didn't come to any harm."

The door opened, and Rakesh looked in.

"Oh, sorry Niraj, I didn't know you had company, I'll come back later."

"No Rakesh, please come in, Suresh, do you mind, he could have some good ideas."

Suresh had met Rakesh several times before and felt comfortable with him. "Yes, please Mr Rakesh, come in."

"What's happened?" said Rakesh, sitting down. He was snacking on devilled manioc and chickpeas from the kade[10] and the smell made Gaya's stomach rumble.

Niraj quickly told him the events leading up to Leela's disappearance.

"Yes, I would say they are telling the truth. It's possible she was able to escape."

"Should we be out looking for her?" Gaya asked.

"I don't think that will be of any use until we know more. I know where that camp is, and it's surrounded by jungle. We have no idea which way she may have gone plus they will probably also be looking for her. There's no point anybody else being

---

[10] Kade – street hut selling food

caught up in it. We will have to wait and hope she can make it out on her own."

Suresh's eyes filled with tears at the thought of his little sister alone in the jungle. He blinked them away. He knew Rakesh was right. He would have no hope of finding her before them.

Niraj spoke softly, "Suresh don't give up hope. Even if they find her, we still have the possibility of making a deal with them. We can still try to get her back."

"Yes, thank you, Mr Niraj, I have my work to do." Suresh got up quickly and left the room. Nobody tried to stop him.

"Keeping busy will do him good for the time being," said Rakesh.

Gaya shifted in her chair. She was feeling unnerved by her own physical reaction to the closeness of this man to her. She tried to pull herself together.

"Niraj, what can we do in the meantime?" she asked.

Niraj turned to Rakesh, "What do you think Rakesh?"

Gaya could feel Rakesh's eyes boring into her. "Gaya isn't it?"

"Hi, yes, that's right," she forced herself to lift her head and keep eye contact but was almost blinded by the intensity of his gaze.

"Well, Gaya, we have a few options…"

She squirmed and coughed to clear her throat, trying to keep Suresh and Leela at the forefront of her mind. 'Get a grip woman' she thought to herself.

"Yes, go on…"

"Well, if we start with the possibility that she may make it out, we can assume she will head for home. We need to warn her family there are likely to be people watching them and if she turns up, they will need to hide her. I don't think she can stay there safely anymore, though I didn't like to say that in front of Suresh. She has seen their camp and will know how to get there. They won't risk that information being leaked. She will need to go underground. She will have to change her name and we can get her false papers. We can try to get her some work on a tea estate or somewhere else where she can be anonymous. I have some contacts."

Rakesh paused for a moment and Gaya, who was watching his face intently, saw his jaw tighten.

"There is also the option of getting her onto a boat to Australia and applying for asylum. The journey is dangerous, however, and there is no guarantee she will make it there. If she does, it is possible we could also get her family to Australia and out of harm's way. But for this, we need money, lots of it. Are there any accessible funds Niraj?"

"There could be, I need to make some enquiries. There are several benefactors who offer assistance for emergencies. It just depends on how much and how quickly we need it."

Rakesh stood up. Gaya felt a jolt in her stomach as if on the precipice of a roller-coaster ride.

"Are you leaving?" she blurted out.

Rakesh looked at her and smiled a playful grin. "As much as I love the company here, there are some people I have to meet."

Gaya blushed inwardly but pulled a poker face. "I mean there might be a few more questions I need to ask you, about getting an action plan together."

"Don't worry, I'll be back in a few hours, you can ask me anything then."

"Great!" said Gaya and then sat on her hands to stop herself from being any more explicit.

Rakesh stopped in front of her on his way out and put his hand on her shoulder. "Gaya, the boat to Australia is the last option. It's so dangerous that many people are dying at sea on vessels not equipped to deal with a journey like that."

Gaya shivered. She wasn't sure if it was his touch or what he was saying, but she couldn't meet his gaze.

"Ok Rakesh, understood," she said, looking at the floor.

As he shut the door behind him, Niraj spoke. "He's very sought after, Rakesh, by both his enemies and his friends."

"Does he have a lot of enemies?"

"He does. He likes to make things public that other people want kept private. He's upset people on all sides of the political spectrum."

"What does he do?"

"He's a journalist. Most journalists have learnt their place in this war, how to keep their jobs and families safe by not rocking any boats. Rakesh is the opposite. He doesn't care whose toes he stands on. He's fearless. He's probably only still alive because of his family connections otherwise they would have got rid of him long ago. He's a threat to all those looking for power."

"Why doesn't he care about his life?"

"He cares passionately about the truth. I don't know whether it's bravery or foolishness. He has been behind many of the leaked undercover news stories that have shocked the world in the last year. He has a network of people around the country that he can rely on, and he doesn't stop until he's found the evidence he needs to send a story to press."

While Gaya processed all this information, alarm bells responded in every crevice of her brain. This was not a man to get entangled with. A man who lived in a constant state of crisis, who was never in one place for more than a few days at a time, especially a man who could turn her to jelly by the crook of his lips.

'Oh, stop behaving like an idiot,' she said to herself. "Right Niraj," she said out loud, "I know what the embassies will say, they have already brushed me off. There is nothing we can do until we have Leela in person. I guess it will be the same with getting false papers. We need to find her first. Only then I'll be able to get her photo to give to them."

She hesitated, remembering the touch of Rakesh's hand on her shoulder. "Do you think I should investigate whether there are any boats leaving?" She ventured.

"I don't know Gaya. I've heard terrible stories about people leaving on boats and never being heard of again."

"You mean like children disappearing into the jungle and never being heard of again?"

Niraj stared at her for a while before replying. "I don't really want to send anyone on a boat. I just don't have a good feeling about it. However, Leela's options are limited if she makes it out of the jungle, so it's probably in her best interest for us to prepare for all eventualities."

He wrote several phone numbers from his phone onto a piece of paper and handed it to Gaya.

"A friend of mine passed these contacts to me. You can try calling and see what information you can find."

It was hard to get any straight answers. The people she spoke to were reluctant to give out information, but she found a local contact, who agreed to meet her and talk face to face. They arranged a meeting on a secluded beach to the north.

"You can't go alone," said Niraj when she hung up. "These people are dangerous. I'll come with you."

"I was hoping you'd say that," said Gaya. "It's one thing making a phone call, it's another being face to face on an empty beach. I might take a swim now and have some lunch. Do you want to join me?"

"No, I have some work to finish up, you can let Marni know I'll be wanting lunch though if you see her."

"Will do. See you later."

Gaya changed quickly and ran through the shallows, diving in when it was deep enough. The water engulfed her, washing away the stress of the morning. She was so lucky. How many other people had paradise as their office? It really was the most incredible place.

Jenny had left that morning to visit a project in the North, returning to Colombo the following day. She liked Jenny. She felt they were similar. She had warned Gaya off Rakesh again, over breakfast. Gaya had laughed and said, "You sound like you talk about him from personal experience."

"Which is exactly why I can recognise the look on your face, Gaya," she had replied, dissolving into cackling laughter. "Learn from my mistakes, don't copy them."

"Thanks for the advice Jenny, but if I had any interest in him, and I'm not saying I do, then I will probably have to make my own mistakes!"

"Don't say I didn't warn you. He doesn't have any time to think about the people around him. He's too busy saving the world. Not that that is a bad thing, I respect what he does, but it's not worth trying to get close to him that's all."

Gaya thought over the conversation as she floated, basking in the sun. Even the thought of having a conversation with him made her groin throb with pleasure. 'It's an idle distraction' she thought. 'There's nothing wrong with that.'

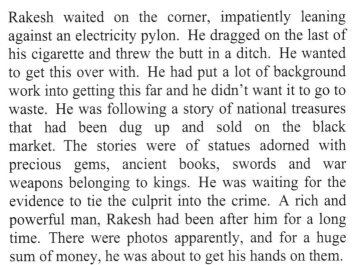

Rakesh waited on the corner, impatiently leaning against an electricity pylon. He dragged on the last of his cigarette and threw the butt in a ditch. He wanted to get this over with. He had put a lot of background work into getting this far and he didn't want it to go to waste. He was following a story of national treasures that had been dug up and sold on the black market. The stories were of statues adorned with precious gems, ancient books, swords and war weapons belonging to kings. He was waiting for the evidence to tie the culprit into the crime. A rich and powerful man, Rakesh had been after him for a long time. There were photos apparently, and for a huge sum of money, he was about to get his hands on them.

His thoughts turned to the pretty, young girl he had met at the hotel. He knew he shouldn't go there, but he also knew he couldn't help himself. He liked the comfort and closeness, even though it was always momentary. He knew she was keen, he could smell it. The thought turned him on.

A gate in the fence behind him opened and an old man beckoned him in. Rakesh stepped inside, and the old man immediately padlocked the gate from the inside.

"Follow me."

Rakesh followed him into a crumbling building and the man motioned for him to sit on a cracked plastic chair.

"Can I see your ID," he asked.

Rakesh handed him his ID card, and the old man peered closely.

"And the money?"

Rakesh opened the satchel he was carrying. The old man called out and a burly young man entered the room.

"This is my son. He can count the money."

Rakesh handed him the satchel, and the man began to count.

"I will bring the photos," the old man said.

He left the room and Rakesh watched the younger man count, one million rupees in total. Rakesh had got the money from an overseas newspaper that wanted exclusive rights to the story. Rakesh was happy with that. As long as it was out there.

He finished counting and left the room with the bag.

'Shit,' thought Rakesh. 'That may be the last I see of that.'

But before long the old man returned and handed him a phone. "The photos are on this," he said.

Rakesh scrolled through the photos. They were out of focus, but you could still make out who was in them. There were a few clear photos of the statues, some cargo containers and the name of a ship. The man in question was clearly visible in one, smoking a cigar with one hand resting idly on the statue.

"It's not right." The old man's voice was quivering. "These treasures belong to Sri Lanka, to the people. They are our history. My son took these photos. Risked his life. Are you going to make sure these statues are returned?"

"I'll do my best," said Rakesh.

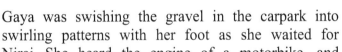

Gaya was swishing the gravel in the carpark into swirling patterns with her foot as she waited for Niraj. She heard the engine of a motorbike, and Rakesh swung through the gates several moments later, squealing to a halt beside her.

"Hey there," he said taking off his helmet.

"Hey yourself. A successful day out hunting?"

"Always," he said. "Where are you off to?"

"Me and Niraj are going to meet the people smugglers to find out when the next boat is leaving, just as a back-up plan in case we need to move her fast."

"Are you sure you know what you're doing?" asked Rakesh.

"Um… no, not exactly."

"I spoke to my friends in the tea estate. They are concerned about hiding an AWOL terrorist."

"She's not a terrorist!" Gaya shouted in disgust.

"We know that, but they don't. All they know is that the Tamil Freedom Fighters will be hot on her trail and they can't afford to have any trouble in their place. They have too much going on as it is."

"So that's a no-go then."

"Hey, Gaya!" Niraj was hurrying towards them. "I need to attend to something that can't wait. I can't come with you. Can you call them and try to postpone?"

"No, don't postpone, I can go with her," said Rakesh. Niraj turned to Gaya. "What do you think Gaya? Are you happy if Rakesh goes instead?"

Gaya swallowed before answering, sure her words would come out in a stutter. "Yeah, sure, no problem, that's fine."

"Hop on then," Rakesh winked before putting his helmet back on.

"Ok, I'll just try and borrow another helmet from Aruna."

She raced off to the kitchen to find him. When she returned, the two men were talking quietly. They stopped as she approached, she had the feeling they were talking about her. She put on her helmet to hide the pink creeping into her cheeks.

"Take care," said Niraj. "These are dangerous men."

Gaya slid her leg over the seat and held onto Rakesh for support. 'This will be an interesting ride,' she thought. She could feel the sexual energy like electric shocks shooting out from his body.

"Hold on tight!" shouted Rakesh as he accelerated onto the main road, dust spinning out from the back wheel.

The scenery was amazing. They sped along the coastal road, the bright blue of the water contrasting with the luscious green of the paddy fields on the other side. Gaya studied the broad back of Rakesh and the curls of hair protruding from the base of his helmet on to his neck. She wanted to kiss his neck so badly. She almost did and was thankful for the bulk of the helmet which would have prevented her anyway. She smiled to herself. 'Pathetic!' she thought.

She had an envelope full of notes, in case she needed to bribe anyone. Niraj had given it to her just before they left. She slid her hand in her bag to check it was still there before attempting to tame her hair, which was flapping wildly around in the wind.

Rakesh knew which beach to head for and made twists and turns down tiny lanes and back alleys to make the journey shorter. They finally arrived, parked up and scoured the beach from left to right. It was deserted, but that was no surprise, being the hottest part of the day. They sat down in the shade of a tree and waited.

"So where are you from Gaya?"

"Borella, Colombo, but I just spent the last four years in the States."

"What's your family name?"

"Somarasekera."

"I knew a Somarasekera when I was at school. Dulip was his name, are you related?"

"Yes, he's my older cousin. Did you go to St Andrews College?"

"Sure did. Say 'Hi' to him from me. I lost touch with him over the years."

"Will do." They sat in silence for a while. Gaya stared at the sand in front of her, wishing she could think of something smart to say.

Finally, Rakesh spoke up, "You're very beautiful Gaya. I haven't been able to take my eyes off you since we met."

Gaya's stomach flipped and she giggled nervously, lifting her head to meet his gaze. She gasped, as over his shoulder, she saw two navy officers striding towards them.

They jumped to their feet as the men approached.

"Gaya?" said the taller of the men.

"Yes," she replied, thinking they must have arrested the smugglers who had given them her name.

"I'm Nishan."

"Oh!" Gaya gasped. "But you're in the Navy!" she exclaimed.

"Yes," he replied with a stony gaze. "And who is this with you?"

"My name is Dulip Somarasekera, I'm her cousin." Rakesh jumped in before Gaya could reply.

"Do you have money with you?"

"Why?" she asked.

"The boat leaves in five days' time on the morning of the 27th. If you want your passenger to be on it, you need to pay now."

"What kind of boat will it be?" Gaya asked.

"It's a cabin cruiser. It's got berths for sleeping, life rafts, life jackets, food and water. The journey will take two to three weeks."

"How much money do you want?"

"The total will be 1,000,000 rupees. How much do you have now?"

Gaya looked at Rakesh. He nodded at her.

"100,000."

"That will have to do."

"Will the passenger need papers?"

"Once they're on the boat, it doesn't matter. Bring the balance, Rs 900,000, with you when you come. You need to be here at 9 am. Don't be late and don't come without the money."

"The men turned on their heels and marched off across the hot sand."

"Ok," Gaya called after them.

"Navy!" Gaya turned to Rakesh, exclaiming in a half-whisper.

"Yup. Who else has the best contacts, knowledge of the sea and can get around undetected? Hopefully, in the meantime, we can find a better solution for Leela but at least this option is there if we need it. That boat won't have cabins, that's for sure, or life rafts, and probably not life jackets either."

"This country never ceases to amaze me. Who doesn't have their hand in something?"

"Well, I know where my hands want to be," he said pushing her back against the tree and bringing his mouth down on hers.

Gaya didn't bother pretending to resist as her knees gave way and they sunk down to the soft sand.

8 Wood Apples

---•---

Jayasuriya had been counting money. Something he liked to do now and then. Not that he had a lot, but he did have a secret stash that he kept all to himself. Not even his wife knew where he hid it. He was grumpy because he'd been ordered to do a state visit, so was soothing his mood with every crinkled note that passed through his fingers. He wasn't overly enamoured with visiting, especially not to the East. It was hot and dry and extremely lacking in the necessities of life such as quality spirits and ice cubes. He huffed as he lost count and picked up the pile to start again.

"Ra-hul," came the shrill voice of his wife up the stairs. "What are you doing up there?"

Jayasuriya gave up on his moment of calm and put the notes back in their hiding place.

"What is it?" he retorted gruffly as he shoved his rough feet into the soft lining of his slippers.

He was not an old man, but he did not move with ease. He pushed himself up from the chair and shuffled out to the landing.

"What, what is it?" he called.

No answer.

Jayasuriya held on to the polished rail and began the descent. He could hear his wife's voice from the kitchen and followed the fumes of stale coconut oil and garlic.

He found her giving a young, frightened domestic an earful about re-using old oil and stood in line waiting for her attention.

"Where have you been?" she turned to face him now. "Didn't you hear me calling you?"

"Yes, I did. That's why I'm standing here."

She scrutinised him a few seconds longer than necessary, abruptly turned on her heel, and left the kitchen.

Jayasuriya looked at the young girl who stared back at him with wide frightened eyes.

"What are you still standing there for?" he shouted, and she scuttled off to retrieve the offending oil from the stove and throw it out for the rats.

Leela cowered in the undergrowth. She listened for the noise again, but she wasn't sure which direction it had come from. Shadows danced around her, playing tricks on her eyes in the moonlight. There it was again, it seemed to be near her now. She jumped as something ran over her foot and then laughed out loud as she realised she was petrified of a mouse.

'Come on Leela,' she said to herself. 'You can do this.'

She had been walking all night and was hungry, but she didn't dare eat any of the food she had brought as she didn't know how long she would need to make it last. She was glad of the clear sky tonight. She had followed the North Star, keeping it to her left, hoping to make her way east and on to the coast. Her feet were blistering in her boots, but she was more grateful to have them than not.

A sweet smell of rotting fruit filled her nostrils carried by a slight breeze. Following the smell, she found a patch of ground covered in fermenting wood apples. There was elephant dung around and Leela smiled to herself at the thought of the elephants feasting on the rotten fruit. Her grandmother had compared her father to these animals. Just as her father would drink his way through a bottle of arrack until he could no longer walk straight, so the elephants would gorge themselves on the fermenting fruit until intoxicated and giddy, stumbling around and hooting with laughter. Leela enjoyed having this picture in her mind as a child. She had thought, if this drunken behaviour was good enough for the elephants then it was good enough for her father.

She picked a wood apple from the tree and cut it open with her knife; she tried some, but it was bitter, so she spat it on the ground. Instead, she opened her sack and took out a piece of coconut. She ate slowly, feeling the energy flow back into her body.

Eventually, she felt able to continue; she picked up her sack and pressed on through the heavy undergrowth.

Dawn was drawing close and as the first patches of light appeared through the trees, Leela's spirits lifted. She felt proud of herself to have made it through the night.

With the day she felt she could relax. There seemed fewer dangers threatening her, and the uneasy feeling had gone. She knew there would be mayhem at the camp. They must have noticed her disappearance and she wondered what they would do. They may send out a search party in which case she shouldn't rest, but without the night sky, and the North Star to follow, she was unsure which direction she should take.

She walked on for a while until her legs felt like they couldn't take another step. She found a thick, shady spot where she wouldn't be seen even if people did pass by. She threw her bag on the ground, laid her head on it, closed her eyes, and was instantly asleep.

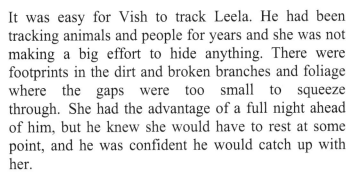

It was easy for Vish to track Leela. He had been tracking animals and people for years and she was not making a big effort to hide anything. There were footprints in the dirt and broken branches and foliage where the gaps were too small to squeeze through. She had the advantage of a full night ahead of him, but he knew she would have to rest at some point, and he was confident he would catch up with her.

He didn't, however, know what to do with her when he found her. Was he going to drag her back to the camp? Unlikely. He didn't want to go back there himself. So, what were they going to do? They would just be standing there like two deer in the headlights. She would probably be frightened and want to run. He would be confused and distressed, because, until he found her, he was on a mission and didn't need to make any decisions. As soon as he found her, he would have to face his future. This would not be an easy task. He wished that she had been more cunning in her escape so he could wander around the jungle in circles for a few days. At least then he could hide in the present and not have to deal with the past or the future.

He thought of his life. He had no idea it was going to turn out like this. He had plans, which he would never see materialise. He was not young anymore and where was the brood of children he had always wanted, a home, people around him who loved him? There were his comrades, but it was always necessary to wear a mask in the field, to keep yourself from breaking. He had missed it all. He had dedicated himself to the idea of freeing his people and had trapped himself. But who were his people? The ordinary people, the people who went about their everyday lives hoping for equality and better rights as civilians? These people had no idea who he was, and if they did, there was a good chance they hated and feared him. What had it all been for?

He needed to pull himself together and focus on the task at hand, his search for a missing child in great danger. This was worthwhile. This he could be proud of himself for doing. This he could take with him to the grave and be ready for his judgment day.

He felt comforted as he pushed his way through the jungle. He distinctly knew the last time he had felt like that. He had only in love once. It was short-lived due to circumstances in each other's lives. But the immense pleasure, of holding someone that he cared for deeply, would never leave him, of caressing her naked flesh and breathing her in.

Many nights in the camp his mind had travelled back to those days. Her body entwined with his, comforting him in his bare, lonely bed.

Leela woke with a jolt. She had been dreaming of serpents slithering all over her body, then wrapping themselves around her and crushing her bone by bone. She stretched and coughed, trying to get the air back in her lungs and her bones back into place. She had slept well into the heat of the day and she imagined it must be about 11 am, by the placement of the sun. She crawled out of her hiding spot, relieved herself in the bushes, turned around and screamed.

Vish was there, sitting on a log and carving a stick with a penknife.

"I didn't want to wake you, so I waited."

"You didn't want to wake me! What do you mean you didn't want to wake me? You kidnap me, and you feel bad about waking me? What kind of logic is that?"

Leela was mad. She was mad at herself for letting him catch up with her. She was mad at him for being so irritatingly calm about it all and now she was back where she started, trapped.

He patted the rock next to him. Why don't you sit down for a bit and we'll talk?

Leela saw no choice really. At least he wasn't tying her up or manhandling her. She could try running, but really how far would she get?

"It's a shame," he was saying. "You really do have all the characteristics of making a first-class soldier."

"Except I don't want to be one," she snapped back.

She accepted his invitation however and sat down on the smooth, hard rock.

"I thought like you once," he said, "but then circumstances change people and you end up following a route laid down for you."

"It seems this is the excuse of someone with no backbone!" Leela could feel herself becoming more confident. 'Who is this man?' she thought. If I'm going to die anyway, I might as well say what I think.

"You may think you have courage, but you might just be stupid and naïve," said Vish. "Do you think life will be good for you if there aren't people fighting for your rights? Do you think there will be Tamil schools or equal employment for Tamils if we don't stand up for ourselves? It is only a few brave soldiers able to offer their lives for the sake of all Tamils and this is the only chance we have of stopping this oppressive government taking what belongs to us."

"And when your brave little soldiers are all dead, do you feel you've stood up for their rights?" Leela's eyes were fierce, challenging.

"And what is your alternative? Do you dream of becoming a chief minister or a managing director? You are clever, you do well at school. But why are there no books in your library, no paper to write on? How can you go to university when you don't have equal access to education? How can you compete?"

"Sacrifice one child for the sake of one thousand? I'm sorry I don't agree with your philosophy. You're a child murderer. It's as plain and clear as that. There are no grey areas however much you want to dress it up and disguise it behind your political ideas."

Vish closed his eyes. The words stung him as only the truth can. Isn't it what he had been saying to himself over and over again, the words he couldn't get out of his head? Child murderer. Child murderer. He let them sink lower and lower until they touched his heart, lungs and bowels, twisting and tightening them into a knot.

Leela watched Vish fall silent, then retreat inside himself. His face contorted, and he clutched at his belly letting out a low moan. She couldn't understand this man. He didn't seem like a violent murderer, but that was what he was, wasn't it? She resisted an urge to reach out and touch him, comfort him through his anguish. Maybe he was having a seizure. Maybe he was going to fall off his log stone-cold dead and she would be free again, to run through the jungle, back to her life and everything she knew.

Eventually, he was calm. He opened his eyes and stood up. His body was tall and muscular, and he towered above her. He must have been very attractive in his youth, thought Leela.

His voice was soft when at last he spoke, "There are many things I have done in my life that I am not proud of. I seem to have less and less justification in myself for my actions. Those things in my life that were clear, predestined, are no longer that. Someone has kicked dirt on my path and I can't see which way to go. I don't know what will happen. I only know that this, right here, right now, is the only real thing in my life. When you went missing, it made me happy. For your sake, for my sake, I don't know which. But now I am here, and I've never felt freer. I will get you out of this jungle alive and then we will see where the wind blows us."

Leela stared at him, open-mouthed. She wasn't sure if she was still curled up in her hiding place, asleep and dreaming. It seemed so surreal. A grown man, dedicated to a life of terrorism, baring his soul to a lost, frightened little girl. This man was no monster. At this moment she saw before her a gentle, sensitive human being. Where were the guns and the bombs, the cyanide and the hand-to-hand combat? Just two people, each willing the other for a second chance.

"Well, I have no choice but to trust what you're saying," said Leela, standing up. "It could just as well be a trap. You could say all this just to get me to come willingly to the road, where you and your comrades can kidnap me all over again."

"In your heart, you will always know what the truth is. The challenge is letting your brain give up the power to your heart. However, I'm not asking you to trust me. I will just walk by your side for as long as you want me there. If you ask me to leave you, I shall."

It's all very unusual, thought the girl, as she stood staring at this man. Was he her enemy or her protector? How was it possible to be so unsure? She thought back to last night. She was confident that she could make another night in the jungle by herself. If you've done one, what's another? But having the choice of company was a bonus. She had felt very frightened at points and maybe this man would help her find her way out. He interested her anyway. She wanted to talk to him more. He was obviously having some kind of personal crisis, and in this present moment, seemed less of a threat and more of an ally.

"Ok then, I guess we'd better push on," she said, getting her bag together. Vish smiled, his worry lines opening up, and his face gaining a new dimension.

"Well, I hope you know some good stories!"

The two figures trekked on through the jungle. Vish was humming to himself with newfound joy. He absorbed the sounds, smells and colours of the jungle as if he hadn't noticed them in the past ten years of living there.

"What do the rest of the camp think you're doing?" Leela asked.

"They're expecting me to drag you back there, kicking and screaming."

"And what will they do when we don't turn up?"

"They will send someone else in after us, I expect. However, seeing as I have had many more years at jungle tracking than you, I concealed the very obvious track that you made through the jungle, so they will take much longer to find us than I did to find you."

Vish was teasing the girl but secretly he was immensely proud of her. He wasn't sure there would be many who could get themselves to where she was. She had guts and determination and seemed to slice through her fears with a razor-sharp sword. He wished he could have half her courage. He was glad when he found her. It had been easy and if it hadn't been him he wasn't so sure she would have remained unharmed.

"Will they look for us in a vehicle or on foot?"

"Both I should think," said Vish.

"So, they may approach us from front or back?"

"Yes."

"And what do we do then?"

Vish hadn't thought that far. Well, to be fair, he had thought that far, but as yet still hadn't come up with an answer. If he was truly honest with himself about what he was doing there, walking through the jungle with this girl, then he would have to admit he was probably deserting. If he was a deserter, then that would mean, most definitely death. He knew they could not trust him anymore. Not with the amount of information he had stored in his head. They would have no choice but to kill him. And then what would happen to the girl? Would they kill her too? Maybe not, he thought. He could lie, say he was bringing her back. That they had travelled too far, and it was easier to come out onto the road and get picked up there.

Vish had no answer for her so he remained silent.

After a while, he spoke, "I will do what I can to save your life," he replied.

The sun had almost disappeared, changing the mood of the canopy that towered above them. Vish had been using a compass to get them through the last section and now they would have a compass and the stars to guide them. The birds that had filled the trees through the day, with their shrieking and calling, had returned home to their beds. The crickets set up their noisy clamour and the night-feeders were venturing out of their hideouts. Vish suddenly stopped. He held onto Leela's arm to prevent her from moving any further forward.

"What is it?" she whispered.

"I'm not sure, I heard something from back there. Be quiet for a moment."

They held their breath for what seemed like an age. Slowly, beginning quietly like a low rumble, there came a noise that unnerved the listening figures. The sound got louder until they could distinctly hear a growl.

"It's a leopard," Vish said. "We're being stalked, probably a female, we must be near her lair, maybe she has young cubs." He could see, from the shoulders of Leela, she was trembling. "Try to stay as still as you can, no sudden movements and look down at the ground." Vish held the strap of his rifle and slowly pulled it off his shoulder. He took off the safety and the leopard growled louder at the sudden noise.

"Are you going to shoot it?" asked Leela.

"Only in self-defence."

There was a movement from behind the trees and the leopard became visible. She came out from the shadows, her head bent low to the ground, displaying the full warning force of her teeth and gums. They glistened in the light from the moon, dripping with saliva. Leela was sobbing now. The beast was undeniably majestic: her flanks, the muscles bulging through the patterns in her fur, the sheer weight and size of her. Vish was in awe. He had never seen a leopard this close and wanted the moment to last.

The leopard took a step towards them. Vish pulled Leela behind him and gently pushed her back so they were retracing the way they had come.

As deftly as he could, Vish fired his rifle into the air. There was an almighty crack and the leopard screeched and flung herself around and back into the bushes.

Vish grabbed Leela's hand and dragged her. They ran and ran as fast as they could, their feet hardly touching the floor.

"We must make a big circle around this area, she's obviously protecting young and doesn't want us anywhere near," said Vish, panting as they ran.

Eventually, when they felt they were a safe distance, they sank down to the ground in a heap and remained silent until they could breathe properly.

"We need to keep moving," Vish said. They may have heard the rifle shot and increase the search.

Vish pulled Leela to her feet. Her knees were shaking, but she made no other reference to her fright or exhaustion. "After you, Uncle," she said.

9   Tomato Curry and Fried Eggs

Marni walked up the beach, shaking the seawater out of her ears and hair. Her morning swim had revived her. The water had washed away her troubled sleep and she felt positive and relaxed.

The INR crew were having a breakfast meeting and Marni caught sight of the steaming bowl of tomato curry on their table. Her empty belly gurgled.

Aruna was standing in the doorway to the kitchen. "Miss Marni, come and eat."

"I'll be right back." She hurried to her cabana to shower and change.

Tomato curry, spicy pol sambol, coconut roti and fried eggs, her favourite breakfast. She helped herself to a generous serving and took her plate back out to the restaurant to sit down. Jake was there with Zoe. She joined him on the plantation chairs facing the sea.

"Good morning, my sweethearts," she said, giving Zoe a kiss on her forehead.

Jake looked at her over the rim of his sunglasses. "You're in a sunny mood this morning."

"Well, it's a beautiful day and I'm counting my blessings that I live in paradise and I've got my wonderful family by my side."

"You weren't saying that last night," Jake replied, grumpily.

They had argued again. Marni had tried to discuss the problems they were having but was called away to deal with a request from a restaurant guest. When she returned Jake didn't want to talk anymore.

"How can we make things better between us if you constantly put the guests and the hotel first?" he had said.

"I can't just make them wait," she had replied.

"You can! That's the whole point. Get the staff to say you're not here, you're sick, you're putting the baby to bed, anything! It's about your priorities, Marni. Zoe and I don't feel you put us first."

Marni could feel herself tense. She didn't like to be accused of bad parenting and she lashed back. "Well, if you helped more around the hotel and weren't out, god knows where I would have more time to devote to Zoe. You can't blame me when you're not here most of the time."

With that, Jake had stormed out, leaving Marni to worry herself to sleep. Today, however, she felt different. She had woken with a feeling of hope, the start of a new day. She knew that some of this was her fault and she wanted to make the effort reconciliation with an olive branch.

"I thought that maybe we could go out tonight?" she ventured.

Jake looked intently at her.

"You mean like on a date?" he asked.

"Well yes, like a date. Rushani is staying over tonight to help with the ministerial dinner, so we can put Zoe to bed, and she can watch her for a few hours. Let's get out of the hotel for a bit, I've been really stressed planning this dinner, I need a break before they all arrive."

"Sure" said Jake, but he didn't look very convinced. Marni bit back the urge to make a sharp remark about him looking more enthusiastic, but she remembered her pledge to herself and contained it.

"Great," she said and turned her focus on the feast that awaited her. She broke off some roti and dipped it into the tomato curry. The flavour was intense. The ripe, juicy red tomatoes, coated in sweet coconut milk and laden with chilli, inflamed her lips and made them tingle. The pol sambol had been prepared with green chillies and lime zest, and the sourness made her salivate all the more. She ate without stopping. The morning swim had made her ravenous. She wiped the last piece of roti around her plate, picking up every drop of sauce. She licked her fingers and sighed.

"Comparative to an orgasm, I would say."

"Thanks a lot," said Jake.

"Don't take offence Jake, if I was to have sex with you, and eat curry simultaneously I'd probably be orbiting the moon."

"We should try it sometime," Jake grinned.

The change in atmosphere dissolved the remaining tension enough for Marni to remember how they used to be.

She laid her hand over his. "I'd better get on, I've got some accounting to do, I look forward to tonight then."

"Yeah, see you later, darl."

As Marni walked back through the restaurant, she smiled a secret smile. It had been a long time since he had called her that.

"Marni, come and join us."

Eva and Jo beckoned her over. They were sitting with a couple that Marni had seen a few times around town and in the building merchants. She sat down and held out her hand.

"Hi, I'm Marni."

"This is Karen and Mark, they've just finished building their house, you know, the white villa on the other side of the lagoon," said Jo.

"Oh, I wondered who built that, it's beautifully designed. Are you here full-time?"

"On and off, we do contract work, so fly-in, fly-out stuff. It's a bit of a tax dodge actually, but we love Sri Lanka and thought we'd like to settle here, eventually."

"Sounds like a great life."

"Yes, we're enjoying ourselves and Australia was getting too overcrowded for our liking."

"Really!" Marni was surprised. "There are more people in Sri Lanka."

"Yes, but we don't have to give up our hard-earned cash to the government to support all those people too lazy to work, not to mention all the illegal immigrants."

Marni started fiddling with the napkin holder, wondering whether she should spoil the good start to the day by getting into an argument with these people. She decided to proceed carefully.

"Which illegal immigrants would those be?"

"All those people claiming asylum, jumping the queues, trying to cash in on Australia's prosperity."

"Do you mean, all those people running for their lives?"

"That's what they say, but of course it's an economic decision. Who wouldn't want to move to a country that will pay them social security for doing nothing?"

Eva stepped in, "I think what Marni is trying to say is that most of those people are not economic migrants, they are genuine asylum seekers whose lives are at risk. I know, because I used to work in this field."

"I just don't believe it," said Karen. "They're just trying to milk our system."

"Isn't that what you're doing?" asked Marni. "You're the ones not paying your taxes. Living in another country, do you even have a visa to reside here? Aren't you the illegal immigrants?"

Karen and Mark looked taken aback and Jo stifled a giggle, with a coughing fit.

"Anyway, lovely to meet you, enjoy the rest of your stay." Marni hopped up and away. No, they were definitely not going to spoil her day!

She found Suresh out the back of the kitchen preparing the tuna.

"How are you, Suresh? Has there been any news?"

"No, Miss Marni, nothing. But now I don't know which is worse. Thinking she is in a camp or knowing that she is by herself, lost in the jungle."

"Do you want to go and be with your family?"

"No Miss Marni, I stay here. Mr Niraj may be telling something, and I busy working."

"Yes, we have a lot of work to do today. We have dinner for twenty booked tonight. They are mostly government officials, the minister Mr Jayasuriya, and some army officers. I wish we didn't have to host them, but when it's the minister's office phoning up, what can you say?"

She ventured out the back door of the kitchen and looked into the deep hole in front of her. They had called in the builders the day before to dig the hole and cement it. The cement was still drying, but the finish looked good. She was pleased they would be able to hide the beer there now and try to avoid any more debts to excise police. There were some old wooden crates, which had been cleverly transformed into a covering and they would hide it with some mats and chairs on top.

Marni headed into the office to deal with the accounts. It was difficult to keep track of expenditure. They paid everything in cash, the honey seller, the chicken man, the fisherman, the beef man, the hopper woman, the vegetables from the market. No receipts exchanged and no accounts given. Marni had asked over and over for some kind of system to be introduced, but it was hard to enforce it. She sighed as she picked up a bunch of scrap papers that were presenting themselves as receipts. Well, at least there are some receipts, she thought. She squinted at the first one, no date and written in Tamil, she hadn't a clue. This will take forever, she thought.

"Saved by the bell!" she exclaimed, as Ali opened the office door and came in.

He laughed as he saw the pile of papers on the desk. "That time of the month! Let me help you."

They fell into an easy rhythm. Marni had always felt comfortable with Ali around. She felt the business was safe with him as her partner. They made a good team.

"How's your wife?" she asked.

"She is good, but her mother is driving me crazy! She has moved in with us since her husband died and now she wants everything done her way. Sometimes I feel like I can't breathe at home."

"I thought we'd been seeing more of you recently," Marni laughed. "Will you be around tonight? Jake and I thought we'd go out for dinner, but we have the minister coming. I don't want to leave the staff by themselves."

"Unfortunately, I won't be able to come. I have to take my mother-in-law to the hospital. She needs some tests done."

"Ok, no problem, I'm sure we'll manage. Can I ask you something, Ali?"

"Anything," he replied.

"Did you ever think about not rebuilding after the tsunami?"

"Well, that's an interesting question, what made you ask that?"

"I don't know, I'm just curious. Was it a decision that you needed to make, or you just knew?"

"I think I just knew. It's really the only chance I have of making decent money to support my family. As the eldest son, I am also looking after my younger siblings financially and my wife's brother and younger sister too. My father left me some paddy land and I have my day job but none of that will ever bring in enough money for us to live off. What about you?"

"I think for me there never any choice. This is where my heart is. I couldn't bear when everything we had was destroyed so violently. I wouldn't have been able to cope if there wasn't hope that we could create it again. But for Jake it's different, I can see it in his eyes. He doesn't feel the same about being here as I do. He would return to England tomorrow if he could."

"He's just worried about his family Marni. He is a father now, and he doesn't know how he will protect you and Zoe if something like that ever happens again. You all nearly died in that tsunami, let alone what's going on with the war. This is a volatile place to be right now. I'm not surprised he wants to return to where it's familiar and less threatening. Men are different Marni. If we don't feel we can look after our loved ones, we feel worthless. That's probably how he's feeling right now."

"I haven't looked at it like that, through his eyes. You're right, he feels like it's all out of his control. But what can we do? I don't want to leave, but I'm not sure he'll ever feel comfortable here again."

"That's something you need to work out together. It's good for you to get out of here tonight. You need to talk. Find the fabric that binds you together."

"You talk a lot of sense Ali, it's hard to think like a man though."

"We are very simple creatures, nothing complicated. We like to eat well, love well, work and protect. At the moment he probably only has one out of those four. Help him find the others and he will be happy wherever you are."

Marni got back to sorting the receipts. She knew they were both still suffering from some version of post-traumatic shock from the tsunami. Their village had been devastated. In the beginning, there was the crisis period to get through. The seriously injured needed to get to hospital, the dead needed a funeral and the living needed to eat. Food and clean water were scarce. Their groundwater was thick with salinity and it was hard to access fresh fruit and vegetables. Marni was pregnant with Zoe. At first, she thought that the baby she was carrying must be dead. She had broken ribs, covered in cuts and bruises and her stomach became rigid like a shell. She couldn't feel the life inside her, so she detached herself from what could have been. It was a week before Marni could get to Colombo to have a scan. It shocked her that the baby's heartbeat was so strong. She had been sure her baby had died along with all the other babies who had lost their lives that day. People would say to her, "You must have such a new lease on life, for surviving a natural disaster." Marni would smile weakly and agree. It was easier than explaining that no, she didn't feel energised. She felt scared, vulnerable, sick to her stomach and worst of all, empty.

Gradually, as the hotel was rebuilt, so Marni's spirits lifted. By her third trimester, there were three cabanas built, a makeshift kitchen and a covered area for the restaurant. Their cabana was nearly finished when they left the coast and headed to Colombo to deliver the baby. When Zoe was born, the love Marni felt exceeded all other twisted up emotions she may have had, and she held her new baby in her arms, crying. Jake was by her side, holding her and crying too. We've got through the worst of it, she thought.

But as time went on, with old emotions not dealt with, Marni and Jake drifted further apart. They had stopped talking, stopped sharing. They were hardly ever alone, and when they were, they argued. They rarely had sex. First, it was because she was pregnant, then it was because she had stitches, after a while, it stopped occurring to them. Marni found it easier sometimes to talk to the guests. Strangers would come and go. Just enough time to share a story and have a laugh. And then they were gone. She didn't need to go deep; she didn't need to open up. They weren't asking anything of her. She didn't know how to be vulnerable anymore. She had clouded herself in armour, waiting for the next shock to hit. And whilst protecting herself from the world, she had cast out the person who wanted to protect her.

She sighed heavily.

"Excuse me, Miss Marni, the army here," said Suresh popping his head around the door.

"Don't worry Marni, I'll see to them," said Ali standing up.

He returned a few minutes later. They need to search the property, give it the all-clear for the dinner tonight. They want a list of all guests, their passport numbers and nationalities, and a list of all staff, their ID numbers and if there are any Tamils working here.

"What did you tell them?" asked Marni.

"I said there are Tamil staff working here, but we have known them for a long time and they have already been cleared by local police."

"Did they accept that?"

"No, they still want to interview all Tamil staff."

"It's so unfair," cried Marni. "As if Suresh doesn't have enough on his plate without this adding to his worries. They can interview him, but I want to be present."

"Fair enough, let's get it over and done with."

They called Suresh out from the kitchen and led him outside. It wasn't as if he hadn't been through this before. He knew the procedure. They asked him his name, address, village, age and previous work experience. Suresh's Sinhala was good, and they got through the questions quickly.

"Have you ever had any dealings with the Tamil Freedom Fighters?" a short stocky officer, with a wide moustache, inquired.

"No," Suresh said, but his voice came out in a whisper.

"What did you say, boy?"

"No," he forced out, louder this time. There was silence as the officers scrutinised him. Marni stared back at them, willing them to leave him alone. After a long minute, the short man spoke again.

"I hope you know how to cook well. We don't want to disappoint our minister. This restaurant was recommended to him. We don't want to haul the chef off to jail!" They all guffawed with laughter.

Marni swallowed hard and looked at the floor.

10 Tiger Prawns

Leela pulled off her boots and plunged her feet into the ice-cold stream. She had followed Vish all day without a rest. He worried that the trackers from his camp would be almost upon them by now. The forest was thick and cutting through it was taking up time they couldn't afford. The path they were leaving behind would be easy to follow. The stream had been a welcome sight. They had finished their water several hours ago and Leela scooped up the clear nectar, drinking in gulps.

"We can rest here for a while and eat," said Vish. He knew they were getting closer to the coast. The air was salty and the terrain was becoming sandy.

Leela was lying on her back on the grassy bank, her eyes closed, bathing in the dappled rays of the sun. She looked so peaceful. Vish didn't want to break the spell, but there was something he needed to say.

"Leela, you know you can't go home don't you?"

Leela sat up, blinking in the light. "You mean not at all?"

"They will be waiting for you there. Although it's not you they are interested in anymore, it's me. But they will do everything they can to find me."

"So where can I go?"

"We will go to your brother's place."

"But surely they will look for me there too?"

"It's our only option. We need to find someone who can help us. You need money and clothes and ID, then we can find a way to get you out. There are people we had contact with, in the past, that work there. They have helped people get out before. They may be able to help you."

"I won't see Amma again." It was more of a statement than a question. Leela's eyes were glistening, but she wiped them dry angrily. "It's not fair for her. She needs me there to help look after my brother and sisters. Why must she suffer?"

Vish looked at the water bouncing from rock to rock, flowing freely towards the sea. It wasn't fair. He agreed with her. But what could he say? He and his politics were to blame. The logic that had brought him to this point was not there anymore. He could no longer convince himself that tearing families apart for the greater good was necessary. The thick knot of dread began to braid itself through his guts. He closed his eyes, waiting for the pain to pass. He felt it tighten in his throat like a lump of molten lava, making him wince.

"Are you ok?" asked Leela.

The pain had passed for now. He splashed water on his face and looked at her.

"I'm sorry for the past, but it is done. There is nothing I can do to change it. But there is your future to protect now. We will do what we can. Come on, let's move."

They picked up their belongings and ruffled the grass where they had been sitting, to eradicate signs they had rested there. They followed the river for several miles until Vish stopped suddenly.

"I can hear cars, we are near to the road now."

They journeyed on more carefully knowing how near they were to civilisation. The sound of traffic was getting closer and they could see the road through the trees. They crouched down in the long grass.

"We need to find out where we are. I don't think it's safe to hitch a lift. We will continue by foot when it gets dark. You get some sleep and I'll keep watch."

Leela lay her head on her bag but couldn't sleep. She thought of her mother and her baby brother, her sisters who would be missing her so much. And she thought of her brother Suresh. What trouble was she about to bring to him? Should she just lose herself in the forest? Get trampled by elephants or a herd of angry buffalo? That would be better for everyone, she thought. She was putting her whole family's life in danger by coming back for help.

"I don't want to find my brother," she said to Vish. "It's too dangerous. They'll find us and kill us and kill him too."

"I won't let that happen," said Vish.

"You can't guarantee that," she cried. "What? Are you going to take on the Sri Lankan Army, your terrorist friends, the local police and anyone else who wants us dead, single-handedly?"

"I will find a way," he said quietly.

"There is nothing you can do. They'll kill you first."

Leela was crying now. She desperately wanted to see her brother, but she was not naïve. There was a whole heap of trouble hurtling towards them.

———————◀ ● ▶———————

Rushani picked up the frangipani from the gravel. It was in perfect condition. White and yellow and uniform. She smelt it and tucked it behind her ear. Humming to herself, she rinsed the soap off the sheets and hung them out to dry. The brightness of the sun on the sheets almost blinded her. A shadow fell across her face and she pulled the sheet aside to see who was there. A soldier stood to attention his rifle slung over his shoulder.

"What do you want?" Rushani asked.

"My orders are to keep an eye on the staff today, look for anything suspicious. You just go about your business. I'll be here, watching." He gave a sneer like a cat getting ready to pounce.

Rushani shivered, despite the scorching sun. "Well, just don't interrupt me from my work. I have a lot to get through today."

The soldier took off his rifle and sat in the shade of the neem tree. He looked young, Rushani thought, younger than her. Where is his family? Were they proud of their army son? Serving his country, protecting the people.

She felt nauseous. She hadn't had her breakfast yet. She pounded the towels that were soaking in the laundry tub and began to wring them. She wanted to get away from this man. She felt threatened by him and everything he stood for. She needed to get back to the bustling kitchen and surround herself with people she knew.

Nausea surged in her belly. She steadied herself on the fencepost of the washing line. The soldier's head was back against the trunk. She watched the slow rise and fall of his chest and listened to his heavy breathing.

Just then she vomited, splashing the soldier's uniform. He jumped awake, cursing her and her forefathers. "You dirty woman, you need to clean my clothes. He was already taking off his shirt and threw it at her feet."

"Wash it yourself" she snapped, wiping the spittle from her mouth.

"How dare you speak to me like that!"

"Who are you that I should speak to you with respect? You are not my god, you are not a teacher, you are not even my protector. You are a man with a gun. I feel no respect, only contempt."

Rushani bowed her head, unused to such public expression of her emotions. She knew that she was not angry with this man. She was afraid. Over the last few weeks, she had felt the swelling of her belly and breasts, and the rising waves of nausea that crashed through her. There was no doubt anymore what was growing inside her.

"What's going on?" The voice startled the pair and Rushani looked up to see another soldier watching them, a frown on his face.

"What is the trouble?" he asked again.

"Nothing," said Rushani, "there's no trouble. I'm sorry." She bowed her head again.

The man turned to his comrade. "The chief is looking for you. He needs you on the perimeter fence."

The soldier got to his feet, picked up his shirt and rinsed the vomit from it, under the running tap. He scowled at Rushani before turning on his boots and marching off toward his chief.

"I'm sorry," said Rushani again.

"What are you sorry for?" said the man. "If that soldier was disturbing you, you need to report him."

"No, no, he wasn't disturbing me."

The man walked closer to Rushani and she flinched.

He spoke again, more gently. "We're not here to harm you. We're here to protect you. If that soldier did something wrong, you must tell me."

Rushani spoke quietly. "He did nothing wrong, he was just resting under the tree. I spoke out of turn."

The man waited for her to speak further, but she said no more.

Eventually, he spoke, "I'm sorry you were upset. If there's anything I can do to help you, please let me know."

Rushani couldn't help the tears welling up in her eyes. She couldn't remember the last time someone had tried to protect her.

"Thank you," she managed to say.

The soldier nodded at her and walked away.

From the commotion coming from the kitchen, it was clear Aruna was not impressed.

"Every corner of my kitchen ransacked! What are they looking for? Arms? Ammunition? Tiny terrorists hiding in the spice jars? They've turned it upside-down and for what? Just so we can wait on them and feed their greedy appetites."

Marni started clearing up the mess. She had felt uneasy all morning with the army in every corner of the hotel. They were all in danger until the politicians and officials had cleared out and left them alone. It was comforting that her guests would be there to act as a buffer. She hoped it would force good behaviour, by having witnesses. The INR would be there, as would Chris, who had such a calm persona, she believed it could diffuse any kind of conflict. Guns, power and arrack were never a good combination.

She and Jake were going out for an early dinner so they could be back before the 'honourable' Mr Jayasuriya arrived. She couldn't stay out when there was so much at stake back at the hotel. She had wanted to cancel altogether but knew Jake was expecting that. She had to see this through. Give Jake the time he deserved.

She saw Gaya approach the restaurant and beckoned to her.

"Hi Gaya, I wanted to ask if you'd be here for dinner tonight?"

"Yes, I will, but I think the INR staff are going to keep a low profile. Niraj wants to avoid meeting Jayasuriya so he will make himself scarce. He has, so far, flown under the radar and as so much of his work is sensitive it's better to keep away from prying eyes and too many questions. If pressed, then I will talk about the rebuilding schemes we are involved in. The rest is too much of a political quagmire."

"Jake and I are going out for a few hours. We need to talk about a few things. But I wondered if you might be able to keep an eye on Suresh while we're gone. I don't want anyone to bully him, especially at the moment."

"Yes, I will."

"Have you heard any more news from your informants?"

"No, Niraj has asked to be notified immediately if there are any developments."

"Where can Leela be? It's been four days now and still nothing. Suresh is beside himself."

"I know Marni, it doesn't look good. But we have to hope." Gaya wrapped her arms around Marni and squeezed tightly. "Hang in there, Marni. If you can stay calm, while everything around you is turning cyclonic, then we will all have something to hang on to!"

Marni managed to crack a smile. "Bring on the cyclone!"

Rushani finished the laundry and returned to the kitchen to prep for the evening's buffet. The business with the soldiers had disturbed her and she wanted to take her mind off it.

She busied herself with shelling tiger prawns in the outside kitchen. She pulled off their heads and legs and peeled the shell from around their bodies. With a sharp knife, she made a cut down the length of the prawn and pulled out the black vein that held the congealed waste. Some people thought of prawns as the waste-disposers of the sea and refused to eat them. They floated around on the seabed looking for scraps that the rest of the ocean had thrown away. She held some empathy for the scavenging prawn. She also felt like she was scraping around at the bottom of the barrel.

She looked up at the crows perched in the branches above, watching every move she made with their beady little eyes. They were so wily, waiting for her to lower her guard for just a minute. Then they would swoop, lunging at the prawns, grabbing as many as they could fit in their beaks.

Not today, she thought. There were too many people wanting to grab what they could from her. She felt it from every angle. If she wasn't on her guard, someone would take something from behind. If she looked behind her, the blow would come from the front. She was tired of the constant battle to keep her head above water.

A voice behind her startled her. She whirled around, the sharp knife still in her hand. "Oh, Suresh, it's you. I'm sorry, my nerves are on edge today, as yours must be."

Suresh stared down at the knife in her hand with wide eyes. He looked pale and drained. "That's ok, I was just going to ask you if you'd managed to get the cellar ready, so we can move the crates of beer down there. Marni's worried about there being so many security forces on site and wants to hide all the alcohol."

"I still haven't got down there today, but I think the cement is dry. Aruna fixed the door on this

afternoon. I covered it in old palm fronds. You'd
never know it was there."

"Ok, I'll get on to moving the crates. All the
soldiers are out on the beach watching some foreign
girls play volleyball. Couldn't have asked for a better
distraction!"

"Suresh, I'm sorry about your sister. If there's
anything I can do…" Rushani's voice trailed off. She
knew there was nothing she could do, or Suresh, or
anyone in fact. They were all powerless, just pawns
waiting to be sacrificed in a game of money and
greed.

Rushani rinsed off the prawns, hissed at the
crows and marched inside. She placed the bowl in the
fridge and looked over at Aruna. He was
concentrating on the measurements to make arrack
and date ice-cream: one capful for the ice-cream
maker, one capful for him. Things didn't look good if
he was starting this early in the day.

"Ayer, don't drink now. You know how upset
Marni will be. She needs you to look after things this
evening."

"You don't need to get involved woman. It's
none of your business. The food will be on the
table. That's my job and it will be done."

"It's not just about the food being on the
table. What if things get out of hand? What if the
minister and his cronies get drunk and rowdy? Who
will look after things?"

"Is it my job to be security for the security
forces? Why are they even coming here? Why don't
they stay in Colombo and have their meetings and
decide on their policies? Nobody benefits when they
are here. All they do is hassle everybody, turn
everything upside down, eat and drink our profits and

ignore all our requests. No, I will not babysit government officials. If they can't look after themselves, how the hell are they going to look after this country!"

Rushani knew the conversation was going nowhere. She could already hear the arrack in his voice. Well, as long as he lasted until the food was ready. At least that was something. Why he thought he had any more of a leg to stand on than the government officials, she did not know. "All a bunch of useless drunks," she muttered, "the lot of you."

She left Aruna ranting by himself and took the broom and mop to the restaurant. There were several guests lying in hammocks. Chris was sitting at a table, working on his laptop. He raised his head and grinned at her.

"Hi Rushani, busy day today I guess."

"Yes, I will be happy when tomorrow comes. Can I get you anything?"

"Yeah, a coffee would be great, and one of those delicious cinnamon biscuits."

Rushani returned to the kitchen and prepared a half pot of fresh coffee. She opened the biscuit jar and put the last two on a plate. She carried out the tray and lowered it gently onto the rickety table.

"Oh superb, thanks," said Chris, closing his laptop. "I'm currently writing a proposal that I'm planning on giving the minister tonight. I have a meeting booked with him when he arrives."

"Oh, what is it?" asked Rushani, slightly embarrassed to be talking to Chris about his work. She took the philosophy of closing her eyes and ears when she moved around the guesthouse.

"Well, I'm hoping to start a de-mining project in this area. The national park has had a lot of terrorist and military activity, as you know, and it is not safe for the elephants, nor for the farmers who live on the edge."

"I hope you can," said Rushani. She noticed the little bubble of excitement that had crept up from below, at the thought of Chris sticking around. Of course, she would want someone to stay who was kind, considerate, respectful and going to benefit her community. Who wouldn't want that? It may also be the twinkling blue of his eyes, his warm smile, his large strong hands and his soft, accented voice. But what did that matter? She would only ever be able to look from afar. It was a nice thought though, a streak of blue on an otherwise black horizon.

"I'd better get on." She turned away from him and began to sweep, a smile playing at her lips, and a hum escaping from her throat.

Chris watched the sweeping movement of her arms, the sound of the sand scuttling across the polished, cement floor. He had never met a woman like her. He felt drawn to her. She appeared so strong, yet he wanted to wrap his arms around her and protect her. There was such a deep sadness that he yearned to dispel. He didn't know how he was going to get close to her. But being in the same location would definitely help.

11 Frangipani

Claudette swept through the restaurant in a shimmer of Indian silks. She felt irritable today and was desperately seeking someone to vent her frustrations on. She spotted Gaya alone with a pot of tea.

"Gaya darling, I must get out of this place soon. It's killing me slowly."

"Yes, you and several hundred thousand other people probably feel that way," Gaya said, raising her eyebrows. She liked Claudette but sometimes she found her just a little too dramatic and self-centred. Gaya wasn't sure how she had got herself into a job position like this in the first place. It just didn't seem to suit her.

"Oh darling, you know what I mean, the heat, the dust, all those boring meetings and the disgusting, sweet tea. I need some luxuries in my life. I mean, look at my fingernails. They need some attention!"

Gaya looked at the long, painted talons and thought, what a world Claudette must live in, where fingernails were a cause for concern.

"Well, maybe you should leave if you are finding it too hard. If we have a choice, we really shouldn't be doing things that make us miserable."

"And why do you want to be here, mon cherie? Aren't there better places for you to be right now? America, for example. Why didn't you want to stay there, away from all this pain and destruction?"

"For what? So I can get a manicure? I have no desire to be anywhere else. Nowhere else makes any sense to me. I can't ignore what's going on here, just because my family is rich enough to educate me overseas. There but for the grace of God go I, as they say."

"I thought it would be different coming here. I imagined the raw edge of life, experiencing the front-line, interesting people and crazy situations. That's why I left my comfortable life in Paris, for the excitement and danger."

"This is people's lives we're talking about Claudette, not a movie set."

"Oh, mon cherie, I'm just telling it like it is. People aren't honest enough these days. I mean, who would prefer to live like this rather than in luxury?"

"Me."

"But it is not preference, Gaya, it's based on the guilt that you have construed about the haves and the have nots, you are being a martyr."

"Claudette, why do you think you know what's going on for me? Guilt is not the reason I chose to work here. Well, there is some guilt on behalf of my race persecuting another race, but it is not personal guilt."

"You feel guilty because you are Sinhalese, because you have led a comfortable life, because you have an overseas education, because you have a way of escaping all this. I know that once you have found the perfect partner to mate with, when you feel life growing in your belly, only then will you allow yourself to return to the comfortable, luxurious life that you were born with. You will use your child as an excuse, that the child needs to be safe, but really you will secretly be relieved you don't need to live like this anymore. You are paying your dues, and when they are paid, you will return to your life."

Gaya stared at Claudette open-mouthed. She was incredulous that Claudette could judge her like this. Claudette didn't know who she was or what her reasons for being here were. But somewhere deep in her gut, she felt the rising sensation that Claudette had touched on a raw nerve.

"Claudette, I really must get on with my emails," she said, turning back to her laptop.

"Sure thing sweetie," Claudette got up and flounced off in the direction of the kitchen, stepping a little lighter than before.

Gaya stared at the screen, drumming her fingers on her teacup. Claudette could be such an A-class bitch sometimes. She really must stop entertaining it. She read the email again, analysing every word and trying to make sense of it. She knew it was from Rakesh, although it was under a different name. He had left a few days ago after what had happened on the beach. Gaya had thought of nothing else since. She'd wished he would have spent the night with her, but he had said it was impossible, that he had some pressing work to do. The email said the following;

'Dear Gaya, I've been having a lovely time but am heading home tonight. I've decided to make a trip overseas to visit my family, before settling down and starting my new job. I was thinking about taking that cruise we were talking about. How's life? I hope to see you soon. Best Wishes Sudini.'

Gaya contemplated all this. What did it mean? Was Rakesh coming here? Was he seriously considering going on the boat to Australia after everything he had said? Was that the only way he could get out of the country? Had he decided to flee before he published his latest report? His life must really be in danger, he must have found out something big. He wouldn't leave unless he really had to.

She felt anxious and a little sick. She knew she was holding his life in her hands right now and the wrong move could lead security forces straight to him. She needed to find Niraj. He would know what to do.

She replied quickly, 'Dear Sudini, it's great to hear from you. Life is good. We've been very busy. We have a state visit tonight so it's all very exciting. The honourable Mr Jayasuriya is coming to dinner. I don't have time to write more today but will try and write again tomorrow when it's calmer around here. Love Gaya.'

She hoped he would delay his arrival until Jayasurya and all his cronies left the area. It was too dangerous for him to arrive in the middle of it. There were at least twenty army officers stationed on the beach and around the hotel, so nobody would be able to get in without valid ID.

She sent the mail and closed down her laptop. Walking past the flowering bougainvillea, she opened the door to the office and spoke quietly to Niraj.

"I need to speak to you about a delicate matter."

Niraj looked up immediately. "What is it Gaya?"

"Shall we take a walk on the beach? It's cooler now and I feel a little sea breeze will do wonders for my head."

"Sure, let's go." He locked up the office and followed her down the path. Once they were through the gates and out of earshot of the patrolling officers, Gaya began to talk.

"I've had an email from Rakesh. He said he was coming here tonight, but I've told him to wait until tomorrow. He wants to leave the country."

"He must have got his story," replied Niraj. "His life won't be worth living here anymore if he publishes it. That is if he's allowed to keep his life."

"We need to help him get out. How do we do that?"

"I have contacts in town who can get him a fake ID for travel, then we can try and get him on a fishing boat or a yacht over to India."

"I think he's planning on getting on the boat to Australia."

"Oh, shit."

Gaya and Niraj walked for a while in silence, contemplating the treacherous road ahead for their friend.

"Do you think he'll be ok?"

"I don't know Gaya. There's a lot stacked against him, but he's faced these odds before and come out on top. We've just got to hope the gods are still smiling down on him. It doesn't seem like there are any other options at this stage. They will hunt him down and kill him if he stays here. There is too much at stake for the politicians and businessmen. They will want his blood if he makes public the information he has."

They had reached the tumbling sand dunes that marked the end of the bay. They turned around and headed back to the hotel. The beach was almost empty. Locals didn't come here anymore. They were too afraid to leave their villages for fear that something might happen to them. Those who lived in Colombo never came. It was like a whole other country to them. The sound of shelling could always be heard somewhere in the distance. It accompanied the night sky, where the sound of birds filled it by day. There were the few brave, intrepid travellers not put off by the war. These young and old backpackers could still be found enjoying the beach, the wildlife, the food and partying till dawn amongst the raw broken remains of a once vibrant community.

Gaya returned to her room. She wanted to be by herself. She felt worried for Rakesh. She had tried to stop herself from feeling this way about him, but it had proven too difficult. She knew where she stood with him. He had never promised her anything, but she couldn't help how she felt. His charisma and charm had won her over and she had so much respect for him. He was brave beyond comparison. Consistently putting his life in danger for people he didn't know. He was 100% committed to his job and to supporting freedom of information, however many obstacles were put in his way and what had he sacrificed in return, a loving relationship, the possibility of family, even a home? These were all things he could now never have in this country. He had pushed too many boundaries, and crossed too many lines, for the powers-that-be to let him slip through the cracks.

Maybe Claudette had been right. Gaya wasn't prepared to cross those boundaries so maybe she was a fake after all. Pretending she cared but not sacrificing any of her freedoms for the cause. What if he made it to Australia? Some people had. Would she follow him there? Start a new life with him? In a safe place where they could raise a family? It was just as Claudette had predicted. She didn't really care about all these nameless faces, not really. Not if her life plan was in jeopardy. Did that make her just the same as Claudette? Was she just better at hiding it? More dishonest, as Claudette would say.

But then again, what was wrong with wanting what every other human wanted from their life? Surely this was what they were all working for anyway: to give people the freedom to love and be loved, to work, to raise families safely. Why wouldn't she want the same thing for herself? Damn Claudette, for making her feel so torn up. What did her opinion matter anyway? She was just a bitter, gin-soaked old crow, only content when putting other people down.

Gaya closed her eyes and fell into a restless sleep. When she opened them again, an hour had passed, and the sun was setting. She looked at the last rays of daylight shining through the cracks in the cadjan[11] roof. The show is about to begin, she thought.

She showered and dressed in her most elegant suit. She needed to keep her wits about her tonight. She was hoping they wouldn't ask too many awkward questions, and she hoped she would be able to give the right answers. She had a lot to talk about

---

[11] Cadjan – woven palm leaf used for roofs, walls or fences

in terms of their rebuilding projects. Some housing estates were nearly complete and they had managed to re-house 350 people after the tsunami had hit almost two years before. That was the main thrust of their work here but Niraj had moved into more sensitive areas that had to be kept unofficial and which took up a lot of his time. Gaya had taken over much of his administrative and project management role.

Mr Jayasuriya would expect her to sit at his table. This visit was a big press opportunity to show the government's caring side. How it was supporting the rebuilding of Tamil communities, to show that the country was working as one. They wouldn't mention of course how the Sinhalese areas were receiving most of the foreign tsunami aid and that these Tamil areas were, in fact, receiving very little. Or how a few miles up the coast everything, from temples to schools, was being blown to smithereens.

The restaurant looked exquisite. Flower garlands decorated the poles and the tables had hand-woven placemats and bowls of frangipani flowers. There were fire sticks burning in every corner and the smell of fried garlic and spices was emanating from the kitchen.

Marni, Jake and Zoe were all scrubbed up and in the restaurant. Gaya approached them.

"Wow, you all look lovely."

"Thanks, Gaya," said Marni. "We're on our way out."

"Well, good for you. It's definitely a good idea to get out of the hotel for a few hours. It must have been a busy day getting everything prepared."

"It was, we're leaving Zoe here with Rushani, but we will only be five minutes away and we'll be back before the big J arrives."

143

"Don't worry, I'll keep an eye on things and let you know if you need to come back sooner. But try and relax and enjoy yourselves while you can!"

"Cheers Gaya," said Jake. "We will definitely try to."

Gaya waved them off after they put Zoe to bed.

"Have fun, and don't worry, everything is under control here!"

Marni smiled in response, but the smile did not quite reach her eyes. Jake took her hand and began to pull her gently through the gates that led to the road. Marni continued to look back over her shoulder as she walked. Gaya could recognize the look that was in her eyes because she was feeling it too, a cold sense of dread.

12 Fish Patties

Vish was relieved they were finally out of the forest. They could move quickly now and easily immerse themselves in the hordes of weekend shoppers who had flocked to the markets.

Leela followed closely behind. She kept her head down and avoided eye contact. She had left her boots in the forest so as not to draw attention to herself. Vish had also changed into civilian clothing: black trousers and a brown, buttoned shirt. They had washed their hands and faces in the stream and wet their hair. They did not look like they had spent the last three days in the jungle.

Vish took out the cash he had in his pocket and counted it. Rs 15,000. He wished he'd thought to take more from the HQ safe before he left. They would need a lot more to get through the next few days. He bought some sandals for Leela and curried fish patties. They were fresh, and Vish was grateful for the hot food. They ate silently, watching the people going about their daily business. The anonymity of the crowded market felt comforting.

"Come on, let's find the bus station," said Vish.

They crossed the main street, passed the waiting tuk-tuks and the betel nut hawkers shouting their wares.

The bus station was dark, covered by an asbestos roof held up by concrete pillars. The smell from the adjoining rubbish tip spread itself through the stale air.

Vish left Leela on a seat and went to buy tickets.

She watched a family shelling peanuts, huddled together, protecting their basket of vegetables. A baby boy tottered about like a drunk, practising his newly formed steps. She yearned for her brother.

"Hello little sister," the voice from behind her startled her. The man spoke to her in Sinhala. "Why is a pretty, young girl like you alone in a bus station?"

She could feel her heart quicken its beat. Her nerves began to pulse, sending pins and needles up the back of her neck and through her scalp. She felt dry, bony fingers brush against her arm and she turned to look at the man.

He was thin and weaselly, with yellowing eyes and several days of grey stubble. He grinned a rotten, toothless smile as he stared down at her.

"Why aren't you talking to me? Are you shy?" He laughed then, a cackle that echoed around the empty space. He dropped his hand down to the growing bulge under his sarong. "I think you know what I want, I think you know how to be a good girl, I think you've made men happy before."

The man was now standing in front of Leela, his groin parallel with her eyes. With one swift movement, she clenched her fist, pulled back her arm and shot it up between his legs with all her strength. The man cried out and buckled before her.

"You bitch!" he cried before dissolving into a sobbing heap. A few of the waiting passengers began to walk forward with curiosity but hesitated a few seconds too long and the urge to help a stranger passed. Vish heard the cries of the man and ran out of the ticket office.

"Leela, what happened?" he half-whispered when he reached her. He looked around at the other people watching them, worried about the attention that was on them.

"I'm sorry Vish, I tried to ignore him, but he just made me so angry with his words and his leering. Why does he think he has the right to do that? I just wanted him to leave me alone."

Vish looked at the choking heap on the floor and then back to Leela. He smiled down at her, the fear erased from his eyes. "You really do have some good skills!"

The bus pulled in, and apart from some odd stares from the other people boarding the bus, the moment seemed to have passed without further consequence. Leela took her seat by the window and watched the man, who had dragged himself onto the seat. He stared up at her with hatred in his eyes. He slid his index finger threateningly along the width of his neck. Leela watched his futile attempt to take the power from her. She threw back her head and laughed and laughed until tears streamed down her cheeks. The bus pulled off and she watched the man getting smaller and smaller, the look of utter confusion on his face.

Several miles later, Leela heaved a sigh that reached the depths of her gut. As she breathed out, she felt the stress she'd been carrying from the last week fall off her, like eroding cliffs relieved to be finally crumbling into the ocean. She stared out of the window at the houses flashing past her, lost in thought of the happy families behind the walls. Were they happy? Or were they all torn apart by the war? Each one with fathers, daughters, brothers, mothers, sons, sisters, lost and missed for eternity.

Vish had fallen asleep, his heavy breathing comforting her. For now, they were safe, but for how long? She had no idea what new challenge she was going to have to face from one minute to the next. She looked at Vish's sleeping features, from foe to friend. They had already been on a huge journey together. She trusted him now. Some things you just knew for sure, deep in your heart. He would try his best for her.

Her thoughts turned to Suresh. She didn't want to bring trouble to his door. But that was exactly where they were headed.

———————●●——————

Marni and Jake found a secluded table amongst the overhanging bougainvillea in the garden of the Tropical Inn. Marni reached for Jake's hand across the table and he responded by linking his fingers in hers.

"What are you thinking?" she asked, studying his face for his present mood.

"I was thinking it's good to be here. To be away from the hotel makes a huge difference in how close I feel to you. I have all of you right now, in this moment."

Marni smiled and squeezed his hand, but the sinking feeling of the truth flickered across her face for just a moment. She knew she was not fully present. Even as he was speaking, her thoughts were filled with others: Zoe, Suresh, Leela, Gaya, Aruna, Jayasuriya, even her father. How could she sit and enjoy the company of her husband when there was so much going on around her? This was the essence of the problem. She knew that. How could she learn to just let go and enjoy the joyful moments when they appeared?

* * *

Jake stood up and crossed to the bar to order their drinks. He waved to a few of the locals and saw some unfamiliar faces. That was always a good sign, that there were still people brave enough to have their holiday in a war zone. He was shocked that Marni had suggested going out. It was very rare that she left the hotel to its own devices, especially when there was an important function being organised.

He loved Marni so much it hurt. As the years went on, she seemed to pull away from him, bit by bit. He felt that he shared her with everybody. He was not a selfish man, but she was his wife. He should be able to expect some intimate moments, some shared private time, a little energy left at the end of the day just for him. But as it was, he felt like the hired help. There, to perform a duty. Look after their child and don't rock the boat. Allow her the freedom to pursue all her desires, whatever they may be and whether they included him. He detested it.

It hadn't started this way. They had dreams, big dreams and they involved each other, in each and every step. They had met at college in London. Marni was studying photography and Jake website design. They planned to work freelance, setting up their own company in the home they rented together. Several years of good marketing, good fortune and good business sense passed by. Their portfolio of clients was on the increase and they had a regular income. But Marni was getting restless. She had often talked about her father and trying to find him. She said that she had never felt complete not knowing who he was. She had lived all her life in London, but she wanted to return to the country she thought of as her home. To Jake, it was just another adventure in the great journey of life. He loved Marni and was happy to follow her to the ends of the earth. They had no family commitments, nothing to tie them to England. They were young, free and full of drive. He agreed immediately to her plans of moving out there and seeing where the wind blew. They had saved some money and had all the equipment they needed to continue working freelance from wherever they were. They had nothing to lose.

They packed up their house, had a huge farewell party with their friends and family and left to find their pot of gold.

They had, initially, travelled the length and breadth of the country, immersing themselves in the culture and seeking their ideal place to set up home. After several months they had walked through the gates of the Moon Rise Hotel. The sight of the ocean had lifted their tired bodies and they raced, squealing and fully clothed into the bluest water they had ever seen.

"Well, this is what you'd call paradise," Jake had said, as they locked bodies in the water, the moment caught forever.

They had met Ali later that evening, Marni practising her pidgin Tamil. He had welcomed them to his part of the island.

They spent several glorious weeks bathing in the sea, gazing at the endless wildlife and gorging themselves on delicious rice and curry.

"We don't want to leave, Ali," they had told him one night.

"Well, why don't you stay?" he replied. "I need extra help here with the season starting. You can have one of the cabanas and free food and you can help me out. Why don't you talk it over with each other and let me know?"

Marni and Jake looked at each other for no more than a second and turned back to Ali. "We don't need to talk about it," said Marni. "Our hearts are already here."

"Well in that case," said Ali, "You can start tomorrow!"

The months rolled by as Marni and Jake fell more and more in love with the place. Each day they woke up in an idyllic dream.

"We are very lucky, we have it all." Jake had said to Marni, on more than one occasion.

Marni made several trips back to Colombo to search public records for any trace of her father. She came to a dead-end every time. It was as if he had vanished. There was no death certificate, so she assumed he must still be alive. She had been to the college where he had been studying when he had met her mother, but he had left before completing his degree. She became more obsessed, checking police records, prisons and even asylums. But all to no avail.

The tsunami had hit them four months later. It came from nowhere. The brightest, blue sky and a calm, inviting sea had welcomed in the day. As the sea began to rise and the water seeped through the gates and across the sand, Marni and Jake looked to the horizon.

"What's happening?" said Jake.

"I don't know," said Marni.

"Fucking run!" screamed Jake.

They ran for their lives, Marni turned back to see a wall of frothy white water twenty feet high, chasing them. Baring down on them, snarling and snapping at their ankles. They tried to outrun it, but it was no use. The water caught them, lifting them off their feet and churning them over and over in the raging river that crossed the land.

Everything seemed to be in slow motion. There were trees, cattle, cars and crumbling buildings all churning towards them and threatening to take their lives. The water was full of sulphur and pitch black. As Marni and Jake fought to hold their breath, they searched frantically for the bright, blue sky they had left only moments before. If they could only see which way was up, they could swim that way. They clung to each other and pushed their way through the water. Suddenly they surfaced, taking gasps of air until they were dragged back down into the whirling black.

They had eventually made it to safety, but not without injuries. Broken ribs, a dislocated shoulder, and cuts and bruises which covered their bodies.

The hotel was completely gone, smashed and dragged into the depths of the ocean. All around them lay the bodies of the dead and the carnage of a once beautiful village.

They had not lost their lives, but they had lost their home and equipment, and therefore the means to an income. Jake wanted to return to England and recuperate from the trauma on the savings they still had in the bank. Marni wanted to stay.

So, they stayed.

All their savings went into rebuilding the hotel. They went into partnership with Ali and spent every penny they had, on a new kitchen, restaurant and four cabanas. It had cost $20,000. $10,000 from their own money and $10,000 borrowed from Marni's mother.

There was no way out for them after that. They had fully committed. Looking back on it now, Jake knew that they had acted in a state of shock. Marni had dug her heels in and tried to turn back the clock because she couldn't bear to see the big, empty space where her dreams had been. Jake had finally agreed because he loved her, and he was tired. He had no fight left.

When Zoe was born, Jake's heart lifted a little out of the dark clouds that surrounded him. They had returned to an 'almost' normal. But the ceasefire that the country had indulged in for the last few years came to an abrupt end, and the country returned to a state of war.

This was no place to bring up a child, Jake had thought. He tried to persuade Marni to pack up and go to England on the promise that they would return when it was safe, but Marni had refused.

"I can't leave here," she had said. "This is our home, our business, it's the only place Zoe's ever known. Our family is not in danger, they won't target foreigners. It's not right to leave. I don't want to jump ship."

There was nothing Jake could do. He couldn't take Zoe away from Marni and he couldn't leave Zoe here without him. For now, this is where they had to stay.

He felt trapped and he resented Marni for it. He looked across at her as she sat picking the candle wax from the ornate holder, a fixed look of concentration on her furrowed brow. He knew it was not candle wax she was thinking about, or him.

He brought his attention to the bartender pouring the drinks, arrack, ginger and lime. The ice cracked, and the soda fizzed, as the liquid found its path of least resistance to the bottom of the glass. 'That's just how I live my life' thought Jake.

"Thanks, Roma," he said, handing over some notes. "Keep the change."

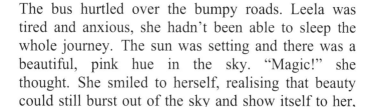

The bus hurtled over the bumpy roads. Leela was tired and anxious, she hadn't been able to sleep the whole journey. The sun was setting and there was a beautiful, pink hue in the sky. "Magic!" she thought. She smiled to herself, realising that beauty could still burst out of the sky and show itself to her, even in the state she was currently in.

"We're nearly there." Vish brought her out of her thoughts. "We need to keep a low profile when we arrive." He was whispering so as not to be heard above the drone of the engine. "It will be better at night. We will need to walk for a while. We can move easier along the beach, only rabid dogs to block our path. I'm not sure yet how we can contact your brother. I don't know if there will be people already there looking for us. We will have to assess the situation when we get there."

Leela said nothing. Her heart was beating fast and her head hurt. She turned to look back out of the window. Night had fallen. The sky was black. The moon, nowhere to be seen.

13 Arrack and Broken Glass

Eva and Jo were watching all the preparations with great interest. Even the thought of a ministerial dinner didn't put them off the joy of tuna curry and fresh barbecued prawns.

Jo was helping Suresh prepare the fire pit. They dug a hole in the sand and lit a fire to create rows of glowing red embers that danced and sizzled in their bed. They placed a grill over the opening and laid the prawns on top. They were wrapped in banana leaves that were stuffed with garlic butter and fresh limes.

They sat around the pit, enjoying the aromas that spiralled towards them and guarding their treasure from prowling cats and dogs.

"I heard about your sister, Suresh," said Eva tentatively, "I'm really sorry. Have you heard any news?"

Suresh stiffened a little. Although he had got to know Eva and Jo quite well, over the last several months, he was anxious about too many people knowing about Leela.

"It's ok Suresh, we understand the severity of the situation and don't worry, we won't be talking to anyone about it, but Niraj has spoken to us about what may happen to your sister if she enters Australia as a refugee. He wanted to know if we might be able to help, which we can."

Suresh relaxed his shoulders and looked at Eva. She had a kind face full of laughter lines, which crinkled up when she smiled. She wasn't smiling now though. She was looking at him intently, with great sadness in her eyes.

"We were supporting refugees in re-settlement programs before we left Australia, and we still have contacts working there. Unfortunately, we can't get through the bureaucracy any quicker to acquire visas, but once she is there, we can certainly help her find her feet."

"Thank you, Madam, it's very nice you giving help, but I don't know where my sister is."

Suresh gazed at the burning embers, glad for the distraction.

"I'll pray we find her soon." Eva got up, stretching her stiff legs. She placed a hand on his shoulder. "Hang in there, Suresh," she said gently, before returning to her cabana to get dressed for dinner.

Suresh and Jo sat silently with their own thoughts, poking at the embers with sticks.

"Minister here!" Rushani called excitedly down the phone. "You come?"

"Yes, of course, stay calm. Just give me a minute."

Jake set the drinks down on the table and slid into his chair.

"I'm sorry Jake, that was Rushani on the phone. The minister's arrived early. We have to go."

All Jake could do was laugh.

Claudette looked at herself in the mirror. 'You scrub up quite well,' she thought to herself, 'even in the middle of this flea pit'. She put on her rouge lipstick and blew a kiss to herself. 'Time to meet the adoring fans,' she said out loud as she grabbed a silk shawl off her bed and unlocked the door.

Claudette didn't think she would be living here much longer. She was over it. There was no-one interesting to play with. Even that Chris, the only possible suitor, seemed to prefer the roughness of the kitchen staff, to her exquisite qualities. 'More fool him,' she thought, as she saw him standing in the restaurant, nursing a beer.

'I'm going to find me some fun tonight. I've had enough of playing the part of someone who cares.' She strode into the restaurant. There was a huddle of shirted men surrounding a large, balding man in a suit. Must be the minister, she thought, as she turned and gave him her most gracious smile. All heads turned in her direction and the minister returned the smile with a slight nod of his head.

She extended her hand out to him, "Claudette Javier, I'm very pleased to meet you."

The group of men parted slightly, and he took her hand. "Rahul Jayasuriya, I hope to have some time to catch up with you later."

His lecherous smile made her recoil, and she tried to slip her hand out of his, but he held onto it firmly and stroked the inside of her palm with his finger, before releasing it.

She turned her back on them and wiped her hand down the front of her dress, trying to rid it of the sleazy touch. She left the restaurant and stuck her head around the kitchen door. "Arrack and soda, plenty of ice, and plenty of arrack."

A drink was placed in her hand within moments, by Suresh, and she took the first sip of the day with relish. She felt the alcohol course through her body, releasing a feeling of euphoria. She lit up a cigarette and inhaled deeply. She stood outside the restaurant, under the stars, looking in. Gaya was there, meeting and greeting everyone with her fake, dutiful smile. Jenny was also there, to back up Gaya, as Niraj had cleared out for the night. The old couple, Eva and Jo, were sitting quietly at a table by themselves, and Chris was discussing his project plans with one of the minister's entourage.

'Nothing to entertain her in that bunch.' She heard voices from behind and her eyes searched through the darkness, towards the gate. She saw Jake and Marni coming down the path. They were talking heatedly. Marni was hurrying along, and Jake was trying to catch hold of her to make her stop.

"Jake, I can't do this now," she heard Marni say. "I'm sorry we didn't get to have our date, I really am, but we're needed here now. We can try again tomorrow."

Marni rushed past Claudette and into the crowded restaurant.

"Tomorrow may be too late," she heard Jake say, from halfway down the path.

'Now this is something I can work with,' she thought. She could spot an opportunity for stirring, a mile off.

"Jake darling, won't you join me for a drink, I have a duty-free bottle of Irish whiskey calling out your name!"

Jake looked so forlorn. He sighed and lifted his eyes to look at Claudette's hopeful expression. "Sure Claudette, why not?"

Marni bustled into the restaurant, her cheeks rosy, from the sudden rush to get home and the closeness of the air that night.

She approached the minister's right-hand man. "How is everything? What can I bring for you?"

"Ice, sodas and some of your famous garlic prawns, to start with. We have several cases of very fine quality arrack to get through!" He laughed a deep, throaty chuckle.

Marni tried to smile but could feel the anxiety of the night ahead overwhelm her. Arguing with Jake didn't help. She wished that he could see it from her point of view and try to understand.

"Sure, I'll send some out immediately."

She hurried into the kitchen, glad to be away from the restaurant. She would try to stay out of it as much as possible tonight unless they needed her. She didn't want to socialise with the politicians and their bodyguards. She just wanted them fed and gone, with no trouble for her, the guests or the staff. Two cases of arrack were certainly not going to help the situation. Alcohol and politics did not mix.

"Hi Rushani, can you serve three plates of garlic prawns and organize ice, sodas and glasses for that table, please. I'm going to check on Zoe."

She walked into their cabana, feeling immediately relaxed as soon as she heard Zoe's quiet breathing. She kissed her daughter and stroked the hair back from her face. "You're what it's all about," she whispered.

She closed the door and headed back to the kitchen. Aruna was drunk, as Marni had feared, and was in the back kitchen, ranting about the state of the government.

"Aruna, I think it's better if you go home," she said gently.

"Why should I go home? Am I not good enough for the great minister?"

"No, Uncle, you know that's not what I'm saying. You're tired and you've had too much to drink and I think it's better if you sleep it off."

Aruna grumbled at her and staggered out of the kitchen.

"He won't go home Miss Marni," said Rushani. "He sleep under palu tree. Always where I find him."

"Well, at least he's out the kitchen and, hopefully, not likely to start any fights with government officials."

Marni took a deep breath and wiped her hands on a tea cloth. "Right, let's get this show on the road."

———————— ● ————————

Jake was lying in a hammock on Claudette's balcony. He felt soothed, by the consistent crashing of the waves, and the joint that Claudette had given him. He sipped his whiskey. He was enjoying the taste of quality, as opposed to the cheap, local alcohol that gave him an awful headache the morning after.

"What are you thinking?" asked Claudette. She had emerged from her room and pulled a chair up close to him so that his thigh brushed against her leg with every swing of the hammock. Jake put his hand lightly on the balcony rail to slow down the swinging.

"Oh, I was just thinking this is the first time I've felt relaxed all day."

Claudette smiled at him with one side of her perfectly lined lips. "Moi aussi."

She stretched her legs out a little further, so they were now under him, and Jake was almost swinging into her lap. Her bracelets tinkled down her arm as she lifted the half-smoked joint to her lips, to relight it. She inhaled heavily and passed it on to Jake.

"Why don't you relax just a little more Jake, you deserve it. Marni doesn't treat you right."

Jake stiffened at the mention of Marni's name. He resented Claudette for bringing up his personal business and for noticing it in the first place.

"Yeah, well, she's been busy today."

"It's not just today, Jake. I saw it the first day I got here."

"Well, it's a private matter between us, and I'd rather not talk about it."

"Hush, hush Jake," said Claudette stroking his bare forearm. "Don't get yourself all heated. I was just trying to help. We don't have to mention Marni's name at all. In fact, I'd rather not. I just think that she should appreciate what she has in you, and if she doesn't, then you should find someone who does. Life's too short to be second best all the time."

Jake twinged in pain at the accurate recognition of his feelings. He felt second best and whatever he tried to do, there seemed to be no way to turn it around. Marni had other priorities now and it didn't seem likely that they would go away anytime soon.

"Well, what would you do Claudette?"

"I would stop trying to live someone else's dream, hoping they would eventually feel satisfied and notice that I was still there. This isn't your dream. Do you even know what your dream is?"

Jake knew what his answer was. It was being with Marni, and making her happy, however lame it sounded.

Well, it had been, until recently. Now it seemed he couldn't make her happy. Only the success of the business and Zoe went anywhere near making Marni happy.

Claudette filled up his empty glass. "Drink-up Jake. Tonight, we don't regret, we take what we deserve."

Jake reluctantly clinked glasses with his companion. He knew she was flirting with him and he had never really trusted her, but what else was he going to do tonight? Get in Marni's way in the kitchen? Join the table of drunk politicians? Go to bed? He didn't fancy any of those options and he figured Claudette was just passing the time with him, entertaining herself with harmless toying.

He looked out over the water. The moon had risen and cast its rays across the ocean. The water shimmered as each wave rose and fell, moving from shadow into moonlight and back again.

A scream awoke Marni from her daydreaming. She ran out of the kitchen door and into the restaurant. Rushani was standing amidst broken glass with the table of men laughing raucously. Chris was hovering at the side of the table, his fists clenched.

"I'm sorry Miss Marni, I drop tray."

"Don't worry Rushani," she said, bending down to pick up the large pieces and put them back on the tray. Marni could see that she was shaking, and she held her hand to steady her. "Come with me to the kitchen."

Once inside the kitchen, she sat her down on a stool. "Suresh, please take a broom and dustpan and sweep up the rest of the glass." She turned to face Rushani. "What happened?"

"I'm sorry, the man touch me and I scared and I drop tray."

"Don't be sorry, it's me who should be sorry for putting you in this position."

Chris came into the kitchen. "Are you ok? I saw what happened."

"Oh," said Rushani, blushing and turning away. "I'm sorry".

"Will you stop saying sorry," said Marni.

"It was all I could do, not to go and punch him, but I figured even if I got out of that with my life, I definitely would have had my visa revoked, so I thought better of it."

"Well, I'm very glad you thought better of it because I couldn't have handled a dead Chris as well," said Marni, laughing away the tension in her throat.

"Ok, that's it, I'm going to do all the waitressing from now on. You stay in the kitchen Rushani."

"No Miss Marni, you can't do that. What if they do something to you?"

"They wouldn't dare, not to a foreigner?"

"I wouldn't be so sure Marni," said Chris. "I'll stay in the restaurant as well, just to be on the safe side. Are you sure you're ok?" Chris said to Rushani again.

"Yes, yes ok," she said, staring at her knotted fingers in her lap.

"Ok, well, let me know if there's anything you need. I'll just go and loiter in the restaurant then," he said, winking as he left the kitchen.

"He's a very nice man," said Marni.

"Yes, he nice," agreed Rushani.

"And I think he likes you," said Marni

"I think he nice to everyone," said Rushani.

"I don't think so," Marni replied.

"Oh, come on Jake, where's your sense of adventure?"

Claudette was trying to persuade Jake to go for a swim.

"I'm very relaxed right here."

"And just think how much more relaxed you'll be in the sea. I'm just so hot and sticky right now. I can't believe you don't feel like that."

"Yeah, well, I'm hot and sticky too, I just can't be bothered."

"You are way too stoned and not enough fun for me. I will have to pull out my secret weapon."

"And what would that be," said Jake, slightly concerned but more worryingly, intrigued.

"Oh, so you're interested then?"

"Depends what it is."

"Oh, don't play hard to get Jake, you know you want it, just say yes or you can't have it."

"Ok, yes then," said Jake, laughing.

Claudette disappeared inside her cabana and opened the fridge. She pulled out a small vial and unscrewed the lid. Attached to the end of the lid was a tiny spoon. She scooped some of the white powder onto the spoon and held it up to Jake's nostril.

"Well, sniff then," she said.

Jake obediently closed his other nostril and sniffed deeply. He felt the white powder hit the back of his nose. Almost immediately his head fizzed, and his eyes began popping.

"Good stuff, eh?"

"Yeah, what is it?"

"It's supposed to be pure MDMA,[12] but it clearly isn't. I don't think it has anything too peculiar

---

[12] MDMA – Methylenedioxymethamphetamine (Ecstasy)

mixed in though. It gives a pretty good buzz. Here, have more."

The tiny spoon was opening him up. Cutting through the haziness of the joint and tipping him into a much lighter, happier, more playful world. There wasn't any need to be serious and maudlin. He'd done enough of that. Claudette was right. It was time he started living for himself. She wasn't so bad. At least she was honest and told it like it is. You knew where you were with Claudette.

"Come on Jake, can't you humour me now? Come for a swim with me."

"Alright, alright, you talked me into it!"

Claudette wasted no time. She grabbed him by the hand and pulled him out the hammock. Together they ran down to the water's edge.

Jake felt delirious with the weight lifted from his shoulders. He didn't need to blame Marni, for anything, or himself. Everything was good. He stripped off his clothes and threw them onto the beach, before diving into the water. The coldness sending shivers of delight through his muscles.

Marni was facing him then. She wrapped her legs around his waist and pressed her body to his. She looked him squarely in the eye, which was when Jake realised it wasn't Marni, but Claudette kissing him fully on the lips.

Jake allowed Claudette's tongue to penetrate his mouth, her hand moving up between his legs. As she wrapped her fingers around him, he could feel himself responding and he pressed himself harder into the palm of her hand. He slipped the strap of her bikini down her shoulder and grabbed at her nipple, now pushing his own tongue deep into her mouth. The drag of the tide pulled Jake off-balance and suddenly he found himself out of his depth.

"No Claudette…," he started to say before he got a mouthful of water. He untangled her legs from around him and pushed her off. He dived into the nearest wave to get to shallower water, taking great strides, to reach the beach as fast as he could. He could hear Claudette calling his name.

"Oh Jake, don't be so serious," she was saying.

Jake grabbed his clothes and headed towards the hotel, shaking his head, trying to erase the last ten minutes of his life.

Claudette tutted and turned her back to the beach. She swam out deep, diving under the water to clear her head. Jake was a fool. Chasing after Marni when she was clearly no longer interested in him. She rolled over and lay on her back, staring at the stars. It was very peaceful. There was not much swell tonight and it felt good to be pulled by the water, this way and that, in its gentle caress. She closed her eyes and put her ears under the surface to block out the noise from the restaurant.

When she opened her eyes again, she saw the lights of the hotel in the distance and realised she had been taken way out to sea by a riptide. "Shit!" she exclaimed and tried to keep herself from panicking.

She knew it was futile to swim against the current, but she had to get to land somehow. She let herself drift horizontally for a while, until she was unable to control her rising fear, and started swimming for shore. The swell was picking up and she caught a few waves inwards, although they dragged her under as they broke over her head. She was swallowing mouthfuls of water as she went out of time with the space between waves. She strove forward, but the rip tried to pull her back into the embrace of the wave behind her. Twice she caught the wave wrong and went under, tumbling and spinning with the force of the water. The second time, however, she hit the sandy bottom and knew then that she was close to shore. The water pushed her up the beach, and then sucked back to where it came from, only to return and lap gently at her ankles. She tried to take deep breaths of air, instead, coughing out a lungful of seawater, her body shaking with the strain.

A hand was placed on her shoulder and Claudette screamed. A soft voice, in broken English, said: "Nona,[13] you ok?"

Claudette turned to the voice and saw a young girl's face, looking down at her.

"I'm not sure," she said, glancing up and down the beach in confusion.

The girl helped her to sit up. She wiped the sand from her face.

"Where you stay?" the girl asked.

"I'm staying at the Moon Rise Hotel, but I went for a swim and got caught in a current and couldn't get back to shore."

"Moon Rise Hotel," the girl repeated.

"Yes," said Claudette. She wasn't sure how much the girl understood.

They both looked back along the beach and could see the lights of the hotel glowing in the distance. Claudette felt immense relief that she would be able to walk back.

---

[13] Nona - madam

"Where did you come from?" she asked the girl, realising that there were only sand dunes and elephants at this end of the beach.

The girl hesitated and looked towards a figure moving out of the shadow of the dunes, into the moonlight.

"Please help me," the girl replied.

14 A Ministerial Feast–Part 1

Gaya saw Jake coming in from the beach. He'd been for a swim and was looking upset. She hurried after him.

"Jake, Marni needs you in the restaurant. The minister and his crew are getting out of hand and she needs back-up."

"What! Ok, I'll just go and put some dry clothes on."

"Are you ok?" asked Gaya.

"Yeah, yeah, I just went for a swim, I'll go and get changed, thanks for the update."

"You're welcome," said Gaya, but Jake was already out of earshot.

She walked back up the stairs to the restaurant and surveyed the group. Chris had commandeered the minister and was in deep conversation with him. The rest of the men at his table were knocking back drinks, singing out of tune and drumming loudly on the table with shockingly bad rhythm. She wished she could turn the volume down. Chris looked up from his conversation and caught her eye. She winked at him and he smiled back. She knew he was just trying to distract the minister with work. Thank goodness for

Chris. He was being a lot more useful than Jake. What was up with Jake tonight anyway?

Her thoughts turned to Rakesh. She was worried about him. She hoped he wouldn't turn up tonight as he had said in his email. She had a bad feeling, a sickening feeling, in the pit of her stomach, which she hoped wasn't anything to do with Rakesh. She wished she knew where he was and if he was ok.

Suresh was arranging the food. Most of the prawns were already devoured but the tuna curry, noodles and various sambols remained untouched.

"Excuse me, gentlemen, dinner is ready." Marni approached their table.

"Just leave it there, we will eat later," said a tall man with oily hair.

Marni was afraid of this. They would keep drinking on empty stomachs until they were so drunk, they would be falling over and causing trouble. Only then would they see fit to eat. The other guests were lining up at the buffet table to take their share.

"Oh, but it is so much better to eat now with everyone else. It might run out." She realised how incompetent that sounded as soon as she said it.

"Why don't you take half back to the kitchen, so we don't make you cook it all again," said the man condescendingly. "We will eat when we are ready," he said slightly more threateningly.

"Right," said Marni, "I'll do that."

She hurried back to the kitchen to get out of sight of the man, so he could not see that he'd affected her. She was angry and scared. How dare they come here and make her feel like this in her own home. Jake came into the kitchen and stood in the doorway.

"What's going on?"

"They're already drunk so it will only get worse from here. They're refusing to eat dinner until after they've finished drinking and I don't think we will ever get rid of them."

"It was pretty obvious this was going to happen, wasn't it?"

"That's not very helpful, Jake. And the minister has already assaulted Rushani."

"What! Where is she?"

"She's in the back kitchen. She's ok, but I'm not letting her go into the restaurant again. I'm clearing the tables tonight with Suresh."

"Oh, so you'll keep your staff out of danger, but not yourself. What is wrong with you, Marni? You let them come here for the sake of the hotel, because you think something bad will happen if you don't, even though you know it will be hell. Then when they assault your staff, you just put yourself in harm's way instead. And that's your solution? That's what you think managing is about? Marni to the rescue! Marni the protector! You're just one person. You need to look after your family, nothing else matters. Don't you get that?"

"Jake, you will never understand."

Jake looked at Marni for a long time before replying, "you have no idea what you're doing to us."

He turned and left the kitchen. Tears welled up in Marni's eyes, but she wiped them away angrily. He was so unsupportive. Why does he have to react like this, especially on a night like tonight? She found the aluminium foil and returned to the restaurant to wrap up half the food.

"What do you mean you need help?" asked Claudette, she could feel the fine hair on the back of her neck rising. "And who is that sitting there?"

"It's ok, he friend. He help me."

"Oh," said Claudette. "So why do you need my help?"

"Suresh, my brother, hotel work."

"Well, why don't you come back with me to the hotel and see him?"

"I can't, army guarding, they no see us."

"Why not?"

"Because danger."

"Why?"

"Because thinking I terrorist."

"Why would they think that?" Claudette was feeling uncomfortable again.

"Because Tamil."

"Oh," said Claudette. "And who is your friend?"

"He help me."

"Is he a terrorist?"

"Now no."

"Now no?" said Claudette quietly. "How does someone stop being a terrorist?"

"Please help me," the girl began to cry. "If you no help, we both die. We run from terrorist, they want kill us. Everybody kill us. You, Suresh, can help me, please."

Claudette looked from the girl to the silent figure, then to the hotel. "I suppose we better meet this friend of yours." She realised that if they were planning on killing or kidnapping her, it wouldn't be very difficult. Her options were limited.

She struggled to get up, leaning on the girl. Her legs were still shaking from her battle with the sea and she felt wobbly as she tried to walk. They reached the figure and he rose from the sand to greet them.

"Hello, my name is Vish," he said, holding out his hand and bending his head slightly. So far so good, thought Claudette.

"And what's your name?" she turned to the girl.

"Leela."

Hadn't she overheard a conversation between Niraj and Gaya mentioning that name? It sounded familiar.

"I don't want to waste any time," said Vish. "We need to get word to Suresh that Leela is here and that she will need money and ID. We won't be able to hide out here much longer because my men will find us."

"Your men?" enquired Claudette.

"I can't explain now, but my main concern is keeping Leela safe. Even if you trust nothing else about me, trust me on that."

Claudette held his gaze for a moment. She felt he was telling the truth. "Alright, what do you want me to do?"

"First, just let Suresh know she is here. Say nothing about me yet, as it may scare him. Ask him if he can get the things she needs and then come back and tell us what he says."

"Ok, I can do that," said Claudette. "And you will wait here?"

"Yes, if we can. Why are there so many guards at the hotel? What's going on?"

"Oh, nothing much, it's just Rahul Jayasuriya visiting. He shouldn't be there all night, but you never know. They're definitely in the party mood."

"I know Jayasuriya, he's a nobody," said the man.

"Well, I'd better get back," said Claudette, her eyes lingering on the man's face. Who was he? And how was he connected to the government?

"Thank you," said Leela.

"Thank me later," said Claudette.

The walk back along the beach to the hotel was hard. Claudette's legs were still not quite right, and she had the added pressure of soft sand sucking her feet down with every step. She was still in shock from her meeting with the two strangers, but on a positive side, it had taken her mind off more mundane matters, such as Jake. She wasn't sure why anyone would want to kill such a young girl though.

Claudette was nearing the hotel. She picked up her sarong from the sand and wrapped it around her waist. A soldier was standing at the entrance, staring at her bikini-clad breasts as she walked up, so she nudged him hard and squeezed past him through the gate. She saw Suresh carrying plates into the kitchen and followed him in.

"Suresh, I need to talk to you."

Suresh put the plates down on the counter and turned to face her. He didn't like Claudette, but she was a guest after all, and he was there to look after her.

"How can I help you?"

"It's your sister, she's here."

"What? Where is my sister?" he said looking around. "Is my mother here and my little brother?"

"No, she's on her own, 'Lila something' she said her name was."

"Leela! Is here? Where is she?"

"Calm down Suresh, she's hiding up the beach a little way. Now I don't know what's going on, but she said she's in some kind of trouble and she needs your help."

"Yes, I help her. I go now."

"I don't think that's a good idea just yet Suresh. There are guards everywhere and they won't bother about me, so much, coming and going. I can go back with a message from you. She said she needs money and ID."

"Money, yes, no ID. Waiting for that."

"She said she can't wait because there are men chasing her and they are not far behind."

"What's going on?" said Marni, coming into the kitchen.

"Leela here, on the beach. I need to help her."

"Ok, let's get her here. We can hide her somewhere. What about the beer cellar? The cement must be dry by now. There's not much air, but we can leave it open until she comes and then we can close it and put something on top."

"How we bring her? Too many guards?" said Suresh

"I don't know," said Marni. "It's going to be difficult."

"We just need to distract them for a few minutes. I think I can do that," said Claudette.

Marni looked at her. Claudette wasn't really a person she would normally rely on, but she seemed to be deeply involved, somehow.

"Ok," said Marni. "What's your plan?"

"I will go and get them, and bring them to just outside the gates, or as near as possible depending on where the guards are. Then I will leave them, enter the hotel and try and distract the guards. You must then slip out the gate Suresh and bring them to their hiding place. But you won't have much time."

"Why do you keep saying 'them'?" asked Marni.

Claudette paused momentarily, "Oh, that's another thing. There's a man with her."

"Who? What man?" cried Suresh.

"I don't know. She said he was her friend and that he was helping her."

"Well, I don't think we can hide him as well," said Marni. "It's too dangerous. We don't know who he is."

"Ok, I'll let them know and I'll just bring Leela to the gate. Wish me luck!"

Claudette flounced off as if she was off on a shopping spree, rather than the volatile situation she was getting herself into. She didn't really care. It was making life more interesting, the danger excited her.

She approached the gate that led out on to the beach. She couldn't see the guard and assumed that he had gone to patrol another area. She slipped through and hurried across the sand, to where the trees loomed large, casting shadows across the dunes.

She didn't see the guard relieving himself in the bushes, his gun resting against the fence. He watched her hurrying down the beach. A foreign woman in a bikini, heading to a remote area, this was too good an opportunity. He zipped up his trousers, slung his gun over his shoulder and followed.

Suresh was casing the restaurant, watching the gate, for the moment Claudette walked back in. He had told no one else about Leela. He thought it best if only he, Marni and Claudette knew, for now. More people may upset the plan. He had checked the cellar. He thought it would be safe for a short time, but it was dark, damp and uncomfortable.

He was glad the minister's people were so drunk. It would be easier to get Leela in unnoticed. He felt sick with nerves. He was so relieved she was alive, but a wrong move now would put them all in danger. Who was the man with her? This troubled him. Would he go and tell someone where she was? Maybe he meant well but if he was forced to tell? He tried to block out his fears. He needed to focus. Leela needed him to hold it together.

Claudette was nearing the point at which she had left the two huddled figures. She called out softly, "Are you there?"

"Shh," the man's voice answered her in a whisper. "Don't turn around, you are being followed."

Claudette winced at her stupidity. She hadn't thought to look behind her. She didn't think anyone had seen her leave. "Shit, I'm sorry."

"Quickly, tell us what Suresh said," came the man's voice again.

"He said he can get money quickly, but not an ID. This will take a few days. He said he can hide Leela in the hotel and to come now, but not you."

"Ok."

"No," hissed Leela's voice. "He come too. I no leaving. They kill him."

"That man is getting close. It's a soldier, I can see the rifle. We need to stop talking."

"Ok, I'm going back to the hotel now," said Claudette. "You both need to follow me when it's safe, and then wait as close as you can to the gate, until Suresh comes out to get you. Good luck."

Claudette turned around and walked towards the man with the gun.

"Hello Madam, where you going?" he said.

"Just out walking. Where are you going?"

"Checking your safety. Very dangerous on the beach, late at night, woman alone. There are very dangerous people."

"Yes, I know about dangerous people. Thank you for your concern. I'm going back to the hotel now."

She began purposefully striding towards the lights. The soldier grabbed her arm.

"Wait, what is your name?"

"Claudette," she said, continuing her pace, so the man had to walk beside her, still holding her arm.

"Wait, I want to talk to you. You are very pretty."

"Thank you."

"Wait, please." The soldier pulled her to a standstill. "Why you running? I like you."

Claudette's heart was quickening. She could see this wasn't going to be as easy as she thought. She forced a smile to appear on her face and said, "I like you too."

The soldier's hand left Claudette's arm and moved to her sarong. He pulled at it and it fell to her feet. He moved towards the elastic around her hips and she grabbed his hand.

"But your minister is waiting for me and I'm sure you don't want to disappoint him, do you? I don't think he will be very happy if we keep him waiting."

The soldier released his grasp. "The minister waiting for you?"

"Yes, I promised to dance with him. Come and watch me dance, and when I have finished with the minister, I will come and find you."

"Good, good, I waiting for you."

His face broke into a boyish grin and Claudette realised that this was not a monster, just a sexually repressed handsome young man, hoping for a good time. 'We are very similar,' she thought.

Claudette let out the breath she was holding and pulled her sarong back over her hips. She hoped that Leela and her friend had not witnessed the scene. She was not used to being at the mercy of a man and she certainly did not want anyone else to think she was.

15 A Ministerial Feast–Part 2

Leela and Vish hung back in the bushes. They were only a few metres from the foreign woman and the soldier, so they slowed down their breathing to not make a sound. They could see that he was being rough with her and Leela bit her lip to stop herself from screaming out at him. She felt awful that she was the cause of all this. Maybe it was time to give herself up.

The two figures moved on and Leela relaxed a little. The soldier seemed to have calmed down and they were picking up the pace back to the hotel. Vish and Leela crept through the undergrowth that lined the beach. They didn't dare stand up and be spotted. There were sticks and sharp edges of shells and broken glass, which the tide had brought in, and Leela felt her skin rip several times. Vish put his hand on her shoulder to make her stop. He motioned to follow his lead. When he signalled, they padded across the soft sand to the next clump of bushes and waited.

"We're making too much noise," he whispered to her. "Even over the sound of the waves, he might hear the rustling. It's safer if we run on the sand in short bursts and then hide."

They were much closer to the hotel now and could hear the music and drumming. Vish said a silent prayer for the noise which would help cover them.

They ran along the sand to the next hiding spot. "I think this is close enough," said Vish. "We can see anyone coming in or out."

They watched the man and the woman disappear through the gates and waited.

Suresh immediately saw Claudette's return. But why was there a soldier with her? She turned and smiled sweetly at him before walking up the steps to the restaurant. The soldier hung back under a palm tree and watched.

As she passed Suresh, she turned for a second, and he thought she mouthed the word 'Go'. She approached the minister's party and sat down on the table, stretching her long legs out and placing her feet on a chair. There was a pause in the drumming as the drunken men feasted their eyes on the smoothness of her limbs, all the way up to her bikini, where her sarong fell open across her hips.

"So, who has a cigarette for me?"

Packets of cigarettes were grabbed, and matches struck, as the men fell over themselves to deliver.

She took a cigarette, lighting it off one of the many flames waving in front of her. She inhaled deeply then swung herself around and jumped off the table.

"Marni, let's have some dancing music!" she called out.

Marni was watching the spectacle, open-mouthed, and took a moment to hear what she said. "Yes, yes, why not Claudette, dancing indeed!" She hit 'Play' on her computer and a Bollywood soundtrack blasted out from the tired speakers. Claudette pulled at the minister's arm, and, one by one she got the men to their feet, laughing and patting each other on the back. In the middle of them, she closed her eyes and danced. She gave herself up to them, lone prey separated from the herd, in a circle of hungry beasts.

Suresh watched the guards slowly moving out of the shadows towards the restaurant, to get closer to the spectacle.

I hope you know what you're doing Claudette, thought Suresh to himself, as he hurried down the steps and out through the gate, to the beach.

Leela's teeth were chattering as she crouched in the bushes waiting for Suresh. She couldn't believe she was about to see him. The minutes had turned into hours and the hours into days, since she had been snatched from her bed, and she had long ago abandoned hope that this day was ever going to come.

She closed her eyes, listening to the fusion of the waves and the thumping bass from the hotel. Maybe she would be able to relax soon, let down her guard, finally be out of danger. But in reality she knew that she was still far from knowing if she would live another tomorrow.

Vish grabbed her arm. "Is that Suresh?" he hissed in her ear.

She looked up and saw her dear brother sprinting down the beach. She made the sound of an owl and he turned and headed towards the bushes. Leela grabbed his hand and pulled him down undercover.

She sobbed and laughed as she clung to him.

"Oh Leela, it's really you," he cried, holding her face in his hands.

"Yes, Anna,[14] and this is my friend, Vish."

It was only then that Suresh noticed the stranger sitting silently nearby.

"Hello," he said, guardedly. "Sorry, only Leela can come with me. It's too dangerous for us. Miss Marni, the owner, has forbidden it."

"It's ok, I understand. I just wanted to get Leela to safety. She will need to leave here as soon as possible. Do you have somewhere she can go?"

"Yes, there is a boa…"

"I won't leave Vish here, Suresh!" Leela interrupted him. "I would be dead if he hadn't helped me, and he will be dead if we don't help him. It's been so horrible…" she started sobbing again.

"Hush Thangai,[15] you don't want anyone to hear us. We must get you to safety and then you can tell me everything that's happened. We will take Vish and try to explain it to Marni. Come on, we'd better go."

---

[14] Anna - older brother (Tamil)

[15] Thangai – younger sister (Tamil)

They followed Suresh through a hole in the fence, broken through by a stray dog. They hid behind the large neem tree that blocked visibility from the restaurant. Most of the guards were gathered to the right of the hotel, watching Claudette on the dance floor.

The three figures crept silently, around the restaurant, behind the toilet block, and through the vegetable patch, to the back of the kitchen.

Suresh pulled back a large wooden grate, exposing a deep hole, cemented on the sides and bottom.

"Climb in," said Suresh.

Vish and Leela obeyed immediately, jumping down into the damp cellar. It was two metres square, large enough for several people. Suresh pulled the grate back over them and covered it with a mat and some chairs.

"You should still be able to get some air through, but I'll come and check on you in about fifteen minutes."

"Ok," said Vish. "And, thank you."

Jake was lying in a hammock in the corner of the restaurant. He felt sick as he watched Claudette parading herself in front of the men. Was she crazy? Just because he had rejected her, she was now trying to make him jealous. She was a complete fool. These men weren't going to take being teased lightly. She was making it worse for Marni. There would definitely be trouble after this.

He reluctantly swung himself out of the hammock and approached the dance floor.

"Hey Claudette," he shouted to her. "Why don't you take a break, sit down for a while?" One of the men stood in front of him.

"She your wife?"

"Well no, but…"

"I don't think you should be telling her what to do then, do you?"

"Oh Jake, are you trying to be a father to me," Claudette called out, mocking him. "There's really no need. I'm a big girl now."

The men guffawed and closed ranks around her, leaving Jake angry, but anxious. He felt partly responsible that she was in this state, but he could see there was no way she was going to listen to his advice.

He joined Gaya, who was also looking on with horror.

"What is she doing?" he asked her.

"I don't know," said Gaya, "but I'm going to have to help her somehow. She won't get out of this easily."

"What are you going to do?" asked Jake.

"I'm not sure."

They looked on in silence for a while. They could see men's hands touching her, but she seemed not to notice. Her eyes were closed, and she was dancing as if in a trance.

"I can't stand it anymore," said Gaya.

She pushed her way into the throng and shook Claudette.

"Oh Gaya, darling, have you come to dance with me?"

"Are you crazy Claudette?" Gaya whispered in her ear. "These men are not going to let you go. What are you doing?"

"Listen to me, Gaya," Claudette whispered back, slowly and clearly. "I know what I'm doing, I'm not drunk, I just needed to create a diversion."

"What, why…?" whispered back Gaya.

"I'll explain in… ah."

Claudette's breath caught in mid-sentence as someone hoisted her up onto their shoulder.

"No, stop!" shouted Gaya. She tried to hold on to Claudette's hand, just as her own legs were grabbed from under her and she fell back into another man standing behind her. This one took hold of her arms and together the two men lifted her up to the sky. She could hear cheering from the watching soldiers, as
Claudette and herself were carried to the beach, like sacrificial lambs.

Marni was in the kitchen with Rushani. She had updated Rushani on the events of the last hour and they were waiting for Suresh to get back safely from the beach with Leela. They heard yelling and rushed out to see what was happening.

They saw the crowd of men leaving the restaurant. Jake was standing alone, looking on in horror.

"They've got Claudette and Gaya!"

"What do you mean they've got them?" Marni's heart was beating at twice the pace.

"They just picked them up and carried them off."

"Shit! Where's Chris?"

"I think he went after them. He was here a minute ago."

"Ok, I'm going to call the OIC,[16] you go after them."

Marni grabbed her mobile and called his direct number, which he had given to her several years ago, when there was a problem with a prowler.

"Yes, Miss Marni, how can I help you?"

"It's... I'm not sure... we have a big problem." Her voice was trembling. "The minister, Mr Jayasuriya is here, with his men. They are very drunk, and, captured two of our female guests and took them to the beach."

"Captured?"

"Yes, captured."

"I will be there with some men in five minutes."

"Ok, thank you."

Marni hung up and rushed out to the beach. The women were being passed around the group, like pass the parcel. Chris was trying to reason with them, but his voice was getting lost in the wind and the waves. All the soldiers were on the beach now, making up a group of about twenty-five hostile men, half of them with guns. They were still laughing and joking, but the sound was sinister, taunting. Claudette and Gaya were shouting, and trying to free themselves, but they were surrounded. Jake and Rushani were on the outside of the fray. Marni went to join them.

---

[16] OIC – Officer In Charge (Police)

"The local police are on their way. They said five minutes, but who knows. I don't think there is anything we can do. This is all my fault."

Jake looked hard at Marni but there was no time to ask her what she meant. A shot went off, and the noise from the men subsided as everyone turned around. The Army Commander was striding towards them, rifle pointed to the sky.

"Release those women!" he ordered in Sinhala.

The group of men parted, and Gaya and Claudette stumbled forward, spat out from the pack. He turned and addressed Marni, Jake, Chris and Rushani. "Take these women back to the hotel."

They put their arms around Claudette and Gaya and hurried back up the beach to the lights of the hotel. They weren't going to argue with this clearly highly effective man.

Eva and Jo were standing at the gate. They had woken when the shot was fired. "What the hell is going on?" asked Eva.

"Come into the restaurant and we'll tell you the whole story," said Marni. She could feel Gaya shaking through her wet clothes. At some point, they had pushed her into the sea.

"Do you know who that man is?" Gaya asked Rushani.

"Yes, it is the Commander of the Special Forces Unit for the East. It is very lucky for us that he arrived when he did."

"Yes, very lucky," murmured Claudette.

"Rushani, please go to the kitchen and get brandy for Gaya and Claudette."

Suresh was waiting for them in the restaurant. "What is happening?" he cried.

"It's a long story," said Marni, "which I'll tell you about in a minute," more quietly she continued, "but what about your sister? Is she safe?"

"Yes, she's safe, she's down in the cellar but..."

"Ok, good. I must take these women to their rooms and make sure they're ok. I will talk with you later."

"Ok Miss Marni." Suresh felt anxious. He liked Marni a lot and felt terrible that he had defied her. She was right. They didn't know who Vish was, except that most likely he was a terrorist on the run, which was about the worst thing he could be, putting them all in immediate danger.

Marni walked Gaya and Claudette to their rooms.

"I think you need to tell me what's going on," said Gaya, facing the two women. "Claudette, what did you mean you were creating a distraction."

"I'm so sorry," said Marni. "This is my fault, and I'm so sorry I put you both at such personal risk."

"It's ok Marni, I made the decision to do this. Unfortunately, Gaya got dragged in as well."

"Will you please tell me what's going on," begged Gaya again.

"Leela is here," said Marni.

"What! Where is she?"

"She's safe, we've hidden her in the cellar. But we had to get the guards away from the beach, to get her in without being seen. That was why Claudette put on her heart-stopping performance in the restaurant."

"Oh my god, that is priceless," Gaya began to laugh, and then to cry, and then to laugh again. "There is never a dull moment around here!"

The three women hugged, letting the adrenalin and emotion run out of their bodies and into the sand.

"Okay, go and get showered, and I'll meet you in the restaurant for a very large brandy."

Marni wandered close to the fence. She could see that the OIC and the local police force had joined the group. A lot of discussion was going on between the men. She could hear some raised voices but couldn't make out what they were saying.

Jake walked up behind her. "How are Gaya and Claudette?" he asked.

"They'll be ok, they're both pretty tough."

"I think that this is all my fault," admitted Jake.

"What do you mean?" asked Marni. "How can it be your fault?"

"Claudette was angry with me."

"Why?"

"Because she tried it on with me tonight and I said no."

"What!"

"I think she must have got really drunk after that and then danced with those men to try to make me jealous."

Marni started laughing.

"Why is that funny?"

"Because it's nothing to do with you. Suresh's sister turned up and we needed a distraction, to get the guards away from their lookout posts, so we could get her into the hotel without being seen."

Jake felt stung. "Why wouldn't you tell me something like that? Something that important which could endanger our daughter is going on, and you don't think I'm important enough to tell?"

"It's not like that Jake. There wasn't enough time. I would have told you if there was time, and if you had been here."

They looked into each other's faces in the moonlight, each with their own self-preserving train of thought. Marni wanted Jake to understand and not to make a big deal of this. She had so much on her plate right now she just needed his support and help. Jake felt embarrassed. He was upset that Marni didn't seem to care that Claudette had made a pass at him and he felt silly that he'd thought this whole commotion could be about him. He was ashamed knowing that he hadn't stopped immediately, and that guilt was at his door, but for now, he was going to keep that buried. He also knew that he didn't have the energy left to carry on the way they were going.

"I will be away for a few days, maybe longer. I need some time to think and work things out. I'm not happy and I need to decide what I'm going to do. I'm going to take Zoe with me because I don't think it's safe for her here at the moment."

Marni breathed deeply before replying. "Well, I could really do with your support around here and I don't really like the idea of you taking Zoe, but if that's what you need to do..."

"Yeah, that's what I need to do," he replied abruptly. "I'm going to check on Zoe."

Marni watched him go. Her heart ached so much that she couldn't reach out to him, but at the moment she was just unable to. She had to keep strong, keep herself walled-up, so she didn't spill out the sides. She just needed to get through the next few days. There were so many people depending on her.

"Miss Marni!" A voice cut through her thoughts. She turned around and saw the OIC, Mr

Fernando, walking towards her. She glanced behind him down the beach and saw the group had dispersed.

"It's all ok now, everything is resolved." He was waving his hands in the air and puffing slightly at having to climb the dune in his heavy boots and full uniform. He was a jolly man with a smiling face and sparkling eyes.

"What happened?" asked Marni.

"Well, the Commander of the Special Forces has ordered all his men back to the base and strongly advised the minister's entourage to go back to their hotel, with the persuasion of an army escort. He has re-arranged their return helicopters to pick them up first-thing tomorrow morning rather than in the afternoon. He is not at all pleased. I think the soldiers who joined in will be severely punished, and he said that he will put in a complaint to the president himself, but I think it highly unlikely to be pursued. Anyhow, we've got them off our doorstep, so that's something to celebrate, don't you think?"

He looked expectantly at Marni and then towards the restaurant.

"Oh, yes, right, um, would you like to join us for a brandy?"

"Oh yes, that's very kind of you, what a good idea," he said, grinning from ear to ear.

"Wonderful," said Marni. Her thoughts returned to Leela, stuck in the deep dark cellar. How long was she going to be down there? Ok, one drink with the OIC, and then she'd send him on his way.

16 Medicinal Brandy

There was a crowd of them in the restaurant now. Eva and Jo huddled together, listening intently to Chris who was bringing them up to speed with the eventful night. Claudette and Gaya were chain-smoking and drowning in neat brandy. Marni was making polite conversation with the OIC, while Rushani cleared away the huge buffet of uneaten food. Suresh caught Marni's eye and signalled that he was going to check on Leela. Marni nodded, her eyes scouring the property, wondering what the hell was going to happen next. Jake was nowhere to be seen.

The OIC was explaining to Marni how tourist crime was on the increase. Guests claimed they had been robbed, to get a police report, so they could get money back on their insurance. This was causing a backlash on hotel owners as they were often accused of theft, with staff being interrogated and sometimes even arrested.

"… so, you see, they think they are not harming anybody except their insurance companies, but in fact, they are causing ripples throughout our community."

Marni tuned back in as the OIC was finishing up his rant.

"Well, thank you, Mr Fernando, that was very enlightening and thank you very much for your help this evening," she said standing up and walking him out. "I must see that all my guests get to bed safely and I myself am exhausted."

"Ah yes, Miss Marni, and please don't hesitate to call me for anything, day or night."

"I won't, thank you, and good night."

The OIC swung his leg over his push-bike and cycled down the path to the road, wobbling as he went.

"Phew!" Marni let out a long sigh.

She looked over at the restaurant and couldn't see Suresh. He must still be with Leela. She was intrigued to meet her, her mind filled with so much worry about her in the last week. She grabbed a torch and headed out the back door of the kitchen. The wooden grate was over the cellar, so she thought maybe Suresh had climbed down with her to keep her company.

She pulled it back and shone her torch down onto the two expectant faces below.

"Suresh, the… huh," she gasped as she saw that it wasn't Suresh.

"Miss Marni!" Suresh came running through the back door at that moment. "There's somebody there, I'm sorry. It's Leela's friend. She not want to leave him. His name is Vish."

Marni stared down at Vish's face without blinking. He stared back at her, waiting for her to shout or order him out. The white light from the torch was blinding him, so he eventually dropped his gaze. He slid his feet into his boots and pulled the laces tight.

"You can come out now. Everybody has gone." Marni felt nervous about this stranger. A young girl was one thing, but allowing a strange man into the hotel was putting everyone's lives at risk.

The man climbed out, turning back to pull Leela up. She ran to Suresh and he cradled her, stroking her hair.

"You can't stay here," said Marni to the man.

"Don't worry, I'm going, but you need to understand that Leela also has to leave. She's in danger, which means you are to."

The man turned towards her and the light from the kitchen lit up his face. Marni twitched, she felt strange like she was getting a fever. Her hands and feet were tingling, and she touched her forehead with the palm of her hand.

"We have a plan for you, Leela," said Suresh.

Marni's legs were trembling and her chest felt constricted. She had to get to her room. "I'm sorry I don't feel well. Suresh please take them to the kitchen and get them some food."

Her eyes had not left the face of the man and he shifted under her stare.

"I don't need food, thank you. I know Leela is safe now. I will leave."

"No!" Marni's voice was louder than she expected. "You will eat something."

She turned towards her room, stumbling in her haste.

In her room she flicked the light on and padded across to her bed, trying not to wake Zoe. She knelt on the floor and pulled out a suitcase. Inside was a wooden box and inside that was a photo. She took the photo out, her hand trembling.

"Fuck!", she whispered to herself.

She took a file out of the suitcase and clutching the photo switched off the light and closed the door quietly behind her. She didn't trust her legs as she made her way to the kitchen and stopped a couple of times to lean against a tree.

Inside the kitchen, Leela and the man sat on stools while Suresh prepared their plates of food. They looked up as Marni walked in.

"I know you." Her words caught, as a sound, somewhere between an animal's cry and a sob, escaped her. "Tell me your name."

The back of Vish's throat was dry. He tried to swallow but ended up coughing. What had he done to this young woman or her family? He couldn't bear to know.

"Tell me," she said again.

"My name is Pravish Thilip."

The sound came again. A guttural cry.

"What's your name? How do you know me?"

"My name is Marnie Clark. I'm the daughter of Lara Clark… and you."

Everyone's eyes were on Vish. He was paralysed, searching her face for comprehension.

Suddenly great gulps and sobbing erupted from Marni and she collapsed to her knees, the papers scattering on the floor.

Vish jumped off the stool and knelt beside her.

"Are you sure?" He asked gently.

She nodded, pointing to the photo. He picked it up and saw an image of himself. Younger and more idealistic, but definitely him. The next piece of paper he picked up was a school report with his name on, the next a list of names from his class at University

"I think we have a lot to talk about Marni, this is all a shock to me. Is there somewhere private we can go?"

"Yes, we can go to my office."

Vish gathered up all the papers and helped Marni off the floor. Together they staggered through to the office.

Suresh and Leela watched them go. "What just happened?" Leela asked.

"A miracle," replied Suresh.

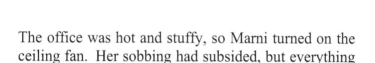

The office was hot and stuffy, so Marni turned on the ceiling fan. Her sobbing had subsided, but everything looked different as if she were a character on a movie set.

"Please, sit down," she said, clearing some toys off a chair.

"Thank you," Vish said. "You have children?"

"Yes, one, a daughter." Marni resisted the urge to say, 'your granddaughter.' It was probably a bit too much for now.

"Marni, I have to tell you, I do know Lara Clark, but this is the first time I know anything about you."

"She wrote to you and told you. When she heard nothing back from you, she presumed that you didn't want to be a part of our lives, so she stopped writing."

"I never got those letters."

They sat in silence, both of them not quite understanding, or believing, what they were seeing before them. Marni had wanted this moment all her life. Her mother had told her about her father, for as long as she could remember. She dreamed of him, holding her in his arms, stroking her hair, rocking her to sleep. And now here he was, flesh and blood, in front of her very eyes.

Vish studied Marni's face. He could see his own mother in her, but maybe he was just imagining it. Wouldn't he have known he had a child? Wouldn't he have felt it in his heart and soul? How could a daughter appear before him, after twenty-seven years, with no warning?

He was confused, but at the same time, he didn't doubt what she was saying. The timing all made sense. She knew all about him. He thought of Lara, as he had done over the years, in the minutes just before he fell asleep, and just before he woke up, that divine moment where everything exists. He had fallen deeply in love with her and he still missed her smile and gentleness. But he had followed his head and thrown himself into his work. He had joined the Tamil Freedom Fighters and worked tirelessly, lobbying the government, trying to pass a Bill of Rights and increase public support for a separate Tamil state. In the end, they had felt there was no alternative but to fight fire with fire.

It was then that Vish had left mainstream society. He no longer had friends or lovers. His whole life had become 'the cause' and that's what he believed he would follow till the day he died.

"How did you recognize me?" Vish asked.

"I saw your scar first. I know every detail of that scar. I know its length, the way it starts just below your cheekbone and bends down towards your ear. My mother gave me this photo of you when I was seven."

It was a Polaroid that Lara had taken of Vish on Galle Face Green. He was wearing a white shirt and looking directly at the camera. The wind had blown the hair over his eyes, but he looked straight into the lens from under it. The scar was very visible.

"I've looked at this photo every day of my life."

Vish let out the breath that he had been holding. He could remember that day. It was the final day they had together. Lara was flying out that evening and they were drawing out every last minute.

He also had a photo from that day of Lara. The wind was whipping her long, sandy-coloured hair around her face, and she was laughing. He had kept that photo in his breast pocket every day until an urgent camp move saw it lost to the jungle. He had mourned for that photo, but the memory was still very much alive.

He came back to the present and looked at the beautiful young woman sitting in front of him. This was his daughter, his own flesh and blood. He knelt in front of her, laid his head in her lap, and cried. She placed her hand on his head and stroked his hair. He cried for the children who had died for his bloody war; he cried for the mothers and fathers left alone, and he cried for himself. For his life robbed of love, family and living, instead, filled with death, fear and battle wounds.

The door flew open and Jake stood there, jaw agape.

"Jake, this is my father Pravish. Pravish, this is Jake, my husband."

Vish wiped the tears from his face with his sleeve and stood up. The two men formally shook each other's hands. There was an awkward silence as they all tried to come to terms with the enormity of the situation.

Finally, Jake spoke. "Suresh just told me that you helped Leela escape. Does that mean you were in the camp yourself? Are you a member of the Tamil Freedom Fighters?"

"I am. I mean I was... I don't know. I just knew I had to help Leela get to safety. She didn't deserve to be there against her will. None of them deserved it. But they'll be looking for me. Which is why I can't stay long."

Marni lurched towards the door of the office and made it outside just in time to be violently sick in the sand. Jake rushed to hold her.

"Take your hands off me! You can't say you're leaving one minute and then try to comfort me the next." Jake backed away, holding his hands up.

Marni wiped the spittle from her mouth and turned to Vish. "You're a fucking terrorist!" She flew at him, pummelling him with clenched fists. Jake grabbed her from behind and wrestled her backwards.

"Marni, stop it. What the hell are you doing?"

Vish stood up, knocking over the chair. "I'm sorry, I shouldn't have come here. They will follow us and then you will all be in danger. I am going. You need to get Leela away from here tonight."

Marni grabbed his arm in reflex. "No, you can't go!" she started crying again. "Please stay."

"It will be too dangerous for you if I stay here. They will know we are here after they have searched Leela's home. I must leave, and Leela also for her own safety, and yours."

"Gaya and Niraj have organised a boat for Leela, but I don't know when it's leaving," stammered Marni.

"Well, if it's not leaving tomorrow, she will have to hide out somewhere until it does. She can't stay here. We just came to get some food, money and ID. My men are too close behind us."

"Your men?" asked Jake.

"My position, that I left, was Commander of the East".

Vish turned to Marni who was shaking her head in disbelief.

"You have to understand, this has been my life for many years. A few months after your mother left Sri Lanka, there was a political rally at the university. The army arrived and disbanded the meeting, arresting several students. I was told to make my way to an address in Colombo that evening, for an emergency action meeting. There, I saw a man, delivering a speech. He was urging us to come to the North to have the time and space to plan our next manoeuvre. He talked of uniting Tamils from all over the country. He said we would not be allowed to form our own Tamil political party in Colombo. He said the army would always disband these meetings to prevent any political strength arising from the Tamil community. I could see it made sense. I strongly believed that we Tamils should have a separate state, but it was becoming impossible to believe in Sri

Lanka's political process. Any opposition would be stamped out. The man who made the speech was Adhikara, now the leader of the Tamil Freedom Fighters. I moved the next day and never looked back."

"That's why my mother's letters never found you," said Marni quietly.

Vish continued, "I'm not proud of many things I have done in my life. There has been too much bloodshed, but I thought that there were no other options."

"What are you going to do now?" Jake asked.

"I don't know. At the moment I can't see past tomorrow. Leela is still very much in danger. After she is safely on the boat, I will look at my options. If it is safe, I will try to return here, but only if I am not going to put you in danger."

Marni held her gaze on him. She was slowly understanding the reality of the situation. Her father was a terrorist. Not someone who had been forced into it but who had chosen it with his own free will. How could she process that information? This was not the story she had made up for him over the years. Half her DNA was from him. There was a big part of her that wanted him to leave so she could pretend to herself that she had never found him. She never thought that she would wish this. That an imaginary father was better than having the real one standing right in front of her. However, the thought that this could be her only chance to spend time with her father, that he might never return to her, was forcing its way through the pain in her head.

"I will make a bed for you in here," she said. "You can leave in the morning."

Suresh came in at that moment, with a plate piled high of left-over buffet. The smell made Vish's stomach grumble loudly.

"Eat and sleep," Marni snapped as she pulled Jake out and shut the door.

When they were outside, Jake pulled Marni in close and wrapped his arms tightly around her. "Are you ok?" he asked.

"I have no idea," she replied pulling out of his embrace. "I can't really comprehend anything that's happened this evening. Are you still leaving in the morning?"

Jake took her hand. "No Marni, I'm not leaving. I love you and want to be here for you. You just have to let me."

Marni made a noise that sounded like a snort. "Can you sort out Pravish's bed? I need to be alone."

———————⬤— ⬤ ⬤————————

A knock at Gaya's door awoke her from her nightmares. "Who is it?" she whispered in the darkness.

"It's me, quick, let me in."

"Oh shit," said Gaya, under her breath. She scrambled out of bed quickly and unlocked the door. She pulled Rakesh in by the arm and shut the door quietly.

"This is not a good ti…" warm, soft lips silenced her anxieties. He slid his hands under her T-shirt and up the smooth skin of her back, then down again, resting on the curve at the base of her spine.

"If you're going to tell me this is not a good time, you're telling me! Unless you are about to inform me you have another man in your bed, then I already know the full story."

"How do you know?"

"I saw it all."

"What! You've been here the whole time?"

"Yup."

"Even the bit on the beach?"

"Yes. Don't worry, I would have rescued you if it had come to that, but lucky for me, it didn't, as I would have had to kiss my freedom goodbye. Anyway, it looked like you weren't doing too badly!"

She thumped him hard, "God, how were you not seen?"

"I'm very discreet!"

Gaya giggled as she moved her hands up his chest to unbutton his shirt. The brandy she had knocked back earlier was still running through her veins and she felt light-headed from lack of sleep.

She pulled the shirt off his body. The moonlight cast rays through the slats of wood on the cabana wall. She ran her fingers over his back, tracing the scars that littered his skin. She kissed his chest, following the line of hair down to his belly button until she was on her knees in front of him. She undid the button on his shorts and slid down the zipper. She eased them down his legs to the floor. Standing up, she pushed him back onto the bed, his body quivering for what was to come. Climbing on top of him, she pulled off her T-shirt and lowered herself down gently. He slid in easily and they made love as if this moment was everything.

When it was over, Gaya lay next to him. She wiped away the sweat from his face. Her feelings for him were overwhelming and she knew he must feel it too.

"Rakesh, when thi…"

"Shh, I can hear something." Rakesh mouthed silently, putting his fingers to her lips and holding her hand tightly.

From behind their hut, they heard footsteps, then whispering, then silence.

17 Pumpkin Soup

Marni watched her father as he slept. The thought that this may be all the time she had with him had kept her from throwing him out, but she wasn't sure she could handle finding out any more about his life. She could still keep some of her imaginary father by her side. The hero, the protector, kept from her by events out of his control. Jake had gone to sleep hours ago, and Suresh had made up a bed for Leela in the kitchen. She could hear a dog barking in the distance, then more. They always did this. One would start barking, then another, then another, until the whole beach of stray dogs had joined in.

It was the light that caught her attention. She thought she saw a match struck, and the red glow of a cigarette. She was sitting in the dark but had the shutters wide open. The window glass of the office was tinted, so you could not see in unless the light was on. Maybe it's Claudette, she thought. Perhaps she couldn't sleep. She left the office to go and see if she could get her anything.

As she approached the lighted cigarette, she called out softly, "Claudette is that you?"

From behind, a hand slammed against her mouth, and another around her body, holding her arms down at her side. She tried to release herself, but the arm around her tightened.

A voice spoke in her ear in Tamil. She could only understand some of the words and she asked him to say it again. "Where are they? Where is the girl, Leela, and the man with her? We know they are here. We don't want to harm you or anyone else. We just want them."

"They aren't here," she said.

A knife glistened in front of her in the moonlight and she felt it against her throat. "I don't have time for this," the voice said. "I will slit your throat first and then find them."

"No, wait, Kumar, I'm here!" They swung around to see Vish standing there. "Don't harm her, I will come with you."

"Where is the girl?"

"You don't need the girl, you only need me."

Kumar released his grip on Marni, and she dropped to the ground. He walked towards Vish, his face twisted in an ugly snarl.

"What do you think you're doing? Are you deserting us? You know what happens to our enemies, especially traitors." Kumar spat on the ground near Vish's bare feet.

"Kumar, I don't care what you think you must do with me. I cannot fight for something that I no longer believe in. This battle will have to go on without me. Our people aren't our ammunition. They deserve better. I don't want to be a part of it anymore."

"You are crazy. You can't see what you are walking away from. You know you can't just leave. Tie him up!" Kumar turned to his men. "And then we will look for the girl."

"No!" Vish shouted again. He started backing away from the two men walking towards him. He turned and sprinted out the gate towards the dunes, all three men tight on his heels.

Marni got to her feet to run after the men, but someone pulled her back.

"Stop Marni." It was Claudette with a firm grip on Marni's arm.

"You don't understand Claudette, that's my father!"

"I know, Suresh told me, but he's got this far without your help, and what exactly are you planning on doing? Are you planning to stand in front of a bullet? Don't be ridiculous."

Marni knew Claudette was right. The men had disappeared into the dunes and any sound was lost in the wind and the waves. She would just have to wait.

Gaya's door opened and she came out with Rakesh.

"Rakesh, what are you doing here?" gasped Marni.

"I'm here to get Leela, it seems. Where is she? I think we need to leave now."

Marni ran to wake Suresh and Leela.

"Wake up," she cried, banging on the kitchen door. The door opened, and a scared face looked out.

"Leela, the men are here. Vish has led them into the dunes, but they are here for you. You have to leave now."

"Oh Miss Marni, I am so sorry for all this trouble." Leela began to cry.

Marni took her by the arms.

"Listen to me Thangai, this is not your fault, none of this. And, if it hadn't happened, I would still not know who my father is. So, don't worry, just go. Please. There is a man called Rakesh here. He will take you into hiding."

Leela put on her sandals, hugged her brother tightly, for the second time that evening, and ran off into the night, again pinning her hopes of survival on a man she didn't know.

Gaya watched Rakesh go. Would she ever see him again? This is exactly what she thought last time she said goodbye to him. It was complete stupidity to get mixed up with a man who could never give you more than a few hours of his time and when he wasn't with you, it was impossible to know if he was alive or dead. Stupid, but it was the reality. She was most definitely in love with this crazy, reckless man. And to top it all off, he was fleeing the country on a boat, that he had already admitted would probably be a death trap.

Gaya's attention returned to Marni. "Come on Marni, let's wake the rest of the guests up and hide in the kitchen. It's secure there and we can bolt all the windows."

"Yes, Gaya, you're right." Marni went to her cabana first. "Jake, wake up." He stirred slightly and then sat up suddenly. "What is it, where's Zoe?"

"It's ok, Zoe's safe, but we need to go to the kitchen and hide. The men from the TFF camp are here. Leela has escaped with Rakesh, but Vish has led the men out onto the dunes, and I don't know what's happened to him."

Jake squeezed Marni's hand tightly, then leapt out of bed to get Zoe. "I'll go and find Aruna," said Marni. "I think he's still asleep under the Palu tree."

Finally, they were all assembled in the kitchen. Aruna was there, groggy but sober, Eva, Jo, Claudette, Chris, Rushani, Suresh, Gaya, Marni, Jake and Zoe.

They looked around at each other in the dark. "What should we do now?" Eva asked.

"Just wait," Chris said. "It's all we can do."

Vish raced up the dunes and headed for the cover of the forest. He was relieved all three men were following him.

"Stop Vish!" Kumar called. "I don't want to shoot you, but I will if you force me too."

'You'll have to find me first,' thought Vish.

He weaved his way deeper into the jungle and headed for a tree to climb. It looked easy enough and was covered in thick foliage, which would hide him well. He grabbed some large rocks from the base of the tree and stuffed them into his pockets. He scampered up the trunk as quick and lithe as a chameleon.

He could see there was a clearing just the other side of him and could make out what looked like huge round boulders at first, but then realised, was a herd of elephants. Some looked like they were sleeping, but others stood around the group as if on guard duty. There were also some young ones amongst the herd. The men were almost below him now. They were whispering to each other. He slowed down his breathing so as not to make a sound. They thought he was in front of them and they were planning on an ambush. They could see the clearing through the trees, bathed in moonlight, and they were hoping to flush him out and then shoot him down, while they had a clear shot.

They moved forward. Vish took a rock from his pocket. He aimed and then chucked it as hard as he could. It skimmed through the leaves of the trees, narrowly missing branches, and landed with a thud, more than thirty metres in front of them.

"Fire!" called Kumar. The men ran forward, firing and shouting. They were already out in the clearing and it was too late before they realised what they'd done.

One elephant had been hit with a bullet and was emitting a screech of indescribable pitch. The other elephants were on their feet now, trunks raised and pacing frantically. The men turned to run, but the elephants were too quick. They stampeded towards the men, trunks high in the air. The two men were caught in the trunks of the two largest and fastest of the herd. One man was flung into the air, falling to the ground like a rag doll. The elephant then reared up on her two hind legs and brought her front feet down on the man, crushing him in a single blow.

The other man was thrashed repeatedly against a tree. His limp body hung from the elephant's trunk, evidently dead well before the rampage stopped.

Vish screwed up his face in horror. He knew these men. He had trained them. It was all so senseless. They had died trying to kill him because he had changed his views. This was not freedom they were fighting for.

Vish scanned through the trees for signs of Kumar. He must have seen the herd before the men and got to safety. He stayed in the tree for a while and watched the elephants. They circled the injured animal. The noise getting fainter. The bullet must have hit an artery or maybe its heart. The animal was dying.

The sound from the elephant ceased and Vish listened to the silence. There was no cracking of sticks underfoot or rustling of leaves, Kumar must be out of earshot, he thought.

He swung out of the tree and lowered himself to the ground. He padded through the forest quietly, listening carefully. The sound of the waves got louder as he neared the dunes.

Then he saw him. Kumar was hiding behind a tree, looking deep into the forest, rifle raised.

Vish circled around him, the noise from the ocean masking his feet as he shuffled through the sand. He closed in, until he was only half a metre behind Kumar and then grabbed him around the throat, his other hand snatching the rifle from Kumar's hands.

Kumar choked, then laughed. "You're an idiot Vish. You've just caused the death of two of your own men and now you're attempting to murder a third. What kind of moral war are you fighting? We'll see how these deaths play on your mind!"

Vish winced. Kumar was right. He didn't want any more deaths, but his actions had resulted in them anyway.

"I don't want to kill you Kumar, and I won't if you return to the camp and stop looking for the girl."

"Why are you so interested in this girl? She's been doing you favours has she?" Kumar started choking again as Vish's grip around his throat grew tighter.

"She doesn't deserve to die."

"Nor did your men. They have families too. You didn't think about that, did you? When you watched them being snapped in two."

"I didn't want that to happen."

"You didn't want it, but it happened anyway. Just like this war. There will be a lot more bloodshed whether or not you like it. But now you're going to die as a traitor and a coward. You've let your people down."

Vish felt the shooting pain as the shiny, sharp tip of Kumar's knife slid into Vish's abdomen, and deep into his stomach. On reflex, Vish's hands choked Kumar's throat tighter and, with one forceful crack, he broke Kumar's neck.

Both men dropped to the ground. Vish removed his shirt and wrapped it tightly around his waist, squeezing the wound shut as best he could. He half-stumbled and half-fell down the sand dunes to the beach. His only thoughts now were of Marni.

He ran along the sand through the water. He was conscious of the trail of blood he was leaving behind him and hoped the tide would wash it away. He didn't want to lead anyone else to the hotel.

He got through the gates and looked around him. The place was deserted. Even the dogs had vanished. Vish called out, repeating his words over and over. "Marni, where are you, it's me, Vish."

He was on his knees now, in the sand. He looked up at the black sky and the silhouette of the leaves against it. They began to swirl around him. He closed his eyes and called out her name one last time, "Marni!"

———————————●◗◖●———————————

The group was silent, except for the gentle purring of Zoe's snores. They weren't sure how long they had been sitting there. Time seemed to move very slowly.

"Oh god, what's happening," Marni whispered under her breath. Jake had Zoe asleep in his lap, with one arm around Marni. She sunk deeper into him.

"What's that?" she said, sitting up. She had heard something but wasn't sure if it was an animal. "There it is again. Can you hear it?"

The others strained to hear above the crashing of the waves. "Oh yes," said Jo, "I can hear it now. Someone's calling."

"Don't go out there," said Eva. "It might be those men coming back."

They listened again. The shouts were getting nearer. "It's Pravish!" cried Marni, leaping up.

"Wait, be careful," Jake tried to grab onto her clothes, to stop her, but she was already half-way out the door.

She saw him then. He was on his knees, face lifted to the sky. He called out her name again. She reached him, just in time to catch him, as he collapsed.

"Quick, help me, someone, he's hurt." The rest of the group came running out of the kitchen. They carried him back in and bolted the door again.

"Let's have a look," said Eva. She had trained as a nurse and had worked for the ambulance service for many years. She looked at the wound. "It's deep," she said. "And it looks like he's lost a lot of blood."

Marni fetched the medical kit. It was huge, from the many donations after the tsunami. Eva cleaned out the wound first. "It's a blessing he's unconscious," she said. "The pain would be unbearable."

She found a needle and thread and stitched him up.

"This is only temporary," she said. He needs to get to a hospital. I don't know what damage there is internally."

She finished stitching and covered the wound with padding and a large waterproof plaster.

Vish began to stir. He opened his eyes and looked at the row of expectant faces. Marni's face was closest. She leant down to hear what he was saying.

"It's ok, you're safe, the men are gone."

"But they might come back?"

"No, they're dead."

The words hung in the air.

Marni felt, at the same time, relieved, and horrified. If they were dead, then Vish must have killed them. She didn't want to think of how many people he had killed throughout his life. It was unbearable. It made her sick to the stomach.

"We need to take you to hospital," she said.

"No, I can't go to hospital. I would be arrested immediately. They will kill me anyway."

"But you might die if you do nothing."

"I would rather die here than in a cell, alone. It is the best thing I could have hoped for, and probably a lot more than I deserve."

Father and daughter held each other's gaze, their faces lit by the candle flame that flickered beside them. The years passed between them; the pain of the past hung in the air, but the bond was undeniable.

"Come, let's find you somewhere more comfortable to rest." They lifted him and carried him to the bed in the office. Marni brought cushions to make him more comfortable.

Vish survived for one more day. Marni didn't leave his side. Jake brought Zoe in to meet her grandfather, and Marni took photos of the two of them together, and then Jake took more of all three of them.

Marni fed her father pumpkin soup and read him excerpts from her mother's letters and emails. They even called Lara, and, for the first time in twenty-seven years, Lara and Vish heard each other's voice, albeit briefly, before he became too tired and his voice too weak. Lara cried, for her long, lost, lover whom she had missed so much over the years, and for Marni, who had only just found her father and would now lose him so quickly.

Marni tried to ask him about his life, but he had not wanted to tell her.

"I'm not proud of the things I've done, and I don't want you to remember me for those things. These few days since I met you are all that are important, nothing else matters now."

He died the next night. He became feverish, as an infection spread through his blood, and in his last hours, he gave instructions that his body must be taken back to the forest, and left close to the others, where they would all be found together so there would be no repercussions for Marni and the others.

They did as he asked. They carried him between them, on a stretcher, made by Suresh and Aruna. The funeral procession weaved up through the dunes as Vish had described, scaring away a pack of wild dogs feeding off one body. Marni had wanted to go, even though Jake had tried to make her stay with him and Zoe. She retched now, at the sight of the body, and turned away.

They laid him on the sand, and she bent to kiss him. "Good-bye," she whispered.

Gaya helped her up as the sobs took a hold of her, and slowly the procession returned to the hotel. Early the next morning she went to the beach and threw frangipani flowers into the water, praying for her father's soul and that he be found before scavengers tore apart his body.

They found him later that day. Soldiers had gone to search the area after seeing buzzards circling overhead. They questioned Marni, as their hotel was the closest to the crime scene. Marni said that they had heard what they thought were bangers going off, which the farmers often let off to scare away the elephants from their paddy fields.

The police investigation was wrapped up quickly and put down to in-house fighting amongst the terrorist party, for leadership. They congratulated each other for the slaying of four terrorist operatives with no one having to leave the barracks. There was some surprise, however, when it was discovered that the wound which had killed one of the men, had been sutured, but further investigation was dismissed on account of more pressing matters.

The camp was quickly moved when news of the deaths filtered back. They assumed that Leela never made it home alive.

18 Vegetable Patties

Leela was sitting on the floor in a cramped kitchen. A toothless old woman was grinning at her and offering her a vegetable patty. She took it gratefully and ate quickly. It tasted stale, but the spices helped with the rancid after-taste.

They had walked along the beach for what seemed like hours, climbing over rocks that jutted out into the ocean. When they arrived on the outskirts of the next town, they had cut across the dunes and into the crowded backstreets, zipping down this lane and cutting through there, until they had reached the door of this woman.

Rakesh had woken her up and given her some instructions in Sinhala. Leela had understood enough to know that he had asked the old woman to look after her. The woman was gazing at her as if she was some kind of doll. Leela smiled nervously. The old woman chuckled back. Leela wondered if she might be a little crazy, not that she minded. She felt quite safe here, for the time being. It was better than the jungle.

She wondered about Vish. She was glad for him, that he had found Marni, and she hoped he was safe. He was a resourceful man; she knew that much. He would be ok.

There was another knock at the door, Rakesh had returned. He was looking brighter than when he had left.

"Good news," he said. "You are leaving, for a boat to Australia, tomorrow morning, and so am I!"

"Australia!" Leela exclaimed. "Why am I going there?"

"Because some kind people thought to pay a lot of money to buy you a ticket for that boat and you are going to take the opportunity to get out of this country, while you can."

"But what about my mother?"

"She will be happy when you're safe. You can't go home, Leela. They will take you again if they hear you made it back. They have already interrogated your family about your whereabouts. Luckily, they know nothing, and that's the way it should stay. Suresh will tell them you're safe when you get on the boat."

Leela was silent. She thought about the severity of what was to happen. A boat to Australia! She couldn't comprehend it. Never to see her mother or brothers and sisters again, to be alone for the rest of her life in a country far away. It was too much. Wouldn't she be better off dead?

"And why are you leaving Sri Lanka?" she asked Rakesh.

"There are so many people that want to see me dead or in jail, it's impossible to count them," he laughed. "Don't worry," he said. "We will have plenty of time to talk about all my misadventures, on the way there. The journey will take about three weeks."

"Three weeks trapped on a boat!" Leela exclaimed. "That sounds awful."

"No, I'm not looking forward to it either," Rakesh said, "but it beats getting shot!" he laughed again.

'Why does he keep laughing about such serious matters?' thought Leela. 'Maybe he's also a little crazy.'

Rakesh left Leela at the old woman's house for most of the day. He returned in the late afternoon with some food supplies and water. "There will be water and food on the boat," he said "but I thought there's no harm in bringing some extra. I received an email from Gaya. She and Suresh are to meet us at the boat. She has the rest of the money to pay for the tickets, and Suresh wanted to say goodbye."

Leela was relieved she would see her brother again. She was confused and terrified. She didn't even know this man who was taking her to Australia. She wanted to check with Suresh that there was really no other choice.

She slept deeply that night, with no dreams disturbing her, and awoke with a renewed feeling of hope. She would do what she had to, she thought. Rakesh had woken her up before the sun had risen. A friend of his was giving them a lift in his tuk-tuk, but they would have to walk the last part as there was a roadblock that they could not pass because Leela had no ID. The old woman pinched Leela's cheeks hard as they left and pushed a package into her hands, nattering to herself and chuckling as she turned away and slammed the door shut.

They climbed into the waiting tuk-tuk and left at high speed. The town and the countryside flashed past Leela and she realised that this would be the last time she would see anything that was familiar. There was a faint flutter of excitement in her stomach. She had, after all, survived.

Suresh and Gaya were waiting expectantly under the tree where Gaya and Rakesh had first kissed. Gaya had sent Rakesh an email to arrange it. Mobiles were often tapped, especially his. The heat of the day had already arrived, and she was nervous about saying good-bye.

She knew he had no other choice but to leave. He would have preferred to stay and carry on his work, but he was now permanently in hiding and too afraid for his life. His idea, he had told her, was to get asylum somewhere else and still carry on his work from there. It would be more difficult for him to be silenced, though still possible.

She saw them hurrying towards the tree from the main road and clutched Suresh's arm. "They're here!" she said, letting out her breath slowly.

Rakesh strode towards her and kissed her long and deeply. She melted instantly. Finally, he pulled away and stroked her face. "I'm sorry to have to say good-bye to you Gaya. I'm going to miss you."

"Me too." Gaya gulped, the words getting stuck in her throat.

"Is Vish ok?" Leela asked, clutching her brother's arm.

"No, I'm sorry Thangai, he died last night."

"No!" Leela cried and covered her mouth in horror. "I should have stayed. I could have helped him. Instead, I ran away like a coward."

"No Thangai. You would also be dead if you had stayed. He died protecting Marni and that will help his soul to rest peacefully. This was his journey. You did not let him down."

Leela let the tears run silently down her cheeks before wiping them away. Vish had saved her life, and now she had to make the most of it. She owed that much to him.

Gaya handed Rakesh the rucksack full of cash and gave him one last, lingering kiss. Suresh and Leela stood some way to the side, awkwardly. Gaya knew she was being unprofessional, but she didn't care.

"Rakesh, the boat," she whispered. "Are you sure you have to go? You said it's not safe, that you might not even make it to Australia."

"Hush now Gaya, me and the girl have no choice. You saw what they did to Vish. You don't want to send her into a blind panic before we're even on board, do you? Don't let her hear you. She needs to believe she will get there."

"Ok, let's go," Rakesh said loudly, turning to Leela. "You ready?"

Leela hugged her brother and followed Rakesh down the beach towards the navy barracks and the waiting boat. She turned and looked back at Suresh every few steps. Gaya waited to give a last wave to Rakesh, but he didn't turn to look back, not even once.

The boat was small and squashed but the navy officer explained that it was taking them to a larger ship, with sleeping compartments and a restaurant. He took the money from Rakesh and counted it. "Okay, climb aboard," he said.

They took a seat on the deck with the others. There were 78 people in total. Rakesh counted them as they waited for the last people to board. He looked across at Leela. She looked composed, but he knew she must be torn up inside. She was a strong girl though, probably strong enough to make it.

The engines started up and the ropes were untied from the jetty. They set off, the whole world lying in front of them. There was excited chatter amongst the passengers as they dared their minds to wander to the hope of a safe future.

Leela opened the plastic bag she was carrying and took out the parcel given to her by the old woman. She unwrapped it carefully and took out a photo frame. She turned it over and saw the face of a young girl smiling back at her.

Rakesh looked over her shoulder at the photo. "That's Aunty Pali's granddaughter. She died several years ago. She was on a bus travelling to her uncle's house when the bus hit a land mine. Aunty Pali's daughter and granddaughter died instantly. You must have reminded her of her granddaughter."

Leela held the frame close to her and stared out over the ocean. She thought of all the wasted lives. So many, and still the body count continued. Was there any hope for Sri Lanka? After the weapons' traders got richer and the population got smaller, then what? Would they stop fighting then?

They had been travelling over an hour. They had followed the coast but were now heading out into the clear, blue sea. A man stood up and called over to the boatman. "How long until we get to the ship?" he asked in Sinhala. The boatman laughed and repeated what the man said to his co-worker, and they both erupted in laughter.

"This is our ship! This is the boat we're going to Australia in." Everyone looked around the tiny boat. There were several twenty-litre bottles of water and a few sacks, presumably containing food. Towards the stern was an old tarpaulin covering one third of the boat in shade.

"There's not enough food and water here for everyone."

The other passengers were standing up to join in the protest too.

"What do you mean 'there's no ship'?" another man said.

"No ship, there's no ship," echoed around the seated passengers, as the terror in their eyes took hold.

"There's not enough shade on this boat," a woman said. "You need to turn us around. I don't want to go. Take me back."

One boatman walked towards her now, holding a pistol. "We're not turning this boat around, do you understand? Now I think you'd all better sit down and shut up otherwise your journey may end sooner than expected. That goes for anyone else who wants to cause me any trouble," he said, waving the gun around. They all remained silent.

Rakesh studied the passengers. About half of them were children, some babies and several elderly and infirm. It was unlikely they were all going to survive the journey. He looked at Leela who was quiet but taking it all in. He hoped she would understand why he didn't tell her before. There were just no other options left for either of them. They would have both been killed if they had stayed in Sri Lanka. At least this way there was hope.

The excited chattering had completely subsided, and the boat continued its journey under the forlorn mood that now encompassed the group.

As the sun passed over midday and began its descent into the west, they handed out biscuits, just two per person. That was the ration. The people ate slowly, breaking off tiny crumbs at a time, trying to make their meagre meal last. Later that evening, a cup of water got passed around, after which, they were told to settle down for the long night ahead.

Leela laid her head on her bag and looked up at the black sky littered with stars. There was some comfort in the way they twinkled, as if they were smiling at her. She silenced her mind of her fears and let herself slip into a deep sleep.

Rushani was watching Marni. She was worried about her. She had been through so much in the last few days and she didn't know what the fallout was going to be.

"Can I make you a tea, Miss Marni?"

"Oh yes, that would be lovely, thank you Rushani."

Rushani moved back into the kitchen to boil the water. She placed her hand on her stomach to settle the nausea that was creeping in.

She grated ginger into a mug for herself and poured the steaming water over the leaves and through the sieve. She poured a cup for Marni and put it on a tray with a biscuit.

She took the tray out to Marni. She was sitting in the porch of her cabana, watching Zoe play in the sand.

"I don't know what I'd do without Zoe," she said. Rushani didn't know whether or not it was to her. "Imagine having a child and never knowing about it. Missing their whole childhood. It would be heart-breaking."

"Yes, Miss Marni. It was a miracle you and Mr Vish found each other."

"Yes," Marni said quietly. Rushani left Marni with her thoughts and returned to the kitchen to drink her own tea. She sat down in a plastic chair and put the hot cup to her lips. She could feel the life inside her growing stronger every day. It wouldn't be long before she would show and then people would start asking questions. She had no idea what she was going to do. She couldn't afford another mouth to feed and there was no way she would get any money from the father. It was so unfair.

The father was a doctor she had been to see in Colombo. Meena had been complaining of headaches and her school had said she was falling behind and that maybe it was her eyes. They had taken the night bus to Colombo to get her eyes tested, having made an appointment with a specialist eye doctor there. He had tested Meena's eyes and informed her that she would need special lenses that would cost Rs20,000. Rushani had cried there and then, saying there was no way she could afford that, and the doctor had said if she would like to return later that evening after the last patient had gone, he could give her the glasses for free. She knew there would be a catch, but she also didn't want her daughter to go without. She returned that evening with Meena and left her in the waiting room with some paper and colouring pencils. Inside his office, the doctor had taken off Rushani's clothes, pushed her over a chair and penetrated her from behind. He had come quickly and efficiently; it was all over within minutes. He handed her the glasses, and she left his office without a word, catching the night bus home.

Within weeks, as the full moon came around, but not her period, she realised what must have happened. She tried to abort, by eating green papaya and pineapple for days, causing sickness, but not a miscarriage. She had run out of options.

Chris came into the kitchen, stirring Rushani from her thoughts. She jumped up from the chair, spilling her tea on her dress.

"Oh, I'm sorry, I didn't mean to startle you," he said.

"What can I get for you?" she asked.

"Oh, I don't want anything," said Chris, "well I do, but nothing to eat," he faltered. "Really, I wanted to ask you if you had a day off then maybe I could take you and Meena somewhere. We could take a picnic and hire a tuk-tuk, go for a drive. What do you think?"

Rushani was looking at him, shocked. Chris knew this would be her reaction, but the events of the last couple of days had pushed him to act. Life was too short to waste. He liked Rushani a lot, and he needed to find out if she felt the same way about him.

"I... um... I think not ok, Miss Marni."

"Don't worry about Marni," said Chris, "I will talk to her. I don't think she will object. The question is, do you object?"

Chris watched her closely. Inside, she was in turmoil. She liked Chris and found him very attractive, but she had secrets to hide. He wouldn't want her if he knew the truth about her. He would think she was damaged, soiled goods. Why lead him along until then?

"I'm sorry Mr Chris. It's very nice you ask but no good idea."

She fled out the backdoor of the kitchen, the empty space she left, pressing against Chris' chest. He felt like she'd slapped him across the face.

19 Scotch on the rocks

———————————— ● ————————————

The sea was grey, the waves slapping up against the side of the boat, as they bounced around in the water. Several of the passengers were leaning over the edge, vomiting, including Leela.

"There's nothing left in my stomach," she complained to Rakesh. "I don't know how I can still be vomiting."

Rakesh looked around. Everyone was suffering. They had been on the boat for a week now. They were given measly quantities of food, twice a day, but it was running low, and they had already drunk half the water.

They were taking it in turns to shade themselves under the tarpaulin, priority being given to the children, but faces were blistering from sunburn, and some were becoming infected. They had left their belongings onshore, as they had been told these would come on another boat and join them on the ship. Precious possessions, mementos of their former lives, along with photos, jewellery and money had all been left behind.

One man was dying. They had heard his groans for days, but he was quiet now. The silence was a relief for the other passengers, but Rakesh knew for the man it was not so fortunate. It only meant that he was too weak to make a sound and it wouldn't be long before his life would leave him altogether. When it did, his daughter was told to say her quick good-byes and the crew tipped him over the edge without hesitation. The woman watched her father float away on the water. Stricken with grief, but with the absence of tears, as dehydration had consumed them.

"It might be time to tell me your story Rakesh," said Leela, wiping the crust forming on her dried-out lips and trying to find a comfortable spot to lie flat.

"Okay, if you're sure you want to hear it," said Rakesh. He looked at the passengers sitting close to him. He didn't really want anyone else to hear what he had to say but no-one really looked like they were listening. He wasn't even sure any of them would get off this boat alive, so what did it matter anyway, he thought.

"Well, it all started like this…"

He spent the next few hours recounting the main events of his life that had led him to this boat. He had worked for a neutral newspaper, committed to writing the facts rather than biased accounts. There were often threats, by both sides, and eventually, it closed down, after a particularly big story, that implied cohesion between kidnappers, and security forces who manned the roadblocks up and down the country. Rakesh had got evidence and first-hand accounts of backhanders and bribery. When the paper had been closed down, Rakesh decided to go freelance. Working on stories that came to his attention, he made contacts throughout the country and an underground network developed. He published them on the internet, funded by private individuals happy to spend their cash on pursuing social justice, or those wanting to take down their political opponents.

He uncovered illegal arms trading, forcing the culprits to be judged in the international arena. He helped individuals as well as taking down those at the top. His latest story had been on the protection rackets up and down the country. Extorting hard-earned cash from the poor, in return for their safety. He had exposed conmen and thugs, on both sides of the war, and sent through the information to their superiors, thus creating a whole spate of internal politics, mistrust and several breakdowns of factions.

He had crossed many people, sparing no race, religion or minority. He had pursued the powerful, in defence of the vulnerable, and now they wanted his head on a plate.

He explained how he had tracked down a ring of treasure hunters, who had been using the country's money and resources to uncover the artefacts and then smuggle them out on the black market. The ring involved politicians, police, and businessmen.

"And this is what it all boils down to," he lifted his shirt and unzipped a travel wallet he had strapped around his waist. He pulled out a plastic bag and held it up to her.

She could see a small, black piece of plastic inside the bag. "What is it?" she asked.

"It's a pen drive that contains all the photos, sworn testaments and documentation I need to expose this ring of corruption. This holds the same value as my life."

Leela stared at the small plastic rectangle.

"I pushed it as far as I could and then had to run. I had a legitimate death threat sent through to me and if they could have found me they would have followed through." He pushed the plastic bag back into his wallet and zipped it up.

"I'm surprised you made it this far," said Leela mockingly. She had enjoyed his tales of bravery and selflessness. They had taken her mind off the boat for several hours and as the sea had calmed, so had her nausea. He had also given her back some faith in society. If there were people like this in the world, willing to do anything they could, to save others, then surely the world could keep on turning, rights would outweigh wrongs, and the people would win through.

The wind took a pause from whipping her face and stinging the blisters that bubbled up under the hot sun. Her lips were cracked and dry and her throat croaky.

A woman sang to her child. Soon the whole boat had joined in. Beauty in the face of adversity, Leela observed. At that moment she felt honoured to be a part of it.

Marni was threading shells onto a thin rope to decorate the lampshades in the restaurant. Her father's body had travelled to Colombo along with the others. She didn't know where he would be buried, and he had made her promise not to ask.

"Don't bring attention to yourself, Marni," he had said. "If anybody knows you are my daughter, you will not be left alone, by either side of this bloody war."

She had promised, even though she could not come to terms with the thought of him dumped in an unmarked grave along with all the other unclaimed bodies, thrown away like garbage.

"Miss Marni?" Rushani sat down on a stool in front of her and picked up some rope to thread. "Can I tell you something?"

"Sure Rushani, what is it?"

"It's Mr Chris...." she began. "He asked me to take a day with him."

"I know, he told me."

Rushani looked up, surprised. "What he say?"

"He told me that he had asked you to come out with him, but you had said no and ran away upset. He was worried he had offended you. He was also confused and thought he must have misread the signals."

"He from different world to me. Everything different."

"It seems to me the language of love is the same the whole world over. I also saw something in your eyes, the way you look at him. Are you sure you're not a little interested in him?"

"He nice but we not same. I am poor, no schooling, I have child," Rushani absent-mindedly put her hand on her belly. "He from a different world. How I interest him?"

"Rushani, why do you put yourself down. You obviously do interest him, a lot. I think you should go, take the day off. Enjoy yourself with Meena. If there is anything that we should have all learnt about life, from recent events, it's that should make the most of it, while we can."

"But there something you not know, Nona." Rushani looked down at the ground.

"That you're pregnant?' said Marni gently.

"How you know?"

"I heard you the other morning, in the toilet, being sick, I also saw you place your hand across your stomach, on several occasions, which reminded me of what I did when I was pregnant. It's an automatic reaction to shield your baby."

"This why I can't go with Mr Chris, he wouldn't want me if he know this."

"Why don't you tell him, see what he says. Is the father involved?"

"No, I not see him again. Bad man."

"Then you must definitely tell Chris, let him decide for himself."

"I don't know. I don't want shame."

"Rushani, I don't know the story behind this baby, but I do know that a baby is not something you should be ashamed about. This is your baby, no one else's, yours and Meena's, you should hold your head up and be proud."

"Thank you, Miss Marni, you very kind."

She stood up and took a deep breath. "I tell him, then we see."

Marni watched Rushani walk away. She was a beautiful, strong woman, so capable, but knocked by life, so many times. Why couldn't she be a princess in a fairy tale? Miracles now seemed possible.

Rushani went to find Chris before she lost her nerve. Marni was right. There really was nothing to lose, except his respect, but she would just have to cope with that.

She found him on the beach. The sun was setting behind the hotel and he was sitting on the sand, looking out to sea.

He turned around as he heard the rustle of her sari and jumped up. "Rushani, won't you join me? It's a beautiful evening."

"I can, but quickly, I cook the fish curry for tonight. Sorry, for…." She was grabbing handfuls of sand and letting it stream through her fingers. She picked up a shell and rubbed the smooth insides with her thumb. "I have baby." She put her hands on her belly to show the roundness.

"Oh," said Chris, glancing down. "I'm sorry, I thought your husband was dead."

"He is, this not my husband baby."

"Oh," said Chris again. He wished he would stop saying that, it made him sound dumb. "I'm sorry, I didn't realise. I didn't want to come between you and another man."

"No other man, he very bad, the baby never see him."

Chris left his gaze on the small round mound in the folds of her sari. He wanted to know more of the story but felt he couldn't press her further. He knew how much it had taken for her to tell him anything.

"Well, in that case, would you, the baby, and Meena, like to join me for a picnic?"

Rushani couldn't help the grin that spread across her face. "Yes, we like, thank you Mr Chris."

"Oh, and Rushani, you must stop calling me Mr Chris."

"Ok, Mr… I mean Chris. I go now. Aruna look for me."

"So how about Saturday?"

"Yes Saturday," she called back over her shoulder.

Chris leant back on his elbows and stared out at the great blue expanse before him. "Magnificent," he said out loud. "Bloody magnificent!" he yelled. The beach dogs paused from their brawl in front of him, to give him an odd look, before carrying on the gnawing of each other's ears.

———————•———

Three hundred miles away in an old colonial house in Kotte, minister Jayasuriya was drinking his way through a bottle of scotch. He rang a bell on his sideboard and a wizened, old man made of skin and bone, in a white shirt and matching sarong, came running in.

"More ice," he barked at the man.

The old man bowed and walked out backwards, tripping over a pile of old newspapers in the doorway.

"Bring it quickly."

Jayasuriya was in a foul mood. He had had his knuckles well and truly rapped by his superior, who also happened to be his wife's Uncle Elmo, and he had suspended him from duties for a week.

"Are you mad, man?" Uncle Elmo had shouted. "Do you want a story like that to get into the international press? This government already makes enough bad press of its own, without you attacking and raping a foreign national."

"I didn't attack her or rape her."

"Only because Colonel Wijesinghe stopped you before it got that far. You were on official business for god's sake. What were you thinking?"

"Why else go to that god-forsaken area, if it's not to enjoy ourselves? Let loose a bit."

"Let loose! Let loose. Get out of my sight. I don't want to see you back here for a week. Wait until it's calmed down and you'd better hope that this woman doesn't make a formal complaint to her employers."

"She is nothing but a foreign whore, she encouraged us."

"Get out of here before you give me a stomach ulcer!"

Jayasuriya marched out of the office and slammed the door. 'Little bitch,' he thought. Because of her he now had a bad reputation in parliament and would not likely get the promotion that he knew should have been his.

Once home, he set about drinking his way through the week. His wife had scowled at him as he tried to explain the suspension. He had told her that his men had got out of hand and they had blamed him; it was deemed his responsibility. She had said, yes it seemed very unfair, and that she would speak to Uncle Elmo herself. She arranged his favourite evening meal, chicken curry, noodles and Chinese chilli paste.

He had left it untouched and gone to bed, bad-tempered and full of revenge.

The next day he awoke with a renewed sense of righteousness. He phoned up the land magistrate in the East and asked for copies of all the deeds and documents relating to the land on which Moon Rise Hotel resided to be couriered to him.

Next, he phoned up the visa office, and with a few name-drops, was put through to the Head of Immigration, from which he extracted the details of the visa on which Claudette, Marni and Jake had entered the country.

Following this, he contacted the tourist board, the pensions department, the inland revenue and lastly, the police.

He chuckled to himself. These foreigners weren't going to get away with stepping on his toes. He would take them all down. Get them out of his beloved country. How dare they dirty it with their ways. Going about half-naked, not treating government officials with the respect that they deserve. That was enough. He would make sure that they were all gone, maybe he could claim the land for himself, build his own hotel there, make his own rules. Yes, that was it, he would get into the hotel industry. There would be fully naked dancing girls every night, but Sinhalese girls with their meek natures and beautiful skin. He closed his eyes at the very thought and wondered if he should retire to his bedroom for half an hour, to iron out the details. More than once that morning he took a quick shot, just a nip, 'hair of the dog' as they say.

He ate a hearty lunch and then slept for the rest of the afternoon. He awoke, just as it was getting dark, with a headache, and a mouth that try as he might, could not moisten. He heaved his legs out of bed and onto the floor. His big, round belly gleaming in the light of the setting sun.

His wife entered the room to bring him a fresh shirt and sarong. "I hope you didn't forget we have company tonight."

"Who?" he said gruffly.

"Mr and Mrs De Silva and their friends the Somarasekera's."

"I can't remember them."

"You haven't met them, but I've told you about them. The husband is a judge. The wife also studied law but never practised, stayed at home to bring up their only daughter. She went off to study in America, does charity work for a living."

"Sounds very boring."

"Maybe so," his wife reprimanded him "but you have a duty to make a good impression for those with influence."

Jayasuriya muttered horrible things about his wife under his breath as she left the room. He had a shower and trimmed his eyebrows, nostrils and toes. He looked at himself in the mirror. He was wearing a black silk shirt and a black, green and gold sarong.

"You are a very handsome man," he said to his reflection.

Downstairs, his wife had already poured him a scotch and soda, and she handed it to him along with his cigarettes and lighter. "They are due here in an hour," she said. "Please try not to be too rude."

God, that woman was insubordinate. He shuffled across the polished red floor and into his study. His large, oak table, an heirloom from Victorian England, was covered in the papers and documents he had received through the fax that morning.

He rifled through them, not looking for anything in particular but trying his best to be out of his wife's company, for as long as possible.

His eyes rested on a photocopy of the deed to the land.

"Aha!" he shouted, leaping up and throwing scotch all over the place. His wife came running in, alarmed at the noise. "They don't own the land, it's permit land, that's it, they don't own it, I can make them leave."

"What on earth are you talking about?" asked his wife. She didn't understand him at the best of times, but this was ridiculous.

"Those foreigners who think they can come here and take money and land that belongs to us. They will have to think again. I will show them who it really belongs to."

His wife smiled tentatively. At least he had come out of his grumpy mood. They might even have a pleasant evening. It was these dinners that she looked forward to, performing her social duties, as a minister's wife. Entertaining their guests in the drawing-room with cocktails and nibbles, then settling them in the grand dining room at the large mahogany table that could seat twelve. Serving wine in crystal glasses with waiting staff, on hand for every whim, and ultimately being the envy of all. Yes, she had got used to this life and not even her frightful husband would knock her off her perch. It was she who had got him the job in the first place. A quiet word in the right ear and a favour repaid had sent them nicely past GO.

20 Juicy Mangoes

As he waited for his guests to arrive, Jayasuriya waddled around his study, excitedly rubbing his belly. He could see it all very clearly, a couple of official visits East and he could wrap this up in no time. The doorbell rang, and his wife came running to his study door, gesturing wildly to make himself presentable and come and meet the guests, whom he could hear chattering in the hallway.

"Alright woman, I'm coming."

She attempted to hush him with a glare, then readjusted into her best hostess face and swished off in a cloud of orange and gold silk, towards her waiting guests.

Once the social pleasantries were exchanged, the group assembled in the garden. They sat down on exquisitely carved chairs, set out in a circle. Drinks were served from a trolley and they settled into comfortable small talk set by the invisible, but highly influential, boundaries of convention. Each person's family was enquired after, ailing relatives, the current state of medical care and the increasing price of food discussed. Jayasuriya tuned out of the sound of his wife Doreen's voice prattling on and on, letting his mind wander to his new ventures and his well thought out plan. His attention returned to the conversation however at the mention of his name.

"Jaya has just returned from a very important trip out East. It's all a bit hush-hush. He doesn't tell me much about it, but they're starting to make official government visits to boost morale and win over supporters. He was checking on some of the development work that's been going on and there's even been some mention of new roads being built."

"Oh, where did you go?" asked the prettier of the two women. The other looked like a horse, thought Jayasuriya, an old, skinny, knackered horse with a huge set of gnashers sticking out of her bony face. "It's just that my daughter's working there, with INR, maybe you met her? Gaya's her name."

Jayasuriya's memory was swamped with the young, attractive girl, that he so wanted to maul on the beach that night. She obviously hadn't mentioned the event to her parents, or perhaps she had, and this was some kind of trick. Maybe they would try to poison his food or slip a knife into his back. He shifted uncomfortably and coughed, mumbling something like, "I might have met her, not sure, met so many people, can't remember everyone's names."

"Oh, yes, it must be difficult remembering everyone," said the woman looking both hurt and a little reproachful.

Doreen poked Rahul in the ribs with her sharp claws, "Wasn't that the place you had that buffet arranged for you? Didn't you say there was an awful French woman there who was very drunk and making an exhibition of herself? Honestly, these foreigners come here for work, but they have no guidance, no moral standards. You see them in the hotels around

Colombo, always drinking and smoking, wearing skimpy clothes and staying up all night long. When they find time to work, I don't know. They have families in their own country, don't you know, but when they are away, well you can only imagine what they get up to." She paused and glanced around her audience. The look on Mrs Somarasekera's face pulled her up sharp.

"Oh, not that I'm implying that your daughter would behave like that. Oh no, not a Sinhalese girl. They know better than to show their parents up like that. They understand the true value of modesty and appropriate behaviour."

Mrs Somarasekera had gone slightly pink and was giving an awful lot of concentration to her soup, though, being so hot, it was burning her mouth, causing her to splutter and drip scalding liquid down her chin.

She grabbed the glass of ice-cold water in front of her, wondering if she could get through this meal without actually having to say another word. She found the fat, egotistical man repulsive and desperately hoped that Gaya had not had to make his acquaintance. His wife seemed equally bad with her quick-fire judgments. The soup was awful too.

She had heard little from Gaya. She received a quick call every few days to tell her she was well and happy, but her mother couldn't help but feel Gaya was holding back. Gaya was someone who liked to give all the details, even down to the food she had eaten, but recently she had been unusually quiet. She hoped that her beloved daughter was not in trouble.

Meena was running backwards and forwards squealing in delight as the tuk-tuk pulled up. Rushani's mother was watching from the front step of the house, scrutinising the proceedings. She wasn't happy about today. She had begged Rushani to cancel the day trip. 'No good will come of this' she tutted. Rushani continued to braid the frangipani petals to wear around the bun she had tied in her hair.

"Ammi, please. I am going, and that's the end."

"You're a fool, Rushani. There's only one thing this foreign man is interested in. You think he's interested in you? No, he just wants to use your body and then he will be on his way."

Rushani tensed slightly at her mother's words. It's not that she hadn't considered this. Maybe she was a fool, blinded by a few compliments and a cheap day out. Maybe he would then think she owed him something. She tried to banish these thoughts from her head. She thought of his smile when they spoke that day on the beach. Chris was a kind, generous man. She'd be a fool not to take the risk.

She heard the tuk-tuk pull up outside. Chris was in the driving seat, looking handsome in a white linen shirt that showed off his tanned skin. Meena jumped in and grabbed the steering wheel. She heard Chris laughing and Meena's excited chatter. She adjusted her sari, grabbed her sun umbrella and an old arrack bottle filled with water and walked into the glaring light.

"Bye Ammi." She bent down and kissed her on the top of the head.

"Look at everyone watching you. The whole village will know your business by lunchtime, that you're letting this foreign man buy you. No eligible man in this village will touch you now."

"Ammi, I don't want them to touch me, so that suits me just fine."

Chris waved at her and climbed out of the tuk-tuk to greet her.

"Rushani, you look beautiful," he said quietly. He knew there were eyes on them, and he didn't want to make a big spectacle. Rushani smiled shyly and climbed in the back, next to Meena.

"I thought we'd go and visit the old monastery and then stop somewhere for lunch. Then, if you're not too tired, we could visit the bird sanctuary and have some tea."

"Yes please, thank you," said Rushani.

They set off, curious eyes following them until they reached the outskirts of Rushani's village. Once on the main road, Rushani visibly relaxed, half-listening to Meena's running commentary. Her eyes rested on the nape of Chris' neck. She liked the way his blond curls hung down from the base of his skull: soft, springy and overgrown. She followed his broad shoulders and could see his taught muscles moving under his shirt as he held the steering wheel. He looked like an adult in a child's toy car. He was a tall man and his knees had to spill out the sides to make his legs fit. His skin had a healthy, golden glow and the hair on his arms bleached blond, so they were almost invisible against his skin.

The bright green of the paddy fields sped past her vision and she settled back against the seat. It seemed strange not to be working. It was rare that she took a day off, and even when she did, it would be to work at home. Her mother was a great help with Meena, otherwise she wouldn't have been able to take this job and they would barely have been able to survive.

She caught Chris's eye in the rear-view mirror and smiled.

"That's better," he said. "You look ten times happier already."

He turned off the main road towards the monastery, a labyrinth of caves that nestled into the hillside.

It was still only mid-morning, but the sun was already scorching. Rushani shielded herself and Meena with the umbrella as they made their way up. Chris was wearing a large-brimmed straw hat that kept some of the heat away. They passed several monks, who nodded a greeting to them. Meena reached the mouth of a cave first and stuck her head in.

"It's dark Ammi," she said, looking inside. Outside the cave was a candle in a glass lantern. Chris took a box of matches out his pocket and lit the candle. He held it up, illuminating the walls.

Meena gasped, "Look Ammi, beautiful pictures."

Paintings covered the walls in beige, red, black and gold. Thousands of years old, the faces beamed down at them. They held the gaze of their observers silently, as though they had centuries of secrets they weren't willing to share.

Feeling parched from the walk up the rock, Rushani opened her mouth, and holding the water bottle a couple of centimetres higher, poured the semi-warm liquid in, swirling it around her mouth before swallowing. She held it out to Meena, who like her mother, drank the water without touching the bottle. Meena passed it on to Chris. He took the bottle and attempted the task, missing by a mile and pouring water down his chin. Meena giggled and Rushani wondered whether he was exaggerating his ineptness for her benefit.

They left the cave and continued on around the hillside where they found a rocky outcrop on which to rest and take in the view. They were above the tallest tree and the forest stretched on into the distance. Chris unwrapped some bananas and mangoes he had brought with him in his backpack. The juicy mangoes were a welcome reprieve from the heat of the day, and the small, sweet bananas satisfied everyone's hungry bellies.

Chris looked across at Rushani's profile: her small ski-slope nose, the wisps of hair that escaped, framing her face, and her beautiful, slender neck. She was perfect. He tried not to focus too much on her lips, as it was all he could do not to kiss them.

"Shall we head back?" he asked, jumping up before he got too carried away with his train of thought.

They followed Meena down. She skipped and jumped all the way, nimble as a mountain goat.

This time they stopped by the monks. Rushani put some money into the collection box and said a prayer.

The seats of the tuk-tuk were burning by the time they reached it, they climbed in, gingerly. Chris had to hold the steering wheel with a towel, it was too hot to touch. They sped off quickly to get some breeze on them and headed towards the town. Chris wished he could know what was in Rushani's prayers.

The winds screeched above, threatening the little boat with each forceful gust. The sun was almost below the horizon and the cool of the night was drawing in. The passengers huddled down further into themselves, as a barricade of rain and sea spray hammered upon the light cotton fabric of their clothes.

Each passenger was wet through. Parents shielded children under them as the boat danced on the waves. Rakesh thought it only a matter of time before the little boat would fling them far into the depths of the fierce ocean.

They hung onto anything that was stuck down. A railing ran along the edge of the boat and a rope had been threaded from one side to the other, weaving a makeshift net over them, like cargo in the back of an open truck. It was a lifeline. Leela held the rope so tightly that she sheared a burn across the palm of her hand from the constant to and fro of her body. Food had long since finished. Water was down to a bare minimum, being drunk only by the sick and the very young. Fever had swept through the passengers like a typhoon, and there had been two more deaths. Leela wondered at which point she may think that death might be a preferable option. She didn't feel that far off.

She couldn't stand the wailing. It coursed through her, like a raging bull, making her want to scream and pull out handfuls of her own hair. It was petrifying. It wasn't just one person either. There were several people around the boat making the same mournful noise, the sound of death. She tried to block it out. She thought of her baby brother. His sweet, smiling face, chuckling as Leela bent to tickle him and plant kisses all over his soft, bulbous cheeks. She wondered about the life he would have. Would the white van come for him also? Stop Leela, she thought. She forced her mind back to the image of her smiling brother. At least she was no longer a threat to her family, that was one good reason to be on this boat. She looked across at Rakesh. His eyes were closed, but she had a sense he wasn't sleeping. His jaw was set and there were frown lines between his eyebrows. She touched his arm gently and his eyes shot open immediately.

"What is it?"

"Sorry, I didn't mean to startle you. I was just wondering what you know about Australia. What will happen to us when we arrive?"

Rakesh sat up now and rubbed his face. He looked at Leela, her expectant eyes and hopeful expression. He didn't want to dash her dreams; her hope. After all, that was all any of them on that boat had been left with and that was fast ebbing away from them. He had heard reports back through his media contacts, of large detention centres and long jail terms. He hoped these stories were exaggerated, but it was unlikely. There were two of his friends he knew were still locked up, after two years, their wives and children facing the same threats, but this time alone. There was no alternative for him. He didn't have a family depending on him, so it was easier for him to make this decision. At least this way there was some hope of staying alive and continuing his work. For Leela, she also had no-one depending on her, but she was a young girl with no family. How she would survive in a detention centre he wasn't at all sure.

"Well?" She pushed him again.

"First, they will give us food and water and then they will take us somewhere we can wash and sleep. The next day they will start trying to sort out who's who. They first need to verify who we are and then they will tell us if we can stay or not."

"So they send some people back again?"

"Yeah sometimes, but you don't need to worry. You have a very good case to stay."

"And what about my family? Will I be able to see them again?"

Rakesh twisted his mouth to the side, not knowing how best to answer.

"It's ok Rakesh, you can tell me the truth, I don't think there is anything much that can truly shock me now."

"I don't know when you will be able to see your family. At the moment you are still fifteen, so it may be possible that your family can join you as you are a dependent, but I don't know how quickly, or how easily these things happen."

"So there is some hope then?"

"Yes, there is some hope."

They had to shout at each other to be heard above the rain. Thunder and lightning scorched their way across the sky. Rakesh was fearful the lightning would hit the boat, it looked so close but somehow, this time, they were spared. The storm raged on throughout the night, but as the blackened sky had its first inkling of light, the winds dropped, and the rain clouds moved away. Bodies began to untangle themselves. One body became two and then three. Some stood and stretched, others sat blinking in the light, still not sure whether they had survived the storm, that this new dawn was real.

"That wasn't even a big storm, was it, Rakesh?" Leela whispered under her breath.

"Don't start wishing a cyclone on us, for god's sake, do you have a death wish or something?" he jested back.

She rolled her eyes at him but couldn't stop the corners of her mouth lifting into a smile. It felt good to find it all a little bit funny.

21 Lemon Puffs

With a long stretch, Gaya opened her eyes and stared at the roof. It had so much more to offer than a white-painted ceiling. It was made from sticks, rope and weaved palm fronds, making the perfect habitat for all kinds of creatures. There was a nest of starlings in permanent residence, squirrels and lizards visited regularly. A small, green frog lived in the weaved fronds that made up her bathroom wall and would spit at her every morning when she brushed her teeth. At first, she was offended, took it as an insult that the frog didn't want her there before she realised that the frog was just imitating her. After that, she grew very attached to their morning ritual. Recently, another frog had joined them, although this one preferred not to play spitting games but jumped on her when she sat down on the toilet. She also enjoyed the bird that called out to her mobile ringtone throughout the day, looking slightly dejected when the silent mobile failed to give it a mating call in return.

Gaya loved living at the Moon Rise Hotel, but she missed Rakesh desperately. She had heard nothing since that day on the beach when they said goodbye, but that was over two weeks ago now. She had called the contact in the navy. He told her that the boat was nearly there, and they would be in touch when they arrived. Gaya stared at the phone in her hand. She really didn't know what else she could do, or who she could ring. She would just have to wait.

The restaurant was empty, except for Suresh, who was sweeping out the sand blown in by the wind during the night. He glanced up as she walked in, giving her a half-smile. He feels just like me, she thought, desperate to hear news and trying to occupy himself until then.

He put down the broom and walked over to where she sat. "Good morning Miss Gaya, what can I get for you?"

"Morning Suresh, a pot of coffee and two cups," she said, as she saw Niraj opening his door and scratching his head. She beckoned him over.

"Hi Niraj, are you feeling any better?"

Niraj had returned to the hotel, over a week ago, with a raging fever, that had him bedridden for most of that time. Gaya had still not properly brought him up to speed with the night of the ministerial visit. She had told him bits and pieces when she had been in to visit him, but due to his hallucinations and confusion, he thought he had dreamt it all.

"I'm feeling a lot better, but you are going to have to start from the beginning with all the news because I really don't have a clue what is real and what's not. I mean I woke up this morning thinking that there was a big shoot-out here like in a Spaghetti Western and that the dog had given birth to kittens."

Gaya giggled, "Well the bit about the shoot-out is true, but not the kittens!"

"Oh, I was hoping it might have been the other way around. Please Gaya start again and tell it to me slowly."

Gaya told the story slowly from beginning to end. They consumed their way through another pot of coffee, papaya and lime juices, eggs, toast and a whole packet of lemon puffs. Niraj's appetite appeared to have returned. Gaya found the end of the story particularly difficult to tell as there was still no conclusion. Leela and Rakesh were lost at sea and there was nothing anybody could do.

Niraj lowered his voice slightly. "You really like him, don't you?"

Gaya looked at Niraj's kind face, worried how unprofessional she sounded, but she really needed to talk about it.

"Yes, I do."

Niraj spoke gently but firmly. "Gaya you are going to have to prepare yourself that you might not be able to see him again. If he does get asylum in Australia, which really is the only thing that can save his life right now, then he won't be able to return here."

"I know Niraj, I am aware, thank you." She didn't tell him about the fantasies that played through her head throughout the day, where he would apply for a visa for her to join him, they would get married and live happily ever after, even if it did have to be in Australia, away from her family. She could cope with that, as long as she was with him.

"Don't worry, I know I'm unlikely to see him again. I just need some time, that's all."

"Well, in the meantime, I think I might help you to take your mind off it by getting you stuck into the backlog of work that's piled up on my desk. Jenny is arriving tomorrow, and we need to get some reports finished for her to look over when she's here."

"I'm all yours," she replied, grateful for the distraction.

Leela had been watching the man for the last few days. He had a kind face, riddled with laughter lines, even when he was sad, like now, he looked as if he was smiling. He was gazing behind her and she turned to look. She could just see the tip of orange rising from the horizon. The water was calm this evening. It grinned up at her, beckoning her to dive in. She stood up, resting her forearms on the ledge that circled the boat, staring out to sea. A hush settled over the group as the great orange moon ascended in the sky.

"It's hard to take your eyes away from it, isn't it?" the voice said over her shoulder in Tamil. She turned to the man. "It's breath-taking," she replied.

"The orange moon is beauty that shines through the dust of chaos."

Leela dragged her eyes away from the spectacle to return her gaze to the man's face. She waited for him to continue.

"When we see a white moon, the air is clean and clear. There are no obstacles in the way and the light passes through to the earth uninterrupted. When the atmosphere is dirty and chaotic, filled with dust and pollution, the light cannot pass through easily. It becomes scattered, and not all the colours are able to cut through the chaos and reach through to the other side. What we see then is something more intense and beautiful than when there is no obstruction. Are you one of those colours that can make it through?" he asked gently.

She smiled at him, unsure of herself.

"I think you are," his hand was on her wrist now, squeezing tightly, "You must believe it."

He was hurting her wrist, but she didn't feel afraid.

"How do you know so much about the moon?" she asked.

"I'm a science teacher."

"Where is your family?"

"I have left my wife and three children in our home in Colombo."

"How old are your children?"

"Three, seven and nine."

"Why did you leave?"

"We were being threatened, letters through our door, badgering the children on the way to school. People were blaming us for the bombs, just because we are Tamil. I didn't think we would be able to stay there much longer. I took this chance in the hope I can get my family visas to join me in Australia, so we can be safe."

"I will pray for them," said Leela. The man released his grasp on her wrist.

"And I will pray for you. You have a future, don't stop believing in it."

The conversation with the man gave Leela the hope she needed. Her stomach no longer growled painfully at her, and she stopped noticing the endless miles of ocean that stretched in front of them every day. Instead, she busied herself with caring for the other people on board. She played with the children and nursed the weak and sick. Rakesh noticed the change in her. He knew from then that she no longer needed him to watch over her.

The very next night she was woken up by the commotion. It was the boat crew; they were pointing and shouting something in Sinhala.

"What are they saying?" Leela asked Rakesh.

"They are saying they can see land. We're almost there."

Roars and cheers could be heard across the water as the little boat heaved and chugged itself through the last stretch of its treacherous journey. As they neared the shore, they could see ominous rocks jutting ugly, black heads out of the water. A swell was picking up, causing the boat to jump around haphazardly, as they approached. Leela's eyes, now adjusted to the darkness of the night, could make out the line of the coast. There was dense forest and cliffs lining the shore.

Rakesh stood beside her, watching the looming rocks. "We can't land here," he said to Leela. "These guys are crazy they'll kill us all." He pushed his way through the people and pulled on the arm of one of the crew.

"Turn the boat around. We can't land here."

"We are going to land here. Look, see the beach? That's where we're heading for."

"It's too dangerous. The wind will push us into the rocks. We won't make it."

"Sit down and stop making a fuss." Rakesh felt the cold steel pressed against his bare stomach. He backed away and looked around the boat. Faces turned to him, willing him to lead them to safety, however it may be.

But what could he do? He could try and ambush the man with the gun, but then what? He had been on boats before but never driven one. How was he going to get the boat to safety then? No, these men were the only people who could handle the boat, and therefore their only chance.

"Okay, do what you have to." He mumbled.

"I wasn't waiting for your permission," the man replied.

The boat heaved and churned as they made their way to the opening in the rocks. There were shrieks and yells as people fell on top of others.

"My baby!", a mother screamed as she tried to push away a body covering her swaddled infant. "You're squashing my baby!"

Leela reached over and pulled the arm of a heavy woman, who had collapsed on top of the child, and was unable to get up. The woman rolled off, and the mother scooped up the screaming infant into her arms. The next moment, with a terrific boom, the boat hit solid rock, and in slow motion Leela watched as the mother and her baby were thrown into the air, and then down into the crashing waves below. Bodies were falling everywhere, screams as they hit the water, silence as they went under. The boat had twisted onto its side and water gushed in. Leela held on to the rail with all her might but could feel her fingers slipping, as the boat's angle turned a few more degrees. She frantically searched around for Rakesh. She couldn't see him anywhere and thought he must be already in the water. As the boat was tossed again and came down on the same rock, Leela thought her arm was going to be ripped from her socket. She closed her eyes and silently prayed. As she hit the water, she thought she heard the man's voice shouting to her, "You will not die today."

The water was black. It felt like the tsunami all over again. She could feel the arms and legs of others, kicking and punching her, as they all fought for survival. Suddenly she surfaced, gulping in air. The huge carcass of the boat lay in the water in front of her, half-submerged. The whole world seemed to have slowed down. She could hear screams, but they were muffled like an out of tune radio. She knew the beach must be behind her. She was not a good swimmer. She turned around and grabbed something floating past in the water. It was one of the large, plastic water containers, long ago emptied. She lay on her back and wrapped her arms around it, so it nestled into her right shoulder. With her eyes on the sinking boat, she kicked towards shore with all her might.

She felt a hand grab her foot and she tried to scream as it pulled her under. Her hands slipped off the bottle and she frantically splashed the water with her arms, trying to keep her head above. The hand was still there, gripping onto her, with all the life it had left in it. She desperately tried to kick it away, free herself so she could come up for air. Suddenly the hand was gone. The bottle was bobbing around innocently when she surfaced. She grabbed hold of it again and looked around her. There was nothing. No head coming out of the water, no bubbles, no splashes, nothing. Where was the person who had grabbed her leg? She could feel the rise of panic in her chest. She suddenly couldn't breathe, and she started to scream.

"No, no," she cried, tears poured down her stricken face, mixing with the salty water splashing up her nose, and into her mouth. She was choking now. She gasped the tiniest breath of air just as she saw the shadow of a wave, before it crashed down on top of her. The bottle was gone, and she was tumbling through the water, scraping along rocks at the bottom. She felt like she was being pinned down, on the seafloor of the treacherous ocean, by the hand of God.

'No,' she silently screamed. 'I am not going to die.' She surfaced long enough to fill her lungs before the last wave carried her in like a piece of driftwood and threw her onto the rocky beach.

She lay there, staring at the sky, trying to find some kind of rhythm of breath that would convince her she was alive. Her body spasmed and she rolled onto her side, vomiting up seawater and saliva. She lay there semi-conscious until the purging subsided, and her breathing returned to normal. The thought could now sink in. She was alive. Somehow, she was still alive.

After the nausea passed, she pushed herself into a sitting position and looked around. There were several other bodies littering the beach. She tried but failed to stand on her shaking legs and eventually managed to crawl. She approached the body nearest to her and shook it. The head fell towards her and she screamed. The bloated face of the heavy woman stared at her, eyes open so wide they were almost popping out of her skull. She scurried backwards on her hands and knees, whimpering.

She forced herself to check the next body. The eyes were closed but she could feel a pulse. It was a boy. He looked about twelve. She had spoken to him a few times on the boat, his name was

Nimal. She thought back to the CPR[17] training they had been given after the tsunami. "You can do this," she said out loud. Five presses on the chest and then blow in the mouth. She rolled him onto his back and began the pressing. She completed six cycles, but nothing happened. Maybe she was doing it too lightly, she thought. She increased the pressure, and within minutes there was a movement in his chest and throat, and water gushed out of him, just as it had done with herself. Of the ten other bodies on the beach, seven of them were still alive. The science teacher was not to be seen, nor was Rakesh.

She looked out to sea. The boat was no longer visible. She could see things floating about on the water but had no idea if they were people or debris.

The group huddled around her. All were silent except one girl who was shaking and uttering the word 'thani'[18] over and over again.

Leela tried to keep the girl warm by putting her arm around her and rubbing her back, but the shuddering worsened.

There seemed to be some expectation in the air that Leela would do or say something. She looked around the group. Some were looking at her, some were gazing into the water.

"I think we should stay here until morning and see if anyone else is alive. We will be able to see more in the light."

There was still silence from the group. Leela took that to mean some kind of cohesion and agreement.

---

[17] CPR – Cardiopulmonary Resuscitation

[18] Thani – water (Tamil)

Where was Rakesh? Surely, he would have made it to shore. She stared out to where the wreck had been. There must be more survivors. She buried her face in her hands, trying to focus, hoping that she would receive a message from the gods, as she had absolutely no idea of what she was supposed to do next.

22 Lamprais

Rushani pushed her plate of food away. She didn't feel like eating. She was upset with herself for thinking that she had choices, that she had the right to make her own decisions. She had taken a big risk and now the tide was turning on her. Her mother was not talking to her and Meena was getting bullied at school.

She gave her daughter a kiss, called goodbye to her mother, although she knew there would be no reply, and hurried out the door to catch the bus to work.

The local village tattletales had coordinated a direct assault at Rushani, over the past week, accusing her of bringing shame on their village. They were keeping their children away from Meena, in case this shamefulness was contagious. There was some talk that Rushani may be pregnant with a foreigner's child, but he had no desire to marry and was using her for his pleasure while he worked out his contract. Rushani's mother was sick of being told that she never should have let Rushani work in a place of such ill-repute and that she was to blame for the catastrophe that had befallen their family.

Rushani's mother tried to shield her granddaughter from the insults, but it was to no avail.

"Why are they saying bad things about Ammi?" Meena asked.

"Because she's making friends with the wrong people," her grandmother replied.

"Do you mean Mr Chris? Why is he wrong when he's so nice?"

"You wouldn't understand, you're just a child. People who seem nice may only pretend to be nice to get what they want."

"Do you mean when you're nice to Ranjit Uncle so that we can get a lift into town on his motorbike?"

"Finish your breakfast Meena, you talk too much and now we're late."

Meena picked up the piece of roti, breaking a piece off. She dipped it in the white potato curry on her plate and put it in her mouth.

She frowned at her grandmother as she chewed. Why wouldn't she answer any of her questions? She wasn't a baby anymore. She could see that Mr Chris was making her mother happy. It wasn't that hard to understand. But why did everyone call him a bad man when he wasn't? He was nice. He smelt nice and he was always laughing.

Meena shoved the last piece of roti into her mouth and grabbed her schoolbag. One or two of the children at school had been mean, calling her mother a coconut, and saying that she was easy. Meena didn't care, she didn't like those children anyway and what was wrong with being easy? Wasn't that a good thing to be? Her grandmother was in a bad mood now and half dragged her by the wrist down the road to the tumbledown village school.

"Archi,[19] stop, you're hurting me."

"It's your fault for being late. Listen, the school bell has just rung."

Most of her lessons were outside, sitting under the giant fig tree that stretched and curled in one corner of the schoolyard. She enjoyed being at school. She especially loved to learn about the world beyond her village.

Her grandmother put her hand on Meena's cheek, then bent down to smell the top of her head, before pushing her roughly between the shoulder blades, towards the school gates. Meena hurried to the waiting lines of children and joined the back of her class. "Honky lover,' the child in front of her hissed. She stood up straight and flicked her plaited pigtails back over her shoulder, pretending not to notice. "Your mother is a dirty whore," the girl continued. Meena kept her head straight, but as the child turned back to face the front, she felt the tears sting her eyelids and she blinked them away. She wasn't sure what a whore was, but a dirty one didn't sound nice at all.

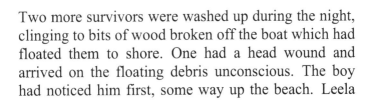

Two more survivors were washed up during the night, clinging to bits of wood broken off the boat which had floated them to shore. One had a head wound and arrived on the floating debris unconscious. The boy had noticed him first, some way up the beach. Leela

---

[19] Archi – grandmother (Sinhala)

thought he was dead, but as they approached, they could hear groaning.

He slowly came too, but his eyes were groggy, and he had still not spoken. The other survivor was the boat captain. He was also not talking. The other passengers tried to abuse him when they recognized him, but Leela encouraged them to hush.

"This is not going to help us now," she had said. "We must pull together to find a way out of here. How we got here is not relevant, the fact is we are all here and we need to help each other."

The other passengers murmured some agreement, but still cast furtive looks his way. The boat captain thought it best to find a spot away from the group. He sat in silence with his head down, coughing and shifting his weight.

There was still no sign of Rakesh. The morning light was creeping in. The group looked around each other, starting to piece together the memories of their features. Faces they had stared at for the last three weeks on their cramped death-trap.

Leela surveyed the rocks that hugged the right-hand side of the bay, penning them in. The boat had sunk a few meters off the point. She wondered whether any survivors had climbed the rocks from where the boat first collided and were there now, trapped or injured.

"Vanga Thambi,"[20] she called to the little boy. "Let's try and climb these rocks."

"Ok," the boy replied.

He looked pleased that she had chosen him to do this important task, and he followed her eagerly.

---

[20] Vanga thambi – come little brother

269

The rocks were slippery with moss, so Leela moved slowly. The boy was nimble and managed to get ahead of her. He scrambled up the rock until he was fifty feet above sea level. Leela caught up to him and they craned their necks to see if they could spot anything. They could see the remains of the wreck under the water. Leela tried not to think of how many bodies might be trapped in the wreck. There was still a lot of debris moving around in a continuous pattern. First in a gentle whirlpool, then up against the rocks, then taken a little way out to sea, then smashed into the rocks again, then back to the whirlpool.

Leela squinted down at the debris, trying to make out any bodies tangled up in it. It was difficult to see, but she was unsure if anyone would have actually survived being thrown against the rocks the whole night.

Suddenly the boy shouted and pointed. Over on the next section of rocks they could see a foot sticking out from behind it. They shouted, but the foot remained motionless.

"We need to get down there," said Leela. The gap between them and the next section was a huge jump. "I don't know if we can."

"Yes, I can," said Nimal.

"No, don't," Leela said and grabbed his arm as he looked like he was about to jump, but too late. He slipped through her fingers, and with a thump, landed on the rock below.

"Are you crazy?" she shouted. "Do you want to end up back in the ocean with all the other bodies?"

He looked hurt at her anger, so she recovered herself quickly. "Sorry, you scared me, that's all."

Nimal started to walk towards the foot. "Wait!" Leela shouted, and without giving herself time to think about it, she jumped. Her heart felt like it was leaving her body through her mouth as she sailed through the air for what seemed an age. She landed badly on the rock below, sending shooting pain up her right leg. She rubbed it, frustrated, and hobbled after Nimal.

She saw him freeze, and put his hand over his mouth, just as she reached the boulder. Looking down, she couldn't stop a scream escaping from her. Staring back up at her, was half the face of the teacher.

Leela grabbed the boy to her and hugged him, half for him and half to force herself to stop looking at the body. She was crying uncontrollably. She thought of his family left behind. What would they do now? No-one was going to be a sending them a visa or coming home to look after them. How would they know what had happened to him? She didn't even know his name.

She looked over Nimal's head, to the gathered group on the beach below. She knew that she had to face up to the reality that Rakesh was not going to appear magically. They were on their own. Thirteen lost souls, looking to her for survival.

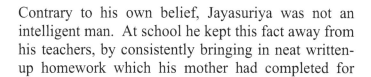

Contrary to his own belief, Jayasuriya was not an intelligent man. At school he kept this fact away from his teachers, by consistently bringing in neat written-up homework which his mother had completed for him. He would be too tired when he got home from school, and as she was sure she had given birth to a little prince, would happily complete his assignments for him.

He was an only child, born to a family of great wealth. His mother was a loving, gentlewoman but, through a series of traumatic events, turned her devotion onto the one gift in her life, her child, in effect making him a useless and lazy human being.

She had servants there for his every whim. If he dropped something on the floor, in would rush a shadow, retrieving the said item and replacing it into his hand before he even knew it had gone. He didn't feed himself, wash himself, nor tie his own shoelaces and especially did not think for himself.

When his mother died, his father, who was horrified at the way his son had turned out, looked to the matchmaker immediately to get him wed and out of the house. He could become someone else's responsibility. The matchmakers and the astrologers weaved their magic and found a suitable match. A wedding was arranged, a lot of money changed hands, and Jayasuriya's father, believing he had done his job well, settled down to retirement in a large, empty and peaceful home.

Jayasuriya's wife was an ambitious woman. After the painful realisation of her new husband's shortcomings, she took it upon herself to become the master of his destiny. She pushed him through a politics degree, which he scraped through, on account of an old friend of her father being on the examination board.

Next, she got him a job, through her uncle, as a junior in the cabinet. She knew he was just there to make up the numbers, an extra vote for her uncle's seat, and as long as he kept his mouth shut and did what he was told, he was destined for a long and lucrative career in politics.

Recently, however, he was causing ripples. Reports were being thread back to her about his behaviour, and concerns were arising as to his suitability to represent parliament. As she had worked hard to make her husband an accomplished man, Doreen took this very badly, vowing to upset the apple cart in their marital home that very night.

"What I want to know is what you think you are achieving by behaving like a complete idiot?"

Jayasuriya looked at her over his paper, a bemused expression on his face. He didn't reply, mainly because he wasn't sure which idiotic behaviour of his she was referring to, and he didn't want to throw the cat amongst the pigeons or let the cat out of the bag. Whichever it was, he thought it best for his mouth to stay firmly shut.

"Well, has the cat got your tongue?"

Jayasuriya stared at the old grandfather clock standing proudly in the corner of the room. The tick of the pendulum was deafening as he waited for his wife to speak again.

"Well, I'll tell you, shall I?" she continued, her voice becoming a shriek as she let her anger meter boil over into rage. "You are a joke, to parliament, to my family, to me. There is nothing you are able to do without making a complete hash of it. Even your own father disowned you because he couldn't handle another minute in your company. How did I end up having to deal with you? You are an imbecile, a fat, lazy, dribbling waste of space. Here I am trapped in this marriage. I have done everything to try and make you into a man but at each turn you fail. You're a stupid, greedy cretin and I can't stand the sight of your ugly face."

Jayasuriya didn't take his eyes off the clock during his wife's tirade. He thought it safer that way. He only looked in her direction when he saw the flash of white, realising she had chucked a marble ashtray at his head to hammer home the last point she had made. He managed to duck in time; the ashtray smashed onto the floor behind him.

She seemed really angry this time. She must have heard about the spot of bother on his trip out East. He wasn't sure how she had heard, but she seemed to have a lot of spies in a lot of places. Well, it can't be helped. If all went to plan, he would be living out there within the year and he wouldn't have to see her at all. Maybe he could run for mayor there, or maybe he wouldn't bother, maybe he should just retire and enjoy himself for a bit, just him and the dancing girls.

He stepped over the chipped, but still usable ashtray, and entered the door to his study. He had applied for a warrant to authorise the local police to remove the squatters from the hotel he now believed to be rightfully his. The Police Commissioner was reluctant to give such authorization without the written request from a senior staff member. This was where it had become a little tricky. Who could he find to write the letter for him? There wasn't really anyone he could honestly call an ally. He wasn't even sure there was anyone who would exchange pleasantries with him if he passed them in the hallway. He may have to get the letter by other means. Perhaps he could somehow persuade one of the secretaries to type him up a letter on official parliamentary letterhead, however that would give them ammunition to turn on him, should anything become sour. No, he would have to steal the paper himself and then type it up at home. The stamp? He would have to get it stamped. The headed paper and the stamp, that's what he needed to complete the task.

The following afternoon he headed off to parliament. His enforced leave had finished a few days ago and they had returned his security pass to him. He arrived at the huge oak-panelled doors and nodded at the security guards as they inspected his pass. His bag was searched, and he was motioned through the turnstile. Once inside the building, he made his way to the Department for Rural Affairs. The office was situated at the end of a long, dark hall. Most of the workers had already gone home for the day and Jayasuriya's footsteps echoed around the quiet space. He knew Miss Gunawardena would still be in the office because he had phoned to make an appointment. He knocked on the door of the office and opened it.

The secretary was a pretty little thing. Not too skinny, with ample bosom and wide innocent eyes, accentuated by the dark ring of black liner around them; a mysterious Eastern princess glancing provocatively at him from under her long, sweeping eyelashes.

He swallowed the saliva that was bubbling up in the corners of his mouth and held out his hand to her, eyeing her admiringly from top to bottom. She offered him a limp shake which she pulled from his grasp almost immediately, balling her hand into a fist in front of her mouth and giving a little cough to mask the involuntary shudder from having to touch him.

Jayasuriya was not put off by her reserved behaviour. She had obviously been brought up well, and the easy ones, well, they just weren't all that attractive. The thrill of the chase made it so much more exciting. He tried to focus on why it was he was here.

"So, Miss Gunawardena, do you have the copy of the letter I requested, outlining the timeline for the implementation of the updated fisheries policy on the East coast?"

"Yes, I have it on file here, I just need to make you a copy." She opened the drawer of the filing cabinet and rummaged through. She found the letter and placed it in the photocopier. From the cupboard behind her she pulled out a piece of headed paper and stuck it in the machine, pressing copy as she did so.

'Oh, the golden chalice', thought Jayasuriya, rubbing his hands together.

She unlocked the drawer under her desk and pulled out the rubber stamp that gave all documents leaving that office, the seal of approval. She pressed it into the ink pad and hammered it down hard on the paper. Jayasuriya's eyes grew wide at the sight of the perfect little circle that was going to lead him to his future.

The secretary handed him the paper and he took it, a lecherous grin spreading over his wide face. He perched his wide bottom on the corner of her desk and leant over her. The remnants of the lamprais, that he had eaten at lunch, oozed out of him. He belched deeply and she gave another polite little cough, turning her head away. He beamed down at her.

"How about we arrange a little meeting of our own, sometime?" He flicked an imaginary piece of lint from her shoulder and as he leant over further, to bring his soft damp lips down on hers, he knocked the cup of tea from her desk, onto her lap.

Miss Gunawardena leapt up from her chair with a squeal. The hot tea had penetrated her skirt and burnt her legs. She ran from the room towards the bathroom.

Jayasuriya smiled to himself, reaching into the cupboard to retrieve one blank, headed piece of paper and then with a resounding thud, he brought down the stamp, to make the circle of perfection.

He whistled as his footsteps thudded back down the corridor, past the toilet where Miss Gunawardena huddled in a cubicle, quietly crying on the phone to her sister, who worked downstairs, begging her to come and rescue her.

23 King Coconut

Leela surveyed the group in front of her. There were thirteen of them altogether; herself, Nimal, the young girl that was severely traumatised, an elderly couple who had clung to each other and the mast of the wreck for survival, the boat captain, three brothers, a middle-aged woman, the man with the head wound (who had made a remarkable recovery), and a mother and her young child. The child had been wrapped on the mother's back when the boat had sunk and the mother, with an intense will to keep her baby alive, had swum the distance to shore, holding only a plank of wood to stop her from going under. She had never swum before in her life.

All the survivors spoke Tamil, except for the boat driver. There were two people amongst them badly injured. The old woman had fallen onto a ruptured floorboard, as the boat capsized, which had pierced her thigh deeply. It was now bandaged with her husband's shirt, and the bleeding had stopped, but she was unable to walk. Two of the brothers went about collecting driftwood and strapping it together with vines, to make a stretcher. The other injured person was the traumatised girl. Not that she had a physical wound, but she was not mobile. She had still not spoken and had a catatonic look in her eyes. She seemed not to understand what anyone was saying to her. They were unsure how they would move her.

Leela looked at the hills looming above them. They would certainly be difficult to climb, but not impossible. They were covered in thick jungle and rose 300m from the beach. Jungle was no longer a threat to Leela, just another obstacle in a long line. She sat down next to the trembling girl and put an arm around her shoulders. She seemed not to notice. Leela began to hum a tune her mother would sing to her at night. She thought she felt the girl's shoulders relax a little. She continued humming the tune. Nimal skimmed up a tree and cut down a bunch of coconuts, with a knife that belonged to the boat captain. It had made it to shore strapped around the captain's waist with a leather belt. As the group feasted on the coconuts, murmurings turned into conversation. The group began to accept their survival. They had not drowned with the others, their lives had been spared, they had a purpose. Nimal approached Leela with a coconut. It was full of sweet, rich liquid and Nimal had cut a hole in the top. Leela drank, closing her eyes as the nectar ran down her throat, giving instant energy throughout her tired body. She couldn't remember when she had last eaten, and the boat's drinking water had run out a couple of days ago. She turned and put the coconut to the lips of the girl. Her lips did not move, but Leela poured anyway, soaking her mouth and chin. The girl quivered and Leela poured some more. This time the girl's tongue protruded from her mouth and she caught some drops. She tried to swallow but the dryness of her mouth made her throat constrict and she made a noise as if she was suffocating. Suddenly she grabbed the coconut from Leela's hands and glugged from it, without taking a breath. As she drank, tears flowed from her eyes, and she spluttered and choked as she tried to get the liquid down her throat, faster than her body could handle. Suddenly she vomited, kneeling over into the sand. Rocking backwards and forwards, she kept retching until all the liquid was out. Finally, she was quiet. She lifted her head and looked Leela in the eye. The look of fear had not left her, but she had come back to her body, from wherever she had fled.

Leela helped her up and took her towards the water. She rinsed the vomit off her face and clothes and returned her to the group. Each person picked up two coconuts and walked in a silent procession to where the trees met the sand. The only way was up.

They clambered around twisted roots and struggled through hanging vines. The brothers were carrying the stretcher. It was hard going and a couple of times they nearly dropped it when it got caught on spindly branches, that reached out and tried to grab their uninvited guests. The woman was groaning throughout the ordeal as fever took hold of her. Her husband walked silently alongside, clutching her hand. More light was filtering through the canopy by the afternoon, and Leela felt they were nearing the top. They stopped to share out some of the coconuts and give a rest to the three young men. They had been travelling with their mother. One brother had held on to her as they hit the water, but something had her trapped. He had pulled and wrenched at her clothing, but she would not budge. He had let go of her to reach the surface to get some air. When he had gone back down, he could no longer find her. He searched and searched but either she had been swept away, or he had been dragged too far from the spot, by the current. Either way, he had eventually given up hope and swam to shore. This brother was holding on to his guilt. He had not done enough to save his mother. It was his fault she had not survived. He did not need to rest; he said. He wanted to keep going, get the woman help before it was too late. He eventually got his way and the group moved on.

The sight of the bright, blue sky filled every heart with hope. The contrast dazzled them as they emerged from the thick forest. They had a panoramic view of the coastline and signs of the inhabitants of the island were clearly visible from where they stood. The journey was downhill from here and with renewed vigour they marched on.

As they approached civilization, Leela began to feel anxious. They needed food and water, but would they be welcomed? She had no idea what to expect and this terrified her. She knew some English, which she had learnt at school, but in her moment of need, she was worried she would forget it all. They were walking on a tarmac road now. They passed some sheds and a few barking dogs but still no sign of any people. Suddenly they all stopped. They heard a car engine approaching from behind and they swung around. A police car had pulled up and two policemen were getting out. A hand in Leela's back pushed her to the front of the group.

"Who are you?" said the first man.

"We… we… from Sri Lanka", stammered Leela. She could feel her legs shaking and she thought her knees would buckle.

"How did you get here?"

"Boat."

"Where is the boat?"

"Broken… finish."

"Where are the other people?"

"Dead. Sir, this Australia?"

The policeman laughed. "Yes, you have arrived in Australia."

The other man was speaking urgently into a radio. Within minutes an ambulance and a bus had arrived. They loaded the old woman and her husband into the ambulance, and the others were herded onto the bus. The young girl held Leela's hand. She didn't want to get onto the bus, and she tried to pull Leela away.

"You need to trust me Thangai, we are family now," she gently pulled her towards the bus and helped her on. She reminded Leela of a fawn, lost from its herd facing a leopard. Her scared eyes darted around her and she almost screamed when the policeman boarded the bus and sat in the seat across the aisle from her. Her fingers dug into Leela's hand, but she stared straight ahead, jaw quivering.

The bus journey was short. They drove through what seemed like the main street. There were a couple of shops, and a Post Office, and a few other buildings with no signs. They took a left off the main street and drove another couple of kilometres, the bus's brakes squealing as they stopped outside huge, locked gates with barbed wire in rolls around the top. A large building stood in front of them. It was yellow, with a flat roof and lots of windows. The driver spoke to a guard and the gates opened. The bus drove in and Leela watched the gates closing behind them, rubbing her chest where a big lump had formed. The bus stopped outside open double doors. They were ushered off and stood in a line. They neither spoke nor were spoken to. After a while, a woman came to the entrance of the building and beckoned them to follow her. They took the men down one corridor and the women down the other. Nimal looked over his shoulder, not taking his eyes off Leela until he disappeared around a corner.

The women entered a room. There was Leela, the young girl, the middle-aged woman and the mother and her baby.

The official woman, who showed them through, was dressed in a brown uniform. It reminded Leela of the uniform she had had to wear when she was in the camp. The woman introduced herself as Margi. She tried to take the young girl through to another room, but the girl fought like a cat, scratching Margi on the arm. Another woman, called Janet, replaced Margi, who went off to get medical treatment.

Leela intervened before any more harm could be done.

"She upset, I come too."

Janet agreed with a brisk nod and the two girls entered another room. They were told to take off their clothes and take a shower. They were given a pile of new clothes to put on. The pile consisted of two T-shirts, one pair of long trousers, one pair of shorts, a pair of rubber shoes and two pairs of underwear.

Janet watched the girls getting changed. She could see they were frightened. They stood close to each other as if covering each other's backs. The younger of the two girls had scars marking her body. Several looked like whip marks, while others could have been burns. She blinked away the water that was threatening to fill her eyes. Damn this menopause, she thought, when did she start getting emotional about their overseas guests? She had a job to do, feeling sorry for everyone she came across, was not useful.

Once dressed, she ushered them through to the medical examiner.

"This one's a wild one, Dr Jakes, Margi has had to go and sterilise the scratch she got from her."

"Ok, I'll approach gently," replied the doctor.

She got the two girls to sit on the bed. First, she checked their eyes and ears. Next, she listened to their heart rates and checked their blood pressure. They both seemed fighting fit, though substantially undernourished. She filled in their paperwork and handed them each a copy.

"Ok, follow Janet to the food hall. A good meal will make you feel better." She smiled kindly at them and Leela muttered a thank you as they trailed off after Janet. The noise of clattering and voices came at them down the corridor, as well as the smell of hot food. Leela's stomach began an angry grumble and she winced as it spasmed in expectation.

They stood in line with a plastic tray. Janet left them to process the rest of the women. The food hall was crammed full of people and the acoustics in the room made the noise overwhelming. Some faces Leela could recognize as Sri Lankan, others she wasn't sure.

Then she saw something that made her cry, and laugh out loud, at the same time. Her young friend turned to her with anguish. "What is it? What's the matter?" Leela couldn't speak, she just pointed. There was Rakesh, with a big, beaming smile directed at her.

She ran over to him and flung her arms around his neck. "I thought you were dead, what happened to you?"

She withdrew her arms almost immediately, a wave of embarrassment creeping over her as she realised everyone in the food hall had stopped eating and was staring at her. Rakesh had a lopsided grin on his face.

"Wow, you must have really missed me," he teased.

"Well, what do you expect? You're the only person I vaguely know in this whole country." Her voice had a slight tremor in it, and she blinked back her emotion.

"Hey, I'm just teasing you," Rakesh put his hand on hers. "I'm really pleased to see you too."

Leela pulled out a chair and sat down.

"Don't you want to get some food?" Rakesh asked.

"I've waited this long, I can wait a bit longer, so tell me what happened to you?"

"I got washed around the rocks into the next bay. I rested for the night and then made my way here in the morning."

"Did you see anyone else?"

"No one alive. There were five bodies washed up on the shore. How many came with you?"

"There was thirteen of us, so fourteen now, including you."

Leela turned around suddenly. Her young friend was standing behind her with a tray, carrying two plates and two mugs.

"I brought you some food," she said shyly.

"Oh thanks," said Leela, "Come and sit down. Rakesh, this is Anoula."

Anoula smiled nervously at Rakesh. "You were on the boat," she said, sitting down.

"Yes, I was," Rakesh replied.

They turned their attention to their food, each momentarily lost in thought.

Leela looked down at her plate, chicken sausages and salad. She picked gingerly at the salad, eating tiny mouthfuls of cucumber and tomato. Her stomach knotted. It was as if she had forgotten how to eat. She picked up the mug of hot, sweet tea, in both hands, and took a sip. Her body immediately responded. It gave her a buzz as the caffeine and sugar hit her bloodstream simultaneously, bringing life back to her exhausted body. Her fingertips and toes tingled, and her body gave an involuntary shiver.

"You ok?" asked Rakesh.

"I am now."

Anoula was gobbling her food, making little snuffling noises. Her head was down, almost in her plate, and she was shovelling the food from plate to mouth with her hand, as if someone was about to steal it from her. She finally looked up, when she'd taken her last mouthful, and saw Rakesh and Leela staring at her.

"What?"

"Oh, no, nothing," said Leela. She pushed her half-eaten plate over to her. "Do you want mine?"

"Why, don't you want it?"

"I've had enough, I don't want to vomit it all up again."

"Oh, ok, thanks." She began the snuffling noises again. Leela giggled. It reminded her of a rat rifling through kitchen scraps.

"Have they spoken to you yet?" asked Rakesh.

"No, not yet, they told us to eat first. What should we say?"

"Just tell them the truth. Tell them the rest of your family is in danger and you also want to get visas for them. Also tell them you're only fifteen. You're a minor. They will need to take that into account."

"And what will you tell them Rakesh?"

"I'll also tell them the truth. That I will be killed if I return."

Someone clapped their hands and the three looked up. Leela spotted Nimal from across the room and raised her hand to wave at him. He tried to smile back but there was fear written all over his face.

A large woman was standing at the doorway beckoning for the room to be silent.

"All those who arrived today, please follow me."

Rakesh stood up, followed by Leela and Anoula. Leela motioned to Nimal and he ran to join them. She glanced around the room and caught the eyes of the other stragglers, whom she now thought of as her family, and signed for them to stand up. Most of them didn't speak English and had no idea what the woman had said. Silently, the group left the room.

They walked down a long corridor and were shown into a room with plastic chairs. They were told to sit down and wait. The official woman left the room and closed the door. No-one spoke, they were all too afraid of what might be about to happen. It seemed like hours before the door opened again and two men walked in. The first man spoke and then stopped, as the second man translated what was being said into Tamil. You could feel the tension release as the group realised they would be able to understand what was happening. They were being taken one-by-one for an interview. They would need to tell their whole story, which would be recorded. Their stories would then need to be verified, before it could be assessed whether or not they would get visas to remain in Australia. They were not told how long this process might take.

The man told the mother and her baby to stand up. As she stood, Leela could see her body trembling beneath her clothes. She hugged her baby tight to her chest. She followed the men out the room and the door closed behind them. Silence descended on the huddled group once more.

24 Gotu Kola

Rakesh looked incredulously at the man seated opposite him. There were three other people in the room. A younger woman with a kind face, a man dressed in a security uniform, stood at the door, and another older woman seated to his right. They were all studying his face intently.

"Why won't you believe me?"

"Mr Cooray, there is nothing you have told us so far, that gives us any evidence that your life is threatened if you return to Sri Lanka. You are of Sinhalese origin. You are not being persecuted by your government, and we are not responsible for career decisions that you may have made along the way."

Rakesh put his head in his hands and heaved a sigh that caused his body to shudder. The young woman flinched and looked down at the floor.

He raised his head and faced the group again, "I will be killed if you deport me to Sri Lanka. I have evidence of corruption at the highest level of government and they know I will print the story. They will not allow that to happen."

"Mr Cooray, you are a journalist. This is your choice. If you want to print your story, go ahead, but you cannot expect our government to protect you if you want to play with fire."

Rakesh put his hand in his pocket and held tightly onto the plastic bag containing the pen drive.

"Well, I think enough has been said. We have only one course of action left to us. There is no option but to deport you. These are our guidelines and we must adhere to them." The man scraped his chair back and stood up. "I don't think we have anything else to discuss." He waited for his colleagues to follow his lead. As he reached the open door, he turned back to the condemned man. "Good-bye Mr Cooray."

Rakesh watched his last hope fade as they filed out the door. The young woman gave him a slight smile as she left, attempting to portray her condolences.

The guard led Rakesh out of the administration block into the bright sunshine where he was left alone. He lay on his back on the grass and stared at the bright, blue sky. Just a few wisps of stray cloud dotted here and there. There was no wind either, stillness all around him. He lay there until he couldn't take the glare from the sun any longer and moved into the shade. His head hurt and the crevices around his eyes were aching. Where was his back-up plan? He always had one. Except, this time, he was already using it and it wasn't working out as he had expected. He always knew if the heat got too much, he would have to skip the country. He had tried, and it seemed he had failed. They would send him back to face the music, but Rakesh already knew the tune that would play.

Jayasuriya was grumpy. His plans were not progressing fast enough for his liking. Doreen was annoying the hell out of him. What was wrong with that stupid woman? Why couldn't she just leave him alone to get on with things? She had already made him visit the temple that morning to give gifts to the monks, fine cloths and a tray of fruit. Why did they deserve anything from him? What did they actually do for him? She was obsessed with that temple, always giving away his money to them. She seemed to think that good karma would bring them results. Well, she was very wrong. The genius of his fine mind would reap them the rewards. Not that he wished to share any of his ill-gotten gains with her. No, this was his project and he would enjoy the fruits all by himself. His lunch was not settling well in his stomach. She had given him heartburn by nagging him all the way through his meal. She really was the most irritating person.

He shuffled to the window and looked out. He could see his wife crouching over the shrub bed weeding, her bulbous bottom sticking out at him like an insult. Maybe he should just bump her off and be done with it. Yes, what a good idea! Surely it wouldn't be that hard. He could do it with poison. Yes, he could cope with that. He couldn't do anything violent like strangle her with his bare hands. No, he was much too refined for that kind of coarse behaviour. A simple poisoning, quick and efficient.

He rubbed his tummy and his body expelled a long loud fart, causing a rush of intense satisfaction. His wife glanced behind her and he moved away from the window. He didn't want her to see him watching her. She might get the wrong idea. He sat down at his desk and switched on his computer. He typed in 'naturally occurring poisons' and settled into his new project with a contented smile across his face.

After several hours of research, Jayasuriya decided on his weapon. He changed out of his sarong, into trousers and a shirt, and called out to his wife that he was going out for a while.

"Don't be late home, we're going to Ammi's for dinner!" she screeched after him in a high-pitched decibel that hurt his ears.

He got into his tiny Fiat and pushed his seat further back to make way for his expanding belly, an accomplishment he was most proud of. He drove into Fort and parked his car as centrally as possible. He got out and surveyed the street ahead. He knew it was down one of these side roads in a small alley. He'd visited the old woman before when he was a young man suffering from issues of virility. She had given him a potion that made him hard for a week. Oh, how he had romped with the girls back then. He paid them, but they were so very appreciative, and a girl needs to eat.

He hoped she had not departed this world; she was an old, wizened woman with knobbly knuckles, even back then. Surely, she must have been making herself strong brews of 'forever young' potions to give her eternal life. He turned down the side street he thought he recognised and came upon a new office building. He was starting to worry now. Maybe they had bulldozed her crumbling shack to make way for new development. Who knows where she may be now? He circled the new building and crossed a bridge over the canal. It was somewhere around here.

A cough from behind him made him jump. He swung round and there she was. How had he missed her?

"You're looking for me."

It wasn't a question, it was a statement. This woman looked exactly the same as he remembered, the same wispy, grey hair hanging down around her face, like curtains, and what looked like the same stained, yellow sari.

"Yes, I am."

She turned on her heel and he followed her to the door of the same crumbling shack. It had a makeshift roof made from pieces of broken asbestos, a blue plastic tarp and some mouldy pieces of cardboard. She took a chair from inside and put it out on the pavement.

"Wait there," she said, through the gaps of her rotten teeth.

Jayasuriya wiped the chair clean with his hanky and sat down. There was a strong stench of sewers wafting down the canal and he tried to take shallower breaths so as not to inhale too much of the filthy air. After some time, the old woman poked her head out the door. "Come," she said.

Jayasuriya bent his head to get through the tiny opening. The room was dark and cramped. There were rows of bottles on the back wall and a stove and gas bottle in the corner.

"What do you want?"

He coughed to clear his throat. He had been practising wording this carefully, on the way there in the car.

"I would like 50mg of Cassava Cyanogenic Glucoside."

"Cyanide?"

He coughed again. "Um yes, that's right."

"Why?" The scrutiny in her eyes made him doubt himself for a moment. He wondered whether to just leave, quickly and quietly now, and abort this latest mission. A picture of his wife flashed into his mind. Her waggling finger pointed at him as she launched into another tirade of abuse designed to make him as insignificant as possible. No, the show must go on.

"It's the rats, in my house. I can't get rid of them. I've tried everything. They appear immune to the general household poisons. I need something stronger, that will definitely get rid of them altogether."

"You want to poison your rats? With cyanide?"

"Um, yes."

"That is very extreme!"

"Yes, I know. Like I said, they are over-running the house. I need to act now."

"Okay."

"Okay?"

She rummaged around on her shelf until she found what she was looking for. She handed him the small bottle. "One drop in food will be enough to kill a human. Be very careful with it."

"Yes, yes, I will, very careful."

He counted out some notes and placed them in her upturned palm. Her palm remained stationary, so he added a few more. After the third attempt, she closed her fingers around the notes and tucked them into her sari blouse, deep down into her leathery cleavage. Jayasuriya's shoulders jolted in disgust.

"Right then, I'll be off."

He tripped over in his haste to leave the cramped space and hit his head on the doorframe. The old woman watched him silently as he cursed and rubbed the bump that was forming on his forehead. Once out in the bright sunshine, Jayasuriya felt better. He walked back to the car with a swing in his step and even managed to whistle a tune. He didn't notice the old woman following him, some way behind. As he got into his car, she flagged down a passing tuk-tuk.

"Follow that car," she said as the little yellow fiat pulled out into the dense traffic.

Oh, how she remembered that smug fat face. It seemed like he had forgotten their last encounter otherwise she couldn't believe he would have ever come back. All her savings she had placed in his sweaty paw on the promise of getting her a visa to work abroad. He had flashed his ministry security pass at her and made her believe he had all the right connections. When she finally realised he wasn't coming back with her documents, she vowed that one day she would make sure he understood what it felt like to have his future snatched away. Her business had slowed down, as the market for potions was not as lucrative as it had been twenty years ago, so she felt like she had some spare time to accomplish her task. When she saw him standing in the street like the gormless oaf that he was, she rubbed her hands in glee. She didn't know it was going to be this easy.

Chris was amazed at how quickly Meena was learning English. They could now have long conversations, usually about the places Chris had travelled to. Meena lapped up the knowledge. Her eyes grew wide at stories of freezing temperatures and big cities where people danced all night long. She would beg him to take her one day, to see it for herself.

"You wouldn't like it, you would be too cold," he joked. "And you'd hate the food!"

"I wouldn't hate the food. I would try everything, and I would go everywhere and see everything."

Rushani laughed and stroked her daughter's wild curls away from her face.

"Maybe one day, my darling, you will be able to do everything and see everywhere."

Today they had planned a trip to the hill country. They would stay in a guesthouse overnight and then return home the next day. Rushani was packing a bag for herself and Meena when the tuk-tuk arrived. Meena ran out squealing and Rushani straightened up to see. She placed her hand under her now generous bump, as she felt a kick near her pelvis. It always made her smile when she saw Chris. He had brought so much to their lives. Her mother was still not happy with their arrangement, but she was holding her tongue more and more.

Chris swung Meena around in the air, dropping her to the ground when he caught sight of Rushani in the doorway. He went to help her with the bags. Her mother was lurking in the room behind. He smiled at her when he saw her.

"Good morning Ammi," he said. She nodded her head but didn't reply. It didn't sway Chris' good mood. He had childish anticipation for the weekend ahead and nothing was going to bring him down today. They loaded up the tuk-tuk and set off.

The journey was long and bumpy and after several hours Chris was beginning to wish he'd hired a decent vehicle, or they'd gone by bus. He wasn't sure though if he'd have been able to handle those windy roads the way the bus drivers took them. They had already met a couple of buses coming the other way, that had nearly run them off the road, down the cliff-side. He glanced down and saw the wreckage of a vehicle on the valley floor. Pulling his eyes up sharply, he increased his concentration.

Finally, they were there. The guesthouse was a bit shabby but had the most spectacular views of the waterfall below. Chris felt like he was on top of the world. They checked into their rooms. Chris had booked one double room for Meena and Rushani, and one single for himself. The hotel receptionist frowned when she saw Rushani's bump but held her tongue.

Chris' room had a double bed with a worn blue blanket covering it. There was an en-suite bathroom with brown patterned tiles and a pink toilet and sink. There was a shower in the corner, with no curtain and a fusty smell in the room, so Chris opened up all the windows. The view was breathtaking. The hills were covered in tea bushes, but to the right was a pine forest that made Chris feel like he was back home. He had a shower, and went down to the restaurant that also overlooked the valley. The restaurant was built out of the side of the hill, so it felt like they were suspended in mid-air. Chris hoped there had been some engineering intervention in the building plans. There were large, glass windows around the circular restaurant that would have once been a great attribute to the guesthouse, before years of grime built up, the only view now through the gaps in the smears.

Rushani and Meena were already seated at a table with a cherry-patterned tablecloth. Meena was excitedly swinging her legs and sucking on a bottle of lemonade through a straw.

"Did you order lunch?" Rushani asked him.

"I did, chicken curry, if I remember right."

The waitress came out of the kitchen and Chris asked her for a cold beer. "Shall I bring your lunch now too, Sir?"

"Yes, that would be great, thanks."

They sat in happy silence until the food was brought out. It smelt great. There was chicken curry, beetroot curry, gotu kola melung,[21] dhal and rice. The waitress kept glancing between Chris and Rushani and her bump. Eventually, she could stand it no longer.

"Gotu kola is very good for pregnancy," she said in Sinhala, nodding at Rushani's bump.

"Yes, I know."

Rushani kept her head down. She didn't want to engage with her.

Is that your husband?"

"No, he's not," Rushani replied.

"Then where is your husband?"

"He's dead."

"Who fathered your baby? Your husband or this man?"

---

[21] Gotu kola melung – green leaf, coconut, onion and spice

"It's none of your business."

"Are you taking money from him?"

Rushani stopped replying. How dare this woman think it was any of her business what was going on in Rushani's life. But it was like this in her own village, the incessant nosiness got her down, being judged all the time by her peers.

They began to eat their meal, and the waitress sloped off to the kitchen, no doubt to report back her findings to the rest of the staff. The food settled Rushani's belly after the travelling and she began to perk up a bit.

"Let's go for a walk after lunch," she said.

"Yes, that would be great if you're up to it"

"Yes, I am, I want to breathe in the mountain air."

They finished their meal with fruit salad and ice cream and set off for their walk. There was a fine mist around and Rushani lifted her face to catch the first spattering of rain.

"Shall we go back to the guesthouse?" Chris asked.

"No, I want to get wet. Let's dance in the rain!"

And so they did. As the heavens opened and the rains came down, the little group danced. They threw up their arms to the sky, they twirled, they squealed, and laughed. Their clothes were soaked, and their hair plastered to their faces. Their eyes twinkled, and their cheeks were flushed. Rushani couldn't remember when she last felt this good.

She closed her eyes and circled around again slowly, her arms sticking straight out to the sides, her face lifted to the sky. When she opened them again,

Chris was on one knee, holding up a little box towards her.

"Rushani will you marry me?" he said.

"What?" she called out.

She didn't know if the words coming from his mouth had been twisted by the wind and the rain, the letters falling, scattering on the ground and realigning into different words that were no longer true. She didn't know if her mind had taken her somewhere else, whether she was still spinning, and if this was all in her wildest dreams.

He said the words again. Meena had stopped dancing and was staring at them both.

"You want to marry me?" asked Rushani.

"Ammi, don't be dumb, that's what he said."

"Why?"

"Ammi!"

Rushani began to cry now, tears mingling with the raindrops running down both sides of her face.

Chris stood up and put his arms around her. They stayed like that for several minutes until her sobbing subsided.

She brought up her head and locked eyes with him. Snot was running from her nose and she was aware how unattractive she must look. She wiped it away with the back of her hand.

"Why you want to marry village girl with daughter and baby? You have any woman in the world."

"And I choose you... and Meena... and the baby."

Rushani felt a small hand slide into hers and she looked down at her daughter.

Meena spoke in English "Please Ammi. Can't we marry Uncle Chris?"

Rushani started laughing, and then she cried, and then she laughed some more.

"Yes, my precious child, we can marry Uncle Chris!"

They hugged, and they danced, until Rushani thought Meena might catch a chill, and they headed back to the guesthouse. Rushani and Chris held hands as they walked back up the hill. Rushani no longer cared who saw them. They got to their bedroom doors, side-by-side on the balcony. Rushani shooed Meena into their bedroom, to have a hot shower. Chris held Rushani's hands and gazed into her face. He inched forward and brought his lips to hers. A soft kiss that spoke of love and protection. The last thing Rushani saw, before she closed her eyes, and surrendered herself, was the shocked look on the face of the cleaner, as she hung onto her broom for support. Rushani allowed herself a secret smile.

25 Instant Coffee

Gaya's grief rose like a Gulf wind. A ball of flames twisted around her intestines, causing her to double up with the pain. She fell to her knees; her head up to the sky, as if in execution, opened her mouth and screamed.

The flight had landed at 13.30. Gaya had arrived at the airport at 12.25, bought herself a sugary, instant coffee and sat watching the arrivals hall with a pain in her stomach. As the minutes ticked by, her trepidation grew, until she saw the board flash LANDED and she allowed herself a flicker of excited anticipation. She watched as passengers filed out. Locals back from working overseas, laden down with their foreign tax-free purchases, tourists hounded by rows of taxi drivers eager to take them to the holiday of their dreams.

She had already bitten all the skin from around her fingernails and she examined them, wondering whether to start on the nails themselves. It was now 14.45. She knew the other passengers from his flight, were already on their way out, because she had checked their luggage tags. Where was he? Maybe they had stopped him at Immigration. It was what she feared most, that they would detain him, or even arrest him, and she wouldn't be able to see him straight away. She had tried to check that he was definitely on the flight, but they had told her they couldn't give out that information until the flight landed, due to security issues. She knew he was on the flight because he had called Niraj just before he boarded. She chewed her fingers a few minutes more, before getting up and walking to the desk again.

"Can you please check the passenger list for flight SL504? I'm looking for my friend, Mr Rakesh Cooray."

She gave what she hoped was an appreciative, coy smile. The man looked at her over the rim of his glasses and paused, wondering whether to aid this pretty damsel in distress. After huffing and puffing a few times, he readjusted his glasses and looked at his computer screen.

"No, he was not on the flight."

"He was definitely on the flight. Please look again."

"You can come around and look yourself. He's not on the list, which means he did not board the plane."

Gaya walked around the desk, her heart leaping around her chest like a panicked bullfrog. She bent down and studied the list. She checked the flight number again, then again scrolled down the list. His name was not there.

"There must be some mistake," she turned to face the man.

"There is no mistake. If his name is not on the list, he was not on the plane. I'm sorry madam, but I can't help you any further. Your friend did not arrive on this plane. Maybe he decided not to come."

Gaya studied the condescending look on his face. He thinks I've been stood up; she thought. Stupid, small-minded...Shit! What should she do? She called Niraj.

"Hi Niraj, it's me, did Rakesh call you again."

"No, why, isn't he there?"

"No, he isn't, and I've checked the passenger list for that flight, he's not on it."

"That's not right, something's not right Gaya."

"I know. If he didn't get on the plane then where is he?"

There was silence at the end of the phone. "Niraj, are you still there?"

"Yes, Gaya, I'm trying to think."

"Let me make some calls and I'll get back to you. You wait there for now."

Gaya hung up the phone and cursed under her breath. Where the fuck was he?

She continued to gaze at the sliding doors. Each time they opened, she prayed it would be Rakesh, but each time, her spirits sunk a little bit more as they confirmed what she knew in her heart of hearts. He was not going to walk through those doors.

The phone rang in her hand, making her jump. She answered it immediately. "Yes, Niraj, tell me."

"I've spoken to a contact I have at the airport. He said there were army officers at the airport today. They arrested somebody, but he doesn't know who. I'm going to try and find out what I can from the army. I think you should head back to Colombo. Go to Jenny's house and I'll call you there."

Gaya left the airport in a daze. She had felt sick since that morning and she realised she hadn't eaten anything. The heat and hustle and bustle outside the airport made her feel faint. She glimpsed her driver waving at her through the crowd and hurried towards the waiting car. She slumped into the back seat, grateful to depart from the new arrivals, pushing and shoving.

Jenny opened the door of her one-bedroom apartment. "Has Niraj called?" Gaya asked, as she stumbled through the door and flopped onto a cushion on the floor.

"Yes, he has Gaya, and it's not good news. There's nothing definite, but there are reports that someone was taken from the airport today, although the army deny any knowledge of it."

"What does that mean?"

Gaya stood up unsteadily and walked to the kitchen to pour herself a glass of water. She drank it in one gulp and stood holding on to the edge of the sink to support herself. Jenny stood in the doorway to the kitchen and when she didn't answer, Gaya turned around to face her.

"What does it mean, Jenny?" she asked again.

"It means that the army may have taken him, but they have covered it up."

"Why would they cover it up?" Gaya asked slowly, and painfully, even though she already knew the answer.

"Because they want him to disappear."

As the words came out of Jenny's mouth, Gaya fell to her knees. The scream was long and guttural and filled every corner of the tiny apartment. Jenny brought her hand to her mouth watching the purge of grief before her.

Leela was sitting on a plastic chair in the garden. She was staring at the barbed-wire fence that surrounded the compound. It was about fifteen feet high with rolls of barbed wire at the top. She wondered about the irony of everything she had been through, that had led her to this point. Detained for an indeterminate length of time. At least she wasn't dead. But she wasn't a criminal either, so why was she imprisoned? She thought that Australia was a country where people had rights, the land of the free. A place where you weren't persecuted for your race or religion. But now she realised that this was only once you had your golden ticket that said you were an Australian. Only Australians had rights. All other races, creeds and colours were criminals until you could prove otherwise. Wasn't that persecution? She had learnt a lot since being incarcerated. Her fellow inmates talked a lot about the United Nations and signing treaties, and the Refugee Convention. At first, she hadn't understood what they were saying; she hadn't known even where she was going when she first boarded the boat. She only knew she couldn't stay in Sri Lanka. Now it seemed there was a reason people were fleeing to Australia. The country had signed a treaty agreeing to take in refugees. They had promised to provide a sanctuary to those who were persecuted in their own countries, however they arrived. She had arrived by boat and she now understood that they considered this illegal entry. This was a concept that she couldn't fully understand. If Australia had agreed to help people, then why were they criminalising the very people they had promised to protect? She had met other inmates who had been there for years. They were pining for their families whom they had left behind. Some had even taken their own lives because the waiting had become unbearable. Lawyers were working tirelessly to speed up the process. They were throwing about phrases such as '... abuse of human rights.' Leela understood what unjust imprisonment felt like. This was nothing new to her. This had happened in her own country. This is what she was fleeing from. And here she was imprisoned for the second time in her young life. She was beginning to think there would be no way out of this particular prison. She gazed again at the barbed wire surrounding her. She missed Rakesh. He was her link to home. She wondered how he was, and where he was? Whether he had met with Suresh and given him her news? Part of her had been jealous when she heard he was being deported. She longed to see her family, even with the danger that this would impose. Would it be worth it to see them for just one day? Even if the very next day they found her and killed her. Maybe.

She remembered the look on Rakesh's face when he said good-bye. He looked drawn and the worry lines in his forehead were more pronounced. He tried to convince them his life was under threat, but they didn't believe him. 'How can a Sinhalese man be persecuted by a Sinhalese government?' they had asked him. They completed his paperwork, stamped him with return to sender and put a line under the case of Rakesh Cooray.

The government officials patted each other on the back over a shot of single malt at the end of their working day.

"Well, that was a job well done. Outrageous that a Sinhalese man would pass himself off as a Tamil refugee and try to trick his way in!"

"He didn't actually try to pretend he was Tamil though, did he?" offered a junior who was still trying to find her feet with her new job. Her question fell unanswered as the bottle made its way around the celebratory group.

"Back on a plane today. That's one less that we have to worry about. That's where you get job satisfaction, weeding out liars and cheats."

The junior sat quietly, nursing her whisky. She had been present in the interview with Rakesh and she was not in agreement with her peers. She thought him genuine. She knew the words of the Refugee Convention off by heart. 'No Contracting State shall expel... a refugee... where his life or freedom would be threatened on account of his... political opinion' (Article 33(1)).

This is exactly what they had done and as such could most definitely be charged with criminal acts in the United Nations Court of Human Rights, if they were ever to find out. She was a diligent employee, anxious to climb the rungs of her career ladder but she was also a woman with high moral values, a lobbyist for the weak and vulnerable. Her superiors had deemed Rakesh not vulnerable. She had got lost in his dark irises and the smooth, deep, velvety tone of his accented voice. She had believed him. They had not.

Zoe gurgled with delight as Marni tried to empty her mouth of the handful of sand she had just shoved into it.

"Do you have the letter? Can I see it?" Ali asked.

Marni wiped her hands on her dress and washed the remaining sand out with water. Zoe returned to her two coconut shells, scooping up more of the alluring sand in her tiny fingers.

"Yes, can you watch Zoe for me? I'll just get it."

She returned minutes later with the offending document and handed it to Ali. She gave him a few minutes to digest the contents. It was from the Land Commission in Colombo. It said that the permit for the land, on which the hotel stood was to be revoked, due to illegal building within the coastal conservation zone of fifty metres from the high-water mark.

"Can they do that?" she asked.

"I don't know. This would never happen on the South or West coast. There would be outrage. They are picking on us because we have no support. They think that we will just buckle under the threat of an official-looking letter. This is our home. We have rights to stay here. We will not accept this. We must fight."

Marni looked at the passion on Ali's face. His grandfather had been granted the permit for the land, which in turn had been passed to his father, and then to him. He had inherited a bare piece of land, stripped of all its flora. It was now a flourishing garden, protected by a wall of mangrove trees, which they had planted post-tsunami, to prepare for a second coming. The hotel, they had rebuilt, since losing it to the wave that nearly destroyed them. Now they were threatened by a human tsunami that wanted to take away everything they had worked for. Marni wondered why they had received this letter. Were they the only ones or was it happening up and down the country?

"Do you think it's personal?" she asked Ali.

"I don't know why. We don't bother anyone. We keep our heads down and mind our own business. Why would anyone want to destroy us?"

"What can we do Ali? It states we must vacate the premises 'forthwith'. Does that mean we have to leave right now? What will they do if we don't? How do we even know if the letter is real, maybe it's someone's idea of a sick joke?"

"I'll take it to the D.S.[22] office in the morning. They can check out its validity. We are not leaving though. There must be a law somewhere that protects us."

"Since when does the law protect people in this country?"

"You're right, unfortunately." Ali got up to leave, brushing the sand from his trousers. "I'll let you know what they say."

"Okay, thank you, Ali."

He stopped, watching her help Zoe arrange the shells that she had collected while they spoke.

"Don't look so sad, Marni. We've survived bigger threats than this," he said, smiling.

As he turned his back to leave, the smile dropped from his face, replaced by a worried frown and a rigid set of his jaw. He marched away from the hotel with grim determination, jumped on his bike and

[22] D.S. – Divisional Secretariat (local government office)

revved it furiously, before zooming off towards town.

Marni heard the bike leave. She knew how worried Ali was. She felt it too. It might be impossible to fight something like this. If the people in power wanted to take them down, then how could they stop them? She took Zoe's hand and led her off the beach into the hotel. The business was only really breaking even. For as long as the war raged on, tourism in the East would remain as a trickle, and who knew how long the war would go on for. Financially, there would be a loss for her, but it was only money. For Ali, it was different. This land had been in his family for three generations. How could the government just take it away on a whim? It was home and livelihood to all the staff, and it had become home to their residents too.

She sat down next to Claudette, who was sunbathing on a plantation chair, her legs akimbo. Marni sat in the eaves of the restaurant, pulling her legs in from the direct glare of the sun. The two women had never talked about what had happened between Claudette and Jake in the sea that night, and Marni doubted if they ever would. Marni didn't care. Claudette was a complicated creature, and Marni believed her methods were borne out of pain. On the other hand, she had shown more guts and fearlessness that night than most people would ever be capable of. At some point, Marni would get around to talking to Jake.

"Marni darling, would you hand me my water bottle?"

Marni passed her the water and studied the horizon.

"Claudette, do you think you're going to leave here soon?"

"Trying to get rid of me are you, darling?"

"No, I just wondered what your plans were?"

"I don't know. Sometimes I think 'get me out of here!' Other times I'm happy to stay a little bit longer. What about yourself, little bird? How long do you plan to keep your family here?"

Marni wondered whether it was a dig at her for seeming to make all the decisions. Jake made the decisions too. Didn't he?

"I don't know Claudette. I don't know where I would be happier."

"It's not just about you though, is it, darling? Where will your family be happier? That's what you should be thinking."

Marni decided not to respond, mainly because she didn't know what to say. Claudette was right, of course, which annoyed her. Jake hadn't pushed her since that night. They had become closer. She had allowed him to give her the comfort she needed, as she grieved for her father. She was forced to let go of the image of Pravish she had created for herself and face the reality of who he was and what he had chosen to do with his life. It felt good to be supported by Jake, to let her vulnerable side show without trying to excuse it. Jake had responded to his new role well, taking on more responsibilities in the day-to-day running of the guest house, and giving her time and space that she needed, to process the events of that night. But nothing had changed really, for Jake. He still didn't want to be here. She knew that. He had just stopped saying it. If they lost the hotel, it would probably be a blessing for her marriage.

26 Tea and Love Cake

The rains had arrived two weeks earlier. There had been almost no reprieve. Farmland and crops were washed away, and the opening in the lagoon had turned the sea to thick brown sludge.

Rushani, however, had not noticed the rain. She was busy making the preparations for her wedding. They had decided not to wait, anxious to touch each other in the privacy and protection of a marital home. No more judgement or prying eyes. They wanted to revel in the feelings that had silently manifested between them. Rushani had not experienced this before. She had respected her first husband. He was a kind, honest man, but she didn't feel the same hunger that she had for Chris. She wanted to be with him all the time. She missed him terribly when he was not there, especially through the nights. He had returned to the North, a few days before, to collect the rest of his belongings, and she longed for his return to soak up more of his affection. He had closed off his project and picked up short-term consultation work for INR. He wasn't sure how long he could count on this coming in though, as aid money was drying up, and smaller organizations had already packed up and gone home. For now, he had savings, and they would worry about the future later.

Rushani unwrapped her wedding sari. It was exquisite. There were sparkling glass diamonds sewn into the silk and swirling patterns of browns and golds. There was fine gold embroidery throughout the cloth. She had a ring for her nose attached to a delicate chain that outlined her cheekbone and attached to her earring. She received in the post a gold hairpiece she had ordered from India. Chris had shown her how to search for whatever she wanted on the internet and she'd spent hours scrolling through the hundreds of pages of bridal wear. Ammi had complained that she should not be ordering all these things. That she would be a goat trying to look like a princess. Her mother did not really think that Rushani looked like a goat, but she was referring to her pregnant belly, and how it would look if she were to be all dressed up like a Bollywood movie star.

Rushani hushed her concerns with the notion that soon her disappointment of a daughter would be the lawful wife of a foreigner, and her baby would have a father. Chris was planning on adopting the baby as soon as it was born, along with Meena for whom they had already put the paperwork in motion.

Meena was over the moon. She adored Chris for making her mother's face light up in a way she had never seen before. The great sadness that had followed Rushani wherever she went seemed to have lifted, and the three of them had an impenetrable cloak of joy surrounding them that touched others they met. The village gossips had even started to back off, their snide remarks replaced with words of congratulations and enquiries whether Chris would be buying any land in their village, and what kind of house he would build. They were moving in to get a piece of the action, feeding off the happiness of Rushani, wondering how her good fortune could benefit them. The head of the village had shaken Chris by the hand and welcomed him into their community, mentioning that their central roundabout with the large statue of Lord Buddha needed some renovations.

The wedding was to take place at the hotel. Marni was preparing the decorations, sari material draped across the roof and a huge archway woven out of fresh palm fronds under which the couple would say their vows. It was to be an evening wedding, the main ceremony out on the beach just before sunset, followed by a dinner party in the restaurant. Rushani smiled to herself as she thought of how Chris had been brought to her, to show her the magic of the world. She could never have imagined before the possibilities that were now in her reach.

She wrapped up the sari carefully and put it in a plastic box with a lid. She didn't want the squirrels and mice getting to it and using her precious silk as padding for their nests. She laid some bricks on top of the box for good measure and finished getting ready for work. Meena was just waking up, and she dropped a kiss on her forehead. Chris had suggested that Rushani leave work, so she could have more time for Meena, the wedding preparations, and to get some rest. She refused, saying that she enjoyed her work and when the baby came, she would be forced to stop, so she wanted to continue while she could. Chris let the matter drop. He would never think that he knew better than she, in matters of her own body.

Rushani was, however, deciding to stay at work mainly due to survival skills she had honed through the course of her bumpy life. There was part of her that was holding back, that was still not sure if fairy tales were true, a part of her she could keep as a back-up plan if everything fell through. She had learnt not to rely on others, and it was not something she could just let go of that easily.

She opened her umbrella and hurried out to the bus stop. There were rivers running down the side of the road and huge puddles that filled the holes in the broken tarmac. The bus soaked her from the knees down when it pulled in to let her on. With the doors closed, the air on the bus was thick with humidity, and steam was radiating off the clothes of her fellow passengers. The bus was already full, and she held onto the seat rail as it lurched off. A man kept glancing at her. She thought his face looked familiar, but she kept her eyes averted whenever he looked, to avoid any kind of misunderstanding that he held her interest. The bus stopped outside the guesthouse and both the man and Rushani pushed their way to the front to get off. Once outside, Rushani braced herself against the rain, fighting with her umbrella to get it open before she got drenched. She was still struggling when a hand appeared on her umbrella and took it from her.

"Let me help you," the man said in Sinhala.

The umbrella sprang to life, and he handed it back to her.

"Thank you," Rushani said. The good look she had got of the man's face when he had taken her umbrella, confirmed to her that she had met this man before, but she still could not place him.

"I'm late for work. I'd better hurry," she said walking away.

The man watched her scuttle across the road and down a path before crossing over himself and following her.

———————————⬤ ● ◗————————

There was still no word from Rakesh. Gaya decided to return to the East and wait for news there. She had done all she could in Colombo. Jenny and Niraj had called every contact they had, to try and find out more information, but it was a dead-end every time. They knew he had definitely left Australia. They had his name on that passenger list. However, the plane had landed in Singapore where he boarded another flight to Colombo. This is where the trail went cold. The airline which was Sri Lankan continued to protest that he had not boarded the plane. There was nowhere else he could have gone. He only had a temporary travel permit to get from Australia back to Sri Lanka. He could not have got through Singapore immigration, so was he still in Singapore airport? It was a big airport, but still. She said goodbye to Jenny, and her parents, and caught the night bus back to the place she now thought of as home.

Her anxiety was relieved momentarily when she woke up to smell the salt in the air and knew they were nearing the coast. She would feel better when she got to the Moon Rise. She would continue the search with Niraj, hopefully he already had news for her. The bus pulled up at the bus station, and she jumped in a tuk-tuk to take her the rest of the way. Dawn was breaking, and the sea looked spectacular, the sun rising into a cloudless sky. She was glad of these moments, to break through her haze, and remind her that the world was still beautiful.

The tuk-tuk turned down the rocky path towards the sea and hooted at some pedestrians to move out the way. The first was a man Gaya didn't recognize, but then she saw Rushani and called out to her.

"You can let me out here," she said to the driver.

She dragged out her suitcase and turned to give Rushani a hug.

"Don't look now Miss Gaya, but I think that man is following me," Rushani whispered, close to her ear.

The tuk-tuk squealed around in a tight circle and sped off back up the path. Gaya glanced up at the man. He had indeed stopped and was tying his shoelaces.

"Can I help you?" called out Gaya

"No, don't," Rushani said quietly, pulling on Gaya's sleeve.

The man stood up and walked towards them.

"Please let me introduce myself. My name is Ranjit Fonseka. We met before when my company was assigned to patrol the hotel on the day that Mr Jayasuriya visited." He turned to face Rushani directly. "We spoke briefly, you were upset. I wondered whether we might speak in private."

Rushani now recognized the soldier who had been kind to her, the day she realized she was pregnant. But what could he want now? Was he expecting her to pay her dues?

"Um, I don't think so."

"It's important, please."

Gaya interrupted. "Would it be possible to say what you have to say to me?"

"It's a very discreet matter, Madam."

"Yes? Well, luckily I'm very discreet. Please follow me."

Gaya wheeled her suitcase through the gates, followed closely by Rushani, and then the man. Niraj was sitting on the veranda outside their office. He jumped up when he saw her.

"Gaya, welcome home." He took her bag and she slumped into a chair.

"Any news?"

"Not since last night."

Niraj turned his attention to Rushani and the man standing behind her.

"Niraj, this is Ranjit Fonseka, he is a soldier in the Eastern Division of the Special Forces Unit, and he has something to tell us."

Ranjit was looking nervous, with so many people now involved.

"It's a very discreet matter, Sir, I'm not sure who I should talk to."

"Don't worry Ranjit, you're safe with us. I think we'd all better go inside the office."

They all took a chair, and everyone looked expectantly at Ranjit.

He cleared his throat. "I think there are plans being made, big plans, and I've come to warn you."

"What plans, what do you mean?" asked Niraj.

"I've seen the faxes. I know it's not legal."

"Go on," urged Gaya.

"The eviction, it's not legal. They can't revoke the permit on this land. It's being pushed through by a minister in the government, and if this person pays the right price, then they will have the muscle to enforce it."

"Which minister?"

"Jayasuriya."

Gaya gasped, "So it is personal, it's revenge!"

"Why are you telling us?" asked Niraj.

"Because it's not right, my family also have beach land. If they can do it to you, then they'll be able to do it to anyone."

"What do you want from us?"

"I don't want anything from you. I just want to stop them."

Niraj contemplated the man before him. He was not used to people putting themselves on the line, for no reward. It was refreshing, but he still felt suspicious.

"Well, what do you think our options are?"

"When they come to evict you, and present you with the documentation, rip it up. I believe they have forged the papers. You must stand your ground."

Niraj picked up the phone to call Ali.

"He's on his way," he said putting down the phone.

"I need to go," said Ranjit standing up. "I've already said too much, and now you must do what you can. The eviction is planned for Saturday."

"But that's my wedding day!" blurted out Rushani.

"I'm very sorry, Madam. It is because of you that I came here today. You looked so sad that day we met, and you reminded me so much of my sister. You will lose your livelihood if they have their way, and I couldn't let that be on my conscience. I'm sorry, I have to go."

Ranjit opened the door and was gone.

Gaya, Niraj and Rushani looked at each other in shock.

"Wow, this country never ceases to amaze me," said Niraj. "I actually think he may be telling the truth."

Gaya put her arm around Rushani. "You will have the wedding of your dreams, don't worry about that."

Gaya and Niraj locked eyes over Rushani's bent head. This was going to be a tough battle to win.

Ali arrived moments later and Rushani ran to find Marni. Niraj filled them both in on the events. Ali had been to the D.S. office that morning, and the local police, but this was a matter they had not been privy to. The letter appeared official and was a directive coming from Colombo. This was not their jurisdiction. They were powerless to do anything if it involved the army.

Ali and Marni left to discuss their options further, leaving Gaya and Niraj alone in the office.

They sat there in silence until Rushani broke their thoughts with a tray of tea and love cake.

"Thank you, Rushani, just what we needed."

Gaya helped herself to a piece of the rich fruitcake and waited until Rushani closed the door behind her before she spoke again.

"What do you think has happened to him?"

"I don't know Gaya. There's no point speculating. We just have to keep looking."

"But wouldn't he have contacted you by now if he could?"

"Not necessarily. He may assume our phones are bugged and not try to contact us."

"But if it wasn't Rakesh who was arrested at the airport, then who was it?"

"We don't know for sure they arrested anyone. It's only the word of one person. Everyone else has denied it."

"But that one person is a good source. You said it yourself. They're reliable."

"Yes, in the past, but people don't always follow the same pattern of behaviour. There are many reasons why this man's loyalty may change."

"So basically, we don't know, and we might never know?"

"Gaya, Rakesh was playing a dangerous game that he believed in enough to risk his life. I hope and pray that he is ok but no, I don't know, and no, we might never know. There are thousands of people missing in Sri Lanka. The families of all those people will probably never know the fate of their loved ones. We will do what we can do, but unfortunately, it may not be enough to uncover the truth."

Gaya looked so downcast that Niraj worried he had said too much. He sat down next to her and placed a hand on her arm. "I'm sorry Gaya, I know what your feelings for Rakesh are, and if I could make it any better for you, I would."

Gaya looked up at him and smiled. "Thank you, Niraj, I know you're doing everything you can. He is your friend too, and you must also be missing him. I just can't bear the powerlessness I feel. That he may or may not be out there somewhere, and there's nothing I can do but wait."

"I can put your waiting to good use. There's a whole heap of work to get on with, many people who need our help. So, go jump in the sea, have a shower, eat, do whatever you need to do and return to me presentable, sparkly, ready and willing for work."

Gaya laughed and stood up, "Well how can a girl say no! I'll be back in five."

Niraj walked back into the office and sat down at his desk. He sighed heavily. He was desperate to find out where Rakesh was and seeing Gaya's pain made it all the harder. If only she had looked at him the way she had looked at Rakesh, when she had first laid eyes on him. But Niraj knew it was not meant to be, and he could accept it. Animal attraction could not be forced. It was simply there, or it was not. How he wished she had felt it too.

27 Egg Hoppers and Katta Sambol

They gave Leela the good news that morning. She was told they had received information back from the Police Commission in Sri Lanka, confirming her identity, that she did not possess a criminal record or had any known links to terrorism. Leela heaved a huge sigh of relief that her kidnapping and short but eventful time in the jungle, had not borne ill effect on this stage of the proceedings. She was also told there was a strong possibility that she could apply for visas for the rest of her family, as she was a minor.

She had kept the kidnapping a secret from the Australian authorities on the advice of Rakesh. He had told her that they would be suspicious if she told them she had spent any time in a terrorist camp. He urged her, however, to make her case strong, that she needed protection, and that her life was under threat. She told them that she had received threats and had run away before anything had happened. They seemed to believe her on the basis that she was a young girl, so unlikely to leave the bosom of her family unless there was a real threat to her life.

Anoula was not having the same level of fortune, bad luck had snapped at her heels for as long as she could remember so she was not particularly affronted by this turn of events. She was first prostituted by her mother at the age of five and forced to learn the ropes of her new career swiftly. Her life had run along a rocky crevice of abuse, violence, sometimes even torture until she had ended up in the lap of a rich trader who took her as his whore and general housekeeper in Colombo. He was cruel and used his hand in most dealings he had with her. The sex was violent, and she often wondered if she would make it through till morning.

Slowly, she pocketed away cash until she saw her opportunity. One morning he sent her on an errand, to pay the balance due to a building contractor working on his holiday house in the mountains. She had taken with her the one treasured item in her possession: a postcard sent to him from a colleague. On the front, was a black-and-white photo of a young girl in old-fashioned clothes and pigtails, sticking out her tongue. He had glanced at it, then thrown it in the bin, useless to him. She had seen it when she was taking out the rubbish later that day. The child reminded Anoula of herself. There she was, the five-year-old girl who hadn't died when her body was sold to a travelling salesman. The girl who stuck her tongue out at the world and all its ugliness, had found her own way to be free.

Her employer was in no doubt that he had sufficiently broken her spirit enough, that she would not take advantage of him, and had not thought twice about entrusting her with a large sum of cash. She had immediately boarded a train to the coast and was never seen by him again. His next housekeeper bore the brunt of her betrayal until she took her own life on the same train tracks that had carried Anoula to freedom.

Anoula's police record had come back blemished, and the jury was out on whether they would grant her a visa to stay. Usually, they would immediately reject an application for asylum if there was a criminal record, but they had agreed time was needed for contemplation in this case due to the extenuating circumstances that Anoula was still only thirteen.

Leela only saw Nimal occasionally, as they were separated into different buildings from the men. She had requested he be placed with her, but the authorities decided to put him under the care of the brothers. Nimal seemed happy with this, and the three brothers become four.

Leela was glad about the division. She and Anoula were the only unmarried women in the centre, and they stood out like beacons amidst the large group of single men, some of whom scared her when they looked at her. She was happy when they were accommodated in the family section, which meant that at least in one area of their lives they were safe.

There were meetings with lawyers and government officials, which Leela found hard to follow, but mainly they just waited. The girls filled their time with looking after the children in the compound and telling each other made-up stories every night before they turned out the lights. They rarely spoke about their past to each other.

The atmosphere in the house was toxic. Jayasuriya knew today would be the day. He had only slight remorse for the fact that he had known his wife for a good number of years, and apart from her, he wasn't sure that he actually had any other friends.

He consoled himself with thoughts of his harem of dancing girls as he wriggled his yellowing toenails into his threadbare slippers and padded downstairs.

His wife had manifested one of her super tantrums already that morning, storming downstairs after throwing a teacup at his head. Luckily, due to her very bad shot, it had bounced off the wall and landed noisily on the floor. He had forgotten to turn up to an awards dinner at her old school the previous night where his wife was expecting a good turnout of Colombo socialites. She wanted to show off her politician husband to all who thought she'd sold out for a no-hoper. She had remained well and truly on the shelf for a good number of years, and it was widely believed she had rushed into marriage with an eejit at the first opportunity.

In his absence, she wove stories of very important political work that had waylaid him, and ultimately, she was relieved that he wasn't there to say something incredibly stupid and undo all of her creative handy work.

This didn't mean however that he was off the hook. He was a lazy fool and she was going to let him know just how much she despised him.

"You're an embarrassment to me!"

She was still screaming as Jayasuriya sat down to his breakfast: a favourite of his, egg hoppers and katta sambol; fried eggs cooked in a crispy bowl-shaped pancake with a hot onion sambol.

"Please woman, I don't have the stomach for this nonsense this morning."

"You don't have the stomach? You don't have the stomach? You have enough stomach for ten buffalos, and a herd of elephants!"

She wasn't far off a rhino or two herself thought Jayasuriya. Heaven knows what the funeral cost will be to heave her cumbersome body into a box and take it away.

Anyhow, he had big plans for the day, and he needed to focus his mind. He tuned out of the stream of verbal abuse and ran through his checklist. After dealing with the messy business of putting Doreen out of her misery, he would jump in the car and head out East. He didn't really want to be around when the domestic found her body anyway. It would all be very tiresome dealing with the practicalities.

His project in the East was costing him a lot more than he expected, which he found highly irritating after going to all that trouble to get an officially stamped letter. He had faxed it through to the Special Forces Eastern Division with a letter requesting back-up for the forthcoming eviction. The letter had gone through to the office as the Deputy Commander sat picking his nose wondering how he was going to trump up for the lavish wedding his wife was planning for the oldest of his four daughters.

He took the letter from the fax machine and read through it. Being that the Minister for Rural Affairs was his second cousin and karaoke partner, he picked up the phone for a chat.

"So, I see the state has actually decided to go through with these forced evictions?"

"Um yes, uh what, evictions?" The Minister for Rural Affairs was a little preoccupied by a window cleaner wobbling precariously on the window ledge outside his office.

"Oh, um nothing, I just thought I heard rumours that maybe we were evicting beach land that didn't have their papers in order." A seed was forming in the Deputy Commander's mind.

"Oh no, we've put that on hold. Too messy, will put the voters off. Anyway, we really don't want the UN to get involved and start throwing about accusations of human rights violations."

"No, no of course not, well I'm planning to be in Colombo next week, better start getting those vocal cords warmed up!"

"Sure, sure, look forward to it."

The Deputy Commander put the phone down and looked at the letter again. It stated that the Department would send Minister Jayasuriya to carry out the eviction.

"Up to some dirty tricks are you Jayasuriya?" he said out loud. Then picked up his mobile to call the number on the letter.

Jayasuriya listened carefully to the terms of the Deputy Commander. He was devastated to be caught out so soon, but the Deputy had a plan that would see both of them benefit. The Commander-in-Chief would be away from the division Friday to Sunday, so they planned the eviction for Saturday. In return for the Deputy turning up with twenty men, and possibly a bulldozer, Jayasuriya would pay him the handsome sum of Rs 500,000 for his trouble. They would evict the permit holders and Jayasuriya would get the permit written in his name, by an Uncle of the Deputy's at the land registry, for another Rs 500,000.

It was this conversation that Ranjit Fonseka was privy to as he passed by the Deputy's door that afternoon. He paused outside, listening to the information. When the Deputy left the room with the newspaper for his clockwork toilet break, Ranjit slipped in and rummaged through his desk until he found the paper he was looking for. "Jayasuriya," he muttered under his breath.

So, as it was, Jayasuriya would be Rs 1,000,000 worse off, but his plan was still on track. He had withdrawn the Rs 500,000 from his wife's bank account the day before. It was money she had inherited from her dead aunt's estate. She wouldn't be checking her bank statements anymore anyway. He packed a bag with a couple of sarongs, beach shorts, three books, from his overly stocked dusty library, and a bottle of aftershave. "What more do I need?" he chuckled to himself and hid the bag in the boot of his car.

So, there he was on that Friday morning, still eating his egg hoppers and katta sambol, his wife still raging on, when the doorbell rang.

His wife answered the door. He could hear the pitch of her voice through the walls, still shrieking incessantly. She slammed back into the dining room.

"There's a woman at the door, she wants you. You've promised her something, apparently. I told her there's fat chance of you keeping your promises, but she's insistent she sees you, and says she's not leaving till she does, so get your fat lazy arse to the door and see what she wants."

Jayasuriya looked at his half-eaten breakfast and sighed heavily. He got up, shuffling his feet over to the sink, and washed the food off his hand. 'Soon' he said to himself, 'Soon'.

He walked down the hall to his front door and pulled it open. There, sitting on his porch, was the old woman from whom he had bought the poison.

"Um yes, what do you want?"

"Well, that's an interesting question. That all depends on what you want."

"I don't have time to talk in riddles woman. What are you doing here?"

"I came to see evidence of your rats, but I think I just saw all I needed. There are no rats are there? It's your wife you're planning on killing, not that I blame you, having met her. However, I am not in the business of murder, so I would like my potion back and some money for my trouble or I may have to tell your wife of your plans."

"Seriously! You're blackmailing me? Why would she believe a crazy old woman?"

"And you're so sure she won't?"

After pondering on this for a moment, Jayasuriya realized that there was no doubt that his wife would believe this crazy old woman over him, and quickly recovered himself to come up with Plan B.

"So, tell me, if you were so sure I wasn't poisoning rats, why did you sell me the poison in the first place? Just so you could blackmail me?"

The woman looked taken aback. Suddenly she started screaming, pulling at her hair, jumping around as if stung by bees, howling and wailing. His wife came running to the door.

"What the hell is going on?"

Jayasuriya was staring at the woman in horror. Doreen poked him in the ribs.

"What's going on you stupid clut? What's wrong with this woman?"

"I don't know she just started screaming."

"Let's get her inside before we have half the neighbours coming outside to watch."

Jayasuriya and Doreen managed to guide the old woman inside. She was still wailing and moaning, but the jumping around had subsided.

Doreen made her a cup of tea. She drank it down with loud slurping noises.

"Can you tell me what happened?" Doreen asked.

The old woman's voice came out in a croaky whisper. "I'm not well Madam, your husband promised me some money to help pay for medicine. I am homeless, he walks by my cardboard box every day on the way to work. He is a very important man, and I know he is so busy, and I am just one very small insignificant person, but he said I should come to his home one day and he will give me some money and a meal."

Doreen looked a bit doubtful that Jayasuriya would have ever offered a beggar anything, but she continued listening.

"I have travelled all the way here by bus, and I am very frail, and I was just so disappointed when your husband said he couldn't help me after all."

Both women looked up at Jayasuriya. His wife looking both confused and annoyed, the old woman with a mocking smile plastered across her bony skull.

"It's not that I said I wouldn't help you…" He started.

"Oh! You're just useless!" said his wife.

She helped the old woman to her feet, and into the kitchen where she asked the cook to look after her and give her a meal. She returned to the dining room.

"And as for you, what are you doing giving beggars our address?" she hissed. Slightly louder she added, "If you promise help to someone then it is your duty to see it through. As a minister, it is an honour to serve the people of your country."

In the kitchen, the cook clucked and raised her eyebrows, and the old woman let out a croaky chuckle.

———————————— ● ◄————————————

Eva and Jo stood on the beach gazing at the ocean one last time. Marni came to join them with her camera slung around her neck. She pointed it towards them and clicked, making sure she had the hotel sign behind them.

"I'll email it to you."

"Thanks, Marni," said Eva, giving her a hug, "Thanks for everything."

"It's me who should be thanking you. It's amazing what you're doing for Suresh."

Suresh had received updates from Leela, but they were sporadic, and he was worried about her. With the deportation of Rakesh and his subsequent disappearance, Suresh's fears had heightened, and he had asked Eva and Jo for their advice.

After a long walk along the beach, and a conversation that went on way into the night, Eva and Jo decided they would fly back to Australia and try to help Leela from there. Their six-month visa was due for renewal and they were missing their children immensely. They were unhappy that they had to leave before Rushani's wedding, but Leela needed them more, and Rushani had told them they must go. They told Suresh the next morning, who hugged them with tears in his eyes.

"Thank you, thank you," was all he could manage to say.

"I don't know how much we will be able to do," Eva had warned, "but at least we can visit her and make sure she is being treated right."

They had told Marni later that day. She too had been emotional, telling them how much it would have meant to her father that someone else was going to look out for Leela now.

They packed up the room that had been home to them for the last six months and went to say goodbye to the staff who had cared for them so well. They left money in their palms as they shook their hands good-bye. First Aruna, then Suresh, and then Rushani who they handed a wrapped-up package as well. 'For your wedding day,' they had said before climbing into Muzil's waiting tuk-tuk. Ali arrived on his motorbike and wished them all the best with their trip. Marni hugged them both and thanked them again for their kindness. The tuk-tuk started up with a loud chug and they were off. Jo took Eva's hand and squeezed it.

"I don't think we'll find a place like that ever again," he said. Eva shook her head as she watched the Moon Rise Hotel disappear from sight.

28 Herbal Medicine

This was not how Jayasuriya had planned today. What was that crazy bitch doing here? He didn't want to pay her. He was shelling out too much money already, and what was he paying her for anyway? He wasn't even going to be able to use the poison. No, he definitely wasn't going to pay her. She could pull all the crazy stunts she liked, but she wasn't going to break his resolve. He left the house with the driver to fill the car with petrol and check the tyres and brakes. It was a long bumpy road out East and they didn't want to have any mishaps along the way. Jayasuriya couldn't stay in the house any longer. He had to get out and clear his head. What was he to do with the old woman? Bump her off too? Then he would have to dispose of the body. He couldn't have two dead women dying of a heart attack in his house on the same day. That would just be too suspicious.

The petrol station was busy. Everyone filling up for weekend trips out of Colombo. Jayasuriya decided he was just going to have to give the poison back. Then there was no evidence anyway. No poison and no dead body. He could wipe the vial clean of his fingerprints and then he would be off the hook. It thwarted his plans quite considerably, but he could always knock off this inconvenience at a later date. Yes, he would give the woman back her stupid vial, tell her where to go with her blackmail, and be off on his journey East with no more ado.

The house was quiet when he returned. He turned his key in the lock, and a rancid smell hit his nostrils as the door opened.

"What the hell!"

He followed the offensive odour to the kitchen and found their cook with a peg on her nose stirring a large pot.

"What the hell are you doing?" he shouted.

"Don't blame me, sir, I would rather not be doing this either," she barked at him with nasal undertones. "It is our new friend. She convinced Madam Doreen that this herbal medicine would lift your mood and give you a new lease of life."

Oh shit, he thought, that bloody woman is trying to poison me now.

"Where have they gone?"

"Madam Doreen has taken her shopping for some new clothes."

Jayasuriya hurried upstairs to shower and change. He would leave now, get away before they tried to stop him. He took the cash out of his sock drawer and placed it in a leather satchel, the poison he wrapped in a sock, and placed in there too. He hurried in and out of the shower and down to the car. His driver was taking a nap in the back seat and he pushed him roughly causing him to roll onto the floor.

"Hurry up man, we're leaving now."

But it was too late. A taxi pulled in and his wife got out along with the amused wicked imp by her side. His wife, however, had her face set rigid in a scowl.

"Where are you going?" She demanded.

"Don't you remember? I have been called to the East to assist with the eviction of some foreigners from a hotel. You know, the one I visited before."

"Ah, yes, the hotel of disrepute. And would you like to explain to me why, when I used my bank card just now, it was rejected?"

"Well, how should I know? Must be some computer error or maybe the card's scratched or something."

"Yes, that's what I thought, that's why I called the bank who told me that the account was cleaned out yesterday. WHERE IS MY MONEY?"

Jayasuriya, as he was not sure what else to do, jumped into the car, slammed the door and yelled "Step on it!" to his startled driver. His driver, who had the engine running and was still slightly asleep, slammed his foot on the accelerator and off they hurtled through the gates and onto the street. His wife, having had to jump out of the way, stared in amazement at the rapidly departing car.

Jayasuriya watched out the back window for a while, then opened the paper and settled himself in for the long ride ahead.

After Doreen had collected herself from the near-miss with her husband's car, she went inside to get one of her pills. The house smelt horrible and she gagged on her way up the stairs.

She popped a pill into her mouth, and then another one for good measure. The phone rang from the hallway, and she heard her housemaid answer it.

"Madam Doreen, it's for you."

Oh hell, who could it be? She didn't want to talk to anyone. She was most perplexed by the day's events, her husband's strange behaviour, the missing money and the peculiar old woman, god only knows where she had got to. She pushed herself off her bed and walked slowly down the stairs. She picked up the receiver and said hello.

"Hello Doreen, it's Elmo here."

"Oh, hello Uncle Elmo, how are you?"

"I've heard some troubling news, actually. Is Jaya there?"

"No, he isn't, he's just left for the East."

"Oh dear, that's not good, not good at all."

"What is it? What's happened?"

"It seems that Jaya is getting himself into more trouble on the East coast. He is attempting to carry out an illegal eviction and has bribed a commanding officer to assist him. To be quite honest Doreen, I believe your husband is having a breakdown."

"Yes. It would appear so."

"Anyway, I was hoping he may not have left yet, so I could stop him. But as it is, I will have to go there myself and put a stop to this, once and for all. I think you need to come with me. I'll be at yours with my driver within the hour."

"Really? Right. I'd better pack a bag then."

Doreen put down the phone. The Valium was kicking in, so she proceeded upstairs again with a new sense of calm. She packed a small bag of clothes and toiletries and carried it downstairs to the front door. She told the cook she would be gone for a few days, who promptly tipped out the cooking pot into the back garden and took the peg off her nose.

Doreen left her house and sat on the bench on the front porch. She surveyed her garden, then got up to pick a beautiful deep red rose from the bush that lined the driveway. She sniffed in the scent and stroked the smooth silky petals, marvelling at its perfection. A moment later, the Rolls Royce, belonging to her Uncle Elmo, turned through the gates. He climbed out of the passenger seat and opened the back door for her. She glided in with her bag and he returned to the front seat. Doreen looked up when the other door opened and in climbed the old woman next to her on the back seat. Doreen started to laugh.

"Who is this Doreen?" asked Elmo.

"Don't worry, it's an old friend, she's coming along for the ride!"

Doreen promptly fell into a deep sleep as the car pulled off. Elmo looked behind him at his two travelling companions; his niece who was snoring like a pneumatic drill, and possibly having a breakdown of her own, and a strange old woman who kept winking at him and grinning toothlessly.

"We're in for an interesting trip," he said to his driver.

"Yes, Sir."

Leela pulled the blanket over her head, trying to block out the noise. It was coming from the room next door. It had been the same last night and the night before. She didn't know whether the woman was sleeping or awake, but the noise was terrible. It began as a low moaning, which would crescendo into a guttural cry. Sometimes the noise would subside again, but occasionally, as it was now, it would erupt into howling, like a wounded animal. Leela couldn't bear it. She hadn't ever spoken to her neighbour; she wasn't sure if the woman spoke at all. She had a daughter who hid in her mother's skirt pleats. Wild frightened eyes would be all you'd catch of her face if you passed them in the corridor. Leela's heart went out to the child. She must have been no more than three or four. The woman also had a son who she guessed was around ten years old. He was a long-limbed boy with a serious face. Someone had told her they'd been there for eighteen months with no sign of discharge. She could hear the whispering tones of the boy now, soothing and comforting his mother from her night terrors.

Anoula tossed in her bed. Leela worried about her. She continually picked at her skin and was now covered in scabs up her legs and arms. She wasn't eating properly, and her frail frame was looking emaciated. Leela had tried to get her to eat more, but whenever she did, she heard her throwing it back up in the toilet soon after.

There was still no good news about Anoula's application. She had been told that she may have to wait a long time before it could be processed. This news had put her on a downturn. Until then she had seemed to cope ok. She never really left Leela's side, but she had been gaining confidence and learning a bit of English. She had learnt to control herself around the guards and so far, not inflicted any more scratches or bites on anyone.

Now, however, Leela could see the same vacant look in her eyes that she had seen on the beach after the crash. She was withdrawing into herself and Leela didn't know how to bring her out before it was too late.

The next morning there was a commotion outside her neighbour's door. As she and Anoula walked back from their showers, they saw a crowd of guards and the doctor standing outside the door. Inside they could see the mother on her knees murmuring and pushing the end of her scarf into her mouth as much as would fit. Her son was standing behind her, holding the hand of her sister. Silent tears ran down his face. He looked up when he saw them watching him, then reached over and pushed the door a little to block their view of his mother.

Leela grabbed Anoula's hand and pulled her towards their room.

"Come on they don't want us staring."

The sound of screaming made them turn back. Three of the guards were dragging the mother out the door. The woman was trying to break free, twisting and turning and kicking out at them. They managed to sit her in a wheelchair and pulled a belt around her upper arms and torso, restraining her to the back of the chair. The doctor pushed a syringe into her hand, and she screamed again and spat at him.

Her two children stood silently watching. The remaining guard tried to usher them back into their room, but the boy pushed her hand away. The young girl made a run for it, towards the chair, crying for her mother. The guards pushed the chair hurriedly away and the boy ran after his sister, catching hold of her and cradling her in his arms.

Leela could feel her own tears escaping. She turned to Anoula who was quietly watching, open-mouthed. There were no tears in her eyes, just that same vacant look.

Leela walked towards the huddled siblings. She bent down and touched the arm of the boy. She didn't know what language he spoke, so she spoke in English.

"Please, can I help you?"

The boy looked up at her. He put his hand over his sister's ears, then screamed, "Leave us alone!"

It was so loud and so emotive that Leela jumped back in shock.

"I'm sorry, I'm sorry," she said backing away from them. She pushed Anoula into their room, as she seemed to be frozen to the spot, and shut the door hurriedly.

"What happened?" Anoula said eventually.

"I don't know."

"Where have they taken her?"

"I don't know."

Leela tried to give Anoula a hug, but her body was stiff, and she didn't respond. They sat like that for some time until Anoula eventually lay down on her pillow and closed her eyes.

Leela watched her. She looked so peaceful, her breathing slow and measured. But in her heart, she knew there was no peace in Anoula's soul, only a barrage of trauma after trauma that was silently closing her down from the inside.

Leela left the room to find the supervisor. She was worried that Anoula would never forgive her, but she didn't know what else to do. She didn't know when there would be a point at which Anoula could never return to herself. She was so young, but so broken.

Leela knocked on the door of the supervisor's office. She had only spoken to her once before, and could feel her heart pounding away in her chest at having to ask for something. All the staff in the centre wore uniforms and they seemed, to Leela, to be the enemy. In their words, they said they were there to help, but to Leela, it didn't feel like help came. Everyone in the centre walked around with their heads down, some screamed to be let out. Most were silent. There were many who had been in there for over a year. Leela could tell the people who had been in for a long time. They had been robbed of the one thing they had clung on to throughout the years of torture, abuse and war, their hope. Without hope they had nothing. The hope of seeing their families again. The hope of their children treading a peaceful, safe path. The hope of walking into or out of a door and not having it locked behind you. The hope of being a free citizen of any country.

"Come in," the voice called from behind the door.

Leela turned the handle and opened it.

"What can I do for you?" the supervisor asked.

"I'm sorry, I need help."

"Why don't you sit down and tell me the problem?"

Leela pulled a chair out and sat down harder than she meant to.

"It's my friend, Anoula. She sick."

"What kind of sick? Why don't you take her to the sickbay?"

"Not fever sick, head sick, thinking problem."

"You mean a mental problem?"

"She very, very sad, too sad, not normal sad. And she no speak and no eat."

The supervisor was writing things down and Leela fell silent.

"Ok, thank you for telling me, Leela. I will get the help she needs."

"Oh ok, thank you. Please help her, thank you."

Leela hurried out the door, glad to be away from the oppressiveness of the office. This was the room where you were told bad news and hope was repeatedly dashed.

She prayed that they would help Anoula. She had become family to Leela, and she felt responsible for her.

Leela walked down the long corridor towards her block, her feet thudding on the concrete floor. As she got nearer, she broke into a run. She could hear Anoula crying and shouting.

She turned the corner and saw Anoula on the ground in front of the two children from next door. A guard was there shouting into a walkie-talkie. The boy was staring at Anoula, pain written all over his face. The little girl had her head buried into her brother's stomach and was shaking.

"What's going on? Anoula, what happened?"

"Their mother, she tried to kill her, she tried to kill her own daughter, she tried to suffocate her with a pillow, he, the boy, he stopped her, but that's why they've taken her, they've taken her away. But you know why... why she tried to kill her?"

Anoula couldn't speak anymore. She was choking on her tears.

Leela knelt down in front of her. "Why Anoula, why did the mother try to kill her daughter?"

Anoula looked up at her then, "Because she wanted to set her free from this... this place."

Leela looked up at the boy. He was still staring at Anoula. He hadn't understood what she had been saying, but it didn't matter. She was just vocalising the pain that was trapped inside him. He had woken up to find his mother holding a pillow on top of his baby sister's face. He had pulled her off, but his mother kept trying to get at her. The guard had come in and called for back-up. Everything moved quickly then. He wasn't to know that would be the last time he would see his mother for several years. Their visa application was successful and came through the following week. The boy and his sister were fostered out into different homes and their mother detained under the mental health act in a high-security unit. It wasn't until several years later, a kindly social worker thought it in the best interests of the children to be brought back together, and to visit their mother. Unfortunately, by then, the irreversible damage had been done.

Anoula was crying again but letting Leela hold her. "We will never get out of this place, they'll never let us out."

"Don't give up hope," she whispered into her hair. But another glimpse at the boy and his sister silenced any more words.

29 The Wedding Feast–Part 1

———————●————————

Marni turned a full 360 degrees, admiring her handy work. There were Indian silks draped from every corner of the restaurant, and lanterns hung from the beams. Every path lined with firelights, to be filled with kerosene and lit at dusk.

The archway of freshly cut palm fronds for the ceremony had been finished and dug deep down into the sand to stop it from toppling over. Aruna had been cooking since dawn, preparing a feast like no other. Kilos of fresh crabs, tiger prawns, calamari and lobster had all been delivered yesterday, along with a lorry load of organic vegetables from the village.

Gaya's parents had arrived from Colombo that morning, and Gaya was excitedly showing them around the grounds.

Jenny and Fawaz had also driven up from Colombo the day before, partly for the wedding, and partly for the threatened eviction.

Ali had spent the morning in meetings with the local police and had been promised support from them if anything happened.

They were of the opinion that the eviction notice had been blown out of all proportions, and that judging by the usual length of time it took to wade through red tape, nothing would actually happen until at least a year from now. It was always best not to take these letters too seriously, the OIC had suggested to Ali.

"Right," said Ali. "Thanks for the advice, but you will support us if the army turns up?"

"Yes, yes, sure, sure. We will come to some peaceful agreement, don't worry."

Ali found that highly amusing but didn't bother trying to explain it to the OIC. He went next to the hardware, on Marni's request, to buy some chains and padlocks. This was just in case the bulldozers did turn up. Marni was going to chain herself to the restaurant poles, and anyone else if they wanted to volunteer. Ali wasn't so sure about this idea, but Marni assured him that she had tried this technique once before in England, when she was protesting about a road being built through her local forest, and that it did definitely work.

He had asked anyone in his family with a van, tractor, 4wd or any other large vehicle to be on hand nearby in case they needed to block off access to enemy bulldozers.

Ali secretly hoped that the OIC was right and this was all going to be unnecessary, but you always had to expect the unexpected in this beloved country of his.

Marni tied the last ribbon around the table leg, then stripped off her sundress down to her bikini and went to find Jake and Zoe on the beach.

They sat at the water's edge and let the waves lap around them, filling up the moat of Zoe's castle with great giggles of delight.

"Are you worried about the eviction?" asked Jake

"I don't know, part of me feels like nothing will happen, but then we've already been through so many roller coasters, that it almost seems inevitable."

"How's Rushani holding up?"

"She was ok when I checked on her last. She's in our room with Meena and her mother getting her sari fitted. Chris is still out with his parents and sister's family. He's taken them on a boat tour of the lagoon to see the crocodiles."

Marni gazed out into the blue of the ocean stretching before her. "Jake, do you still want to leave here?"

Jake was silent for a moment before replying.

"Yes Marni, I do, but more than that I want us all to be happy. I don't want to drag you away from here if that's not what you want. It's all Zoe's ever known, so she's perfectly happy."

"But you're not?"

"Like I said Marni, I'm happy if my family's happy."

They sat together, each with their own thoughts, their dreams, the past, and the direction their lives may turn from this day forth.

"Let's get this day over with first," said Marni pushing herself up.

She ran into the water and dived under a wave to wash the sand off her body. She looked back to the beach at her precious family playing in the sand, then behind them to the hotel nestled between the trees, which had provided them a home for the last three years. This place that filled them with equal amounts of laughter, pain, joy and heartbreak.

"The show must go on!" Marni shouted to the sky. Jake looked up and she blew him a kiss across the water. She caught a wave back into shore and planted another kiss on Zoe's head and one on Jake's lips. She then climbed the steep bank of sand and entered her stage.

———————————● ●————————————

Jayasuriya had arrived in the early hours of the morning and booked himself into a cheap and extremely grotty hotel to get some sleep. He tossed and turned on the uncomfortable bed for an hour, before deciding to get up and go in search of the Deputy Commander.

He arrived at the barracks and gave his name. They radioed through, and he was let in.

"Mr Jayasuriya, how very nice to meet you again," said the Deputy Commander, rising from his desk and holding out his hand.

Jayasuriya shook it and slumped down into a chair. "I hope everything is organized?"

"Of course, just tell us when you want to make your move. I trust you have the money?"

"Yes, yes, here it is." Jayasuriya threw the wad of cash across the desk. He was grumpy from the journey and irritated by having to hand over so much cash.

The Deputy Commander counted it and slipped it into his drawer.

"So, what time shall we reconvene? I was thinking early evening would be a good time, maybe around 4 pm?"

"Yes, fine. How many men will you bring?"

"Twenty."

"And a bulldozer?"

"I have one on standby."

"Right, well I'll be back here at 4 pm sharp."

"I'll look forward to it."

Jayasuriya didn't bother to reply. He had the feeling this man was mocking him. He was a government minister for god's sake. This man worked for him.

He got back to the car and woke his weary driver up. "Back to the hotel," he muttered.

As they drove through town, Jayasuriya was beginning to wonder if he did actually want to live in this godforsaken place. It was just so backward. There were no bars, nice hotels or fancy restaurants. No decent shops, they might as well be living in the jungle. Oh well, he would have to seek out some decent women. Beautiful women could be found anywhere, even in the jungle. This thought soothed him as he settled down on his lumpy mattress, and drifted into a mosquito-ridden sleep, to the slow creaking of the faulty ceiling fan.

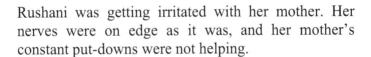

Rushani was getting irritated with her mother. Her nerves were on edge as it was, and her mother's constant put-downs were not helping.

"How can you look like a bride with a big pregnant belly? And you've put fat on your back and your breasts are too large to get the blouse done up."

"Ammi, please try and be a bit more supportive."

Meena stroked her arm. "You look beautiful, Ammi. When I get married, I hope I look as beautiful as you."

Rushani smiled down at her daughter. "You already are beautiful, my princess."

"Well, this will not get the blouse done up, I'll have to put pins in it," came her mother's voice from behind her back.

"Ok Ammi. Do what you have to do," she said winking at Meena.

The blouse was finally in place, and her mother moved on to the folding of the sari around her waist. She weaved the silk cloth around her daughter, starting just above her swollen belly. Around and around the cloth swirled. She folded it in pleats at the front and then pinned it to hold the pleats in place. The last length of cloth she folded over Rushani's shoulder, to hang down her back.

"Ok, you better look."

Rushani stood in front of the mirror and let out a gasp. "Oh Ammi, you've done an amazing job."

Her mother smiled despite the scowl she was attempting to hold in place. "You do look nice," she conceded.

Rushani turned around and gave her mother a hug. "Thank you! And thank you for all the help you've given me, especially looking after Meena for me all these years. It's my turn to look after you now."

"Let's see if you can keep this husband first before you go making any promises."

Rushani let the comment ride on the wind. This was her day, her wedding day. She never thought that life would bring her this kind of fortune and she was going to enjoy it, however long it lasted, even if her mother couldn't.

She applied her makeup carefully with Meena's face an inch from her own. Thick black eyeliner and gold lipstick that matched the gold thread in her sari. She attached the nose stud and the gold chain, and lastly the hairpiece. She was complete. She placed her hand on the baby growing inside her and said a silent prayer for its health and future.

"Come on Meena, let's get you ready."

She dressed her daughter in a satin dress that matched the colours in her own sari and tied a flower garland into her hair.

The door opened, and Marni popped her head around. "Wow Rushani, you look amazing. I just wanted to let you know that Chris and his family have returned and are getting ready. The Registrar has also arrived and would like to get the paperwork done before the ceremony."

"Ok, thanks Marni, I'll be out in a minute."

Marni came into the room and held Rushani's hands. "I'm so happy for you, Rushani. You deserve this."

Rushani squeezed Marni's hands and thanked her with her eyes. She took one last look in the mirror and walked through the open door to her new life.

The registrar was seated at a table in the restaurant. Chris was sitting opposite in a white suit, with his father next to him. Rushani walked along the path towards them, shy now in all her splendour. Chris looked up, a smile spreading across his face. He jumped up from the table and approached her.

"You are so beautiful. I am the luckiest man in the world."

Chris' father had also stood up and pulled out a seat for his soon to be daughter-in-law. Although his parents were at first concerned that Chris was taking on too much with the responsibility of a new wife and two new children all at once, they also knew that he was a man who knew what was good for him, and he had the courage of his convictions. They were proud of him for that.

Rushani sat down and turned her attention on the registrar who was asking her some questions. She saw some movement in the corner of her eye and looked up to see if more guests had arrived. She froze, the blood draining from her face. Chris felt her tense and looked up as well. There, at the gates, stood a squadron of soldiers with guns pointed at them, and in the middle, was the squat, chubby frame of Jayasuriya.

Everything moved quickly. Marni marched towards them, followed by Ali, his phone to his ear, and then Niraj. The body of soldiers moved forward until they met in the middle of the hotel grounds. The battle commenced.

The Deputy Commander spoke first. "We have been authorised to carry out an eviction of these premises. We will deal with anyone resisting this eviction in the proper manner by the police."

He ordered his men to take up position around the hotel.

"You may take some small personal items with you now, and the rest can be packed up under supervision, at a time that is suitable to Mr Jayasuriya."

At the first mention of his superiority, Jayasuriya puffed out his chest and twiddled the corner of his moustache, a wide grin exaggerating his pudgy cheeks. He caught Claudette's scowling glare, and for a moment he faltered, the smile dropping from his face.

He cleared his throat to speak, but Ali cut in first.

"Under whose authorisation?" he asked.

"Right, yes," said Jayasuriya, waving the papers in his hand. He walked towards Ali and handed them to him. Ali put his phone in his pocket and took the papers. Without looking at them, he ripped them up into shreds and threw them on the ground.

"Huh, how dare you?" spluttered Jayasuriya.

He looked around him for support. The Deputy Commander stepped forward and held out his hand to Ali. Ali declined the offer.

"We are here to ensure the safe eviction of this land and withdrawal of your permit to reside here, on the grounds of unsafe and illegal buildings."

"You and whose army?" said Ali taking a step closer.

"The army of Sri Lanka sir."

"We are not moving."

"Then we will be forced to bring in the bulldozer."

At that point, Chris stepped forward. "Excuse me everybody, but this is my wedding day. Surely this matter can be resolved at another time, in another way."

"This is a government matter," said Jayasuriya. "Not that we can expect a foreigner to understand the gravity of this situation. You think that your social engagements are more important than matters of the state?"

Gaya's mother, who had been brought up to speed of the situation that morning by her daughter, was trying to decide if she could bear to talk to this repugnant little man again, after her first experience of him. Gaya had asked her if there was anything she could remember from her law degree that they could use against the eviction. As it was well over thirty years since she had studied law, and, seeing as she had never made a career out of it, she felt a little rusty. However, she was not short of a few brain cells. Finally, she spoke up.

"Rahul, Mr Jayasuriya. As I am the legal representative for this hotel, I can assure you that as the required amount of notification of this eviction is not until tomorrow, we will not be vacating the premises today, and a forced eviction today will be against the law."

Gaya looked at her mum with pride. She wasn't sure that she had ever heard her mother lie, even if it was for the greater good.

Jayasuriya was spluttering again and turned to the Deputy Commander. "Tell her, this is a legal eviction, tell her."

"Madam, we really don't want this situation to get out of hand, but we will get the bulldozers in if we have to."

"I'm not going anywhere!"

The shout from behind the wedding guests made them all turn around. Rushani was standing in the middle of the restaurant, splendent in her wedding glory, attached to the central pillar by a chain and padlock.

"What the…?" Jayasuriya began his face puce red with anger. "I will have you arrested. I don't care if it is your wedding day. I will make sure you never see sunlight again… foreigner whore!" he blurted out.

Chris moved in front of Jayasuriya as he tried to move towards Rushani. "Why are you just standing there?" Jayasuriya shouted at the Deputy Commander.

"I think we should leave," said the Deputy Commander who was fast realising that a) this wasn't going to be an easy eviction and b) Jayasuriya was quite mad, as well as greedy.

"Leave? Leave? We are here to carry out government orders. They must be obeyed!"

"Actually, that's not really true Jayasuriya, is it?" said another voice behind them. They all turned around to see the Commander-in-Chief, closely followed by Ranjit Fonseka striding towards them.

"Wait, wait!" said another voice. In through the gates marched Uncle Elmo, bringing up his rear came Doreen, and an old lady with no teeth.

"Good Lord!" muttered Jayasuriya.

"Jaya enough is enough. This is the end of this ridiculous behaviour. You need to come home with us right now."

Uncle Elmo turned his attentions then on the Commander-in-Chief.

"I'm very sorry for this disturbance. My nephew has been under enormous pressure, resulting in a breakdown. As you can see, this is a personal matter, and I would be grateful if we can handle this as such."

"As you wish Sir," said the Commander-in-Chief. He turned to the Deputy Commander, "Not you, however."

The Deputy Commander looked down at his boots and muttered something incomprehensible.

Jayasuriya looked from his Uncle Elmo, to the Commander-in-Chief and lastly to his wife.

"You won't take me alive," he yelled, pulling a rolled-up sock out of his satchel and recovering a glass vial. He pulled out the cork stopper and put it to his lips.

"Down the hatch and fuck you all."

With that, he took off running through the restaurant, down to the beach, and into the sea.

"Get him would you," said the Commander to Ranjit.

"Yes Sir," said Ranjit, and took off after him.

"Stop, everyone, stop what you're doing." In the gates came Mr Fernando, the OIC of the local constabulary, followed by six of his men.

"It's ok," Ali said, "It seems the matter is resolved."

"Oh," said the OIC, looking slightly put out.

Ranjit arrived back, dragging with him a very drenched but very much alive Jayasuriya. He couldn't understand it. One drop, the woman had said. He'd drunk the whole bottle.

The old woman cackled so hard it turned into a coughing fit. "Aloe Vera juice, I gave you Aloe Vera juice!" she screamed, dissolving into another bout of hysterical laughter. "You fool, you're such a fool!"

Doreen and Uncle Elmo were looking a bit concerned about their charges. Both a little too mad to be undertaking another ten-hour drive with. They had no idea what all this talk about Aloe Vera juice was.

The Commander-in-Chief sent his soldiers back to the barracks and told the Deputy Commander that he would deal with him in the morning.

Elmo and Doreen made their deepest apologies to the staff of the Moon Rise Hotel and headed back to Colombo: Doreen and Elmo in one car, Jayasuriya and the old woman in the other.

An appointment with the psychiatrist had been set for that afternoon. Anoula assumed it was just another in the long line of health checks and assessments they had been put through since they arrived. Leela was glad that she didn't know it was her who had requested it. She didn't want Anoula to think she had been disloyal to her. They would have a translator present, but Leela would not be allowed to attend. Leela was glad about that. She knew she was out of her depth with Anoula's problems. She needed a doctor to help her, someone who knew what they were doing.

Leela was late for dinner as she'd been out in the yard trying to soak up the last rays from a rapidly departing sun. She wandered into the noisy room and lined up in the queue. She looked for Anoula at their usual table, but there was no sign of her.

She stared at the plates of food in front of her. There was something called beef goulash, a large tray of lasagne and a pie that looked like it was made of beans and potato. She chose the pie. What would she give for the taste of curry from back home, especially one made by her mother? To fill her belly with the sumptuous pleasure of fresh ground spices, full to the brim of flavour, crushed and fried up with onion and garlic, and left to simmer in a pot, with fresh fish or vegetables, and coconut milk. Her mouth salivated at the thought. She was sick of the bland food they were served. It was not to her taste at all, and sometimes it was hard to swallow. She forced herself though. She knew that if she stopped eating like Anoula, then she too would start losing hope.

She finished up her dinner and went back to her room to see if Anoula was there. She found her sitting on her bed staring at the wall.

"Hi, how did it go?" she asked.

"Ok," Anoula said, not looking at her.

"What happened?"

"They asked me lots of questions."

"What about?"

"Different things."

"Like what?"

"I can't remember."

"Oh, ok" replied Leela.

"Was the doctor nice?"

"Yes."

"Good."

"Why didn't you come for dinner?"

"I wasn't hungry."

The girls went about their nightly routines in silence after that. Leela went to shower and by the time she came back, Anoula was asleep. Leela lay awake for a while listening to the silence outside their room. The children next door had left the centre and she wondered about them now. She hoped they had gone to a better life on the outside. She had tried, in the past, to imagine what it would be like leaving here, but she couldn't. She had no idea what Australia was like, the schools, the people, what they did every day. She couldn't imagine what would happen to her the day she walked out of the gates forever.

There was shouting, and a bright light shone into Leela's face. She screamed, immediately reminded of the day she was dragged from her bed, and her family, adrenalin pumped through her veins, but she uncurled her fists.

"Come on, out your bed, we need to do a headcount."

Anoula was already out of her bed, looking small and frail in her nightdress, quivering at the sound of the guard's voice.

Leela jumped out of bed. "Ok, number 4074 and 4076 are here." The guard called to her companions. "Alright back into bed, you two. There were several people who didn't turn up for dinner and we needed to check everyone was ok."

"I'm sorry," Anoula whispered so faintly that the guard missed it as she closed the door. The girls climbed back into bed, but neither could sleep. They tossed and turned until eventually, Leela fell asleep. Anoula stared at the ceiling, rarely blinking until the morning light made a pattern on the blank walls of the room.

After breakfast, Anoula was called into the supervisor's office. Leela tried to read an English book that someone had lent her, but her mind wouldn't focus. After an hour, she went looking for her. She checked their room and then the bathroom. A guard caught up with her on her return.

"The supervisor wants to see you."

Leela felt a small tremor of panic, but she pushed it aside and followed the guard down the corridor.

She knocked on the door and waited.

"Come in."

She turned the handle and went in.

"Where's Anoula?" she asked.

"Please sit down."

Leela did what she was told. The supervisor looked at her and smiled.

"We've removed Anoula from the centre."

"What! Why?"

"The psychiatrist has recommended that she be placed into foster care for the time being, while she receives medical treatment. She has been given a temporary bridging visa on medical grounds."

"But… she not like that," Leela said, her voice quivering.

"It's out of our hands now. She needs to be somewhere she can be looked after. Your friend is very ill." She added.

"But she need me. You not understand. She not want to be alone."

The supervisor smiled again. "Leela, you need to concentrate on you now. It looks like your visa application is in its final stages, and you'll also be leaving here soon. You'll be able to visit her on the outside. You've been very kind looking after her, but you are just a child yourself and so is she. It's not your responsibility to look after her. She said to tell you she was sorry."

Leela pushed herself up from the chair. She needed air.

"This not right," she said to the supervisor as she left. "She my family."

30 The Wedding Feast–Part 2

———————————● ● ●———————————

Ali and Marni invited the Commander-in-Chief and the OIC to stay for the celebrations. They accepted with pleasure.

Rushani and Chris got back to signing the marriage register and Marni started the music. They had hired Kandyan dancers and the air was consumed by the hypnotic rhythm of the drummers. The garden firelights were lit, and the atmosphere lifted all the people present.

"I can't believe what just happened!" shouted Marni to Ali over the music.

"The power of the people," grinned back Ali who was, unusually for him, jiggling on the dance floor and waving his hands in the air.

"We were lucky the Commander turned up when he did. That's twice now he's saved us from that man."

"I think this will be the last time. I don't think Jayasuriya will work again after this."

"Who was the old woman with him?"

"I don't know, maybe his mother or a relative. Anyway, they're safely on their way back to Colombo."

The party moved down to the beach for the ceremony. Rushani looked so beautiful, sparkling in the last wisps of the setting sun, and the firelights that surrounded the ceremonial arch. Chris was lost in awe at his new bride, and Meena was dancing wildly around them, throwing bougainvillea petals in their vague direction. They exchanged vows amongst rapturous applause, and Chris moved in to place a kiss on his wife's mouth. Meena cheered and jumped up and down, and Chris's mother shed a small tear. Even Rushani's mother managed a smile for the newlyweds. Marni wrapped her arms around Jake, and they basked in the night's romance.

"Let's eat!" shouted Chris,

The party followed the couple up to the restaurant as the Kandyan drummers played on.

"It's all turned out so perfectly," said Gaya linking arms with her mother and father. "Wow Ammi, you really rocked it earlier when you stood up to the Minister."

"Oh, he's a pig of a man," said her mother. "Do you know, me and your father had to sit through a whole dinner at his house, with him and his frightful wife?"

"That must have been awful!"

"And I asked after you because it was just after he'd visited here, but he said he didn't think he'd met you."

"Oh, we met!" said Gaya, but decided not to elaborate any further on the matter.

Jenny joined them at their table. "What a wonderful wedding. It's so nice to have something to celebrate, and a double whammy today. Two for the price of one!"

"Yeah it's been a tough year all in all," said Gaya. Jenny found her hand under the table and gave it a big squeeze. "Hopefully this is the turning point, and everything will become brighter."

"Yeah, I hope so," said Gaya, lost in thoughts of Rakesh.

The wedding feast was laid out on the tables. There were fifteen different dishes, each with their own aroma infusing the air. The greenest organic vegetables, pink juicy beetroot, two different kinds of rice, spicy chicken curry, grilled prawns, lobster, crab, fried calamari and a twelve-kilogram seer fish cooked on the BBQ stuffed with garlic and lime. All topped off with homemade lime pickle, seeni sambol and a lime and curd[23] dressing. They congratulated Aruna on the fine spread, and he slipped off to the kitchen to indulge in his celebratory bottle of arrack.

Claudette was looking her finest in an indigo silk trouser suit. She had commandeered the attention of the recently widowed Commander-in-Chief and was regaling him with stories of Parisian high society. The Commander looked flushed, not only by the champagne, that was being topped up frequently in his glass, but also the company. He wasn't sure that he had ever in his life met someone like Claudette.

Rushani and Chris slipped off to the beach for a moment alone.

---

[23] Curd – yoghurt made from buffalo milk

"Are you happy?" asked Chris

"I am more happy than possible!"

Chris pulled Rushani in close to him. "You know, I had dreams about you long before I met you."

Rushani buried her head deep into Chris's chest and breathed in his scent. "I'm not scared anymore," she said.

Leela was in the waiting area. She had been informed there was a visitor to see her and she was waiting anxiously biting her nails. She hadn't received any visitors so far and was excited to meet someone new, who wasn't a lawyer, or a social worker, or anything else official. Part of her was hoping it might be Anoula. She had heard nothing about her, even though she kept asking for news. There had been several meetings regarding her own application, but she was struggling to keep up with all the proceedings. Her English was improving, and she could access a translator when necessary, but she still didn't really understand, even when it was translated.

The visitor's door swung open and a guard beckoned her through. She walked in and two friendly faces smiled up at her.

"You must be Leela," the man said. "We've heard so much about you. It's wonderful to finally meet."

"I'm sorry, I don't know…?"

"Oh, we're sorry," said the woman, "We must introduce ourselves. My name is Eva, and this is

Jo. We've come from Sri Lanka. We were staying at the Moon Rise Hotel where your brother works."

"You know Suresh?" Tears sprang into Leela's eyes.

"We do know him, and we promised we would come and find you, and do what we could to help you."

"You come to help me?" Leela's jaw started quivering and the tears sprung out of her eyes and down her cheeks.

"Yes, we did sweetheart," said Eva gently, putting her hand over the young girl's. "We were in the hotel the night you came there with Marni's father, but you were gone again so quickly we didn't get a chance to meet. Suresh is so proud of you and wishes with all his heart that he could have come too."

Leela thought back to that night. It seemed so long ago now. She thought of Vish and started crying again.

"How have you been?" asked Jo, pushing a bag towards her containing jaggery and sesame seed balls. "Just a little something from home. What has it been like since you got here? Suresh has been so worried about you."

Leela told them the whole story. The journey on the boat, the accident, arriving at the camp, Anoula, Nimal, everything she could think of. Eva and Jo listened without speaking. Once or twice Leela's words bought tears to their eyes and they squeezed each other's hand under the table.

"There's more," said Leela, "Even before I left Sri Lanka, but I'll tell you the rest another time," she added glancing towards the guard.

Eva took down the names of Leela's lawyer and social worker. She promised to contact them and find out how things were progressing. They stood up and Eva pulled her close, hugging her tightly. Leela allowed herself to be small for a moment. Jo wrapped his arms around the pair of them and they stood huddled like that until the guard impatiently cleared his throat.

"We'll be back tomorrow," Jo told her.

"Really? Tomorrow?"

Leela's heart gave a little skip of joy. A feeling she hadn't had for a long time.

"Yes, sweetheart, tomorrow."

They returned the next day as promised, and with news of Leela's application.

"We have spoken to your lawyer," said Eva. "She said that they are in the final process of arranging your release. They have been trying to find a foster home for you."

"I'm scared of going somewhere. What if they not like me?"

Jo spoke then, "Well we thought you might have already been through enough to last a lifetime which is why we asked your lawyer to find out if we could apply to be your foster parents. That's if you would like that?"

Leela's eyes filled to the brim. "Yes, please," she managed to say.

Eva and Jo smiled and held her hands in theirs. "We'll hear back tomorrow so we'll come and see you again then."

Eva and Jo were given the green light on account of them being friends of Leela's brother. They had previously fostered, so were already in the system and easy to run checks on. There was a mountain of paperwork to tie up but eventually, one week later, Leela was waiting behind a locked gate, a small plastic bag in her hand containing several items that had been given to her or left behind by other people.

She had burst into tears when she walked out of her room for the last time, so happy that she would not be returning to the tiny cell. She shifted from foot to foot, anxious that all this anticipation would not come crashing down, and the carpet whipped out from under her, as she had come to expect in her short life. She began to feel nauseous as the clock ticked loudly in the waiting area.

The doors suddenly swung open, and Eva and Jo were standing there, beaming smiles across both their faces. She walked towards them, her legs trembling. She felt they might give way. Eva wrapped her arms around her, and squeezed her tight, calming her quivering nerves.

"Come on, let's get you home," she said. The word rebounded over and over in her head 'home!'

They walked through the large metal gates without talking. The noise as they clanged shut behind her sent Leela's nerves into orbit. She hoped she would never have to hear the noise of keys jangling and doors being locked ever again.

Leela remained silent throughout the journey to the hotel. They would fly to Brisbane the next day and then drive up to the Sunshine Coast where Eva and Jo's children lived.

Jo opened the hotel door and they trooped in.

"I hope you'll be comfortable on the sofa bed," Jo said.

"Yes, it very nice, thank you," said Leela, shy now in her new surroundings.

"Tell us what you'd like to do most?" said Eva. "We can do anything you want."

"What I want is find Anoula, my friend. I want know how is she?"

"Of course, we can do that," replied Eva, although it will be too late to call now. I'll send out some emails but then we'll have to wait until we get to the Sunshine Coast to chase it up if we haven't heard anything. Is that ok?" she said gently.

Leela nodded. She had waited this long.

Marni was enjoying the peace and quiet of an empty restaurant. The few guests that were staying had retired early, giving Marni some time to herself. The stress from the threatened eviction was slowly ebbing away, and the wedding, which had been truly magnificent, had taken it out of her. She was feeling quite depleted of energy reserves and was wondering if she might suggest to Jake that they take a holiday.

They had heard the news yesterday that Leela had been released into the care of Eva and Jo. Suresh was over the moon and had gone to stay with his family for a few days to update them with everything that had happened. Marni knew that he would return refreshed and would be able to look after the hotel with Ali's back-up. Chris and Rushani were having a honeymoon on the West Coast but would also be back by the end of the week. Rushani wanted to continue working until the end of her pregnancy, and Marni was happy to still have her there.

She thought back to the last conversation she had with Jake about leaving. He wanted to; she knew that. She thought of how committed she had been, when she couldn't even contemplate leaving. This was especially true after the tsunami, when the hotel was rebuilt. She had poured her heart and soul into each brick and couldn't turn her back on it. But recently she felt the reasons to keep her there didn't seem important anymore. She had found the part of her past she had been searching for and she knew the hotel would survive without her. Maybe she could see herself and her family somewhere else. Start again somewhere new. She heaved a heavy sigh as she turned all the lights off in the restaurant. She rested her hand on the thick wooden pole that held up the roof of her kingdom. She loved every inch of this place. It would be very hard to leave.

The flight to Brisbane was smooth and Leela's face was stuck to the window the entire journey. When they took off, she thought her stomach was going to erupt out of her mouth and she couldn't help a small scream escape. Eva held on to her hand and reassured her they would be fine. As the plane ascended, Leela was utterly amazed. She had experienced nothing like it. She thought if the plane were to crash now, she would die happy because she knew what it was to float in the clouds. To be so high in the sky that nothing could touch you. Where the world and all its problems were just little dots below. There was no other feeling like it and Leela didn't want it to end.

When they arrived at Brisbane airport, the hustle and bustle sent Leela into another shock, but she stuck close to Eva and Jo, taking in everything and everyone around her.

When they got to the hire car, Eva turned around and smiled. "First, we're going to visit our new house. We saw it on the Internet and thought it would be perfect for us. We hope to pick up the keys for it today so we can check it out when we get there, and then we'll stay at our daughter's house tonight."

Leela couldn't believe it, a house that she would be able to call home, however temporary it may be.

When they arrived at the new house, the estate agent was there to let them in. Leela ran through and out into the back garden, Eva and Jo followed her laughing. But out in the back garden, Leela had stopped in silence and was shaking.

"What? What is it?" Eva cried

Leela dropped to her knees and started wailing. Eva ran and put her arms around her small frame. "What is it Leela, tell me, what's wrong?"

"The sea, all the water, I can't look. I can't, I can't."

Eva looked up at the view stretching before her and realized her mistake. Leela had spent three weeks on that wretched boat that had almost taken her life. This view was all she had looked at for weeks, as her body starved, and her hopes faded away.

"Oh, my darling, I am so sorry. I just didn't think."

"You get this house for me, I not like, you send me back." Leela was still crying.

"No Leela, don't be silly. We don't have to live here. We can live anywhere. Don't worry. Let's go and look at another house tomorrow."

Leela turned her back on the view. They left the house and climbed back into the car. Eva promised herself she would not make the same mistake again. She still had no idea of the extent of this child's trauma and was damned if she was going to make it worse than it already was.

They drove the short distance to Eva and Jo's daughter's house. Leela felt ashamed of herself and wished she could make it up to these kind people, who had tried to give her a home. Their daughter Elsie came running out the door as they turned the car into the driveway, followed by two toddlers, a boy and a girl. There was a lot of hugging and squealing and Leela stood back shyly. Eva introduced her to Elsie who immediately gave her a big bear hug, followed by the twins. Leela laughed out loud. The twins were a bundle of love and affection and she felt instantly part of the family.

After dinner, the twins were put to bed and Leela was ushered upstairs to have a bath. This was another new experience for her, and she stayed in it for as long as she could until all the bubbles had popped, and the water was getting cold. She got dressed in the pyjamas that Eva had given her the day before and padded downstairs.

She saw the back of Eva sitting at the desk with her computer. She put her hand on the door to push it open, but stopped when she heard Eva gasp.

"What is it?" Jo said, standing up and hurrying over to look at the screen.

"Oh god, Jo. It's Leela's friend Anoula, she died three weeks ago."

EPILOGUE

Ice Cream and Mangosteen

———————— ● ————————

"Ammi! Come on we're leaving."

Rushani's mother smoothed down her skirt and put her handbag over her shoulder. She looked around her room for the last time before closing the door behind her. They had moved to the city and this house in Dehiwela, six months ago, when Chris had got himself a desk job in his old company. He would be based in the head office in Colombo and spend only a few days each month in the North. They found Meena a place in a private girl's school and she was settling in well.

The house was a large four-bedroom colonial-style villa with substantial gardens and a veranda with a swing chair.

Rushani's mother had moved with them, tutting when she'd seen all the lavish extras around the house.

She'd refused to sleep on the mattress in her exquisitely hand-carved antique bed, choosing instead a mat with a pillow on the floor.

The baby arrived. It was a boy and they named him Anton after Chris' father. His first ever smile was at Chris, which filled Rushani's heart with love, when she saw the bond between them.

They squashed themselves into the waiting van along with a pram and three suitcases and headed to the airport. Meena chattered excitedly about the plane, and everything they would do when they arrived. Rushani kept glancing at her mother who was very quiet and sat looking out the window, her hands clasped in her lap.

This was to be the first time any of them except Chris had been on a plane. As the porters unloaded their luggage onto trolleys, Rushani put her arm around her mother.

"Are you nervous Ammi?"

"Of course I'm nervous, silly girl, a big hunk of metal floating in the sky, it's crazy to even think of going on a plane. I'll just be glad when I'm back on the ground again."

"Are you happy Ammi?"

"What a question to ask! How can I answer that? That's not a question you ask people."

Rushani accepted that her mother was not going to let herself relax, even on a special day like this. They were crossing the oceans for three weeks to visit Chris' friends and family in Norway. Why couldn't her mother embrace life, let herself enjoy the last years that she had left? Her struggles were over, couldn't she see that?

Rushani turned away from her mother and bent down to strap Anton into his pram, before tuning back into Meena's continuous chatter.

Rushani's mother watched her daughter. She looked at her two grandchildren and son-in-law, a picture of a happy family. But how could this family ever be happy? Two children from two different men, and now married to a third man, who was a foreigner. This was not destined to be a happy union. Their worlds were too opposing, their cultures would soon clash. When Chris becomes aware of the responsibilities of fatherhood, he will be off. Probably just after he impregnates her daughter with a third child.

There was nothing she could do now. She would have to bite her tongue and then pick up the pieces when it happened, just like she'd done all her daughter's life.

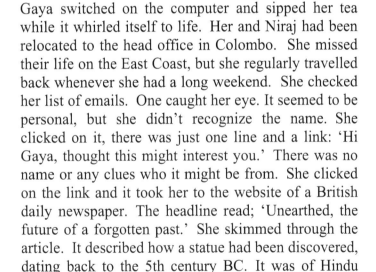

Gaya switched on the computer and sipped her tea while it whirled itself to life. Her and Niraj had been relocated to the head office in Colombo. She missed their life on the East Coast, but she regularly travelled back whenever she had a long weekend. She checked her list of emails. One caught her eye. It seemed to be personal, but she didn't recognize the name. She clicked on it, there was just one line and a link: 'Hi Gaya, thought this might interest you.' There was no name or any clues who it might be from. She clicked on the link and it took her to the website of a British daily newspaper. The headline read; 'Unearthed, the future of a forgotten past.' She skimmed through the article. It described how a statue had been discovered, dating back to the 5th century BC. It was of Hindu origin and believed to be carved from the stone found in Tamil Nadu in India. The article provided a timeline correlating with the arrival of the Sinhalese in Sri Lanka, thus bringing the first real evidence that the Tamils and Sinhalese migrated to Sri Lanka at the same time. The article went on to describe the many other artefacts intercepted on their way out of Sri Lanka to the black market. The high-ranking officers and politicians involved in the illegal trading had been named in the article, along with photos.

Gaya slumped back in her chair. There was his name in black and white. Rakesh Cooray. He had been named as one of the eyewitnesses, but the article had been written anonymously. What did this mean? Was he still alive? Was it written by him? Did he send it to her? Was he thinking about her?

She picked up the phone, Niraj answered immediately as he always did.

"Tell me Gaya?"

"You're never going to believe this."

"What?"

"Rakesh's story has been published in the UK."

"What! Give me five minutes, I'm almost at the office."

She sat staring at the computer screen until she heard Niraj's footsteps. He stood behind her chair reading the article. After a while, he put his hand on her shoulder.

"Are you ok?" He asked her.

"I don't know... I don't know because I don't know what it means."

Niraj sat down and swivelled her chair around to face him. "We still don't know Gaya. We can try and investigate this, see if we can trace the author of the article or this email address, but we still might never know. What we do know, however, is that the story Rakesh risked his life to make public, is out. That is the legacy that he wanted to leave. Even if he is alive, he will be living under a false name, and he will never be able to return home, so we will never know what happened. If he is dead, he will be smiling from his grave."

Gaya felt the tears roll down her cheeks, making her lips salty. Niraj pulled her chair towards him and wrapped his arms around her. Huge sobs racked her body, Niraj made no moves to stem their flow. With tears and snot playing havoc with her composure, she excused herself and headed for the bathroom. She looked in the mirror. Her face was swollen and blotchy. She blew her nose loudly and splashed water on her face. She wiped the panda eyes away as best she could and headed back out to the office. As she swung open the toilet door into the corridor, she bumped straight into Niraj who was waiting for her.

"Are you ok?" he asked as he moved a strand of wet hair away from her face. She nodded and squeezed a smile out. His hand hadn't left the strand and he quickly pulled it away before the temptation overcame him to touch her face. They stood like that, not moving, not even blinking. Niraj cleared his throat and took control of himself just in time to grab her as her legs buckled and she fell to the floor.

"Shall I take you home?" he asked gently.

"Yes, please."

He helped her up and they walked back along the corridor towards their office, both mourning their lost friend, both saying their silent good-byes.

The autumn trees were shedding their leaves and leaving great mounds of reds and purples around the city. Claudette's knee-high leather boots crunched through them as she hurried along the bank of the River Seine. She had left her job in Sri Lanka and returned to Paris over a year ago. She had missed the change of seasons and the hint of a cold wind on her face made her toes curl in pleasure.

She was late for her lover. He had arrived by plane that day and they were meeting at the Eiffel Tower. Her friends would be horrified by her lack of imagination, but she didn't care. She pushed through the crowds of people who had descended from the tower, and then she saw him. He still had that magnificent air of command that had first attracted her, although looking slightly out of place in a coat and scarf.

She ran into his arms and he lifted her up, embracing passionately, with encouraging looks and the odd photo from passers-by. A Paris romance; the tourists were delighted by the explicitness of the act.

Once their immediate rapture subsided, they ran huddled together to the nearest café and ordered coffees and aperitifs.

"It's so good to see you," said the recently retired Commander-in-Chief of the Special Forces Unit, Eastern Division.

"And you, my sweet Mohan."

"Here, I have something for you," said Mohan taking out a round purple fruit from his pocket.

"A mangosteen!" exclaimed Claudette. "How wonderful!" She squeezed the fruit till the skin burst.

Mohan watched her as she savoured each segment of the ripe, white flesh. When the last piece was eaten, he reached over and took her face in his hands, kissing her deeply, tasting the sweet juice on her tongue.

They filled in the gaps since they had last seen each other. Mohan's youngest daughter had left for university, so now all three of his children were living abroad. Mohan had taken early retirement from the army to visit his children in England and America, stopping to see Claudette on the way. It was only his second trip out of Sri Lanka, and he had a lot to see. They spent the rest of the afternoon in Claudette's four-poster bed, eating, drinking and making vigorous love. Later that night they dragged themselves from the envelope of their desire and walked hand-in-hand through the streets of Paris.

"Will I see you again?" asked Claudette. She was secretly becoming fond of this man whom she had only a brief love affair with at the end of her time in Sri Lanka, and then missed terribly when she left, which both surprised and unbalanced her. She was not a woman accustomed to grieving over lost love, and she tried to put him out of her mind.

But he was unlike any man she had met before. He had saved her from danger, and she couldn't help hero-worshipping him for that. Not that she would ever let on. She preferred to keep her girlish fantasies to herself.

When he emailed her saying he would like to visit, butterflies exploded in her stomach. She was too old to be turning away opportunities for happiness.

"Yes, I believe you will see me again, Claudette."

Claudette smiled, turning her face from the biting wind.

Jayasuriya picked up the ringing phone. "Hello?"

"Hello Jaya, it's Elmo here."

Jayasuriya froze. What had he done wrong now?

"Yes, Elmo Uncle, how are you?"

"Let me get right to the point."

Oh hell, thought Jayasuriya.

"Doreen has asked that you vacate the house. She wants to sell it."

"Bu... but where will I live?"

"I'm not sure she's too bothered about that."

"And what will she do if I refuse?"

"I think she might bring along one or two friends to help you on your way."

"Oh."

"And one last thing, she wants you out by Saturday."

Jayasuriya contemplated the phone in his hand, long after Elmo hung up.

He wasn't exactly sure what he was going to do. None of his plans seemed to be transpiring, and nothing new was coming to mind. He wandered in and out of the empty rooms of the large house. The staff had long since moved on to other households. Doreen was living with her spinster sister and had filed for divorce.

'What's the use of staying till Saturday?' he thought. He went upstairs to pack. In his leather satchel, he put his toothbrush, a change of underwear and a sarong (no aftershave), and walked out the front door, leaving it wide open. When Doreen arrived on Saturday morning, they had to evict two stray cats and an abandoned litter of puppies.

Jayasuriya wandered the streets for several hours before ending up at the YMCA in Fort to bed down for the night. As he crossed the square, he thought he saw a familiar wisp of long grey hair and looked again. That same cackle of laughter made him wince.

"I should have killed you when I had the chance you wretched woman," boomed Jayasuriya.

He had tried to, in the car, on the way back from the East. He had several times attempted to wring her scrawny neck, but his driver had stopped at a police station and had him locked up for the night. The driver and the old lady continued their journey to Colombo where they parted company and the driver looked for a new job.

She cackled again. "I've never met such an idiot in my life. You've been a complete failure from the moment you came screaming out of your mother's belly to the day you will die. What have you contributed to the world? Nothing!"

"Why should I contribute anything to the world? Why do I owe anything to anybody? What have they done for me?"

"That's why you've ended up alone with nothing. You're a selfish imbecile and you've got what you deserve."

"I don't see your hordes of friends and family, your lavish house," he retaliated. "You live in a shack with a cardboard roof for fuck's sake, preying on people you can manipulate."

The unlikely couple glared furiously at each other.

"I think we shall agree to disagree," the old woman said getting off the wall she was sitting on and walking away.

Jayasuriya watched her go, smoothed down his ruffled receding hair and strode towards his current abode to think of a new plan.

Marni sunk her toes into the soft grass and grinned as she saw Zoe bounding through the back door and running towards her.

"Mummy we got ice creams!"

Jake was striding behind her. When he reached her, he bent down, dropping a kiss on her forehead and handed her an ice cream with a chocolate flake.

"Are you ready to go home?"

"Sure am!" Marni gathered up the blanket she'd been lying on in the garden and stuffed the tickets into her bag. "Give me a minute, I'll meet you in the car."

It was a beautiful Cornish summer's evening and Marni was on cloud nine. She was excited to be starting on their next adventure and more importantly that she and Jake had decided together. They were finally united in their dreams for the future.

After a long-overdue holiday, and with time to think away from the hotel and everyday commitments, Marni and Jake had come to the decision to leave Sri Lanka and return to England. They packed up their belongings in two suitcases and said a very teary goodbye to the staff of the Moon Rise Hotel and their dear friend Ali to whom they promised to return soon. Rushani had held on to her, thanking her for her friendship and promising to stay in touch.

They stayed with Marni's mum in London when they first arrived back from Sri Lanka but soon realized that the big city was no longer for them. They loaded their few possessions into the boot of an old station wagon and headed southwest to Cornwall where they found a gloriously run-down two-bedroom cottage to rent in a small rural village. They cleaned, painted, fixed, bought basic furniture and hung photos of their life together all over the walls. The photo that Jake had taken of Marni and her father taking pride of place over the mantelpiece.

Jake found a job with a web design company and surfed the icy waters of the Atlantic Ocean. Marni began a degree in Business Management and studied when Zoe was in day-care.

Life changed dramatically for Marni, Jake and Zoe, in that their life was no longer dramatic. They had swapped their days filled with army, politics, guns and fear. There was no other noise in their world now, except them. Zoe's voice would be the first thing Marni would hear when she woke up. She enjoyed making her and Jake's breakfast in the peace of her own kitchen, rather than the hustle and bustle of the hotel. She enjoyed the process of taking time, not rushing, listening and hearing the needs of her family, and letting them know hers in return.

She often thought of the Moon Rise Hotel. That time for her was the most momentous part of her life. She had changed so much through meeting her father and coming to terms with the reality that had brought

She knew her heart would always belong on the East Coast of Sri Lanka, in the earth and in the sea, the trees and the wind. She had never felt more alive than she did when she lived there.

She thought of all the people who had wandered in and out of the gates, the stories, and the energy they bought with them. She remembered the chaos and the peace that had rained down in equal measure, and all the love, lost and found under its roof. She prayed that the terror and trauma were behind them, and she wished for a future of hope for the little kingdom of the Moon Rise Hotel and all the people that walked within its walls.

It was these memories that hammered and pushed their way out of Marni, demanding to be heard, until she couldn't keep quiet any longer. One year after they arrived in England, it erupted out of her, as they sat quietly watching television.

"I want to go back." She waited, eyes fixed forward, not daring to glance across to see Jake's reaction.

"I thought you might say that," Jake eventually replied.

"Well?"

"Well…"

Marni's eyes filled with tears and her voice came out in sobs. "I thought that finding my father was the reason I had to be in Sri Lanka, but I can't shake it off. I don't know what it is. Maybe it's the craziness, the adventure, the weather, the beauty. Maybe it's because there are no limits. I know the other side too; the frustrations, the remoteness, the politics, but they don't seem to weigh as much. It's where I feel alive."

Jake turned to face her and took her hands in his. "Marni, I have loved being here with you. I've soaked up every second of time and attention that you have given to me. I love the privacy that we can enjoy in this house, just the three of us, and I love that our family feels whole again. But I love you more. I can see that the fire in you has burnt out. I want to see that fire again."

Marni's tears came thick and fast now. "Do you mean…"

"Yes." Jake was laughing as he wiped away her tears. "Yes, we can move back home."

Marni took the last look around the house before pulling the door tightly shut. She handed the keys to the agent and walked towards the taxi where Jake and Zoe were waiting for her.

Leela couldn't stand still. She had tried sitting down, then standing up. She'd been to the bathroom three times and now it was time. The flight had arrived, and she would finally be wrapped in her mother's arms. Eva was with her and she grinned widely as 'landed' was displayed on the board. The visas had been issued before they left Sri Lanka, so she hoped there wouldn't be any problem with immigration.

Leela chewed her fingernails impatiently.

Then suddenly there they were, a huddle of people wide-eyed and nervous.

"Amma!" Leela screamed and jumped under the barrier to hug her mother. Tears streamed from all their faces as she hugged each of her family; her grandmother, her sisters and lastly her baby brother.

The doors behind them swung open again and a voice said, "Don't forget me!" She looked up and couldn't stop another scream escaping from her mouth.

"Suresh, I can't believe it! I didn't know you were coming too." She threw her arms around his neck and hugged him, thinking she would never let go.

Eventually, the security guards moved them on as they were blocking up the arrival doors. They were all introduced to Eva, and Suresh took both her hands in his telling her how he could never pay her back for everything she had done for Leela.

"Watching that reunion is all the payback I will ever need," said Eva, wiping away her own tears.

It was a while before Leela could let go of her family, much to the entertainment of the rest of the people in arrivals. Every time one would try to move, she would grab onto them harder. She was laughing and crying all at once. Eventually, her younger brother shouted up at her.

"I can't breathe!"

Leela jumped back still laughing and took his face in her hands.

"I have missed you so much."

"I've missed you too, Akka.[24] I thought I wouldn't see you again. People told me I'd never see you again."

He started to cry and Leela held him tight.

"It's ok," she stroked his hair, comforting him. "It's all over now, it's all over."

It had taken a long time for Leela to come to terms with the death of Anoula. She blamed herself for her part in her friend's death. They had removed Anoula from the centre into the care of foster parents, inexperienced in dealing with such a severe state of depression. They had taken her the next morning for her outpatient treatment at the hospital but had broken down the bathroom door later that afternoon to find her surrounded by a pool of her own blood. They themselves were now being treated for post-traumatic stress and had taken up the vacancy left in the treatment program by Anoula's hasty exit. Leela didn't think she would ever forgive herself for her mistake, even though Eva had tried to help her to understand that it was not her fault.

But for now, Leela's mind was somewhere else. As she looked around her, standing there in the Arrivals Hall, surrounded by the familiar faces of those she loved the most, there were no dark spaces, no empty moments. Her whole being felt its way out of her body, like the roots of a dying plant, sensing the nourishment that was suddenly available to her. The roots curled around her family members, embedding themselves deep into their hearts. She felt them flow into her veins, bringing life back into her. She stretched out her spine, absorbing the sun's rays that pressed through the huge glass windows of the

---

[24] Akka – big sister (Tamil and Sinhala)

terminal building. At that moment there was not one part of her that felt any other emotion but love. She had survived. She would heal. She had hope.

Srianjali Gunasena is mixed race Sri Lankan and English. Born in London, she moved to the East Coast of Sri Lanka in 2003. In 2004 she survived the Asian Tsunami, along with her husband and first son who was born in 2005. She moved to Australia in 2008 where her second son was born. Her wanderlust has led her to live and work around the world, but she always returns to Sri Lanka, the place she calls home. She exhibits her love for the country in her writing, her first book *Luk in Sri Lanka; a children's travel guide* was published in 2013.

Printed by Amazon Italia Logistica S.r.l.
Torrazza Piemonte (TO), Italy

10773245R00228